CANDIDE

broadview editions
series editor: L.W. Conolly

Voltaire's Morning, Jean Huber (1721-86). Oil on canvas, 52.5 x 44.5 cm. Image courtesy of The State Hermitage Museum, St. Petersburg.

CANDIDE,
or
All for the Best

The 1759 Nourse (London)
Translation, revised

Voltaire

edited by Eric Palmer

broadview editions

Library and Archives Canada Cataloguing in Publication

Voltaire, 1694-1778.
    Candide, or all for the best / Voltaire ; edited by Eric Palmer.

(Broadview editions)
This 1759 English translation released concurrently with Voltaire's first French edition.
Includes bibliographical references.
ISBN 978-1-55111-746-1

    I. Palmer, Eric, 1964-   II. Title.   III. Series: Broadview editions

PQ2082.C313 2009   843'.5   C2009-903272-4

Broadview Editions
The Broadview Editions series represents the ever-changing canon of literature in English by bringing together texts long regarded as classics with valuable lesser-known works.

Advisory editor for this volume: Michel Pharand

Broadview Press is an independent, international publishing house, incorporated in 1985. Broadview believes in shared ownership, both with its employees and with the general public; since the year 2000 Broadview shares have traded publicly on the Toronto Venture Exchange under the symbol BDP.

We welcome comments and suggestions regarding any aspect of our publications— please feel free to contact us at the addresses below or at broadview@broadviewpress.com.

North America
Post Office Box 1243, Peterborough, Ontario, Canada K9J 7H5
2215 Kenmore Avenue, Buffalo, NY, USA 14207
Tel: (705) 743-8990; Fax: (705) 743-8353
email: customerservice@broadviewpress.com

UK, Ireland, and continental Europe
NBN International, Estover Road, Plymouth, UK PL6 7PY
Tel: 44 (0) 1752 202300   Fax: 44 (0) 1752 202330
email: enquiries@nbninternational.com

Australia and New Zealand
NewSouth Books
c/o TL Distribution, 15-23 Helles Ave., Moorebank, NSW, 2170
Tel: (02) 8778 9999; Fax: (02) 8778 9944
email: orders@tldistribution.com.au

www.broadviewpress.com

This book is printed on paper containing 100% post-consumer fibre.

Typesetting and assembly: True to Type Inc., Claremont, Canada.

PRINTED IN CANADA

Contents

Preface and Acknowledgements

This is an edition of *Candide* with introduction and primary sources meant to engage readers in intellectual history and philosophy. *Candide* itself, the most popular piece of comic writing in history, should be read with pleasure for its humor. Throughout the plot and parody, Voltaire entertains a topic that he visits numerous times in other writing, and that he shares in discussion with his contemporaries. The topic is a philosophical one, reflected in a simple and durable question: If there is a benevolent God in the world, then why is there evil? A rich and remarkable variety of candidates for answers to that question populate the following pages.

Voltaire considers the significance of evil through three forms of writing: fiction, poetry, and philosophical essay. *Candide* (1759), the *Poem upon the Destruction of Lisbon* (1756), and *We Must Take Sides* (1772), are the best paths to choose within these different rhetorical approaches. Very different kinds of argument are found in these three works, as I suggest in my introduction, but roughly the same humanistic concerns prevail, and the same practical solutions occupy Voltaire in all three treatments. One author, three literary styles, and one answer.

Good intellectual history can serve at least two useful purposes. First, it can explain the motivation that drives the development of a topic: who writes for whom, and why. Motivation is sketched in this volume initially in my introduction, which provides detailed history and an interpretation of the times and of individuals who wrote for those times. The reader may judge and re-interpret my presentation in light of the words of several of those directly involved in the discussion, in the primary source material that follows *Candide*. A second task for intellectual history is to make past efforts relevant for present concerns. Voltaire and the other authors translated in this edition can provide *any* reader with new and challenging food for thought on evil and the possible responses to it.

The final selection, a brief vignette of Voltaire and James Boswell in full battle, sets the stage for this drama as well as it serves to close the curtain.

My thanks for aid in the preparation of this text go to a number of students at Allegheny College, including Geoff Seaman, Tibor Solymosi, Carolyn Roncolato, and Kira Hartger; and of course thanks goes to the College itself, in the persons of

Dean Linda DeMeritt and members of the Academic Support Committee, for much research support, including release time as a Humanities Chair. I am grateful for the help of the Hunt Institute for Botanical Documentation and its senior librarian, Charlotte Tancin, and the help of many at the Pelletier Library of Allegheny College. I am also indebted to my fine colleagues Eric Boynton, Bill Bywater, Nicholas Cronk, Sean Greenberg, Glenn Holland, Carl Olson, Laura Reeck, and Phillip Wolfe, as well as my dearest colleague, Carolyn Butler Palmer.

Detail of a contemporary engraved depiction of the Lisbon earth-
quake of 1755. The scene is reminiscent of the opening scene in
Candide, chapter five. Image courtesy of the National Information
Service for Earthquake Engineering, EERC, University of California,
Berkeley.

Introduction

Candide was an illegitimate offspring, like its protagonist and perhaps its author as well. The book popped into print sometime in January 1759, with just one of numerous publishing houses selling over six thousand copies by late February. Voltaire did not claim responsibility and went so far as to create a smokescreen, sending letters to his primary publisher indicating that "there are impertinent persons attributing to me this book that I have never seen!" The title page included an attribution of authorship to a fictional "Mr. Doctor Ralph," but the illusion did not stand for long, given the attention it received. Voltaire's authorship became an open secret and soon thereafter one edition, probably a pirate issue not authorized by him, indicated "Volt★★★" as author. At least sixteen distinct French language editions appeared during that year, published in several cities, including Geneva, Amsterdam, and London.

Voltaire would not claim his popular child in public, presumably, because of its difficult disposition. *Candide*'s very disrespectful satirical treatment of many national and religious institutions of Europe, combined with thinly disguised references to public figures, and occasionally undisguised ones, made it contraband in many lands. Voltaire had, earlier in his life, been sent to prison for less. Publishing surreptitiously under his pseudonym, and having arranged the affair through many presses and collaborators from his perch in the Swiss countryside, Voltaire anticipated that the book would be very controversial and very popular. He knew that it would also be rapidly reproduced in pirate editions, with market share lost to his own publishers as a consequence. Piracy could not be prevented, partly because any enforcement would be undercut when the book came to be banned in various European cities; and it was banned in Paris and Geneva, perhaps forty days after publication, and placed on the Roman Catholic index of prohibited books shortly thereafter. *Candide*'s production, then, was rapid and meticulously orchestrated. Copies printed in Geneva were sold elsewhere exclusively, to allow deniability for Voltaire's Geneva printer concerning the copies sold in Geneva, and copies that entered the gates of Paris after the ban were smuggled through, then sold surreptitiously, *sous le manteau*—from "under the cloak"—of booksellers and peddlers. The penalty for owning the book in Paris was confiscation upon discovery; the penalties for selling contraband books ranged from fines to incarceration, and even, rarely, sentence of death by exhaustion or disease, as a rowing slave on a French galleon of war. This was very serious business for a work of light comedy, but *Candide* also had its serious aspects, which contributed to its inflammatory nature.

A Life Worthy of a Book: Voltaire

What was inflammatory? First, we might consider the setting, and, especially, Voltaire's own history and reputation. The author was born François-Marie Arouet in 1694, the second son, and the third and last child to survive infancy, in the family of François Arouet and Marie Marguerite Arouet (born Daumart). François-Marie was, at least later in life, convinced that his father was in fact a minor poet named Roquebrune, and after 1719 he would distance himself from any lineage, choosing to live by no name but Voltaire, an approximate anagram of 'Arouet.' François Arouet hoped that the youth would take to the study of law and then to the role of a public servant after completing a primary education at the finest school in Paris, the *Collège Louis-le-Grand*. François-Marie neglected his study of law and concentrated instead on poetry, despite many efforts on his father's part to set him on a proper road, up to 1714. Voltaire had already decided to become a writer, however, and had connected with a hedonistic literary circle gathered by Guillaume, Abbé de Chaulieu (1639-1720). Chaulieu's circle sharpened the young writer's wit, which allowed him entry to the French court, and also drove him out of it. In 1716, he was exiled from Paris for three months as payback for his scandalous writing about the Regent of France, and a year later he would serve eleven months in the Bastille Prison for a similar offence.

Voltaire's life was varied and vivacious from his release up to *Candide*'s publication in 1759, and an abbreviated history, focusing especially upon Voltaire's literary development and the formative influences yielding *Candide*, is all that can be provided here.[1] While in Chaulieu's circle, Voltaire began writing for the stage. His first and very successful play, *Oedipus*, opened at the *Comédie Française* in 1718, and returned him to favor with the Prince Regent. A string of successes in the theatre established him very quickly as a cultural superstar of Paris, opening the

---

1 A chronology of important events, including the publication of many of Voltaire's works and their correct French language titles, follows this introduction.

doors to society parties, to a variety of lovers, to investment deals, and to substantial government stipends in recognition of his artistic work. A satirical view of this lifestyle may be found in chapter twenty-two of *Candide*, and homage to Chaulieu, and perhaps to his own older self, lies in chapter twenty-five, in the character Pococurante.

Voltaire's success in Parisian society was dashed in 1726 by a simple verbal offense, directed at a member of the French peerage. One evening shortly thereafter, the Chevalier de Rohan had Voltaire called down from the dinner he was enjoying with the Duc de Sully, and the Chevalier, still seated in his carriage, instructed his servants to beat Voltaire. Voltaire found his noble friends impassive to the abuse, and this provided him with his most humiliating lesson in the functioning of civil order, and in the limited power a mere author and wit could command. His challenge of a duel to settle the matter was reported to the authorities by the Chevalier—which would have reflected very poorly on the Chevalier, had Voltaire been of high birth—and Voltaire found himself in the Bastille a third time. Though not his final official arrest warrant, it was the final prison sentence of Voltaire's long life. Mercifully brief, it was followed by banishment from Paris, and Voltaire chose life in England for two years.

Voltaire's expulsion and subsequent tour in England led to a new political cast in his writing as well as a new form, the published essay, which supported more direct political criticism than could be clothed in the garb of a poem, or of a French play of the time, which required embroidery upon classical themes. The *Philosophical Letters* or *Letters Concerning the English Nation* (1733), appearing first in English translation, and shortly thereafter in French, provided indirect criticism of French society by highlighting progressive aspects of English civility. Voltaire focused especially upon English tolerance of variety in expression of religions, an abiding division in French society that Voltaire would consider especially later in life. Subtle criticism also infused the representation of England, however, in passages such as the following:

Take a view of the *Royal* [Mercantile] *Exchange* in *London*, a place more venerable than many courts of justice, where the representatives of all nations meet for the benefit of mankind. There the Jew, the Mahometan, and the Christian transact together, as tho' they all profess'd the same religion, and give the name of Infidel to none but bankrupts. There the Presbyterian confides in the Anabaptist, and the Churchman depends on the Quaker's word....

If one religion only were allowed in *England*, the government would very possibly become arbitrary; if there were but two, the people wou'd cut one another's throats; but as there are such a multitude, they all live happy and in peace....

Nevertheless, tho' every one is permitted to serve God in whatever mode or fashion he thinks proper, yet their true religion, that in which a man makes his fortune, is the sect of Episcoparians or Churchmen, call'd the Church of *England*, or simply the church, by way of eminence. No person can possess an employment either in *England* or *Ireland* unless he be rank'd among the faithful, that is, professes himself a member of the Church of *England*. This reason (which carries mathematical evidence with it) has converted such numbers of dissenters of all persuasions, that not a twentieth part of the nation is out of the pale of the establish'd church.[1]

In English exile, Voltaire visited literary figures, including Alexander Pope, whom he esteemed very highly as a poet, but did not connect well with personally. He formed a firmer, but eventually ambivalent, attachment to Lord Henry St. John Bolingbroke, an English peer and once an ambitious parliamentarian and secretary of war. Bolingbroke, who had been exiled to France from 1715 to 1724, wrote copiously on politics, statecraft, religion, and epistemology. He and Pope developed their optimistic philosophies concerning the human condition together, and both men became targets of Voltaire's criticism in some of the writing presented in the Appendix to this volume.

Voltaire received permission to return to Paris in 1728, and there led a grand life. He continued to write many plays, poems, and essays; he also joined others in a successful scheme for exploiting a government lottery, the first of a number of ventures that ensured a very great financial future. In 1733 Voltaire met and soon fell for his first great love, Emilie de Breteuil, eight years married to the Marquis du Châtelet-Lomont. A warrant for

---

1   Letters VI, V of Voltaire, *Letters Concerning the English Nation*, ed. Nicholas Cronk, (Oxford: Oxford UP, 1994) pp. 30, 26. The archaic expression 'Mahometan,' which may suggest incorrectly that Muslims worship Muhammad as God rather than Prophet, will be replaced elsewhere in this volume with 'Muslim.'

Voltaire's arrest concerning the *Philosophical Letters* led him to choose exile at her retreat in Cirey, far from the Marquis's home, where Voltaire and Emilie, Marquise du Châtelet, loved, entertained visitors lavishly, and wrote as a pair. Voltaire re-acquainted himself with English thought, reviving an interest in Isaac Newton and English science that du Châtelet encouraged. The pair hosted prominent scientists and conducted a few experiments of their own; du Châtelet developed her influential scientific and mathematical writing, and Voltaire wrote the popular and influential *Elements of the Philosophy of Newton* (1738). Voltaire also began about this time to greatly expand upon efforts begun in England within another literary form: history. His topics for political and national history varied greatly over the course of his life, building a remarkable background from which he continuously drew. His most ambitious work was the *Essay on Mores* (1756),[1] a world history that ran from prehistory right to his own century. That work was fifteen years in production and completed only a few years before *Candide*. Its composition provided much of the material used to flesh out the travels of the fictional character Candide, especially in the New World and Turkey.

Voltaire spent wonderful years at Cirey with du Châtelet, venturing out occasionally, and, from 1745 to 1747, making his last unsuccessful stab at returning to Paris and its court culture. In 1749, however, du Châtelet died while giving birth to the child of another lover. Her death was a profound blow and sent Voltaire wandering for most of a year, until yet another arrest warrant for yet another publication provided him with a good reason to choose deeper exile, in another court, at the invitation of Frederick II of Prussia. Voltaire had once seen the makings of an enlightened ruler in the Emperor, but had long since had his doubts, and his few years in Berlin were not enjoyable. He finally settled in 1755 on an estate that he named "Les Délices" in the area of Geneva, Switzerland, and returned to a happy equilibrium, beginning the highly productive final stage of his life.

For five years before du Châtelet's death, Voltaire had taken another lover whom he saw occasionally, his widowed niece Marie-Louise Denis. She joined him a number of times in Berlin, then permanently at Les Délices, and finally, at their even larger paired estates at Ferney and Tournay, both of which were just far

---

1 *Essai sur les Mœurs*, or full title: *Essai sur l'Histoire Générale et sur les Mœurs et l'Esprit des Nations*. The word "mœurs" is perhaps best translated as "ways of life," or with the out-of-use English expression "mores," rather than "morals."

enough from the city of Geneva to be politically comfortable residences. The wealthy pair set up what amounted to a very small court of their own, often hosting a dozen or so long-term residents and sometimes hundreds of visitors who would come to watch Voltaire's plays at his private theatre. That venue often provided a workshop in which Voltaire fine-tuned his dramatic productions before their release in Paris.

Late in 1755, an event—an earthquake, near the Bay of Lisbon in Portugal—caught Voltaire's attention. The Lisbon earthquake, and a consequent tsunami, erased perhaps 30,000 lives—a tenth of the population of one of the largest and most Roman Catholic of Europe's cities. It occurred on a Sunday morning, as many attended services for All Saints Day, November 1. The event galvanized Europe. John Wesley warned, "Why should we not now, before London is as Lisbon ... acknowledge the hand of the Almighty, arising to maintain his own cause?"[1] For, if God has a plan, then that event would appear to be part of the plan, as is evident in Psalm 148: "fire and hail, snow and vapour, wind and storm, fulfill his word."

Wesley's comment indicates two features that concerned Voltaire. First, he quite agreed with the suggestion contained within Wesley's question, that God had reasons for the tragic event. The *Poem upon the Destruction of Lisbon*, which Voltaire wrote just days after learning of the disaster, provides a response, a lament that displays that he cannot comprehend any reason behind such a divine plan. The earthquake led Voltaire to promote more resolutely than before a theological view that is reflected in many of his works, and might easily be read into *Candide*. Voltaire suggested the position of deism, which denies any credence to knowledge through revelation, but maintains that the world is a divine creation with an evident ordering that can be understood through reason.[2] Yet Voltaire found that, though

---

1   "Serious thoughts occasioned by the late earthquake at Lisbon" (1755) in *The Works of the Reverend John Wesley, A.M.*, ed. John Emory (New York: T. Mason and G. Lane, 1839) vol. 6, p. 242.

2   Voltaire appears to have used the terms "theism" and "deism" interchangeably; for example, as the title of the same article in different editions of his *Philosophical Dictionary*. In this introduction the term "deism" will not indicate any commitment as to whether human reason could possibly discover a divine plan or refute claims concerning divine providence. This use reflects the *Oxford Dictionary*: "belief in the existence of a Supreme Being as the source of finite existence, with the rejection of revelation and the supernatural doctrines of Christianity; [also know as] 'natural religion'."

God's order is evident—for example, in the laws of nature—nevertheless, whatever plans God might have could not concern human happiness or any conception of a goodness that humans might fathom. So, Voltaire's answer was very different from what we might expect Wesley had in mind, for Wesley wished to motivate the action of his followers in light of his interpretation of God's will. By aligning God with what he saw to be a just cause, Wesley verges upon the sort of religious fanaticism that reflects a second concern of Voltaire. Voltaire blamed many of the worst crimes of recent history on fanaticism, most notably the slaughter of French Protestants following St. Bartholomew's Day in 1572, the assassination of the French king Henri IV in 1610 by a Catholic fanatic, and the Catholic and Protestant sentiments that fueled the Thirty Years' War (1618-48). Voltaire found the most dangerous fanaticism to be that which aligned with the machinery of state power, as in the first and final of these examples.

The stage has now been set up to the composition of *Candide*, and the biographical details considered above should make it apparent that Voltaire learned a great deal about human callousness, indiscretion, and duplicity through his own experiences. Many of these events and others in Voltaire's life and in European history would find their way into passages of *Candide*, and the resulting picture that Voltaire paints of his fellow creatures, not to exclude himself, is rich in detail and far from flattering. Yet the deepest blow to Voltaire's belief in goodness may have instead been his observation of evil in nature, particularly in the Lisbon earthquake. Voltaire would visit evil in both of these aspects repeatedly in his writing, and he would also repeatedly suggest the remedies that he could discover.

Voltaire's Humanism Through Poetry, Philosophy, and Fiction

Voltaire's varied discussion of evil is featured in three very different literary forms: poetry, philosophical essay, and fiction. Each form has its own rules or rhetorical setting, each demanding of Voltaire substance and style that is worthy of distinct consideration. Each form is also of great significance in Enlightenment culture. For these reasons, all are represented in this volume and are accompanied by a collection of writings that either inspired Voltaire to think about these problems or presented responses to his views. What is lightly sketched, but present in *Candide*, is more clearly delineated in writing from the other forms, and the reverse holds true as well; consequently, a study of the three forms affords a much clearer understanding of Voltaire's purposes.[1]

Poetry is the best place to start, for it is the form to which Voltaire first turns when his sensibilities are rattled by the Lisbon earthquake. Earlier, Voltaire had been delighted by Alexander Pope's *Essay on Man* (1733-34), and he swiftly commenced his own imitation, the *Discourse in Verse on Man*. Two decades later, immediately following the earthquake, Voltaire writes a very different reply, the *Poem upon the Destruction of Lisbon* (1756). He continues to respect Pope's poetic ability, which he had praised to the skies in the *Philosophical Letters*, and in a preface to the *Poem* Voltaire writes that he also respects Pope's philosophy; indeed, he "agrees with him, on almost every question." Yet Voltaire demurs from and challenges Pope's central purpose, the attempt to "vindicate the ways of God to Man," which is a goal that echoes one thesis in Milton's *Paradise Lost*.

Pope's *Essay* is the most remarkable work of philosophical argument in the form of poetry since the Classical era. The argument is well and clearly represented in Pope's own words, in the selection for this edition (Appendix A1). Here we can sketch the terrain contested between Pope and Voltaire, as the latter takes up a challenge offered in Pope's lines. Pope maintains that our efforts to understand God (and consequently, to judge God) show overblown pride that puts us out of our place. He asks,

> Is the great chain, that draws all to agree,
> And drawn supports, upheld by God, or thee? (p. 144)

Pope reinforces his concern regarding our inherent limitations with the question, "... can the part contain the whole?" and concludes by explaining our place and proper purview,

> That Reason, Passion answer one great aim;
> That true Self-Love and Social are the same;
> That Virtue only makes our Bliss below;
> And all our Knowledge is, Ourselves to Know. (p. 156)

---

1 A greater grasp of Voltaire's thoughts on evil may be gained by adding three other literary dimensions to the view: Voltaire's plays, historical writing, and correspondence. There are limits to what a short introduction and a small collection can contain, however, and relevant works in these other literary forms are noted briefly in the Select Bibliography of this volume.

Voltaire's poem is a fitting reply to these particular passages. His challenge is clear:

All's right, you answer, the eternal cause
Rules not by partial, but by general laws.
Say what advantage can result to all,
From wretched Lisbon's lamentable fall? (p. 159)

Voltaire does not answer this question. He does not reflect the arrogant pride that Pope warns against, and that a claim to knowledge of God's purposes would suggest. Instead, he draws a judicious humanistic conclusion early in the poem that makes no attempt to vindicate God:

God my respect, my love weak mortals claim;
When man groans under such a load of woe,
He is not proud, he only feels the blow. (pp. 159-60)

Voltaire neglects a good deal of Pope's argument and conclusion, which are encapsulated in Parts Three and Four of the *Essay on Man*. Those lines include what may be used as a rejoinder to Voltaire's conclusion ("God loves from whole to parts ..." p. 156 lines 97-118). They also present Pope's broader argument about human vanity, and about how to be, and why to be, a virtuous person. In its presentation in this volume, the *Essay* has been trimmed to one third of its size to show, at a similar length, the argument most relevant to Voltaire's *Poem upon the Destruction of Lisbon*. Voltaire's composition is certainly not as complex, allusive to tradition and ideas, or as clever as Pope's, and so Voltaire's argument appears the weaker in an over-all comparison. But Voltaire's poem was an occasional work, not intended to be of great significance, whereas the *Essay* is Pope's masterwork.

Voltaire bookends his poem with a prose preface and a conclusion of sorts: a lengthy final footnote. The final footnote gives great weight to revelation concerning an afterlife, which provides a light of hope for humanity, but Voltaire sees it as false hope. Some claims voiced by Voltaire, such as the statement concerning the value of religious revelation in the final sentence of the footnote, are either irony or dissimulation, for Voltaire believes quite the opposite of what he writes. His true view on the lack of value of revelation becomes very clear in the *Poem on Natural Law*, which was published together with the *Poem upon the Destruction of Lisbon* in their first appearance. Voltaire's *Philosophical Diction-ary* articles, "Theist," included in this volume (Appendix B4), and "Theism," also suggest that he had ideas concerning revela-tion, God, and providence that were quite different from what Catholic or Protestant views required.

Jean-Jacques Rousseau replied to Voltaire's *Poem* in the *Letter on Providence*, which Voltaire received within months of the appearance of the *Poem*, and which saw publication, perhaps without the assent of either party, in 1759. Selections from Rousseau's *Letter*, reproduced as Appendix A3, show diverse, even scattered arguments, and in places he contradicts his own apparent purposes. For example, Rousseau is at odds to claim, "I do not see that one could look for the origins of moral evil any-where but in man," and then to attempt to support that position just two sentences further along with the suggestion, "I believe I have shown that ... most of the physical evils we experience are really of our own making." "Most" is just not to the point, for if a single one of those evils is not of our making, then it would appear that its origin, its moral source, lies elsewhere. Rousseau makes it clear late in the *Letter* that he himself has little faith in arguments such as he has developed, for "they depend on topics about which human beings have no real idea." Rousseau, however, was the writer who initated the philosophical folly sur-rounding the *Poem*, for Voltaire's work is neither a philosophical discourse, nor a denunciation of God; rather, it is a poetic lament.

Rousseau's effort teaches an important negative lesson: it shows the ineptitude of replying to poetry with a prose essay. Even if his effort were done well, a rebuttal that treats poetry as if it were prose argument would be like shooting fish in a barrel, simply because the prose essayist has the opportunity to expand with less concern for beauty, and so can work to rule out false interpretations wherever necessary.[1] The poet, mindful of the art necessary to balance the piece, does not have this luxury. Voltaire's reply to Pope—pitching poetry against poetry—is by contrast a balanced challenge, a rhetorical match; and literary criticism of poetry would also be a very different thing from what Rousseau has attempted. One charge from Rousseau—that

---

1   For an example of such a prose reply, directed at Pope's *Essay*, see Jean-Pierre de Crousaz, *A Commentary on Mr. Pope's Principles of Morality* (New York: Garland Publishing, 1974). This is a translation from the French dated 1739, in facsimile reprint.

Voltaire's poem leaves no space for hope—does appear a more just ground, as literary criticism, for his attack. The charge may be valid as a specific criticism of the *Poem*, but one can find hope, and a significant, practical social conscience, in many of Voltaire's other works, as I will attempt to indicate below.

The debate over Pope's *Essay* only scratches the surface of the problem of evil in relation to the nature of God, and much more digging into Voltaire's ideas, and into the broader history of ideas, is required to clarify Voltaire's philosophy. Aid comes from the brief article "Of Good and Evil, Physical and Moral" (Appendix B2); one from among over five hundred polemical entries in Voltaire's *Philosophical Dictionary*, a work meant to infect society with radical ideas by means of brief, witty, and memorable articles arranged alphabetically by topic. There Voltaire focuses upon two strains of thought that were of great importance to eighteenth-century intellectuals: Manicheism, the view that the world is ruled by two gods, one good and one evil, and that the creatures of the earth are playing out a battle between the two; and philosophical optimism, an effort to account for the events of the world in order to cast light on the apparent obscurity of divine providence. Manicheism was introduced to many in the culture by the writing of Pierre Bayle just around 1700 (Appendix B1), and optimism was detailed by Gottfried Leibniz in his *Essays of Theodicy* of 1710 (Appendix B3), and would also feature in Pope's *Essay*.

Pierre Bayle was not necessarily a Manichean himself, but he provided a battery of brief skeptical arguments intended to unsettle received views about God. He deserves the title of skeptic, regarding both the power of reason and the accuracy of authoritative opinions. Though he regularly rounds out his discussions by promoting relatively orthodox theological views, the whole was invariably laced with claims that free thinkers read as invitations to reject those explicit conclusions. Like Voltaire's irony, Bayle's skeptical technique very effectively promoted free thought. Thus, early in the article "Paulicians" (Appendix B1) Bayle explicitly states that heretical views are "more agreeable to the ideas we have of order" than are traditional Christian views, some of which, he later states, simply "will not satisfy reason." Bayle concludes that "Men must captivate their understandings to the obedience of faith, and never dispute about some things," but leading to that point in the article, he has already engaged in such dispute at great length, and he similarly takes issue with Leibniz and many other authors, in other articles and other books. In an article (also excerpted in Appendix B1) that is meant to "clarify" his writing, Bayle states quite the opposite of his earlier caution: "It is by a lively sense of those difficulties [that] we learn the excellency of Faith ...." Bayle's varied twists might be unified into one clear view, but many, from his own time forward, have found in him a clear skeptic and a closet atheist, or perhaps a Manichean. As Bayle's writing could be all things to all people, it was even more slippery than Voltaire's, and was very actively discussed in the intellectual culture of the early eighteenth century. He may be read for the power of his argument, without settling upon a definitive conclusion on what his own views actually were.

Bayle's discussion of Manicheism is probably his most significant contribution to Enlightenment culture. Ranged against his broad, disruptive skepticism is Gottfried Leibniz's meticulous effort (Appendix B3) to return the discussion to one God alone, and to reconcile that account with the apparent disarray of our world. Leibniz would title his lengthy essay *Theodicy*, and that word would become the technical term used thereafter to describe any similar philosophical effort to show, through reason and the available evidence, that God is just. Responding directly to the Manichean assessment in Bayle, Leibniz proposes the perhaps surprising thesis that things in the world could not be better than they are, as the world is the construction of a single perfectly good creator, all-seeing and suffering neither interference nor imperfection; that is, an omniscient, omni-benevolent, and omnipotent God.

Which philosopher has the better arguments, and which is right about God, if either? The debate is reflected in *Candide* through two characters whom young Candide takes as his instructors. Martin, who is explicitly identified as a Manichean, appears in chapter nineteen, but we find little of real substance on the topic in his character. Martin's comments are more marked by pessimism and misanthropy, which are lightly supplemented by his self-proclaimed Manicheism in the hypothesis that, "when I cast an eye on this globe, or rather on this little ball, I cannot help thinking, but that God has abandoned it to some malignant being" (p. 100, this edition). Martin provides little specific discussion in matters metaphysical; he never even claims to be a philosopher, though he is identified as one by Candide, and is always happy to respond to a challenge. Voltaire took Manichean ideas much further in other writing, including *We Must Take Sides* (Appendix C1), but in *Candide* Manicheism is primarily a foil: an indication of a lightly noted radical alternative to contrast the optimistic philosophy of Pangloss. From Voltaire's perspective, neither philosopher has much in the way of good argument, and his solution will be a third, practical humanistic alternative to such philosophy, placed in Candide's mouth, that will be considered in the following section of this introduction.

Bayle was the primary expositor of Manicheism for Voltaire's time, but the opposite view represented in Pangloss has multiple sources. We see the first glimpse of the character in Leibniz, who coined a phrase that famously proceeds from the mouths first of Pangloss, then of his student Candide: the claim that this is "the best of all possible worlds." But how could that be? How could the goodness of God, and the horrors evident in this world, be reconciled? Leibniz's answer reflects a concern frequently noted in the history of theodicy: that the world, though created by God, nevertheless may resist God's will, or be impervious to it, in certain respects. Some Manicheans held that matter itself was an aspect of the evil principle, but Leibniz suggests that the resistance to simple good that we see is not an evil opposition, but instead, what might be thought of as a conceptual limitation upon God's power. Such limitation is not active opposition to the work of the creator, and it is not an external constraint either, unless we consider mere coherence to be a constraint. Earlier thinkers had already considered the relevance of such limitations in the abstract: perhaps even God could not make blue apart from a blue *substance*, or add a corner to a triangle, and still keep it a triangle. Leibniz carries this concern through by asking whether such limits, which he refers to as eternal truths or Verities, might explain the complications of this world, as compared with the apparent—but only apparent—simplicity of perfection. Thus Leibniz concludes:

> ... as this vast Region of Verities contains all possibilities it is necessary that there be an infinitude of possible worlds, that evil enter into diverse of them, and that even the best of all contain a measure thereof. Thus has God been induced to permit evil.[1]

The problem of theodicy is actually twofold, as Leibniz and many of his contemporaries see it, since it may concern two dis-

---

1 Gottfried Leibniz, *Theodicy*, trans. E.M. Huggard (New Haven: Yale UP, 1952). Part 1, Section 21, p. 136.

tinguishable sorts of evil, either produced by God, or produced by humans. Earthquakes might be a simple case of God-induced evil, which was called 'physical evil.' Earthquakes are straightforward, undeserved suffering that humans are in no way the authors of—at least, not before the era when seismology and building codes were feasible—but somehow, in the grand scheme, they might be a complication that must enter into the best of worlds. War, on the other hand, seems to be of *our* manufacture: the physical evil of suffering is bound up within it, but we ourselves choose to inflict the suffering, so we are responsible for what has been named the 'moral evil' of the world. The division is clear enough, but are humans the only source of moral evil? How could a good God present us with the choice of evil, and how could a good, omniscient and omnipotent God allow us to do such evil, to sin, rather than foreseeing and forestalling our damaging choices? Given God's omniscience, it would seem that our fates are predestined, with God effectively paving the road to suffering, and damning the sinner and blessing the saint before the race has been run.

These are classic problems of free will and of theodicy that were debated across Europe, particularly from the period of the Protestant reformation to the French revolution. Bayle suggests that, even if free choice is the greatest of gifts with which God favors humanity, it seems inconsistent that a good God would contain within that gift the means for our own suffering. "There is no enemy so inveterate who would not upon these terms load his enemy with favours," Bayle writes (Appendix B1, p. 182). Leibniz again steps forward to reply. First, he admits that reason may not be adequate to solve all of these "mysteries," and he even suggests that those of little faith might rightly "be content with instruction on faith ... offering to God a sacrifice of their curiosity." Second, for the incurably inquisitive, Leibniz suggests that "Mysteries may be *explained* sufficiently to justify belief in them; but one cannot *comprehend* them, nor give understanding of how they come to pass."[1] To support the idea of impassable limits to comprehension, Leibniz argues that all explanation is limited: in natural science, as in theology, explanations come to an end, and there is no final satisfying resting place for inquiry.

In a third effort to reconcile human will and God's goodness, Leibniz returns to the strategy shown in the eternal truths discus-

---

1 Leibniz, *Theodicy*, Preliminary Dissertation, sections 40 and 5, pp. 97, 76. The same sentiments are also expressed in Bayle, within a quotation from Jesuit theologian René Rapin (1621-87), see p. 188, this volume.

sion, arguing that God is not the author of moral evil, after sketching a distinction between the antecedent and the consequent causes of moral evil. Leibniz has already argued that some features of the world may arise as constraints upon the not-so-simple perfection that is the best of all possible worlds. Human freedom and sin may be included among those constraints, and in an earlier work, Leibniz had referred to sin as a necessary part of the best of worlds, a part that provides the required context for good. He wrote, in a metaphor, "Sins occur to bring forth a universal harmony of things, thus distinguishing the light by means of shadows."[1] On the one hand, he argues, God is the creator of human will, and so, indirectly or antecedently, produces those shadows, and is the author of all of our evil choices. On the other hand, God produces us as complex wholes, and we, rather than God, make the choices that we ourselves do make. It is a fine point—perhaps too fine to be satisfying—but it might be improved by considering an analogy. The situation is much like that in which a king appoints a general to lead his army: the king does not directly appoint lower officers to other posts, since that is the general's role, yet the king is the antecedent cause of their appointment, and, consequently, he might well be in a position to anticipate who will be appointed to those posts by the general.[2] An omniscient God, then, might well arrange things according to the best plan, fully knowing what will arise (and not merely anticipating, as the king must do). But God is not the author of the individual's action, even if God permits the action to occur, because it is through the individual's choice that the action is done. With the antecedent/consequent distinction in place, as well as the restriction posed by the eternal truths, Leibniz can construct a general argument for theodicy that includes human will and sin, showing God's benevolent role. Leibniz summarizes his findings:

it must be concluded that God wills all good in itself *antecedently*, that He wills the best *consequently* as an end, that

---

1 "The confession of a philosopher," in Leibniz, *Confessio philosophi: Papers Concerning the Problem of Evil, 1671-1678*, ed. Robert C. Sleigh (New Haven: Yale UP, 2005), p. 45.

2 I have here modified an example that Leibniz used in correspondence (Section 3 of the letter to Hessen-Rheinfels, 12 April 1686) along the way to a conclusion similar to the one that I draw (Section 5 of the letter to Arnauld, 14 July 1686). The correspondence may be found in G.W. Leibniz, *Philosophical Texts*, ed. R.S. Woolhouse and Richard Francks (Oxford: Oxford UP, 1998), pp. 98ff.

He sometimes wills the indifferent and physical evil as a means, but that He will only permit moral evil if it is absolutely required or from some hypothetical necessity that links it with the best. This is why the *consequent will* of God, which has sin as its object, is only permissive.[1]

God permits sin and physical evil, then, allowing these constraints as the necessary means to the realization of this best of all possible worlds. Leibniz's argument to this effect is presented in a new translation for this edition by Sean Greenberg as Appendix B3.

Though it is not evident from the jocular style of *Candide*, which contains brief musings on human free will, Voltaire also maintained a serious concern for many, though not all, of the problems Leibniz poses. What he jokes about in *Candide*, he writes of more seriously in the *Elements of the Philosophy of Newton*, and in *We Must Take Sides*. Essentially, Voltaire agrees with both Leibniz and Bayle that reason may not be satisfied when we inquire into the divine purpose for earthquakes and war. Yet Leibniz breaks from the others by asserting nevertheless that reason indicates that God is good, and that the best among worlds is all that a good God would choose to make. Must the best of all possible worlds, then, contain these evils? Leibniz replies to all such requests with a general capitulation, not to the presence of unaccounted evil, but to the limits of human reason:

> It is true that possible worlds without sin and without unhappiness can be imagined ... but these very worlds would be very much inferior in goodness to our own. I cannot make you see this in detail, for can I know and can I represent to you infinities and compare them together?[2]

Leibniz's blanket limitation upon reason is not reflected in the character of Pangloss in the least. Pangloss would provide us with detailed solutions to unravel the tangle of evil in this world; in a memorable passage in chapter four of *Candide*, he concludes that the evil that is syphilis is merely a negative shadow, more than made up for in this world by the virtuous presence of chocolate and cochineal dye. Though Leibniz claims, "I cannot show ... in detail" why God allowed syphilis, earthquakes and more into this best of possible worlds, others have tried, and they provide

---

1 *Theodicy*, Part 1, Section 25 (p. 207, this edition).
2 *Theodicy*, Part 1, Section 10 (p. 205, this edition).

further material for Pangloss. The most remarkable among them was Noël Pluche, who made such analysis his specialty, in popular science texts of Voltaire's time.

Pluche's most famous work, *The Spectacle of Nature* (8 volumes, 1732-50), was one of the most common volumes to be found in personal libraries in France and across Europe in the mid-eighteenth century (see Appendix B5). *Spectacle* contains vivid explanations of just why earthquakes happen, why carrion-eating animals roam, and even why burrowing worms destroy ships at sea. Each is for humanity's benefit, the author suggests, compliments of a benevolent God. Pluche's conclusions are decidedly more anthropocentric than Pope's claims, such as this one from the *Essay on Man*:

While man exclaims, "See all things for my use!"
"See man for mine!" replies a pamper'd goose:
And just as short of reason he must fall,
Who thinks all made for one, not one for all. (p. 153)

Pluche's focus upon the purposes behind God's design rests at the intersection of theology and natural science. He relies very heavily on careful direct observation of nature and an understanding of the scientific writing of his time. Pluche is eager to solve these puzzles, and such effort remained a legitimate form of explanation during his time in some natural sciences, such as geology, though it had lost currency in other fields, such as physics. The attempt to find traces of God in nature, natural theology, is a close cousin to more narrowly philosophical theodicy, and it would continue as an adjunct to science for much longer, with some of the most eminent English scientists of many fields even trying their hands at it a century later in eight books with the series title *Bridgewater Treatises on the Power, Wisdom and Goodness of God, as Manifested in the Creation* (1833-36). Today, vestiges of such a strategy for explanation may still be found in earnest discussions regarding God's intentions concerning the creation, in the hypotheses of anthropic cosmology, and intelligent design.[1]

---

1 For an introduction to the *Bridgewater Treatises*, see John Robson, "The Fiat and Finger of God: The Bridgewater Treatises," in Bernard Lightman and Frank Turner, eds., *Victorian Faith in Crisis: Essays on Continuity and Change in Nineteenth-Century Religious Belief* (Stanford UP, 1990), pp. 71-125. On anthropic cosmology, see John Barrow and Frank Tipler, *The Anthropic Cosmological Principle* (Oxford: Oxford UP, 1987). (Continued)

Voltaire, like many now familiar figures of the Enlightenment, was thoroughly unimpressed with Pluche's work, but not quite able to ignore it. Pangloss explains, "Observe, that the nose is formed for spectacles, and therefore we come to wear spectacles. The legs are visibly designed for stockings, and therefore we come to wear stockings" (p. 48). Voltaire reiterates the point, referring explicitly to Pluche's book, in the *Philosophical Dictionary* article "Final Causes":

"The Spectator of Nature," contends in vain that the tides were attached to the ocean to enable ships to enter more easily into their ports, and to preserve the water from corruption; he might just as probably and successfully have urged that legs were made to wear boots, and noses to bear spectacles.[1]

Voltaire's article on "Final Causes," portions of which appear as Appendix B6, presents a helpful complement to *Candide*, as it contains Voltaire's own philosophical lesson on how to correct the obvious mistake in Pangloss's oft-repeated argument structure, which puts the effect (the design of spectacles) before the conditions that contribute to the causes of that effect (one of which is the shape of the nose).

Though a flaw of logic is put on display in *Candide* and addressed in "Final Causes," it is clear from the bulk of *Candide* that Pangloss's optimism, rather than his logic, is the more important target of the comedy. By Pluche's account, catastrophes are a godsend. We find that river systems helpfully wash our land, but along with them must come earthquakes, which arise because of the volatile materials brought into the earth by the rivers. To reduce the violence of the earthquakes, God has happily provided volcanoes. Pangloss, similarly, produces many compound reflections on the order of the world and the evil within it, in service of the general and simple lesson that we must take the bad with the good, for all to be for the best.

The argument against this approach, represented through

Unlike anthropic cosmology, intelligent design arguments generally challenge some aspects of received evolutionary science; see William Dembski and Michael Ruse, eds., *Debating Design: From Darwin to DNA* (Cambridge: Cambridge UP, 2007).

1   *The Works of Voltaire, A Contemporary Version*, trans. William F. Fleming, 22 vols. (New York: E.R. DuMont, 1901) vol. V, 83. "Spectator of Nature" is a translation of Pluche's title (*Spectacle de la Nature*), as other indications on the page of Voltaire's text indicate.

parody, is clearest in the opening events of chapter four, as Pangloss persuades Candide not to save someone from drowning, since Pangloss "demonstrated to him that the bay of Lisbon had been made on purpose for the anabaptist to be drowned." Candide's choice should shock, for metaphysics might be about examining the structure of the world in order to aid living, but it does not lead quite so directly to conclusions about how to live in that world. Metaphysics and natural theology could aid or hamper one in this life, depending on how they are taken to illuminate problems, and Leibniz and Pluche both have their say concerning how metaphysics might help. Leibniz actually finds limited use for metaphysics, beyond enlightenment and solace: for practical matters, "we should act according to *the presumptive will of God*, striving with all our power to contribute to the general good ..."[1] Pluche seems to find the attraction of displaying our understanding still more invigorating, if it can inspire yet more understanding of the clues that God has placed at our disposal, to allow us to develop technologies and improve our condition. Voltaire, ever the Enlightenment figure, appears to believe that these efforts certainly do have their places, but they also do not serve more important purposes: good choices of action. His position is suggested in the irony of chapter four, is expressed through many of his writings, and appears in a particularly original, detailed, and elegant way in one of his late works, presented in an abridgment in this edition (Appendix C1), entitled, *We Must Take Sides, or The Principle of Action and the Eternity of Things: A Diatribe* (1772).

We Must Take Sides is a relatively long and challenging essay, with a complex structure. Brief mentions of an ongoing war between the Russians and the Turks and of religious factions open the work, and the significance of those passages only becomes apparent in the final chapter. Three identifiable sections, represented in reverse order in the work's convoluted full title, follow the opening. The first section (chapters 1 to 6) attempts to prove the continuing existence of a god, a "great artisan of things, ... necessary, eternal, intelligent, powerful, possessed of will, and free." Voltaire takes philosophical argument concerning God very seriously here, as he does in the *Poem upon the Destruction of Lisbon*; he even touches lightly upon natural theology, referring to God as an artisan who fashions all to function

---

1 "Discourse on Metaphysics," Section 4, p. 56, in G.W. Leibniz, *Philosophical Texts*, ed. R.S. Woolhouse and Richard Francks (Oxford: Oxford UP, 1998).

according to design. But Voltaire is clearly no optimist, and though Pluche explains how all is arranged for the good of humanity, and Leibniz gestures at the usefulness of faith, Voltaire will not agree. He does rule out the Manichean option by suggesting, too swiftly for serious argument, that the presence of physical laws in nature rules out the disharmony that would result from either cooperative or oppositional action of two gods. Voltaire argues for a "very powerful" single God, who should be an object of respect, but not of love. His position, then, is a deism that reflects his views in the *Poem*: good and evil are not obviously a concern of this God. "It is just as absurd to say ... that God is just or unjust as to say that God is blue or square," he writes in an earlier essay, his *Treatise on Metaphysics* (1734).[1]

The second section of *We Must Take Sides* (chapters 7 to 19) concerns the "principle of action" in both inanimate and sentient beings that operate under eternal, or natural, law, and its connection to evil. Voltaire considers especially human freedom, our "principle of action"—Voltaire's analysis of the meaningful aspect of our concept of the soul—and the natural and human-made evils that we face. He relentlessly attacks Alexander Pope and others who hold that "all is well." He does not turn to a discussion of God at this point, or anywhere further along in the work, so the charge that there is evil in the world stands unchallenged, and the question of its origins is left hanging. The discussion turns to the third and final section (chapters 20 to 25), in which an atheist comments on the significance of the presence of evil for proving his beliefs. The atheist is followed by religious partisans—a Manichean, a pagan, a Jew, a Turk, and a theist—who provide similar comment, and who respond to the previous speakers' answers. The final spot does not go to the theist, however, but to "the citizen," who asks the others to intermarry their children, burn their divisive books, and then read a bit of Cicero, Montaigne, and La Fontaine—all humanists, the first a Stoic philosopher, the second an enigmatic Christian, and the third an early Enlightenment moralist with hedonistic ideals. So, Voltaire does not, ultimately, repudiate the theology and metaphysics that he has developed in the first and second sections, but it is very important to note that those discussions also do not ultimately bear fruit. Voltaire begins with metaphysics and natural

---

1   *Traité de Métaphysique*, in *The Complete Works of Voltaire*, vol. 14, ed.
    T.E.D. Braun, Colin Duckworth, W.H. Barber, Sylvain Menant (Oxford:
    Voltaire Foundation, 1989).

theology, but he ends by leaving them aside, instead going on to a more important subject that ties back to the brief mention of war that opens the work: his closing concerns how we can get along. The cause of humanism is the side we must take.

We Must Take Sides is an essay that closely reflects, in the form of philosophical argument, the concerns that Voltaire considers in a more literary form in *Candide*. It is important to see that neither piece of writing is intended to point us toward more than a very basic level of philosophy, or grasp of literature. *Candide* reflects and arises from the problems of theodicy that were suddenly brought to the fore by the earthquake of 1755, but explaining God's place is not, ultimately, its purpose. The story begins with allusions and jests concerning the manifold sources of evil, and with Pangloss's ridiculous attempts to make sense of it all. These efforts are followed by Martin's parallel attempts to fit all the world into a pessimistic mold. Pangloss is also permitted to complete a final summation concerning the best of possible worlds in the closing paragraph of the work, cheerfully recalling the staggering quantity of death and destruction that has led up to their current relative comfort, and so, he thinks, has been a necessary precursor to it. But Candide, no longer the student, sits at last among his several friends, including the two contrary philosophers, and he delivers the final words: "All that is very well ... but let us take care of our garden." The practical supplants the philosophical, as it does also in *We Must Take Sides*.

The Argument of *Candide*

Candide presents a search for wisdom nevertheless, within a mocking reflection on a traditional romance in which the hero overcomes great obstacles to prove himself worthy of his beloved. Cunegonde, named after an obscure saint who stood for fidelity and chastity, lacks the qualities of her namesake and so presents a stark contrast to Candide. His kindred spirit at the start, she is similarly battered by the world but invariably settles for imperfect compromise. Candide's quest degrades to absurdity, as his most precious prize is hollowed out before he finally obtains her in the last chapter. As a story of education and self-development, *Candide* is similarly parody, with practically all of the youth's learning also compressed into the final chapter. But the route that leads to this close is a path out of philosophy, taking the young hero away from his role as a student, through experience, and into practical action. Pangloss has his say almost exclusively in the first five chapters of the story, and he stands for little but brief comic relief thereafter. Martin, introduced in the middle of the book, hardly gets beyond anecdote. In the final chapter, both Pangloss and Martin learn from Candide's lead, and have already joined the effort to cultivate the garden.

Candide has two other practical guides, however: the old woman (who is never named in the text) and Cacambo, the native of the New World. If we peer through the comedy of their portrayal, we see very different advice and action from these two characters. When the old woman is present, she is consulted at practically every turn. She generally provides sound advice directed in the narrow interests of whomever she counsels, and she suggests the purchase of the farm late in the story. She has the wisdom of age, and is always ready to observe that all have suffered trials, like the main characters of the story, and herself not the least. Cacambo, much like the old woman, pulls Candide from the tightest scrapes efficiently, showing practical wisdom and a particular fascination with the practical wisdom of others. He also remains true to Candide—whom he seems to consider his lord and master, though he is merely in Candide's employ as a valet—even when entrusted with substantial funds that most other characters in the story would surely steal. These guides of practicality and fidelity provide cross-lighting to the ineffectual philosophers, showing a wisdom of sorts that the philosophers— the designated lovers of wisdom—do not show.

But none of the guides will do. None contain the moral compass that is patently missing from the world that Candide encounters. Where can he find it? Apparently not through religion, for the representatives of that sphere are some of the worst that he encounters. Similarly, not from the old man of Eldorado, in chapter fourteen, who lives in a different land, where the human quality of avarice is very simply inverted as generosity. The dervish and the old man of chapter thirty present limited theological and worldly advice, respectively; nevertheless, their wisdom hardly suffices to resolve the concerns that the story is meant to prompt. Candide's final state is clear, from his final statement, "let us take care of our garden." But what is the argument of *Candide* as a whole?

Candide ultimately leads us to ask two very simple questions: Where can we find the moral compass for our actions, and why are our lives, on balance, as ugly as they are? I believe Voltaire's answer becomes clear when *Candide* is placed in historical context, and is set against Voltaire's other writings, as I have attempted in this introduction. The evil in the make-up of the world we might never understand, but human-induced evil we can prevent, and the bulk of Candide's experience is of human evil. Pangloss the philosopher is no help: he has forsaken another, in the Bay of Lisbon, for metaphysical reasons, and when faced with other victims of the disaster, "Pangloss endeavoured to console them by affirming that things could not be otherwise than as they were" (p. 59). Implicit in this vignette is an attack by Voltaire on passive responses, excuses, and false consolation. Leibniz is perhaps a target, though, in all fairness, Leibniz also cautions that "we should not be quietists about the future, and stupidly wait with folded arms for what God will do...."[1] In the preface to the *Poem upon the Destruction of Lisbon*, Voltaire excuses Leibniz, but does charge "the supporters of Leibniz and Pope" with Pangloss's error. Voltaire writes:

If, when *Lisbon, Moquinxa, Tetuan*, and other cities were swallowed up with a great number of their inhabitants in the month of November 1755, Philosophers had cried out to the wretches, who with difficulty escaped from the ruins, "*all this is productive of general good; the heirs of those who have perished will increase their fortune; masons will earn money by rebuilding the houses; beasts will feed upon the carcasses buried under the ruins, it is the necessary effect of necessary causes, your particular misfortune is nothing, it contributes to universal good.*" Such an harangue would doubtless have been as cruel as the earthquake was fatal....[2]

Natural theology will not suffice. But *We Must Take Sides* and other works show that Voltaire actually engaged in metaphysics and natural theology, so it is clear that he did not find such efforts entirely corrupt.

Voltaire's position, then, is that the application of the intellect in theodicy and natural theology could promote four evils, if applied inappropriately. It might produce confusion about what divine goodness is, and confusion about the roles people should play in realizing that goodness and in improving their own con-

1 "Discourse on Metaphysics," Section 4, p. 56.
2 *The Works of M. de Voltaire. Translated from the French with Notes, Historical and Critical by T. Smollett, M.D., T. Francklin, M.A., and Others*. Printed for J. Newbery [*et al.*], at Salisbury (1761-74, 34 vols.). Vol. 33. For other sections of Voltaire's preface see Appendix A2.

dition. It could also lead to inaction in the face of those confusions, and to inappropriate efforts at consoling the victims of tragedy or evil. Furthermore, since Voltaire doubted the applicability of any conception of divine goodness or divine love, he would reduce the general usefulness of these efforts to a deistic minimum that also denies providence, as is found in the *Poem upon the Destruction of Lisbon*, and in *We Must Take Sides*.

The Lisbon earthquake may suggest that God having humanity's purposes solely in view in the design of all minutiae of the universe is absurd, though the mere suggestion of absurdity clearly lacks as substantive argument. But again, such debate about providence does not seem to be Voltaire's central point in *Candide*, though it is key in the *Poem*. Instead, Voltaire retains a theological aspect and shifts the argument, suggesting that we each bear the responsibility to determine which of our choices coordinate with the right universal order. He puts this most plainly in "Final Causes":

> Sheep, undoubtedly, were not made expressly to be roasted and eaten, since many nations abstain from such food with horror. Mankind are not created essentially to massacre one another, since the Brahmins, and the respectable primitives called Quakers, kill no one. But the clay out of which we are kneaded frequently produces massacres, as it produces calumnies, vanities, persecutions, and impertinences. It is not precisely that the formation of man is the final cause of our madnesses and follies, for a final cause is universal, and invariable in every age and place; but the horrors and absurdities of the human race are not at all the less included in the eternal order of things.[1]

Here we have an argument that reflects the heart of Voltaire. There is an "eternal order of things" that is not evident in *Candide*, but is explained further in *We Must Take Sides*. It shows very modest limits, however, that do not even clearly encompass the categories of good and evil. This shows the maximum extent to which Voltaire will extend his deism. His position is that this is not the best of possible worlds: all is decidedly not well, but it is our job to make it so. Voltaire supplements "let us take care of our garden" with an implicit argument for an Enlightenment ideal, represented in his own massive literary effort, and shown pointedly in the quotation from "Final Causes." Reason, and the

---

1 "Final Causes," pp. 221-22, this edition.

persuasive use of reason in writing, can lead us to our better natures.

After *Candide*

Following the Lisbon earthquake, Voltaire shifted from his somewhat cynical worldliness to a partial disengagement, as he withdrew into his gardens at Les Délices, as reflected in the last chapters of *Candide*, and then at a new residence at Ferney. That contented and comfortable retreat was followed by a burst into activism that took up the humanistic standard implicit in *Candide*. Voltaire would adopt *"écrasez l'infâme"*[1] as the catchphrase for his long battle, carried through in correspondence and in print, to challenge offenses against humanity by the powerful, and in particular, offenses linked to religious persecution. The campaign has its anticipations—for an example, see the reference to the fate of Admiral Byng in chapter twenty-three— and it gained momentum, and its name, just after *Candide* was published.

The first great move in Voltaire's campaign shows his concerns best. It was prompted by news in 1762 of the torture on the wheel and execution of a father, Jean Calas, who was accused of hanging his own son, Marc-Antoine, allegedly because he was contemplating a shift of religious faith, from Calvinism to the politically dominant Catholic church. Marc-Antoine had in fact committed suicide, and the public face of the events concealed a still deeper tragedy: the body of Marc-Antoine had been discovered by the family, who resolved to make his suicide appear an accident, so that he might be buried in consecrated ground. Voltaire's own detailed investigation, following an appeal addressed to him by the family, convinced him of fabrication and fanaticism by the Catholic authorities in Toulouse. Voltaire built a program of enormous political pressure to right the wrong, through a correspondence over three years that approached one thousand letters directed to his many friends and connections of rank across Europe, such as Frederick II and Catherine the Great of Russia. He also represented the affair in several publications, including his most important work on justice, the *Treatise on Tolerance* (1763). Voltaire campaigned for the Calas family until Jean

---

1 Voltaire's famous phrase does not translate well. Against the unobstructed power of Church and nobility he directed the command: "rub out the infamous thing." But it hardly catches the spirit; perhaps "fight the power" would do a bit better.

was exonerated, and the family was compensated by the Crown. Voltaire's choice of action in the Calas affair, and in a number of others over the next fifteen years, reflects the deliberately naïve and independent image of the enlightened citizen chosen for *We Must Take Sides*. Voltaire sees himself as just that citizen, wielding the power of reason through his pen, chipping away at inhumanity one case at a time through his voluminous correspondence, and writing plays, poems, and pamphlets that would lead his vast audience to think. Voltaire felt and found that things could become better (though perhaps not necessarily *good*) through a persuasive use of reason. This was his conception of Enlightenment, and it remains a plausible one today. It dictated Voltaire's role as *philosophe*, a term he came to use as an honorific, bestowed selectively upon those he found to be practically engaged thinkers.

Positive and productive as his humanistic campaign was, Voltaire was also a man with limits to his purview, who remained uncharacteristically blind to some forms of inhumanity within his sphere. Voltaire's treatment of Jews in *Candide* and elsewhere in his writing is a particularly clear case that deserves a special note. From Voltaire, one would expect criticism of any oppression carried out in the name of Judaism that parallels his criticism of Christianity and of other dominant organized religions. Voltaire discusses, for example, the inhumanity of the massacre of the worshippers of the golden calf that is ordered by Moses in Exodus 32. Since vicious but cleverly tweaked stereotypes are very much the stuff of Voltaire's chosen comedic approach, one might also expect a sharp and ungenerous satire of Jews that indicates areas in which such figures hold unchecked power, such as we find in Voltaire's portrayal of Jesuits as pedophiles and colonialist manipulators. Alongside the brief references to victimization of Jews by the authorities, however, we find them represented in *Candide* simply as vicious moneylenders and scheming traders. The portraits are less nuanced and not more fresh than Shakespeare's representation of Shylock in *The Merchant of Venice*, over one hundred and sixty years earlier. It may be fair to say, then, that Voltaire's spirit of humanity comes across as truncated, in this case. More humane attitudes than Voltaire would express were clearly available to any Enlightenment thinker: near to the time of composition of *Candide*, England had actively debated the political status of immigrant Jews, and Montesquieu, in *The Spirit of Laws* (1748), had shown a clearer grasp of the oppression suffered by this group than Voltaire ever would.

Overall, however, Voltaire promoted tolerance, and all would fit under his umbrella, except to the extent that their actions promoted division, or constituted abuse of power. Voltaire was unstoppable against such abuse, and he might be seen, in retrospect, as the first European human rights activist. *Candide* may be seen as an early literary effort in that campaign, and *We Must Take Sides* was one of Voltaire's last. As his work developed, Voltaire saw the effects. The man beaten by the servants of French nobility in his youth found his pen to be very powerful later in life, and he would write with great hope: "In the final analysis, opinion rules the world, and in the long run, the *philosophes* rule the opinions of men."[1]

---

1 Voltaire to Count and Countess d'Argental, 27 January 1766, in Besterman, ed., *The Complete Works of Voltaire* (Oxford: Voltaire Foundation, 1972).

Voltaire: A Brief Chronology

[handwritten: 1649 Charles I beheaded (Swot)]

1694	22 November: François-Marie Arouet baptized in Paris (he will adopt his famous name, Voltaire, in 1718).
1697	Pierre Bayle publishes the first of numerous editions of the *Dictionnaire Historique et Critique* (Historical and Critical Dictionary).
1704	Death of mother, Marie Marguerite Arouet (born Daumart).
1704-11	Attends the Jesuit-run school, Collège Louis-le-Grand (Paris).
1710	Gottfried Leibniz publishes *Essais de Théodicée* (Essays of Theodicy).
1711	François-Marie begins study of Law.
1713	September-December: Sent by father to Caen, to remove him from the bad influences of Parisian literary culture. Then sent as secretary to the ambassador to The Hague; the visit ends after a failed elopement. Returns to commence legal articling in Paris.
1714	Competes for poetry prize of the *French Academy* with *Voeux de Louis XIII*, but does not win.
1716	May-October: Exile to Sully-sur-Loire, by order of the Prince Regent, for writing satirical poetry about rumors of the Prince Regent's incestuous activities. Voltaire disavows authorship.
1717	May-March 1718: Accused of further satire against the Prince Regent; serves eleven months in Bastille prison, then six month exile at Châtenay.
1718	Stages first play, *Oédipe* (Oedipus), at the *Comédie Française*.
1722	Death of father (perhaps not biological father), François Arouet.
1723	Voltaire publishes *La Ligue*, an epic poem, later retitled *La Henriade* (Henriad), about French King Henry IV.
1726	Voltaire quarrels with the Chevalier de Rohan, is imprisoned for two weeks in the Bastille, then exiled from Paris. Travels to England.
1728	Returns to France. Voltaire is permitted to return to Paris five months later, spring 1729.

1732-50	Noël-Antoine Pluche publishes *Spectacle de la Nature* (Spectacle of Nature, 8 volumes).
1733	Alexander Pope publishes *Essay on Man*.
1733	Voltaire publishes *Letters Concerning the English Nation* in London. The work is republished in French shortly thereafter as *Lettres Philosophiques*.
1734	*Lettres Philosophiques* is condemned by the *Parlement* of Paris, and Voltaire flees to Cirey, setting up house with Madame Marie du Châtelet.
1735	Warrant for Voltaire's arrest rescinded: Voltaire remains at Cirey, for the most part, for the next decade.
1736	Voltaire begins his correspondence with crown-prince Frederick of Prussia (who becomes King Frederick II, "Frederick the Great," in 1740).
1738	Voltaire publishes an important work to popularize science, *Eléments de la Philosophie de Newton* (Elements of the Philosophy of Newton).
1741	Voltaire writes *Mahomet* (Muhammad), a play produced in Lille, and produced (then banned as sacrilege) the next year, in Paris. Voltaire begins work on the *Essai sur les Mœurs* (Essay on Mores), his universal history.
1745	Voltaire returns to Paris society, is appointed historiographer to King Louis XV, and begins work on a history of the king. The husband of Madame Marie-Louise Denis dies, and she and Voltaire (her uncle) become intimate.
1746	Voltaire is elected to the *Académie Française*.
1747	Voltaire falls from favor at the French court, and will not return to Paris for any great length of time thereafter. Continues work on *Siècle de Louis XV*, and publishes the short fantastic tale *Zadig*.
1749	Death of Madame du Châtelet, in childbirth.
1750	Voltaire's last visit to Paris before his death year. Voltaire moves, with the title of Chamberlain, to the Court of Fredrick the Great at Berlin and Potsdam. He will not return to Paris until shortly before his death.
1753	Leaves Frederick's court, largely due to a public disagreement with another intellectual, Pierre Louis Maupertuis. Voltaire is arrested and briefly detained under Frederick's orders at Frankfurt.

1754	Arrives in Geneva in December, soon to move into the château Les Délices with Madame Denis.
1756	Publishes *Essai sur les Mœurs* (Essay on Mores) and the *Poème sur le Désastre de Lisbonne* (Poem upon the Destruction of Lisbon); Rousseau replies to the *Poème* with *Lettre à Voltaire sur la Providence* (Letter to Voltaire on Optimism, or Letter to Voltaire on Providence). Voltaire attempts unsuccessfully to stay the 1757 execution for neglect of duty of British Admiral Byng.
1759	Publishes *Candide*; moves to his final home, the château of Ferney in France, very near Geneva. Begins the war on infamy, with the *Relation de la Maladie ... du Jésuite Berthier*.
1763	Voltaire publishes the *Traité sur la Tolérance* (Treatise on Tolerance), his major work on political and religious tolerance, after the torture and execution in Toulouse of the protestant Jean Calas, who is exonerated in 1765.
1764	Publishes the *Dictionnaire Philosophique Portatif* (Portable Philosophical Dictionary) in its first form (in 1770, "*Portatif*" is dropped, and a much expanded version is published as *Questions sur l'Encyclopédie*).
1772	Publishes *Il Faut Prendre un Parti* (We Must Take Sides).
1778	Voltaire returns to Paris in February with his last play, *Irène*. He dies on 30 May and is buried secretly at the Abbey de Seillières in Champagne.
1789	Beginning of the French Revolution.
1791	Voltaire's body is transferred to the Panthéon in Paris.

1793 Louis XVI behaded
(guilotine)

A Note on the Text

There are currently over a dozen translations of *Candide* readily available to the English reader. Is a new one needed? No. The translation for the Nourse edition published in London in 1759 (the copy text for this edition) holds a special place, however, for a number of reasons. First of all, because it is contemporary with Voltaire's own effort, the Nourse version presents historical style and language that recent translations simply cannot match. Second, it can lay a claim to being the authoritative English edition, the version that Voltaire agreed to publish. It may also be the first: either the Nourse edition, or a pirated edition that also appeared in 1759, was the first published English translation. With clandestine publications such as these, records may be too scarce to allow for a final judgment.

Some features of this translation are challenging, partly because of archaic usage and grammar, but also because of the translator's choices for crafting a rapid and immediate style, very much like Voltaire's own. This Broadview edition introduces modern punctuation, and modern and regular spelling (including the name "Candide," where the original edition has "Candid"), for the ease of the contemporary reader. Archaic terms have not been replaced by modern alternatives, but some of the more obscure words are explained in the notes to the text. Where possible, contemporary translations of supplementary texts have also been provided. Spelling and punctuation have been left in their original state in some cases, and particularly in poetry, because such changes occasionally affect rhyme or meter.

Voltaire made a few very minor changes to the French text for the 1761 edition and later ones, and he augmented chapter twenty-two, making further jabs at Paris and its culture. The changes appear to have been insignificant for English-speaking audiences, since they were not included in corrected second editions of either of the English translations that then existed. The augmented chapter is provided, following this translation (p. 134), in its form in the next known translation of about 1762.

CANDIDE,

O U

L'OPTIMISME,

TRADUIT DE L'ALLEMAND.

D E

Mr. le Docteur RALPH.

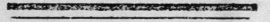

M D C C L I X.

Title page of the first London edition of *Candide*. See the introduction for an explanation of the deliberate misattribution of Voltaire's writing as "translated from the German of Mr. Doctor Ralph." Image courtesy Eric Palmer.

CONTENTS

Chapter I

How Candide was brought up in a magnificent castle, and how he was expelled from thence

Chapter II

What became of Candide among the Bulgarians

Chapter III

How Candide made his escape from the Bulgarians, and what afterwards became of him

Chapter IV

How Candide found his old master Pangloss, and what happened to them

Chapter V

Tempest, shipwreck, earthquake, and what became of Doctor Pangloss, Candide, and James the Anabaptist

Chapter VI

How the Portuguese made a beautiful Auto-da-fé, to prevent any further earthquakes; and how Candide was publicly whipped

Chapter VII

How the old woman took care of Candide, and how he found the object he loved

Chapter VIII

The History of Cunegonde

Chapter IX

What became of Cunegonde, Candide, the grand inquisitor, and the Jew

Chapter X

In what distress Candide, Cunegonde, and the old woman arrived at Cadiz; and of their embarkation

Chapter XI

History of the old woman

Chapter XII

The adventures of the old woman continued

Chapter XIII

How Candide was forced away from his fair Cunegonde, and the old woman

Chapter XIV

How Candide and Cacambo were received by the Jesuits of Paraguay

CANDIDE,

O U

L'OPTIMISME.

CHAPITRE PREMIER.

Comment Candide fut élevé dans un beau Château, & comment il fut chassé d'icelui.

 I L y avait en Westphalie, dans le Château de Mr. le Baron de Thunder-ten-tronckh, un jeune garçon à qui la nature avait donné les mœurs les plus douces.

A 2   Sa

First page of *Candide*. Image courtesy Eric Palmer.

Chapter I
How Candide was brought up in a magnificent castle, and how he was expelled from thence

In a castle of Westphalia, belonging to the Baron of Thunder-ten-tronckh,[1] lived a youth, whom nature had endued[2] with the most gentle manners. His countenance was a true picture of his mind. He had a sound judgment, with great frankness and simplicity, which was the reason, I apprehend, of his being called *Candide*. The old servants of the family suspected him to have been the son of the Baron's sister, by a good honest gentleman of the neighbourhood, whom that young lady refused to marry, because he could produce no more than seventy-one quarterings[3] in his arms, the rest having been lost through the injuries of time.

The Baron was one of the most powerful lords in Westphalia, for his castle had not only a gate, but even windows, and his great hall was hung with tapestry. He used to go a hunting with his mastiffs and spaniels, instead of hounds; his grooms were his huntsmen, and the country curate was his great almoner.[4] They all called him, My Lord, and were sure to laugh whenever he was pleased to tell a story.

The Baron's lady weighed about three hundred and fifty pounds, and upon that consideration was greatly revered, but she did the honours of the house with a dignity that commanded still greater respect. Her daughter Cunegonde was seventeen years of age, fresh coloured, comely, plump, and desirable. The Baron's son seemed to be a youth in every respect worthy of his father. Pangloss, the preceptor, was the oracle of his family, and little Candide gave ear to his instructions with all the simplicity becoming his age, and natural temper of mind.

Pangloss was professor of metaphysico-theologo-cosmolo-

---

1   Westphalia is a province in western Germany; Thunder-ten-tronckh is a make-believe Baronial estate, probably invented by Voltaire because the syllables sound vaguely Germanic, and unpleasant.
2   Endowed.
3   A measure of noble intermarriage that appears as divisions upon an individual's heraldic shield. Eight quarterings would be uncommon among nobility.
4   A curate holds the lowest level of authority among clergy; an almoner is employed by a noble family to lead them in prayer and to distribute alms to the poor.

nigology.[1] He could prove most admirably that there is no effect without a cause, and that in this world, the best of all possible worlds, the Baron's castle was the most magnificent of castles, and his lady the best of Baronesses that could possibly exist.

"It is demonstrable," said he, "that things cannot be otherwise than as they are, for all things having been created for some end, they must consequently be created for the best. Observe, that the nose is formed for spectacles, and therefore we come to wear spectacles. The legs are visibly designed for stockings, and therefore we come to wear stockings. Stones were made to be hewn, and to construct castles; therefore my lord has a magnificent castle: for the greatest baron in the province ought to be the best lodged. Swine were intended to be eaten; therefore we eat pork all the year round, and they who assert that everything is right, do not express themselves correctly; they should say that everything is for the best."

Candide listened attentively, and believed implicitly, for he thought Miss Cunegonde excessively handsome, though he never had the courage to tell her so. He concluded that after the happiness of being Baron of Thunder-ten-tronckh, the next was that of being Miss Cunegonde, the next that of seeing her every day, the next that of hearing the instructions of Master Pangloss, the greatest philosopher of the whole province, and consequently of the whole world.

One day that Cunegonde went to take a walk in a little neighbouring wood, which they called the park, looking through the bushes, she espied the Doctor Pangloss giving a lecture of experimental philosophy to her mother's chambermaid, a little brown wench, very pretty, and very docile. As Miss Cunegonde had a great disposition for the sciences, she observed with the utmost attention the experiments repeated before her eyes. She clearly perceived the force of the Doctor's reasons, the causes, and effects; she turned back greatly flurried, quite pensive, and filled

---

1 Pangloss, as his name suggests, is knowledgeable on every subject, and so his area of study is a pastiche of fashionable philosophical and scientific terms of the time. The root 'cosmolo' refers especially to a term used by contemporary philosophers that has since become familiar ('cosmology'); 'nigolo' means 'insignificant'. Other technical terms to follow, such as 'sufficient reason' and 'best of all possible worlds,' refer especially to the philosophy of Gottfried Leibniz. Frequent mention of "cause and effect" also indicates that Pangloss maintains an interest in natural science.

with the desire of knowledge, imagining that she might be a *sufficient reason*[1] for young Candide, and he for her.

On her way back she met the youth, and blushed; Candide also blushed. She wished him good morrow in a faltering tone, and he returned the salute without knowing what he said. The next day, as they rose from dinner, Cunegonde and Candide happened to get behind the screen, when Cunegonde dropped her handkerchief, and Candide took it up. She innocently laid hold of his hand, and the youth as innocently kissed the young lady's hand with an eagerness, sensibility, and grace, all very particular. Their lips met, their eyes sparkled, their knees trembled, their hands strayed.... Baron Thunder-ten-tronckh happened to come by, and beholding this cause and effect, gave Candide a kick on the backside, and drove him out of doors. Miss Cunegonde fainted away, and as soon as she came to herself, the Baroness boxed her ears. Thus a general consternation[2] was spread over this most magnificent and most agreeable castle that possibly could be.

Chapter II
What became of Candide among the Bulgarians

Candide being driven out of terrestrial paradise, rambled a long while without knowing where he was. His eyes, bedewed with tears, were sometimes raised towards heaven, and sometimes turned towards the magnificent castle, where lived the fairest of young ladies. Though it snowed very hard, he laid himself down to sleep, without his supper, in the middle of a ploughed field. In the morning he awoke almost frozen to death, and made a shift to crawl to the next town, which was called Waldberghoff-trarbk-dikdorff. Having no money, and being ready to perish with hunger and fatigue, he placed himself in a melancholy posture before an inn-keeper's door. In this situation he was taken notice of by two men dressed in blue,[3] one of whom said to the other, *"See here is a well built young fellow, and of a proper size,"* upon

---

1 A reason that serves to explain why another thing is present in the world. A technical term of Leibniz's philosophy.
2 Distress, alarm.
3 Guards of the Prussian Army. In French, the term 'Bulgares' presents a pun connoting homosexuality, a jest built upon throughout this chapter. Voltaire himself knew well, and may have known intimately, the Prussian King Frederick II, who is represented later in this chapter.

which they made up to Candide, and very civilly invited him to dinner.

"Gentlemen," replied Candide with a most engaging modesty, "you do me a great deal of honour, but I have no money."

"O, sir," said one of the blues to him, "lads of your appearance and merit should never pay anything. Are not you five feet five inches high?"

"Yes, gentlemen, that is my size," answered he, making a low bow.

"Come, sir, sit down along with us. We will not only pay your reckoning, but we will never suffer such a clever fellow as you to want money; mankind were born to assist one another."

"You are right," said Candide. "This is what I was always taught by Mr. Pangloss, and I see plainly, that everything is for the best." They beg of him to accept of a few crowns, which he complies with; he wants to give them his note, but they refuse it, and place themselves at a table.

"Are you not deeply in love?"

"O yes!" answered he, "I am deeply in love with Miss Cunegonde."

"No," replied one of the blues, "we ask you whether you are not deeply in love with the king of the Bulgarians?"

"Not at all," said Candide, "I never saw him in my life."

"Is it possible! O, he is the best of kings; we must drink his health."

"With all my heart, gentlemen," and he drinks.

"That is enough," they tell him, "now you are the support, the defender, the hero of the Bulgarians. Your fortune is made, you are on the high road to glory."

Instantly they handcuff him, and carry him away to the regiment. There he is made to wheel about to the right, and to the left, to draw his rammer,[1] to return his rammer, to present, to fire, to march, and they give him thirty blows with a cudgel.[2] The next day he does his exercise a little better, and he receives twenty; the day following they let him off with ten, and his comrades look upon him as a surprising young fellow.

Candide was thunder-struck, and could not for the life of him conceive what made him a hero. It came into his head upon a very fine day in the spring to take a walk and he marched straight forward, looking upon it as a privilege of the human as well as of

---

1 Ram-rod, used for packing the charge in a muzzle-loading firearm.
2 Bat, club.

the animal species to make use of their legs in what manner they pleased. He had not advanced two leagues,[1] when he was overtook by four other heroes six feet high, who bound him and carried him to a dungeon.

A court-martial[2] sat upon him, and he was asked which he would choose: either to be whipped six and thirty times through the whole regiment, or to have his brains blown out at once with twelve musket balls. In vain was it for him to tell them that the human will is free, and that he chose neither; they obliged him to make a choice, and he determined, in virtue of that divine gift called liberty, to run the gauntlet[3] six and thirty times.

He had gone through this discipline twice, and the regiment being composed of two thousand men, that composed for him four thousand strokes, which laid bare all his muscles and nerves, from the nape of the neck quite down to his rump. As they were going to proceed to a third whipping, Candide, unable to withstand the operation any longer, begged as a favour that they would be so good as to shoot him. The favour being granted, they pull a cap over his eyes, and bid him kneel down.

At this very instant the king of the Bulgarians happening to pass by, inquires into the nature of the crime. Being a prince of great penetration, he found that Candide was a young metaphysician, extremely ignorant of the world, and therefore, out of his great clemency,[4] he condescended to pardon him, for which his name will be celebrated in all the journals, and throughout all ages.

An able surgeon makes a cure of Candide in three weeks by means of emollients[5] taught by Dioscorides.[6] His wounds were now skinned over, and he was able to march, when the king of the Bulgarians gave battle to the king of the Abares.[7]

---

1   A league is a distance of approximately three miles or five kilometers.
2   A military court of law.
3   A military punishment in which the offender runs between two rows of men, each of whom administers a stroke.
4   Forgiveness or leniency.
5   Medicinal ointments.
6   A medical theorist of the 1st century CE.
7   Abar and Bulgar are references to two opposed cultures of ancient history. Voltaire deliberately mixes historical periods throughout as part of the fantasy of this story, and many references to events result from Voltaire's detailed reading in world history, which is expressed especially in his *Essai sur les Mœurs*. The opposing factions are, consequently, most likely meant to bring to mind France and Prussia respectively, in the context of an ongoing terrible war (the Seven Years' War, 1756-63).

Chapter III
How Candide made his escape from the Bulgarians, and what afterwards became of him

There was never anything so gallant, so well accoutered,[1] so brilliant, and so well disposed, as the two armies were. Trumpets, fifes, oboes, drums and cannon made such music as the devil himself never heard in hell. The cannonading first of all laid flat about six thousand men on each side; the musket-balls swept away out of the best of worlds nine or ten thousand ruffians that infected the surface of the earth. The bayonet was next a *sufficient reason* for the death of several thousands. The whole might amount to thirty thousand souls. Candide trembled like a philosopher, and concealed himself as well as he could during this heroic butchery.

At length, while the two kings were causing Te Deum[2] to be sung in each of their camps, Candide took a resolution to go and reason somewhere else about effects and causes. After he had passed over heaps of dead or dying men, the first place he came to was a neighbouring village, which belonged to the Abares, and had been set on fire by the Bulgarians, according to the laws of war. Here you might see old men covered with wounds, who beheld their wives—hugging their children to their bloody breasts—massacred before their faces. There you might behold young virgins with their bellies ripped open and breathing their last after they had satisfied the natural wants of Bulgarian heroes, while others, half burnt in the flames, begged to be dispatched out of the world. The earth was strewn with the brains, arms, and legs of dead men.

Candide made all the haste he could to another village, which belonged to the Bulgarians, and there he found that the heroic Abares had acted the same tragedy. From thence continuing to walk over shattered palpitating limbs, or through ruined buildings, he arrived at last beyond the seat of war, with a few provisions in his knapsack, and Miss Cunegonde always in his heart.

At his arrival in Holland, his provisions failed him. But having heard that the inhabitants of this country were all rich, and Christians, he made no doubt but he should meet with the same treatment from them as he had met with in the Baron's castle, before Miss Cunegonde's bright eyes were the cause of his expul-

---

1 Outfitted, equipped.
2 A hymn to God; in this context, a celebration of victory.

sion from thence. He asked charity of several grave looking people, who unanimously answered him that if he continued this trade, they would confine him to the house of correction, where he should be taught to get his bread.

The next he addressed himself to was a person who had been haranguing[1] a large assembly for a whole hour on the subject of charity. But the orator, looking askew, said, "What brought you hither? Are you for the good cause?"

"There can be no effect without a cause," answered Candide, in a submissive manner. "The whole is necessarily concatenated,[2] and arranged for the best. It was necessary for me to have been banished from the presence of Miss Cunegonde, to have afterwards run the gauntlet, and now it is necessary I should beg my bread, till I learn to earn it; all this cannot be otherwise."

"My friend," said the orator to him, "do you believe the Pope to be antichrist?"

"I never knew he was," answered Candide, "but whether he is or not, I have not a morsel of bread."

"Thou deservest none, said the other. Be gone, varlet, wretch; never come near me while thou livest."

The orator's wife, putting her head out of the window, and— spying a man that doubted whether the Pope was antichrist—she saluted him with a full—.[3] O heavens, to what excess does religious zeal transport the fair!

A man who had never been christened, a good Anabaptist, named James, beheld the cruel and ignominious[4] treatment shown to one of his brethren, to an implumed biped endued with a rational soul.[5] Moved with pity, he carried him home, cleaned

---

1 Speaking at great length, or delivering a tongue-lashing.
2 Combined in a specific order.
3 The word "chamber-pot" often fills this break in recent editions of Voltaire's text. A half-dozen other obscene words are partly expurgated in Voltaire, or in some French editions and not others (e.g., "p*x*d"). They will be filled in henceforth ("poxed"), because some expressions are obscure enough for current readers as to leave them guessing.
4 Shameful, disgraceful.
5 Anabaptist Christians do not hold that baptism is genuine unless it is performed on a competent, consenting adult. James, however, appears to be unbaptized, and Voltaire's development of this good character suggests no religious affiliation whatever. The reference to "implumed biped with a rational soul" is a tossed-off mention of ancient philosophical discussions of inessential and essential features of the human being, respectively.

him, refreshed him with bread and beer, made him a present of two florins, and intended to instruct him in his silk manufacture. Candide threw himself at his feet and cried out, "Master Pangloss was in the right, when he said that everything was for the best in this world, for I am infinitely more affected with your extraordinary generosity, than with the inhumanity of that gentleman in the black cloak, and his lady."

The next day as he took a walk out, he met a beggar all covered with scabs, his eyes sunk in his head, the end of his nose corroded, his mouth distorted, his teeth black, snuffling through his nose, coughing most violently, and spitting out a tooth every time he tried to expectorate.[1]

Chapter IV
How Candide found his old master Pangloss, and what happened to them

Candide, more touched with compassion than struck with horror, gave to this shocking figure the two florins which he had received of honest James the Anabaptist. The spectre[2] looked at him very earnestly, dropped a few tears, and was going to embrace him. Candide drew back, aghast.

"Alas!" said one wretch to the other, "don't you know your dear Pangloss?"

"What sound is this? Is it you, my dear master? You in this terrible plight! And what misfortune has happened to you? What brought you away from that most magnificent of all castles? What's become of Miss Cunegonde, the mirrour of young ladies, and nature's masterpiece?"

"I am so weak that I cannot stand," said Pangloss, upon which Candide carried him to the Anabaptist's stable, and gave him a crust of bread.

As soon as Pangloss had refreshed himself a little, "Well," said Candide, "what news of Cunegonde?"

"She is dead," replied the other.

Candide fainted away; but his friend brought him to himself again by the help of a little vinegar that happened to be in the stable. Candide, opening his eyes once more, cried out, "Cunegonde is dead! Ah, best of worlds, where art thou? But of what

---

1 Cough or spit.
2 Ghost or shadow.

illness did she die? Was it not for grief, upon seeing her father kick me out of his magnificent castle?"

"No," said Pangloss, "her belly was ripped open by the Bulgarian soldiers, after they had most barbarously ravished her. They knocked the Baron her father on the head, for attempting to defend her. My lady her mother was cut in pieces. My poor pupil was served just in the same manner as his sister, and as for the castle, they have not left one stone of it standing, no nor a barn, nor a sheep, nor a duck, nor a tree. But we have had our revenge, for the Abares have done the very same thing to a neighbouring Barony, which belonged to a Bulgarian lord."

This discourse threw Candid into a second swoon, but coming to himself, and having said all that it became him to say, he enquired into the cause and effect, as well as into the *sufficient reason* that had reduced Pangloss to so miserable a plight.

"Alas!" said the other, "it was love: love, the comfort of the human species, the preserver of the universe, the soul of all sensible beings, love, tender love."

"Alas!" said Candide, "I have some knowledge of love, that sovereign of hearts, that soul of our souls, yet it never cost me more than a kiss and twenty kicks on the backside. But how could this beautiful cause produce so hideous an effect?"

Pangloss made answer in these terms: "O my dear Candide, you remember Paquette, that pretty wench who waited on our noble Baroness. In her arms I tasted the pleasure of paradise, which produced those hellish torments with which you see me devoured. She was infected with the distemper,[1] and perhaps she has died of it since. This present Paquette received of a learned Cordelier,[2] who had traced it to the source; he was indebted for it to an old countess, who had it of a captain of horse, who had it of a marchioness,[3] who had it of a page, who had it of a Jesuit, who in his novitiate had it in a direct line from one of the companions of Christopher Columbus. For my part I shall give it to nobody, I am dying."

"O Pangloss!" cried Candide, "what a strange genealogy! Is not the devil the original source of it?"

"Not at all," replied this great man, "it was a thing unavoidable, a necessary ingredient, in the best of worlds! For if Columbus had not landed upon an island in America, and there catched

---

1 A euphemism for syphilis or the pox.
2 A Franciscan monk; the term refers to the cord belt of the monk's habit.
3 Marquise, a noblewoman of middle rank.

this disease—which contaminates the source of life, frequently hinders generation, and is evidently opposite to the great end of nature—we should have neither chocolate nor cochineal.[1] We are also to observe that upon our continent this distemper is, like religious controversy, confined to a particular spot. The Turks, the Indians, the Persians, the Chinese, the Siamese, the Japanese, know nothing of it; but there is a sufficient reason to make us conclude that they will be acquainted with it in a few centuries. In the mean time, it has made prodigious havoc among us, especially in those armies composed of well disciplined hirelings[2] who determine the fate of nations, for we may safely affirm, that when an army of thirty thousand men fights another of an equal number, there are about twenty thousand of them poxed[3] on each side."

"Surprising!" said Candide. "But you must get cured."

"Alas! How can I?" said Pangloss. "I have not a farthing, my friend, and this I know, that all over the globe, there is no possibility of being let blood, or of taking a glister[4] without a fee."

This last speech had its effect on Candide. He went and flung himself at the feet of James, the charitable Anabaptist, and gave him so striking a picture of the situation of his poor friend, that the good man did not scruple[5] to take Dr. Pangloss into his house, and had him cured at his own expense. Under the operation Pangloss lost only an eye and an ear. As he wrote a good hand, and understood accounts very well, the Anabaptist made him his bookkeeper.

At the expiration of two months, being obliged to go to Lisbon about some mercantile affairs, he took the two philosophers with him in the same ship. Pangloss explained to him how everything was so constituted as it could not be better. James was not of this opinion.

"Mankind," said he, "must, in some things, have deviated from their original innocence, for they were not born wolves, and yet they worry one another like those beasts of prey. God had given them neither cannon of four and twenty pounders, nor bayonets, and yet they have made cannon and bayonets to destroy one another. Into this account I might throw not only bankrupts,

---

1 A clothing dye produced from crushed insects.
2 Employees, or, in this case, recruits.
3 Covered with sores, due to syphilis.
4 Enema.
5 Conscience, sense of responsibility.

but the law which seizes on the effects of bankrupts only to cheat the creditors."

"All this was indispensably necessary," replied the one-eyed Doctor, "for private misfortunes constitute the general good, so that the more private misfortunes there are, the greater is the general good."

While he was arguing in this manner, the sky darkened, the winds blew from the four quarters of the compass, and the ship was assailed by a most terrible tempest within sight of the port of Lisbon.

Chapter V
Tempest, shipwreck, earthquake, and what became of Doctor Pangloss, Candide, and James the Anabaptist

One half of the passengers were so sick, and their nerves so greatly convulsed from the rolling of the ship, that they were not even sensible of the danger. The other half, either made loud outcries, or fell to their prayers.

The sheets[1] were rent, the masts broke down, and the gaping vessel sucked in the rushing ocean. All hands aloft, but nobody could be either heard, or obeyed. The Anabaptist, being upon deck, bore a hand, when a brutish sailor gave him a knock, and laid him sprawling. But with the violence of the blow, he himself tumbled head foremost over board, and stuck upon a piece of broken mast. Honest James flies to his assistance, and with great difficulty hauls him up again; but in the attempt he falls into the sea himself, and though the sailor might have saved him from drowning, he was so barbarous as to let him perish. Candide draws near, and sees his benefactor one moment rising above water, and the next swallowed up by the merciless deep. He was just going to jump after him, but was prevented by the philosopher Pangloss, who demonstrated to him that the bay of Lisbon had been made on purpose for the Anabaptist to be drowned. While he was proving this a priori,[2] the ship foundered, and the whole crew perished, except Pangloss, Candide, and the sailor, who drowned the good Anabaptist. The villain swam ashore, but Pangloss and Candide escaped upon a plank. As soon as they recovered themselves a little, they walked towards Lisbon. They

---

1 Sails.

2. Independent of experience (a Latin philosophical term).

had some money left, with which they hoped to save themselves from starving, after they had escaped drowning.

As they were lamenting the death of their benefactor they reached the city, when all of a sudden the earth trembled under their feet, the sea swelled and foamed in the harbour, and beat to pieces the vessels riding at anchor. The streets and public squares were involved in clouds of fire and smoke, the houses tottered and tumbled down, and thirty thousand inhabitants of all ages and sexes were buried in the ruins. The sailor at this sight set up a whistling and swore there was some booty to be got there.

"What can be the *sufficient reason* of this phenomenon?" said Pangloss.

"This is certainly the day of judgment," cried Candide.

The sailor ran among the ruins, defying death in the pursuit of plunder. He found some money and got drunk with it, and after he had slept himself sober, he purchased the favours of the first good natured wench that fell in his way.

As he was thus wantonly rioting in the ruins of demolished houses, and amidst the groans of dying persons, Pangloss came and pulled him by the sleeve, saying, "This is not right, my friend, you trespass against the *universal reason* and fitness of things; this is not a proper time for such extravagancies."

"S'blood[1] and fury," answered the other, "I am a sailor, and born at Batavia;[2] four times have I trampled upon the crucifix in four voyages to Japan; a fig[3] for thy universal reason and fitness of things."[4]

In the mean time Candide—being wounded by some stones that fell from houses—lay stretched in the street, almost covered with rubbish. "For God's sake," said he to Pangloss, "get me a little wine and oil, I am a dying."

"This concussion of the earth is no new thing," answered Pangloss. "The city of Lima, in America, experienced the same convulsions last year. The same cause, the same effects; there is certainly a train of sulphur[5] under ground from Lima to Lisbon."

---

1 An irreligious oath, a contraction of "God's Blood".

2 Capital of Indonesia; a town founded by the Dutch. Now Jakarta.

3 An obscene oath, contraction of "I don't give a fig;" that is, "I don't care."

4 Stepping on a crucifix, which might discourage entry of missionaries, was thought by some to be an act required of Dutch traders entering port in Japan during part of the seventeenth century.

5 An explosive (sulfurous) compound thought by some to be the cause of earthquakes.

"Nothing more probable," said Candide, "but for the love of God, a little oil and wine."

"Probable?" replied the philosopher, "I maintain that the point is capable of being demonstrated." Candide fainted away, and Pangloss fetched him some water from a neighbouring fountain.

The day following they rummaged among the ruins and found provisions, with which they repaired their exhausted strength. After this they joined the rest of the inhabitants in relieving the distressed and wounded. Some, whom they had humanely assisted, gave them as good a dinner as could be expected under such terrible circumstances. True, the repast was mournful, and the company moistened their bread with tears. But Pangloss endeavoured to console them by affirming that things could not be otherwise than as they were. "Because," said he, "all this is fittest and best. For if there is a volcano at Lisbon, it could be in no other spot, for it is impossible but things should be as they are, for everything is right."

Near him sat a little man dressed in black, belonging to the inquisition,[1] who, taking him up with great complaisance, said, "Very likely, sir, you do not believe in original sin. For if everything is best and fittest, consequently there was no such thing as the fall, or punishment of man."

"I humbly ask your excellency's pardon," answered Pangloss still more politely, "for the fall and curse of man, necessarily entered into the system of the best of worlds."

"Therefore, sir," said the other, "you do not believe any such thing as liberty."

"Your excellency will be so good as to excuse me," said Pangloss. "Liberty is consistent with absolute necessity, for it was necessary we should be free; for in short, the determinate will ..."

Pangloss was in the middle of his proposition when the little inquisitor beckoned to his footman to help him get a glass of wine.

Chapter VI
How the Portuguese made a beautiful Auto-da-fé, to prevent any further earthquakes; and how Candide was publicly whipped

After the earthquake had destroyed three fourths of the city of Lisbon, the sages of that country could think of no means more

---

1 A Catholic policing institution, notorious for its pursuit of heretics and ill treatment of suspects.

effectual to preserve the kingdom from utter ruin, than to entertain the people with an Auto-da-fé.[1] For it had been decided by
the University of Coimbra,[2] that the burning of a few people
alive, by a slow fire, and with great ceremony, is an infallible
secret to hinder the earth from quaking.

In consequence hereof, they had seized on a Biscayner,[3] for
marrying his godmother, and on two Portuguese, for stripping a
chicken, as they were at dinner, of a little lard. After dinner, they
came and secured Doctor Pangloss and his disciple Candide: the
one for speaking his mind, the other for seeming to approve of
what he said.

They were conducted to separate apartments, extremely fresh
and cool, being never incommoded[4] by the sun. Eight days after
they were dressed in a *sanbenito*, and their heads were crowned
with paper mitres. The mitre and *sanbenito* belonging to Candide
were painted with inverse flames, and with devils that had neither
tails nor claws. But Pangloss's devils had claws, and the flames
were upright.[5] In this habit they marched in procession and heard
a very pathetic sermon, which was followed by an anthem set to
music. Candide was whipped in cadence while they were singing.
The Biscayner and the two men who refused to eat hog's lard, were
burnt, and Pangloss, though contrary to custom, was hanged. The
same day the earth sustained a most violent concussion.

Candide, terrified and amazed at the shocking bloody scene,
said to himself with some trepidation, "If this is the best of pos-

---

1 "Act of faith." A public punishment for crimes against the Roman
   Catholic Church, made infamous by the Spanish Inquisition. The last
   public *auto-da-fé* in Portugal in which an individual was burned
   occurred in 1761; in Spain, the last execution for heresy (by hanging)
   occurred in 1826, according to Henry Charles Lea in *A History of the
   Inquisition in Spain*. The heretics in Voltaire's story include an unfortunate individual who, in Catholic doctrine, has married a spiritual parent,
   and two others suspected of being Jewish, due to their choice to remove
   pig fat from their provisions. Voltaire draws some of the details of the
   ritual that he invents from seventeenth-century written sources.
2 The oldest and most authoritative university in Portugal.
3 From the Biscay region of northern Spain.
4 Made uncomfortable, inconvenienced.
5 The *sanbenito* (Spanish: Saint Benedict) is a simple garment the convict
   wears, and the mitre is a pointed hat: both are degraded representations
   of the garb of religious orders. The differences between the costume of
   Candide and Pangloss may indicate repentant and unrepentant individuals, respectively.

sible worlds, what must we think of the rest? Well, if I had been only whipped, I could put up with it, for I met with the same usage among the Bulgarians. But O my dear Pangloss! Thou greatest of philosophers, that it should be my hard fate to see thee hanged, without knowing for what! O my dear Anabaptist! Thou best of men, that it should be thy fate to be drowned in the very harbour! O Miss Cunegonde, thou mirrour of young ladies! That it should be thy fate to have thy belly ripped open!"

Thus he was musing, though scarce able to stand, after sermon, flagellation, absolution, and benediction, when an old woman accosted him, and said, "Child, take courage, and follow me."

Chapter VII
How the old woman took care of Candide, and how he found the object he loved

Candide did not take courage, but followed the old woman to a decayed house, where she gave him a pot of pomatum[1] to anoint his sores, showed him a very neat bed with a suit of clothes hanging up, and left him victuals[2] and drink. "Eat, drink, and take your rest," said she, "and may our lady of Atocha, the great St. Antony of Padua, and the great St. James of Compostella, receive you under their protection. I shall be back tomorrow."

Candide, amazed at all he had seen, at all he had suffered, and, more than all, at the charity of the old woman, wanted to kiss her hand. "It is not my hand you must kiss," said the old woman. "I shall be back to-morrow. Anoint yourself with the pomatum, eat, and go to sleep."

Candide, notwithstanding so many disasters, ate and slept. The next morning the old woman brought him his breakfast, looked at his back, and rubbed it herself with another ointment. In like manner she brought him his dinner, and at night she returned with his supper. The day following she went through the very same ceremonies.

"Who are you?" said Candide. "What deity has inspired you with so much goodness? What return can I make you?"

The good woman made him no answer, but came back in the evening, and brought him his supper. "Come along with me,"

---

1 A salve of medicinal ointment.
2 Food.

said she, "and do not say a word." She took him by the hand, and walked with him about a quarter of a mile into the country, where they arrived at a lonely house, surrounded with gardens and canals. The old woman knocked at a little door, which opened directly, and she showed Candide up by a back-stairs into a small apartment, richly furnished.

She left him on a brocaded sofa, shut the door, and went away. Candide thought himself in a dream, and indeed, that he had been dreaming all his life, but that the present moment was the only agreeable part of it all.

The old woman returned very soon, supporting a lady of a majestic mien[1] and stature. Her attire was rich, and glittering with diamonds; she seemed to tremble very much, and wore a veil. "Take off that veil," said the old woman to Candide. The young man approaches, and with awful reverence takes off the veil. But O what joy! What surprise! When he beheld Miss Cunegonde, for it was she herself in person. His strength fails him, he is incapable of uttering a word, but drops down at her feet. Cunegonde falls upon the sofa.

The old woman applies a smelling bottle; they come to themselves, and recover their speech. As they began with broken accents, with questions and answers interchangeably interrupted, with sighs, with tears, and cries, the old woman desired they would make less noise, and then she left them to themselves.

"And is it you?" said Candide. "Are you then alive? And is it my good fortune to meet with you in Portugal? Then you have not been ravished? Then they did not rip open your belly as Doctor Pangloss informed me?"

"Yes they did," said Cunegonde. "But those two accidents are not always mortal."

"But were your father and mother killed?"

"It is but too true," answered Cunegonde, in tears.

"And your brother?"

"My brother was also killed."

"And how came you here in Portugal? And how did you know of my being here? And by what strange adventure did you contrive to bring me to this house?"

"I will tell you," replied the lady. "But first of all let me know your history, since the innocent kiss you gave me at my father's house, and the rude kicking you received in return."

Candide respectfully obeyed her, and though he was still in a

---

1 Bearing or manner.

surprise, though he faltered in his speech, though his back still pained him, yet he gave her a most ingenuous account of everything that had befallen him, since the moment of their separation. Cunegonde lifted up her eyes to heaven, and shed tears upon the death of the honest Anabaptist, and of Pangloss, after which she made the following speech to Candide, who had his eyes fixed upon her the whole time, and listened to her with the utmost attention.

Chapter VIII
The History of Cunegonde

"I was in bed and fast asleep, when it pleased God to send the Bulgarians to our delightful castle of Thunder-ten-tronckh. They slew my father and brother and cut my mother in pieces. A tall Bulgarian, six feet high, perceiving that I had fainted away at this sight, began to ravish me. The violence of the ruffian brought me to my senses; I cried, I struggled, I bit, I scratched, I wanted to tear the tall Bulgarian's eyes out, not knowing what happened at my father's house was the usual practice of war. The brute gave me a cut in the left side with his hanger,[1] and the mark is still upon me."

"Ah! I hope I shall see it," says honest Candide.

"You shall," said Cunegonde, "but let us continue."

"Do so," replied Candide.

And thus she resumed the thread of her story. "A Bulgarian captain came in, and saw me weltering in my blood, and the soldier not in the least disconcerted. The captain flew into a passion at the disrespectful behaviour of the brute, and killed him, just as I was sinking into insensibility.

"He ordered my wound to be dressed, and took me with him to his quarters as a prisoner of war. I washed what little linen he was master of, and dressed his victuals. He thought me very pretty; on the other hand I must own he had a good shape, and an excellent complexion; but he had little or no sense or philosophy; and you might see plainly that he had never been instructed by Doctor Pangloss.

"In three months time, having lost all his money, and being grown tired of my company, he sold me to a Jew, named Don Issachar, who traded to Holland and Portugal, and had a strong

---

1 Short sword, hung from belt.

passion for women. This Jew grew extremely fond of me, but never could make me yield to his desires; I made a better resistance against him than against the Bulgarian soldier. A modest woman may be ravished, but the violence only strengthens her virtue. In order to render me more tractable, he brought me to this country house. Hitherto I had imagined that nothing could equal the beauty of Thunder-ten-tronckh castle, but I found I was mistaken.

"The grand inquisitor, happening to spy me one day at mass, was smitten with my person, and sent to let me know he wanted to speak with me about private business. I was conducted to his palace, where I acquainted him with the history of my family; he represented to me how much beneath it was a person of my birth, to belong to a circumcised Israelite.

"A proposal then was made to Don Issachar, that he should resign me to my lord. Don Issachar, being the court banker and a man of credit, would not acquiesce.[1] The inquisitor threatened him with an Auto-da-fé. In short, my Jew was frightened so as to come into a composition,[2] that the house and I should be held by them both in common; that the Jew should have Monday, Wednesday, and Saturday to himself, and the rest of the week I should be enjoyed by the inquisitor. It is now six months since this agreement was made, during which time they have often quarreled to know, whether the space from Saturday night to Sunday morning, belonged to the old or new law.[3] For my part I have hitherto held out against them both, and I verily believe that this is the reason why I am still beloved.

"At length, to avert the scourge of earthquakes, and to intimidate Don Issachar, my lord inquisitor was pleased to celebrate an Auto-da-fé. He did me the honour to invite me to the ceremony. I had a very good seat, and the ladies were served with refreshments between mass and the execution. I was shocked at the burning of those two Jews, and the honest Biscayner that married his godmother, but how great my surprise, my consternation, when I beheld a person to look like Pangloss, dressed in a sanbenito and mitre! I rubbed my eyes, to see whether I was right; I saw him hanging, and I fainted away. But, no sooner was I recovered, than I beheld you stark naked, and this was the full measure

---

1   Relent or consent.
2   An agreement, a contract.
3   That is, the man adhering to the Old Testament, or the man adhering to the New Testament.

of horror, pity and despair. I shall ingenuously own to you that your skin is far whiter than that of my Bulgarian captain.

"This spectacle worked me up to a pitch of distraction. I screamed out, and was going to say, 'Stop, barbarians!' but my voice failed me, and my cries would have signified nothing. After you had been severely whipped, 'How is it possible,' said I, 'that the lovely Candide, and the sage Pangloss, should both be at Lisbon, the one to receive a hundred lashes, and the other to be hanged by the order of my lord the inquisitor, who is my lover? Pangloss most cruelly deceived me, in saying that everything is fittest and best.'

"In this hurry and agitation of spirits, now distracted and lost, and now ready to sink under the weight of my affliction, I revolved in my mind the massacre of my father, mother, and brother, the insolence of the vile Bulgarian soldier, the wound he gave me with his hanger, my servitude under the Bulgarian captain, my subjection to the filthy Don Issachar, the abominable inquisitor, the execution of Doctor Pangloss, the *miserere*[1] sung to music while you was whipped, and especially, the kiss I gave you behind the screen, before you left Westphalia. I gave thanks to God for bringing you back to me after so many trials, and I charged my old woman to take care of you and to conduct you hither as soon as possible. She has executed her commission perfectly well, and I have had the inexpressible satisfaction of enjoying your company again. But you must be very hungry, and so am I. Let us go to supper."

They both sat down to table, and when supper was over, they placed themselves once more on the sofa. There they were, when signor Don Issachar, one of the masters of the house, surprised them. It was the Jewish Sabbath, and Issachar was come to assert his prerogative, and to explain his tender sentiments to Cunegonde.

Chapter IX
What became of Cunegonde, Candide, the grand inquisitor, and the Jew

This Issachar was the most choleric[2] Hebrew that had been ever seen in Israel since the captivity of Babylon. "What!" said he,

---

1 A musical setting of Psalm 50 (Psalm 51 as it is numbered in the Tanak) that is intended to encourage or express penitence.
2 Irascible, hotheaded.

"Thou bitch of a Galilean,[1] was not the inquisitor enough for thee? Must this rascal also come in for a share with me?"

As he was uttering these words, he drew out a long poniard,[2] which he always carried with him, and not imagining that his adversary had any arms, he attacked him most furiously. But our honest Westphalian had received a handsome sword of the old woman along with the suit of clothes. Candide draws his rapier,[3] and though he was of so humane and gentle disposition, he laid the Israelite sprawling at Cunegonde's feet.

"Good God!" cried she, "What will become of us? A man killed in my apartment! If the peace officers come, we are undone."

"Had not Pangloss been hanged," replied Candide, "he would give us good counsel in this emergency, for he was a profound philosopher. But let us consult the old woman."

She, as a prudent person, began to give her opinion, when suddenly another little door burst open. It was now one o'clock in the morning, and of course the beginning of Sunday, which by agreement was allotted to my lord the inquisitor. Entering the room he beholds a shocking spectacle: Candide standing with his drawn sword, after having just undergone the discipline of the inquisition, a man dead upon the floor; Cunegonde frightened out of her wits, and the old woman giving counsel.

At that very instant the following thought occurred to Candide: "If this holy man calls in assistance, he will surely consign me to the flames; and Cunegonde, perhaps, will be served in the same manner; besides, he was the cause of my being cruelly whipped. He is my rival, and as I have now begun to kill, I will kill away, for there is no time to hesitate." This whole reasoning was clear and instantaneous, so that without giving time to the inquisitor to recover from his surprise, he run him through the body.

"Now indeed we are ruined," said Cunegonde, "There is no mercy for us, we are excommunicated, our last hour is come. But how could you, who are of so mild a temper, prevail on yourself to kill a Jew and a prelate in two minutes?"

"My fair creature," answered Candide, "when love, jealousy, and the terror of the inquisition, act upon a man's brain, they are enough to drive him distracted."

---

1 From Galilee (and, by implication, Jewish).
2 A straight dagger.
3 A light, straight sword.

The old woman then put in her word, saying, "There are three Andalusian[1] horses in the stable with bridles and saddles! Let the brave Candide get them ready! Madam has moydores[2] and jewels; let us therefore mount quickly on horseback, though I can sit only on one buttock; let us set out for Cadiz,[3] it is the finest weather in the world, and there is great pleasure in traveling in the cool of the night."

Immediately Candide saddles the three horses, and Cunegonde, the old woman, and he travel thirty miles of a stretch. While they were making the best of their way, the St. *Hermandad*[4] enters the house, my lord the inquisitor is interred in a handsome church, and Issachar's body is thrown upon a dunghill.

Candide, Cunegonde, and the old woman had now reached the little town of Avacena in the midst of the mountains of La Sierra Morena, and were holding the following dialogue in a public inn.

Chapter X

In what distress Candide, Cunegonde, and the old woman,
arrived at Cadiz; and of their embarkation

"Who was it that robbed me of my moydores and jewels?" said Cunegonde all bathed in tears. "How shall we live? What shall we do? Where shall I find inquisitors or Jews to supply my wants?"

"Alas!" said the old woman, "I have a shrewd suspicion of a reverend Cordelier, who lay last night in the same inn with us at Badajos. God preserve me from making a rash judgment, but he came into our room twice,[5] and he set out upon his journey long before us."

"Alas!" said Candide, "Pangloss has often demonstrated to me, that the goods of this world are common to mankind, and that they all have equal right to enjoy them. But, according to these principles, the Cordelier ought to have left us enough to carry us through our journey. Have you nothing at all left, my dear Cunegonde?"

"Not a farthing," said she.

---

1 From Andalusia, southern Spain.
2 Portuguese gold coins, valued in England at twenty-seven shillings.
3 A port city on the Atlantic coast in southern Spain.
4 An auxiliary police force (Spanish: Brotherhood).
5 That is, he passed through their rooms in order to get to his own: there was no corridor in the house.

"What then must we do?" said Candide.

"Sell one of the horses," replied the old woman. "I will get behind Miss Cunegonde, though I can hold myself only on one buttock, and we shall reach Cadiz."

In the same inn there was a Benedictine prior,[1] who bought the horse very cheap. Candide, Cunegonde, and the old woman, having passed through Lucena, Chillas, and Lebrixa, arrived at length at Cadiz.

A fleet was then getting ready, and troops were assembling in order to reduce the Jesuits of Paraguay, who were accused of having excited one of the Indian tribes in the neighbourhood of the town of the Holy Sacrament to revolt against the kings of Spain and Portugal. Candide, having been in the Bulgarian service, performed the military exercise of that nation, with so graceful an address, with so intrepid an air, and with such agility and expedition, that the general of this little army gave him the command of a company of foot. Being now made a captain, he sets sail with Miss Cunegonde, the old woman, two valets, and two Andalusian horses, which had belonged to the grand inquisitor of Portugal.

During their voyage, they reasoned a good deal in regard to poor Pangloss's philosophy. "We are going into another world," said Candide, "and surely it must be there that everything is best. For I must confess, there is reason to complain a little of what passeth in our world, in regard both to natural and moral government."

"I have a sincere value for you," said Cunegonde, "but I shudder still to think of what I have seen and experienced."

"All will be well," replied Candide. "The sea of this new world is already preferable to our European seas; it is smoother, and the winds blow more regularly. Certainly the new world must be the best and fittest of worlds."

"God grant it," said Cunegonde. "But I have met with such terrible treatment in this, that I have almost lost all hopes of a better."

"You murmur and complain," said the old woman. "But alas! You have not gone through half the misfortunes that I have done."

Cunegonde was ready to burst out a laughing at the good old woman for pretending to have gone through as many scenes of

---

1 A monk who directs a monastery, of lower rank than abbot.

adversity as herself. "Alas!" said Cunegonde, "My good mother, unless you had been ravished by two Bulgarians, had received two deep wounds in your belly, had had two castles demolished, had lost two fathers and two mothers, and seen both of them cruelly murdered before your eyes, and lastly, had two lovers whipped at an Auto-da-fé, I do not conceive how you could be more unfortunate than I. Besides, though born a Baroness, and able to prove seventy-two quarterings, I have been obliged to submit to the drudgery of a cook."

"Miss," replied the old woman, "you do not know my family as yet, and were I to show you my backside, you would not talk in that manner, but would suspend your judgment."

This speech having raised a high curiosity in Cunegonde and Candide, the old woman spoke to them as follows.

Chapter XI
History of the old woman

"I had not always sore eyes, neither did my nose always touch my chin, nor was I always a servant. I am the daughter of pope Urban X[1] and of the princess of Palestrina.[2] To the age of fourteen, I was brought up in a palace, in comparison of which, all the castles of your German Barons would be no better than stables, and one of my robes was worth all the magnificence of Westphalia. As I grew up I improved in beauty, wit and every graceful accomplishment, in the centre of pleasure and encompassed by flatterers and admirers. Now I began to inspire the men with love. My neck was come to its right shape, and such a neck—white, erect, and exactly formed like that of the Venus of Medicis![3] My eye-brows were as black as jet, and as for my eyes, they darted flames, and eclipsed the twinkling of the stars, as I was told by the poets in our part of the world. My waiting-women, in dressing and undressing me, used to fall into ecstasy, whether they viewed me before or behind, and how glad would the gentlemen have been to perform that office for them!

"I was affianced[4] to a sovereign prince of Massa Carara. Such a prince! As handsome as myself, sweet tempered, agreeable,

---

1 A fictional pope.
2 A principality near Rome.
3 A particularly well-executed classical statue of the Roman goddess of Love.
4 Made a fiancée, betrothed.

witty, and desperately in love. I loved him as one is apt to love for the first time, with transport, with idolatry. The nuptials were prepared with surprising pomp and magnificence. The ceremony was attended with feasts, carousals, and operas and all Italy composed sonnets in my praise, though not one of them was tolerable. I was just upon the point of reaching the summit of bliss when an old marchioness, who had been the mistress to the prince my husband, invited him to drink chocolate. He went, and died of most terrible convulsions in less than two hours. But this is only a bagatelle.[1] My mother—distracted in the highest degree, and yet less afflicted than me—determined to absent herself for some time from so fatal a place. As she had a very fine estate in the neighbourhood of Cajeta, we embarked on board a galley, which was decorated like the great altar of St. Peter's at Rome. No sooner were we out at sea than a Sallee rover came up, and boarded us. Our men defended themselves like the pope's soldiers: they flung themselves upon their knees, and laid down their arms, begging of the Corsair[2] an absolution *in articulo mortis*.[3]

"Instantly the Moors[4] stripped us as bare as monkeys; my mother, my maids of honour and myself were served all in the same manner. It is amazing with what expedition those gentry undress people. But what surprised me most was that they thrust their fingers into that part of our bodies — which the generality of women suffer no other instrument but pipes to enter. It appeared to me a very strange kind of ceremony, and thus we are apt to judge of things, when we have not seen the world. I afterwards learnt that it was to try whether we had concealed any diamonds. This is the practice established time immemorial among civilized nations that scour the seas. I was informed that the very religious Knights of Malta never fail to make this search when they take any Turkish prisoners of

---

1 A small matter; of little importance.
2 A government-sanctioned pirate, or privateer, of the Barbary Coast; also the privateer's ship.
3 The Barbary states—Morocco, Algeria, Tunisia and Tripolitania (now Libya)—were territories of the Ottoman Empire, a Muslim power generally at war with Christian Europe in the eighteenth century. Consequently, laying down weapons to request Christian articles of absolution just before death (Latin: *in articulo mortis*) would appear to be a futile request.
4 Individuals from western North Africa, usually dark skinned.

either sex.[1] It is a branch of the law of nations from which they never deviate.

"I need not tell you how great a hardship it was for a young princess and her mother to be made slaves and carried to Morocco. You may easily imagine what we must have suffered on board the Moorish vessel. My mother was still very handsome; our maids of honour, and even our waiting-women had more charms than are to be found in all Africa. As for myself, I was an exquisite beauty; I was grace itself, and a virgin. I did not remain so long; this flower, which had been reserved for the handsome prince of Massa Carara, was plucked by the captain of the Sallee rover, a frightful negro, who imagined he did me a great deal of honour. And indeed both the princess of Palestrina and myself must have had a very strong constitution, to go through all the hardships we suffered till our arrival at Morocco. But I proceed, these are such common things as not to be worth mentioning.

"Upon our arrival at Morocco, we found the whole kingdom a scene of blood and confusion. Fifty sons of the emperor Muley-Ismael[2] had each their adherents. This produced fifty civil wars, of blacks against blacks, of tawnies[3] against tawnies, and of mulattos against mulattos. In short, it was a continual carnage throughout the empire.

"No sooner were we landed than the blacks of a contrary faction to that of my captain's attempted to rob him of his booty. Next to jewels and gold, we were the most valuable things he had. I was witness on this occasion to such a battle as you never beheld in any part of Europe. The northern nations have not that fermentation in their blood, nor that raging lust for women so common in Africa. The natives of Europe seem to have their veins only filled with milk, but those of the inhabitants of mount Atlas, and the neighbouring provinces, are impregnated with vitriol and fire. They fought with the fury of lions, tigers, and serpents of the country, to see who should have us for their prey. A Moor seized

---

1 The Knights of Malta, originally the Knights Hospitaller, is a Christian medical organization founded in Jerusalem that gained military and monastic dimensions as a result of the First Crusade (1096-99). Closer to Voltaire's time, the Knights patrolled the Mediterranean, suppressing Barbary piracy and engaging in piracy against Turkish and, occasionally, Christian vessels.
2 Sultan of Morocco, 1672-1727.
3 Brown-skinned persons, particularly of North Africa.

my mother by the right arm while my captain's lieutenant held her by the left; another Moor had hold of her by the right leg, and one of our Corsairs held her by the other. Thus almost all our women were drawn in quarters by soldiers. My captain concealed me behind him, and with his drawn scimitar[1] he cut and slashed every one that opposed his fury. At length I saw all our Italian women and my mother herself torn and mangled by those inhuman monsters.

"The slaves made on board our galley. The Moors who took them—the soldiers, the sailors, the blacks, the whites, the mulattos, and lastly my captain himself—were all killed, and I remained alone, expiring upon a heap of dead bodies. The like barbarous scenes were transacted every day all over the country, through an extent of three hundred leagues, and yet they never missed the five prayers a day ordained by Mahomet.[2]

"With difficulty, I disengaged myself from such a heap of slaughtered bodies and made a shift to crawl to a large orange tree on the bank of a neighbouring rivulet, where, oppressed with fatigue, horror, despair, and hunger, I tumbled down. My senses being overpowered, I fell asleep, or rather, seemed to be in a trance. Thus I lay in a state of weakness and insensibility, or between life and death, when I felt myself pressed by something that moved upon my body. This brought me to myself, and I saw a very good looking man, of a fair complexion, who sighed and muttered these words in his teeth, '*O che sciagura d'essere senza coglioni!*'"[3]

Chapter XII
The adventures of the old woman continued

"Surprised and pleased in a high degree to hear my native language, and no less astonished at what the man said, I made answer that there were much greater misfortunes than that which he complained of. I gave him a compendious account of the horrid scenes I had undergone, and I fainted away a second time. He removed me to a neighbouring house, put me to bed, gave me victuals, waited upon me, did all he could to ease and comfort

---

1 Curved sword.
2 Archaic variant spelling of Mohammed or Muhammad, the prophet of Islam.
3 Italian: "Oh, what tragedy to have no balls!"

me, saying that he had never seen so fine a woman, and that he never regretted so much the loss of what it was impossible for him to recover. 'I was born at Naples,' said he. 'There they geld[1] two or three thousand children every year. Some die of the operation, others acquire a fine voice, and others are raised to be prime-ministers.[2] This operation was performed on me with great success, and I was chapel-musician to madam the princess of Palestrina.'

"'To my mother!' cried I.

"'Your mother!' cried he, the tears trickling down his cheeks. 'Is it possible that you should be the young princess, whom I had the care of bringing up till she was six years old, and who promised so early to be as fair as you?'

"'It is I, indeed, but my mother lies four hundred yards from hence, torn in four quarters, under a heap of dead bodies.'

"I told him all my adventures, and he made me acquainted with his, letting me know that he had been sent to the emperor of Morocco by a Christian power to conclude a treaty with that prince, in consequence of which he was to be furnished with military stores and ships to help to demolish the commerce of other Christian governments. 'I have executed my commission,' said the honest eunuch.[3] 'I am going to take shipping at Ceuta,[4] and I'll take you along with me to Italy. *Ma che sciagura d'essere senza coglioni!'*

"With tears of joy I thanked him, but instead of reconducting me to Italy, he carried me to Algiers, where he sold me to the Dey.[5] No sooner was I sold into slavery than the plague, which made such havoc over Africa, Asia, and Europe, broke out with great malignancy in Algiers. You have seen earthquakes, but pray, Miss, have you ever seen the plague?"

"Never," answered Cunegonde.

"If you had," said the old woman, "you would acknowledge that it is far more terrible than an earthquake. It is common in Africa and I caught it. Imagine to yourself the distressed situation

---

1 Castrate.

2 The eunuch's story below loosely alludes to the career of Carlo Broschi, a.k.a. Farinelli (1705-82), and to an unrelated series of political negotiations between European powers and the Sultan of Morocco in 1703.

3 Man who was castrated as a child.

4 North African port directly south of Gibraltar.

5 Title of the governor of the state of Algiers, a territory of the Ottoman Empire (more recently, Algeria).

of the daughter of a pope only fifteen years old, and who, in less than three months, had felt the miseries of poverty and slavery, had been ravished almost every day, had beheld her mother drawn in quarters, had experienced the scourges of famine and war, and now was dying of the plague in Algiers. Yet I recovered, but my eunuch and the Dey, and almost the whole seraglio[1] of Algiers, perished.

"As soon as the first fury of this terrible pestilence was over, a sale was made of the Dey's slaves. I was purchased by a merchant, and carried to Tunis. This man sold me to another merchant, who sold me again to another at Tripoli. From Tripoli I was sold to Alexandria, from Alexandria to Smyrna, and from Smyrna to Constantinople. At length I became the property of an aga of the janissaries, who was soon ordered away to the defense of Asoph, then besieged by the Turks.[2]

"The aga, who was a very gallant man, took his whole seraglio with him, and lodged us in a small fort on the Palus Maeotis, guarded by two black eunuchs and twenty soldiers. The Turks killed a great number of the Russians, but the latter had their revenge. Asoph was taken by storm and the inhabitants, without any distinction of age or sex, were all put to the sword. There remained only our little fort, and the enemy wanted to starve us out. The twenty janissaries had sworn they would never surrender. Being reduced to the extremity of famine, they found themselves under a necessity of eating our two eunuchs, for fear of violating their oath. And in the course of a few days, they resolved also to devour the women.

"We had a very pious and humane imam,[3] who preached an excellent sermon, exhorting them not to kill us all at once. 'Only cut off a buttock of each of those ladies,' said he, 'and you'll fare extremely well. If you must go to it again, there will be the same entertainment a few days hence. Heaven will accept of so charitable an action, and send you relief.'

"Being a man of great eloquence, he succeeded, and we underwent the terrible operation. The imam applied the same balsam[4]

---

1 Harem.
2 'Aga' is the title of a leader of the Janissaries, the elite troops of the Ottoman Empire. Asoph was captured from the Ottomans for Russia by the army of Peter the Great in 1697 (now Azov, at the mouth of the Don River on the Palus Maeotis or the Sea of Azov).
3 Spiritual leader of Islam; usually the leader within a community and in a mosque.
4 A balm, a medicinal ointment.

to us as he does to children after circumcision, and we were all in a very dangerous way.

"No sooner had the janissaries finished the repast with which we had supplied them, than the Russians attacked them in flat-bottomed boats, and not one janissary escaped. As for the Russians, they did not seem to mind the condition we were in. But there are French surgeons in all parts of the world. A very skilful operator of that nation took us under his care, and cured us, and as long as I live I shall remember that as soon as my wounds were healed he made love to me. He bid us all have a good heart, telling us that the like had happened in many sieges, and that it was according to the laws of war.

"As soon as my companions were able to walk, they were obliged to set out for Moscow. It was my fate to belong to a boiard,[1] who made me his gardener and gave me twenty lashes a day. But this nobleman having in two years time been broken upon the wheel along with thirty more boiards for some broils at court, I took advantage of this event, and made my escape. After traversing all Russia, I was a long time an innholder's servant at Riga: the same at Rostock, Wismar, Leipsick, Cassel, Utrecht, Leyden, The Hague, Rotterdam. I waxed old in misery and disgrace, having only one half of my posteriors, and always remembering I was a pope's daughter. A hundred times was I upon the point of killing myself, but still I was fond of life. This is one of the most ridiculous foibles[2] our nature is subject to. For what can be more absurd than to persist in carrying a burden of which we would willingly be eased? To detest, and yet to strive to preserve our existence? In a word, to caress the serpent that devours us, till he has gnawed our very entrails?

"In the different countries which it has been my fate to traverse, and the numerous inns where I have been servant, I have taken notice of a vast number of people who held their own existence in abhorrence, and yet I never knew of more than eight who put an end to their misery by laying violent hands on themselves, viz. three negroes, four Englishmen, and a German professor, named Robek.[3] My last scene was being servant to Don Issachar, who placed me near your person, my fair lady. I am determined to share your fate, and have been much more affected with your misfortunes than with my own.

---

1 A high member of the Russian aristocracy.
2 Character faults.
3 Johann Robeck (1672-1739) wrote and spoke publicly of the absurdity of life and advocated, then eventually committed, suicide.

"I should never have troubled you with the narrative of my adventures if you had not incited me to it, and if it was not customary to tell stories on board a ship, in order to pass away the time. In short, Miss Cunegonde, I have a good deal of experience and knowledge of the world; therefore I advise you to divert yourself, and prevail upon each passenger to tell his story, and if there is one of them all that has not cursed his stars many a time, that has not frequently looked upon himself as the unhappiest of mortals, I give you leave to throw me headforemost into the sea."

Chapter XIII
How Candide was forced away from his fair Cunegonde, and the old woman

The beautiful Cunegonde, having heard the narrative of the old woman's adventures, paid her all the civilities due to a person of her rank and merit. She likewise accepted the proposal, and engaged all the passengers to relate their adventures and then both Candide and she allowed that the old woman was in the right. "It is great pity," said Candide, "that the sage Pangloss was hanged contrary to custom at an Auto-da-fé. He would tell us most amazing things in regard to the natural and moral evil that overspread the earth, and I should be able, with due respect, to make a few objections."

While each passenger was recounting his story, the ship made her way, and they landed at Buenos Aires. Cunegonde, captain Candide, and the old woman waited on the governor, Don Fernando d'Ibara y Figueora y Mascarenes y Lampourdos y Souza. This nobleman had a stateliness becoming a person dignified with such a string of names. He spoke with so noble a disdain, carried his snout so lofty, strained his voice to such a pitch, assumed so imperious an air, and stalked with such intolerable pride, that those who saluted him were strongly inclined to give him a good drubbing.[1] His lust was insatiable, and Cunegonde appeared in his eye the choicest morsel he had ever beheld.

The first thing he did was to ask whether she was not the captain's wife. The manner in which he asked the question alarmed Candide; he durst not say she was his wife, because indeed she was not; neither durst he say she was his sister, because it was not so, and though his lie might have been of

---

1 Beating.

service to him, and did no hurt to any body, still he was too ingenuous to betray the truth. "Miss Cunegonde," said he, "is to do the honour to marry me, and we beseech your excellency to grace our nuptials with your presence."

Don Fernando d'Ibara y Figueora y Mascarenes y Lampourdos y Souza, turning up his whiskers, sneered and gave order to captain Candide to go and review his company. Candide obeyed, and the governor remained alone with Miss Cunegonde. Immediately he declared his passion, protesting he would marry her the next day in the face of the church, or otherwise, just as should be agreeable to herself. Cunegonde asked a quarter of an hour to consider of it, to consult the old woman, and to take her resolution.

The old woman spoke thus to Cunegonde: "Miss, you have seventy-two quarterings in your arms, and not one farthing in your pocket; it is now in your power to be wife to the greatest lord in America, who has besides a very clever pair of whiskers. And what occasion has such a one as you to pique herself upon inviolable fidelity? You have been ravished by Bulgarians; a Jew and an inquisitor have enjoyed your favours. Misfortunes are a very good plea.[1] I own that if I was in your place, I should have no scruple to marry the governor, and to make the captain's fortune."

While the old woman was thus giving her advice, with all the prudence that can be expected from age and experience, behold a sloop arrives from Spain, on board of which were an Alcalde and his Alguazils;[2] the occasion of their voyage was this: the old woman had shrewdly guessed, that it was a Cordelier who purloined[3] Cunegonde's money and jewels in the town of Badajos when she and Candide were making their escape. The friar wanted to sell some of the diamonds to a jeweler; the jeweler knew them to be the grand inquisitor's. The friar, before he was hanged, confessed he had stolen them. He likewise mentioned the persons he had stole them from, and the route they had taken. It was by this time publicly known that Cunegonde and Candide fled together. They were traced to Cadiz; a vessel was immediately got ready, and sent in pursuit of them, and now the vessel was in Buenos Aires. A report was spread that the Alcalde was going to land, and that he was in pursuit of murderers of my lord the grand inquisitor.

---

1 That is, your past misfortunes provide reasonable claims against your fidelity to Candide.

2 The Alcalde (Spanish) is mayor or chief magistrate of a town; the Alguazil is a lesser official, perhaps a police officer.

3 Stole.

The sage old woman immediately saw what was to be done. "You cannot run away," said she to Cunegonde, "and you have nothing to fear, for it was not you that killed my lord. Besides, as the governor is in love with you, he will not suffer you to be ill treated; therefore stay." Then hurrying away to Candide, "Be gone," said she, "from hence, or in an hour you will be burnt alive." There was not a moment to lose, but how could he part from Cunegonde, and where could he fly for shelter?

Chapter XIV
How Candide and Cacambo were received by the Jesuits of Paraguay

Candide had brought such a valet with him from Cadiz as one often meets with on the coasts of Spain and in the American colonies. He was the fourth part of a Spaniard, of a mongrel breed, and born in Tucuman.[1] He had successively gone through the professions of singing-boy, sexton, sailor, monk, pedlar, soldier, and lackey. His name was Cacambo and he loved his master, because his master was a very good man.

He got the two Andalusian horses saddled with all expedition. "Come, master, let us follow the old woman's advice. Let us set off, and make what haste we can, without ever looking behind us."

Candide dropped a few tears. "O my dear Cunegonde! Must I leave you just at a time when the governor was going to celebrate our nuptials? Cunegonde, what will become of you, in this remote part of the world?"

"She will do as well as she can," said Cacambo. "The women are never at a loss. God provides for everybody. Let's be gone."

"Whither art thou carrying me? Where art thou going? What shall we do without Cunegonde?" said Candide.

"By St. James of Compostella,[2] you was going to fight against the Jesuits. Now let's go and fight in their defence. I know the road perfectly well; I'll conduct you to their kingdom, where they will be charmed to have a captain, that understands the Bulgarian exercise. You'll certainly make a prodigious fortune; if we cannot find our account in one world, we shall find another. It is

---

1   A region, now a province of northwest Argentina.
2   Saint James the Apostle, whose body is held to lie at Compostela, Spain, following miraculous transportation after his martyrdom in Judea.

a great pleasure to see variety of objects, and to perform new exploits."

"Then you have been in Paraguay?" said Candide.

"Ay sure," answered Cacambo, "I was servant in the college of the Assumption, and am acquainted with the government of the good fathers as well as I am with the streets of Cadiz. It is an admirable government. The kingdom is upwards of three hundred leagues in diameter, and divided into thirty provinces. There the fathers are masters of everything. The people have nothing; it is founded on the laws of reason and justice. For my part I see nothing so divine as good fathers who wage war in this part of the world against the kings of Spain and Portugal at the same time that they hear the confessions of those princes in Europe, who kill Spaniards in America, and send them to heaven at Madrid. This pleases me above all things. Let us push forward; you are going to be the happiest of mortals. What pleasure will it be to those fathers to hear that a captain who understands the Bulgarian exercise is come to offer his service to the society!"[1]

As soon as they reached their first barrier, Cacambo told the advanced guard that a captain wanted to speak with my lord the commandant. Notice was given to the main-guard, and immediately a Paraguayan officer ran and laid himself at the feet of the commandant to impart this news to him. Candide and Cacambo were disarmed and their two Andalusian horses seized. The strangers were introduced between two files of musketeers; the commandant was at the further end, with the three-cornered cap on his head, his gown tucked up, a sword by his side, and a spontoon[2] in his hand. He beckoned, and strait-away the newcomers were encompassed by four and twenty soldiers. A sergeant told them they must wait, that the commandant could not speak to them, and that the reverend father provincial does not suffer any Spaniard to open his mouth but in his presence, or to stay above three hours in the province.

"And where is the reverend father provincial?" said Cacambo.

"He is upon the parade just after celebrating mass," answered the sergeant, "and you cannot kiss his spurs till three hours hence."

---

1 This organization of the Spanish territory of Paraguay is exaggerated, but based in several reports concerning the military structure and political power of the Jesuit order in Paraguay and Peru. As it was in chapter two, "Bulgarian exercise" is here meant to imply what at the time was referred to as sexual non-conformism.

2 A short lance.

"However," said Cacambo, "the captain is not a Spaniard, but a German; he is ready to perish with hunger as well as myself. Cannot we have something for breakfast, while we wait for his reverence?"

The sergeant went immediately to acquaint the commandant with what he had heard. "God be praised," said the reverend commandant. "Since he is a German, I may speak to him. Take him to my arbour."

No sooner said, than Candide was conducted to a beautiful pavilion, adorned with a colonnade of green marble intermixed with yellow and with an intertexture of vines, abounding with parrots, humming birds, fly-birds, Guiney hens, and all other sorts of exotic birds. An excellent breakfast was provided in vessels of gold, and while the Paraguayans were eating Indian corn out of wooden dishes in the open fields and exposed to the heat of the sun, the reverend father commandant retires to his arbour.

He was a very handsome young man, with a full visage and excellent complexion. He had an arched eye-brow, a lively eye, red ears, vermilion lips, a bold air—but such a boldness, as neither belonged to a Spaniard nor to a Jesuit. Candide and Cacambo had their arms and the two Andalusian horses restored; Cacambo gave them some oats to eat just by the arbour, having an eye upon them all the while for fear of a surprise.

Candide began with kissing the commandant's robe, and they sat down to table. "Are you then a German?" said the Jesuit to him in that language.

"Yes, reverend father," answered Candide. As they pronounced these words, they looked at each other with great amazement, and with such emotion as they could not conceal.

"And from what part of Germany do you come?" said the Jesuit.

"I am from the dirty province of Westphalia," answered Candide. "I was born in the castle of Thunder-ten-tronckh."

"O heavens! Is it possible!" cried the commandant.

"What a miracle!" cried Candide.

"Is it really you?" said the commandant.

"It is not possible," said Candide. In uttering those words they fainted away, then coming to themselves they embraced each other, and dissolved in tears. "What, is it you, reverend father? You, the brother of the fair Cunegonde! You, that was slain by the Bulgarians! You, the Baron's son! You, a Jesuit in Paraguay! I must confess this is a strange world that we live in. O Pangloss! Pangloss! Pangloss! How glad you would be, if you had not been hanged!"

The commandant sent away the negro slaves and the Paraguayans, who presented them with liquors in crystal goblets. He thanked God and St. Ignatius a thousand times; he clasped Candide in his arms, and their faces were all bathed with tears.

"You will be more surprised, more affected, and transported," said Candide, "when I tell you that Miss Cunegonde your sister, whose belly you imagined to have been ripped open, is in perfect health."

"Where?"

"In your neighbourhood, with the governor of Buenos Aires, and I was going to fight against you."

Every word they uttered during this long conversation was productive of astonishment. Their souls fluttered on their tongue, listened in their ears, and sparkled in their eyes. As they were Germans, they sat a good while at table, waiting for the reverend father provincial, and the commandant spoke to his dear Candide as follows.

Chapter XV
How Candide killed the brother of his dear Cunegonde

"I shall have ever present to my memory the dreadful day on which I saw my father and mother barbarously killed and my sister ravished. When the Bulgarians retired my dear sister could not be found, but the slaughtered bodies of my father, mother, and myself, with two maid-servants and three little boys, were put in a hearse, to be conveyed to a chapel belonging to the Jesuits, within two leagues of our family seat. A Jesuit sprinkled us with some holy water, which was confoundedly salty, and a few drops of it went in my eyes. The father perceived that my eyelids stirred a little; he put his hand upon my heart, and felt it beat, upon which I had proper assistance, and at the expiration of three weeks I recovered. You know, my dear Candide, I was very handsome, but I grew much handsomer, and the revered father Didrie,[1] superior

---

1 There are no known associations for this name. In other editions, Voltaire names father Croust, after Antoine Croust, who failed to send along Voltaire's baggage after a visit to Colmar in 1754. Voltaire (Continued)

of that house, took a great liking to me. He gave me the habit of the order, and some years afterwards I was sent to Rome.

"Our general had great need of new levies[1] of German Jesuits. The sovereigns of Paraguay admit of as few Spanish Jesuits as possible; they prefer those of other nations, as being more subordinate to their commands. The reverend father general looked upon me as a proper person to be employed in cultivating this vineyard. We set out upon our mission: a Polander, a Tyrolese,[2] and myself. Upon my arrival I was honoured with a subdeaconship,[3] and a lieutenancy. Now I am colonel and priest. We shall give a warm reception to the king of Spain's troops; I will answer for it, that they shall be excommunicated and well banged. Providence has sent you hither to our assistance. But is it true that my dear sister Cunegonde is in the neighbourhood, with the governor of Buenos Aires?" Candide swore that nothing could be more true and the tears began again to trickle down their cheeks.

The Baron could not refrain from embracing Candide. He called him his brother, his saviour. "Perhaps," said he, "we shall be able, my dear Candide, to take the town sword in hand, and to recover my sister Cunegonde."

"That is all I want," said Candide, "for I intended to marry her, and I still hope I shall be able to effect it."

"Thou insolent fellow!" replied the Baron. "Wouldst thou have the assurance to marry my sister, who can show seventy-two quarterings in her coat of arms! I find thou hast the most consummate effrontery to dare to mention so presumptuous a design!"

Candide, thunder-struck at this speech, made answer, "Reverend father, all the quarterings in the world would signify not a straw. I rescued your sister out of the hands of a Jew and an inquisitor; she has great obligations to me and she is desirous of having me for her husband. Master Pangloss always told me that mankind are by nature equal; I assure you therefore I will marry her."

"Say you so? We shall see, thou scoundrel!" said the Jesuit-Baron de Thunder-ten-tronckh, and that instant he struck him across the face with the flat side of his sword.

---

was apt to suggest that child sexual abuse was a regular occurrence in monastic orders and Church schools, and he suggested that he himself was a victim of such abuse. See David Wooton, "Unhappy Voltaire, or 'I Shall Never Get Over It as Long as I Live,'" *History Workshop Journal*, No. 50 (2000), 137-55.

1   Recruitments of men in a military draft.
2   An individual from the Tyrol Mountains of Austria and northern Italy.
3   Lowest post in the Roman Catholic Church.

Candide in an instant draws out his rapier, and plunges it up to the hilt in the Jesuit's guts, but in pulling it out, reeking hot, he burst into tears. "Good God!" said he, "I have killed my old master, my friend, my brother-in-law. I am the best natured creature in the world, and yet I have already killed three men, and of these three, two were priests."

As Cacambo stood sentry near the arbour, he instantly ran up. "We have nothing more for it than to sell our lives as dear as we can," says his master to him. "There will be people presently coming into the arbour, so that we must die sword in hand."

Cacambo had been in a great many scrapes in his lifetime. He therefore did not lose his presence of mind, but took the Baron's Jesuitical habit and put it on Candide, then gave him the square cap, and made him mount on horseback. All this was done in the twinkling of an eye. "Let us gallop fast, master. Everybody will take you for a Jesuit going to give directions to your men, and we shall have passed the frontiers before they will be able to overtake us."

He flew as he spoke these words, crying out aloud in Spanish, "Make way, make way for the reverend father colonel."

Chapter XVI
Adventures of the two travellers, with two girls, two monkeys, and the savages called Oreillons

Candide and his valet had got beyond the barrier before it was known in the camp that the German Jesuit was dead. The wary Cacambo had taken care to fill his wallet with bread, chocolate, bacon, fruit, and a few bottles of wine. With their Andalusian horses they penetrated into an unknown country where they perceived no beaten track. At length they came to a beautiful meadow, intersected with purling rills.[1] Here our two adventurers fed their horses.

Cacambo proposed to his master to take some nourishment, and he set him an example. "How can you ask me to eat," said Candide, "after killing the Baron's son, and being doomed never more to see the beautiful Cunegonde? What will it avail me to spin out my wretched ways, and drag them far from her in remorse and despair? And what will the Journal of Trevoux say?"[2]

---

1 Brooks, rivulets.
2 The *Journal de Trévoux* was an important intellectual periodical edited by a Jesuit and frequently editorially opposed to Voltaire's writing.

While he was thus lamenting his fate, he went on eating. The sun had reached the horizon when the two adventurers heard some cries, which seemed to be a female voice. They could not tell whether they were cries of pain or joy, but immediately they started up with that inquietude and alarm which every shadow is apt to raise in the minds of persons who have got out of their latitude. The noise was made by two naked girls, who tripped along the mead,[1] while two monkeys were pursuing them close, and biting their buttocks. Candide was moved with pity. He had learned to fire a gun in the Bulgarian service, and he was so clever at it that he could hit a filbert in a hedge without touching a leaf of the tree. He takes up his double barrel Spanish fusil,[2] lets it off, and kills the two monkeys.

"God be praised, my dear Cacambo, I have rescued those two poor creatures from a most perilous situation. If I have committed a sin in killing an inquisitor and a Jesuit, I have made ample amends by saving the lives of these girls. Perhaps they are young ladies of a family; and this adventure may procure us great advantages in this country."

He was going on, but stopped short when he saw the two girls dissolved in tears over the dead bodies of the monkeys, embracing them in the tenderest manner and rending the air with the most dismal lamentations.

"Little did I expect to see such good nature," says he at length to Cacambo, who made answer, "Master, you have done for yourself and me. You have slain the sweethearts of those two young ladies."

"The sweethearts! Is it possible! You are jesting, Cacambo. I can never believe it."

"Dear master," replied Cacambo, "you are surprised at everything. Why should you think it so strange that in some countries there are monkeys which insinuate themselves in the good graces of the ladies; they are the fourth part of a human being, as I am the fourth part of a Spaniard."

"Alas!" replies Candide, "I remember to have heard master Pangloss say that the like accidents used to happen formerly, that these commixtures are productive of Centaurs, Fauns, and Satyrs, and that many ancients had seen such monsters, but I looked upon the whole as fabulous."

"Now you are convinced," said Cacambo, "that it is very true,

---

1 Meadow.
2 Musket.

and you see what use is made of those creatures, by persons that have not had a proper education. All I am afraid of is that those ladies will play you some ugly trick."[1]

These reflections were well founded, so that Candide was prevailed upon to quit the meadow, and to pierce into a thicket. There he and Cacambo supped, and after cursing the Portuguese inquisitor, the governor of Buenos Aires, and the Baron, they fell asleep on the bare ground.

When they awaked in the morning, they could neither stir nor move, for the Oreillons,[2] who inhabit that country, and to whom the ladies had given information of these strangers, had bound them with cords made of the bark of trees. They were encompassed by fifty naked Oreillons, armed with bows and arrows, with clubs, and hatchets of flint. Some were making a large cauldron boil; others were preparing spits.

"A Jesuit! A Jesuit! We shall be revenged," cried they. "We shall have excellent cheer. Let us eat the Jesuit, let us eat him up! "

"I told you, master," cried Cacambo in a most sorrowful tone, "that those two girls would play you some ugly trick."

Candide seeing the cauldron and the spits, cried out, "I fancy we are going to be either roasted or boiled. Ah! What would master Pangloss say were he to see how pure nature is formed? Everything is right, be it so, but I own it is very hard to be bereft of dear Miss Cunegonde, and to be put upon a spit by barbarous Oreillons."

Cacambo had always his wits about him. "Do not despair," said he to the disconsolate Candide, "I understand a little of the jargon of those people, and I will speak to them."

"Be sure," said Candide, "you make them sensible of the horrid barbarity of boiling human creatures, and how repugnant such a practice is to Christianity."

"Gentlemen," said Cacambo, "you reckon you are going to feast upon a Jesuit. It is all very well; nothing more just than thus

---

1 All of these topics received some discussion in the mid-seventeenth century. In *Essai sur les Mœurs,* Voltaire speculates about interspecies sex and the fantastic creatures, such as satyrs, that are reported in ancient history. Cacambo's reference to those "not properly educated," along with two references later in the chapter to "pure nature," satirize Iau's speculations concerning the inherently simple and good desires and actions of the natives of the New World and of uncultured humanity in the pure State of Nature. See Rousseau, *Discourse on Inequality* (1754) and earlier prize essays.

2 A South American people, then called *Orejones* ("big ears") by the Spanish.

to treat your enemies. Indeed the law of nature teaches us to kill our neighbour, and such is the practice all over the world. If we do not make use of the same privilege, it is because we have much better fare than human flesh.

"But for your part, you have not such resources as we, and certainly it is much better to devour your enemies, than to resign them to the crows. But, gentlemen, surely you would not choose to eat your friends. You think you shall spit a Jesuit, whereas he is your friend and defender: you are going to roast the very man who has been fighting against your enemies. In regard to myself, I am your countryman, that gentleman is my master, and, far from being a Jesuit, he has just now killed one of that order, whose spoils he wears, and thence comes your mistake. To convince you of the bit of truth of what I have affirmed, take his habit, and carry it to the first barrier of the Jesuits' kingdom, and inform yourselves whether my master did not kill a Jesuit officer. No great time is requisite for this, and you may still feast upon our bodies if you find I have deceived you. But if I have apprized[1] you of the truth, you are too well acquainted with the principles of public law, humanity, and justice to take away our lives."

The Oreillons, finding this speech very reasonable, deputed two of their principal people with all expedition to inquire into the truth of the matter; these executed their commission like men of sense, and soon returned with good news to the prisoners.[2] They untied them both, showed them all sorts of civilities, offered them girls, gave them refreshments, and reconducted them to the confines of their territories, proclaiming with great joy, "He is no Jesuit, he is no Jesuit."

Candide could not help being surprised at the cause of his deliverance. "What sort of people," said he, "are these! How strange their manners! If I had not been so lucky as to run Miss Cunegonde's brother through the body, I should have been devoured without redemption. But after all, pure nature is right, since those people, instead of feasting upon my flesh, have shown me a thousand civilities, when they knew I was not a Jesuit."

---

1 Apprised, made aware of.
2 Voltaire is notorious as an early exponent of scientific racism, arguing in the first half-dozen chapters of his *Essai sur les Mœurs* for an essential difference and general inferiority of African and American to European races (and, arguably, a superiority to both of Asian). At this turn of *Candide*, however, he brings forth quite another theme of the *Essai*: the universal reasoning capacity of all humans.

Chapter XVII
*Candide and his valet arrive at the country of the El Dorado,
and what they saw there*

"You see," said Cacambo to Candide as soon as they had reached
the frontiers of the Oreillons, "this hemisphere is not a pin better
than the other. Take my word for it, let us go back to Europe the
shortest way possible."

"How go back?" said Candide. "And where shall we go? To my
own country? The Bulgarians and Abares are laying it waste with
fire and sword. To Portugal? There I shall be burnt. And if we
abide here, we are every moment in danger of being spitted. But
how can I resolve to quit a part of the world, where my dear
Cunegonde resides?"

"Let us turn towards Cayenne," said Cacambo. "There we
shall find Frenchmen, who ramble over all parts of the globe. They
may assist us, and God perhaps will have pity on our distress."

It was not easy to get to Cayenne. They knew which way to
direct their steps, but mountains, rivers, precipices, robbers,
savages, obstructed their passage. Their horses were killed with
fatigue, and their provisions consumed. They fed a whole month
upon wild fruit, till at length they came to a little river lined with
cocoa-trees, which raised their spirits and supplied them with
nourishment.

Cacambo, who was as good a counselor as the old woman,
said to Candide, "We are able to hold out no longer. We have
travelled enough on foot; I spy an empty canoe near the river-
side. Let us fill it with cocoa-nuts and get into it. The stream will
carry us down, for a river always leads to some inhabited place.
In case we do not find things to our mind, at least we shall meet
with something new."

"With all my heart," said Candide, "let us recommend ourselves to Providence."

They rowed a few leagues down the river, the banks of which
were in some places flowery, in others barren, in some parts
smooth, in others steep and rocky. The stream widened as they
advanced, till at length it ran under an arch of frightful rocks
which reared their lofty heads to the sky. Under this arch the two
travellers had the courage to commit themselves to the stream.
The river contracting itself hereabouts, whirled them along with
a dreadful noise and rapidity. At the end of four-and-twenty
hours they saw daylight again, but their canoe was dashed to
pieces against the rocks.

They were obliged to creep along those rocks the space of a league, till at length they discovered a very large plain, bounded by inaccessible mountains. The country was cultivated as much for pleasure, as for the necessaries of life; the useful and the agreeable were completely mixed. The roads were covered, or rather adorned, with carriages of a glittering form and substance, in which men and women of surprising beauty were drawn by red sheep of a very large size, which for fleetness surpassed the finest coursers[1] of Andalusia, Tetuan, or Mequinez.[2]

"Here is a country however," said Candide, "preferable to Westphalia." He stepped along with Cacambo to a neighbouring village, and the first thing they saw was children dressed in tattered brocades,[3] and playing at quoits.[4] Our travellers from the other world amused themselves greatly with this sight. The quoits were large round pieces, yellow, red, and green, which cast a surprising lustre. The travellers picked a few of them off the ground, and they proved to be either gold, emeralds, or rubies, the least of which would have been the greatest ornament of the Mogul's[5] imperial crown.

"Without doubt," said Cacambo, "these children must be the king's sons, that are playing at quoits." Just as he had spoke these words, the schoolmaster of the village came and called them to school.

"There," said Candide, "is the preceptor of the royal family."

The little beggars immediately quitted their diversion, leaving the quoits on the ground with all their other playthings. Candide gathers them up, runs to the master, and presents them to him in a most humble manner, giving him to understand signs, that their royal highnesses had forgot their gold and their jewels. The schoolmaster, smiling, flung them upon the ground. Then looking at Candide with a good deal of surprise, he went about his business.

---

1 An especially swift or powerful horse, a charger.
2 The red sheep would seem to be the llamas of the New World. Llamas, coconuts, and even some of the political organization of El Dorado, are drawn from Voltaire's extensive reading of world history and travel literature, which he used in composing his *Essai sur les Mœurs*. The most important sources are Garcilaso de la Vega, *Royal Commentaries of the Incas and General History of Peru* (1617) and the (perhaps fictional or pseudonymous) *Relation of the Voyages of François Coreal* (1722).
3 Richly woven tapestry fabrics.
4 A game of throwing stones or rings across a field, similar to lawn bowling.
5 Emperor (usually of India).

The travellers took care however to gather up the gold, the rubies, and the emeralds. "Where are we?" cried Candide. "The king's children in this country must have an excellent education, since they are taught to despise gold and precious stones." Cacambo was as much surprised as Candide.

At length they drew near to the first house in the village, and they found it as magnificent as a European palace. A multitude of people stood crowding at the door and there was a much greater number in the house. Their ears were delighted with most agreeable music, and a fragrant odour came from the kitchen.

Cacambo went up to the door, and heard they were talking Peruvian, which was his mother-tongue, for it is well known that Cacambo was born in Tucuman in a village where no other language but this was spoke. "I will be your interpreter here," said he to Candide. "Let us go in; it is a public house."

Immediately, two waiters and two girls dressed in cloth of gold and their hair tied up with ribbons accost the strangers, and invite them to sit down to table with the landlord. Their dinner was: four dishes of soup, each garnished with two young parrots; a tureen of bouillé,[1] that weighed two hundred pounds; two roasted monkeys, exquisitely well tasted; three hundred humming birds in one dish, and six hundred fly-birds in another; excellent ragouts; delightful pasties[2]—the whole served up in dishes of rock-crystal. The servants of the inn poured out several liquors drawn from the sugar cane.

Most of the company were chapmen[3] and waggoners,[4] all extremely polite; they asked Cacambo a few questions with the greatest circumspection, and answered his in the most obliging manner.

As soon as dinner was over, Candide, as well as Cacambo, thought it would be very handsome if to pay their reckoning they laid down two of those large gold pieces which they had picked off the ground. But the landlord and landlady burst out a laughing. When the fit was over, "Gentlemen," said the landlord, "it is plain you are strangers, and such guests we are not accustomed to see. Pardon use therefore if we fell a laughing when you tendered us the common pebbles of our country, in payment of your reckoning. To be sure, you have none of the coin of this kingdom,

---

1 Bouillabaisse broth soup.
2 Savory pastries.
3 Merchants or traders.
4 Horse-drawn cart or wagon drivers.

but it is not necessary to have money at all to dine in this house. All our inns are established for the conveniency of commerce and paid by the government. You have fared but very indifferently, because this is a poor village, but everywhere else, you will meet with a reception suitable to persons of your merit."

Cacambo explained this whole discourse of the landlord with great astonishment to Candide, who was as greatly astonished to hear it. "What sort of a country then is this," said they to one another, "a country unknown to all the world, a country of so different a nature from ours? Very likely this is the part of the globe where everything is right, for there must certainly be some such place. And let master Pangloss say what he would, I often found that things went very ill in Westphalia."

Chapter XVIII
What they saw in the country of El Dorado

Cacambo asked a great many curious questions of the landlord, who made answer. "I am very ignorant, but not the worse on that account; however, we have in this neighbourhood an old man retired from court, who is the most learned and most communicative person in the kingdom." This said, he carries Cacambo to the old man.

Candide acted now only a second character, and attended his valet. They entered a very plain house, for the door was only of silver and the ceilings were only of gold, but wrought in so elegant a taste as to vie with the richest ceilings. The antechamber, indeed, was only encrusted with rubies and emeralds, but the order in which everything was arranged made amends for this great simplicity.

The old man received the strangers on his sofa, which was stuffed with humming birds' feathers, and ordered his servants to present them with liquors in diamond goblets, after which he satisfied their curiosity in the following terms:

"I am now one hundred and seventy two years old, and I learnt of my late father, master of the horse to the king, the amazing revolutions of Peru, of which he had been eyewitness. The kingdom we now inhabit is the ancient patrimony of the Incas, who quitted it very imprudently to conquer another part of the world, and were at length destroyed by the Spaniards.

"More wise by far were the princes of their family, who remained in their native country. They ordained, with the consent of the whole nation, that none of the inhabitants should ever be permitted to quit our little kingdom, and this has preserved our innocence and happiness. The Spaniards had a confused notion of this country, and called it *El Dorado*, and an Englishman, whose name was Walter Raleigh,[1] came very near it about a hundred years ago. But being surrounded with inaccessible rocks and precipices, we have hitherto been sheltered from the rapaciousness of European nations, who have an inconceivable passion for our pebbles and dirt, for the sake of which they would murder us all, to the very last man."

The conversation lasted some time, and turned chiefly on their form of government, their manners, their women, their public entertainments, and the arts. At length Candide, having had always a taste for metaphysics, made Cacambo ask whether there was any religion in that country.

The old man, reddening a little, said, "How can you ask such a question? Do you take us for ungrateful wretches?"

Cacambo humbly asked, "What was the established religion of El Dorado?"

The old man, reddening once more, made answer. "Can there be two religions? We have the religion of the whole world; we worship God from morning till night."

"Do you worship but one God?" said Cacambo, who still acted as interpreter in representing Candide's doubts.

"Sure," says the old man, "there are not two, nor three, nor four. I must confess, the people from your side of the world ask very extraordinary questions."

Candide was not yet tired of interrogating the good old man; he wanted to know in what manner they prayed to God in El Dorado.

"We do not pray to him at all," said the respectable sage. "We have nothing to ask of him; he has given us all we need, and we incessantly return him thanks."

Candide having a curiosity to see the priests, asked where they were, at which the good old man smiling, said, "My friends, we are all priests; the king and all the heads of families sing solemn canticles of thanksgiving every morning, accompanied by five or sixth thousand musicians."

"What! Have you no monks to teach, to dispute, to govern, to cabal, and to burn people that are not of their opinion?"

"We must be mad, indeed, if that were the case," said the old

---

1 English explorer and courtier (*ca.* 1552-1618).

man. "Here we are all of one opinion, and we know not what you mean by monks."

During the whole discourse Candide was in raptures, and he said to himself, "This is vastly different from Westphalia and the Baron's castle. Had our friend Pangloss seen El Dorado, he would no longer have said that the castle of Thunder-ten-tronckh was the finest thing upon earth; there is no knowing anything without traveling."

This long conversation being ended, the old man ordered a coach and six sheep to be got ready and twelve of his domestics to conduct the travellers to court. "Excuse me," said he, "if my age deprives me of the honour of attending you. The king will receive you in such a manner, as you will not complain, and no doubt but you will make an allowance for the customs of the country, if some things should not be to your liking."

Candide and Cacambo got into the coach, the six sheep flew, and in less than four hours they reached the king's palace, situated at the extremity of the capital. The portal was two hundred and twenty feet high, and one hundred wide, but words are wanting to express the materials of which it was built. It is plain such materials must have a prodigious superiority over those pebbles and sand which we call gold and precious stones.

Twenty beautiful damsels of the king's guard were ready to receive Candide and Cacambo as they alighted from the coach, from whence they conducted them to the bath, and dressed them in robes of tissue interwoven with the down of humming birds. The great officers of the crown led them to the king's apartment, according to custom, between two files of musicians, a thousand on each side.

When they drew near to the audience-hall, Cacambo asked one of the great officers in what manner he should pay his obeisance to his majesty: whether it was customary to fall upon their knees, or to prostrate themselves upon the ground; whether they put their hands upon their head, or behind their back; whether they licked the dust off the floor; in short, what was the ceremony observed on such occasions. "The custom," said the great officer, "is to embrace the king, and to kiss him on each cheek." Candide and Cacambo threw themselves round his majesty's neck, who received them with all the goodness imaginable, and very politely begged they would sup with him.

In the mean time they took a walk about the city and saw the public structures rearing their lofty heads to the clouds; the market-places decorated with a thousand columns; the fountains of spring water, those of rose-water and those of liquors drawn from sugar-cane, incessantly flowing in the great squares, which were paved with a kind of precious stone, from whence issued a delicious fragrance like that of cloves and cinnamon. Candide asked to see the parliament, or the court of justice; they told him they had none, and that they were strangers to lawsuits. He enquired whether there were any prisons, and he was told there were not. But what surprised him most, and gave him the greatest pleasure, was the palace of sciences, where he saw a gallery two thousand feet long, and filled with physical experiments.[1]

After rambling about the city the whole afternoon and seeing but a thousandth part of it, they were reconducted to the royal palace, where Candide sat down to table with his majesty, his valet Cacambo, and several ladies. Never was there a better entertainment, and never was more wit shown at table than what fell from his majesty. Cacambo explained the king's *bon mots*[2] to Candide, and notwithstanding they were translated, they still appeared to be *bon mots*. Of all the things that surprised Candide, this was not the least.

In this manner they spent a whole month, during which time Candide used to say to Cacambo, "I own, my friend, once more, that the castle where I was born is nothing in comparison of the place where we are at present. But, after all, Cunegonde is not here, and no doubt but you have some sweetheart in Europe. If we abide here, we shall only be upon a footing with the rest. Whereas if we return to our old world, only with twelve sheep laden with the pebbles of El Dorado, we shall be richer than all the kings in Europe; we shall have no more inquisitors to fear, and we may easily recover Miss Cunegonde."

This speech was agreeable to Cacambo. Mankind are so fond of roving, of making a figure in their own country and of boasting of what they have seen in their travels that the two happy strangers resolved to be no longer so, but to ask his majesty's leave to quit the country.

"You are very indiscreet," said the king. "I am sensible that my kingdom is but a trifling place, but when a person is tolerably well settled in any part, he should abide there. I have no right to detain strangers against their will. This would be tyranny, and therefore

---

1 This touch adds to El Dorado elements from Francis Bacon's utopia of scientists, *The New Atlantis* (1627). It stands as a great improvement upon Pangloss's experiments, carried out in chapter one.

2 Jokes, especially wordplay; French: *bons mots* (good words).

inconsistent both with our manners and our laws. Mankind are all by nature free; therefore go whenever you please, but you will meet with very great difficulty in passing the frontiers. It is impossible to ascend that rapid river, which runs under vaulted rocks, and on which you were conveyed to El Dorado in the most surprising manner. The mountains round my kingdom are ten thousand feet high, and as steep as a perpendicular. They are each above ten leagues in breadth, and there is no other way to descend them than by precipices. However, since you absolutely insist upon departing, I shall give orders to my engineers to construct a machine that will convey you very safe. When they have conducted you back to the mountains, nobody is to attend you farther, for my subjects have made a vow never to quit the kingdom, and they are too wise to break it. Ask me whatever you please."

"We desire nothing of your majesty," said Cacambo, "but a few sheep laden with provisions, pebbles, and this country clay."

The king smiled and said, "I cannot conceive what pleasure you Europeans find in our yellow clay, but take as much of it as you have a mind to, and much good may it do you."

Hereupon he gave directions that his engineers should construct a machine to hoist up these two extraordinary men out of the kingdom. Three thousand mathematicians went to work, and finished it in fifteen days; it did not cost above twenty millions sterling in the specie[1] of that country. Candide and Cacambo were put into the machine, together with two large red sheep to ride upon as soon as they got over the mountains, twenty sheep laden with provisions, thirty with presents of the several curiosities of the country, and fifty with gold, diamonds, and precious stones. The king embraced the two wanderers very tenderly.

It was a curious spectacle to see them set off, and the ingenious manner in which they and their sheep were hoisted over the mountains. The mathematicians, after conveying them to a place of safety, took their leave, and Candide had no other desire, no other aim, than to present his treasure to Miss Cunegonde. "Now," said he, "we are able to pay the governor of Buenos Aires, if Miss Cunegonde can be ransomed. Let us move towards Cayenne, where we may take shipping, and then we shall see what kingdom we shall be able to purchase."

---

1 Coin or coins.

Chapter XIX
What happened to them at Surinam, and how
Candid got acquainted with Martin

Our travellers spent the first day very agreeably. They were delighted with the notion of possessing more treasure, than all Asia, Europe and Africa could scrape together. Candide in his raptures cut Cunegonde's name on trees. The second day, two of their sheep plunged into a morass, where they and their burthens were lost, two more died of fatigued a few days after, seven or eight perished with hunger in a desert, and others a few days after tumbled down from precipices. At length, after traveling a hundred days, only two sheep remained.

Said Candide to Cacambo, "You see how perishable are the riches of this world; there is nothing solid but virtue, and the happiness of seeing Cunegonde once more."

"I grant all you say," said Cacambo, "but we have still two sheep remaining, with more treasure than the king of Spain will ever be possessed of, and I espy[1] a town, which I take to be Surinam, belonging to the Dutch. We are at the end of all our troubles, and at the beginning of happiness."

As they drew near the town they saw a negro stretched upon the ground, with only one moiety[2] of his habit, that is, of his blue linen drawers; the poor man had lost his left leg and his right arm. "Good God!" said Candide, in Dutch. "What art thou doing there, friend, in that shocking condition?"

"I am waiting for my master mynheer[3] Vanderdendur, the famous merchant," answered the negro.[4]

"Was it mynheer Vanderdendur," said Candide, "that used thee in this manner?"

"Yes, sir," said the negro, "it is the custom of our country. They give us a pair of linen drawers for our whole garment twice a year. When we work at the sugar-canes and the mill snatches hold of a finger, they cut off our hand, and when we attempt to run away, they cut off our leg. Both cases have hap-

---

1 See.
2 Half.
3 Dutch: Mister.
4 This name may relate to Jean Van Duren, an Amsterdam publisher who had angered Voltaire almost twenty years before by not accepting his changes to a book in the process of publication. Note also the story of Martin, below: "a slave ten years to the booksellers of Amsterdam."

pened to me. This is what we suffer for your eating sugar in Europe.[1]

"Yet when my mother sold me for ten patacoons[2] on the coast of Guinea, she said to me, 'My dear child, bless our Fetiches.[3] Adore them forever; they will make thee live happy. Thou hast the honour of being the slave of our lords the whites, which is making the fortune of thy father and mother.' Alas! I know not whether I have made their fortune; this I know, that they have not made mine. Dogs, monkeys and parrots are a thousand times less wretched than I. The Dutch Fetiches who converted me, declare every Sunday, that we are all of us children of Adam, blacks as well as whites. I am not skilled in genealogy, but if those preachers tell the truth, we are all second cousins. Now you must allow me that it is impossible to treat one's relations in a more barbarous manner."

"O Pangloss!" cried Candide, "You never thought of this horrid scene; there is an end of the matter. I see I must renounce your doctrine at last."[4]

"What is his doctrine?" said Cacambo.

"Alas!" said Candide, "It is the folly of maintaining that everything is right, when it is wrong!" At these words he looked at the negro, and with tears in his eyes, he entered Surinam.

The first thing they inquire after is whether there is ever a vessel in the harbour which they could send to Buenos Aires. The person to whom they applied was a Spanish sea captain, who offered to agree with them upon reasonable terms. He appointed to meet them at a public house, whither Candide and the faithful Cacambo went with their two sheep, and waited for his coming.

---

1 Voltaire wrote against slavery, and he and the rest of Europe read about such treatment, some of which was codified in law, under Louis XIV, in Père Jean Baptiste Labat, *Nouveaux Voyages aux Isles de l'Amérique* (1742). It is worth noting that it does not occur to Candide, laden with riches at this point in his journey, to offer aid to this miserable fellow. Voltaire, like others, consumed sugar copiously; humanitarian and anti-slavery boycotts and actions against the sugar trade followed in Europe in the 1790s.

2 Spanish coins; the dollar, or eight "pieces of eight" of the new world.

3 Original Portuguese name for priests of the African Voodoo religion, which utilizes fetish objects.

4 In the original French text, Voltaire names the doctrine "optimisme." This is the only appearance of the word in the text of *Candide*, alongside its use in the title. The word derives from a mathematical use (optimum) and was new to popular use in France. Consequently, it was translated in the title as "all for the best" in two of three English translations of 1759.

Candide being extremely frank and open, told the Spaniard all his adventures, and owned to him that he intended to run away with Miss Cunegonde.

"Take my word, for it then," said the captain, "I will not carry you to Buenos Aires for I should be hanged, and so would you. The fair Cunegonde is my lord's favourite mistress."

Candide was thunderstruck at this discovery, but after he had vented his grief in a flood of tears, he called Cacambo aside, and spoke to him thus: "I'll tell you, my dear friend, what you must do. We have each of us in our pockets to the value of five or six millions in diamonds. You are cleverer at these matters than I; you must go and bring Miss Cunegonde from Buenos Aires. If the governor makes any difficulty, give him a million. If this will not soften him, give him two. As you have not killed an inquisitor, they will have no suspicion of you. I'll get another ship, and go and wait for you at Venice; that's a free country, where there is no danger either from Bulgarians, Abares, Jews, or inquisitors."

Cacambo greatly applauded this sage resolution. It grieved him to the very heart to part with so good a master, who has become his intimate friend, but the desire of being serviceable to him prevailed over the pain he felt from the separation. In embracing each other they shed tears. Candide charged him not to forget the good old woman, and Cacambo set out that very same day. This Cacambo was a very honest fellow.

Candide stayed some days longer at Surinam, waiting for another captain to carry him and the two remaining sheep to Italy. After he had hired domestics and purchased everything necessary for a long voyage, mynheer Vanderdendur, captain of a large vessel, came and offered his service. "What will you have," said he to the Dutch skipper, "to carry me and my servants, my baggage, and these two sheep directly to Venice, without touching at any other port." The skipper said ten thousand piasters; and Candide immediately agreed to let him have the money.[1]

"Zdsucks!"[2] said the prudent Vanderdendur. "This stranger gives me ten thousand piasters without making a single word. He must therefore be immensely rich." Returning a little while after, he let him know that upon second consideration, he could not undertake the voyage for less than twenty thousand.

"Well, you shall have them," said Candide.

"Ay," said the skipper to himself, "this man agrees to pay

---

1 The Spanish piaster was equal to one "piece of eight."
2 An oath indicating surprise; variant of gadzooks.

twenty thousand piasters, with as much ease as ten." He went back to him again, and declared he could not carry him to Venice for less than thirty thousand piasters.

"Then you shall have thirty thousand," replied Candide.

"Odso,"[1] said the Dutch skipper once more to himself, "thirty thousand piasters are a trifle to this man. Surely these sheep must be laden with an immense treasure. Let us say no more about it. First of all let him pay down the thirty thousand piasters, and then we shall see."

Candide sold two small diamonds, the least of which was worth more than what the skipper asked for his freight. He paid him before hand. The two sheep were put on board, and he hired a boat to follow them at his leisure. But before he arrived, the skipper seized the opportunity to unmoor, and stretched out to sea with a favourable gale. Candide, losing sight of the Dutchman, was greatly dismayed. "Alas!" said he, "what a sad trick! A trick worthy of the ancient hemisphere." He puts back overwhelmed with sorrow, for indeed he had been robbed of a treasure sufficient for twenty monarchs.

No sooner was he landed, than he waited upon the Dutch magistrate. In his perturbation of mind, he knocked very loud at the door, which being opened, he goes in, tells his case, and raises his voice with great vehemence. The magistrate began with fining him ten thousand piasters, for making a noise. Then he listened patiently to what he had to say, promised to examine into his affair at the skipper's return, and ordered him to pay ten thousand piasters for the expense of the present hearing.

Candide lost all patience at this behaviour. He had indeed experienced much greater vicissitudes, but the insensibility of the magistrate, and the cruelty of the skipper, flung him into a deep melancholy. The villainy of mankind presented itself before his imagination in all its deformity, and his mind was filled with gloomy ideas. At length hearing that a French captain was ready to set sail for Bordeaux, as he had no sheep nor diamonds to take along with him, he hired the cabin for the usual price. But before he went on board, he published an advertisement, that if any honest man would favour him with his company during the voyage, he would pay his passage and board, and, moreover, give him ten thousand piasters, upon condition that this man was the most dissatisfied with his state, and the most unfortunate in the whole province.

Such a multitude of candidates appeared on this occasion that a fleet of ships would have been hardly able to contain them all.

---

1 An oath indicating surprise; Italian origin: *cazzo*.

Candide being desirous to select from among the best, marked out about twenty who seemed to be sociable men, and all pretended to deserve the preference. He assembled them at an inn, where he treated them with a supper, on condition that every man should ingenuously relate his own history. He promised, moreover, to choose the person who to him should appear most deserving of compassion, and most justly dissatisfied with his station of life, and to bestow some presents upon the rest.

They sat till four o'clock in the morning, as they were telling their adventures, Candide recollected what the old woman had said to him in their voyage to Buenos Aires, and of her wager that there was not a person on board the ship but had met with very great misfortunes. At every adventure he heard, he thought of Pangloss. "My old master," said he, "would be greatly puzzled to demonstrate his system. I wish he was here. Certainly if everything is for the best, it is in El Dorado, and not in the other parts of the globe." At length, he made choice of a poor man of letters, who had been a slave ten years for the booksellers at Amsterdam. He determined that there was not a greater drudgery in the whole world.

This philosopher was an honest man, but he had been robbed by his wife, buffeted and abused by his son, and forsaken by his daughter who got a Portuguese to run away with her. He had been also deprived of a small employment, on which he subsisted, and he was persecuted by the preachers of Surinam, who took him for a Socinian.[1] We must allow that the others were at least as wretched as he, but Candide was in hopes that a man of letters would contribute more than the rest to divert him in his passage. All the other candidates complained that Candide had done them great injustice, but he stopped their mouths, by giving one hundred piasters to each.

Chapter XX
What happened at sea to Candide and Martin

The old philosopher, whose name was Martin, embarked for Bordeaux in company with Candide. They had both seen and

---

1 The Socinians were antitrinitarian Christians named after Fausto Sozzini (1539-1604), who maintained that Christ was human, rather than identical with God. Socinianism began to develop into what is now a familiar established form, called Utilitarianism, in the late seventeenth century.

suffered a great deal, and if the vessel had been to sail from Surinam to Japan, round the cape of Good Hope, the subject of moral and natural evil would have enabled them to entertain one another during the whole voyage.

Candide, however, had one great advantage over Martin—that he always hoped to see miss Cunegonde—whereas Martin had nothing at all to hope. Besides, Candide was possessed of money and jewels, and though he had lost one hundred large red sheep, laden with the greatest treasure of the earth—though the knavery[1] of the Dutch skipper still sat heavy upon his mind—yet when he reflected upon what he had still left, and when he mentioned the name of Cunegonde, especially towards the latter end of a repast, he inclined to Pangloss's doctrine.

"But what think you, Mr. Martin," said he to the philosopher, "of this whole system? What is your notion of moral and natural evil?"

"Sir," answered Martin, "our priests accused me of being a Socinian, but the real fact is, I am a Manichean."[2]

"You jest," said Candide. "There are no Manicheans in the world."

"I am one," said Martin. "I cannot help it; I know not how to think otherwise."

"Surely the devil must be in you," said Candide.

"He is so deeply concerned in the affairs of this world," answered Martin, "that he may very well be in me, as well as in everybody else. But I own to you that when I cast an eye on this globe—or rather on this little ball—I cannot help thinking but that God has abandoned it to some malignant being, yet we must always except El Dorado. I scarce ever knew a city that did not desire the destruction of the next city to it. Scarce a family that did not wish to exterminate some other family. The poor in all

---

1 Action of a knave, a dishonest individual, or a crafty rogue.

2 A Socinian doubts the divinity of Christ, but the greater heresy of a Manichean is the belief that there are two gods of similar standing ruling the creation: one corresponding to good, the other to evil. Candide doubts that there are Manicheans because believers were heavily persecuted in Europe; for example, in 1209 the papal legate Arnaud-Amaury, a leader against the Cathars, is reputed to have given the following counsel concerning the uncooperative people of Béziers, a tenth of whom were heretics: "Kill them all, God will recognize his own." Note that the devil may be a lesser figure—the archangel Beelzebub, vanquished by God—but Martin does not concede this. See Pierre Bayle's selections in Appendix B for more concerning the Manicheans.

parts of the world abominate the rich, to whom they are obliged to creep and cringe, and the rich treat the poor like sheep, whose wool and flesh they barter for money. A million of disciplined assassins are spread from one extremity of Europe to the other, getting their bread by regular depredation and murder, for want of honester employment. Even in those cities which seem to enjoy the blessings of peace, and where the arts and sciences flourish, the inhabitants are devoured with envy, care, inquietude, and other plagues much greater than those which are felt at the siege of a town. Private chagrins are still more shocking than public calamities. In a word, I have seen and suffered so much, that I am a Manichean."

"Yet there is something good in this world," replied Candide.

"That may be," said Martin, "but I know it not."

In the middle of this dispute, they heard the report of cannon, which redoubled every instant. Each man takes out his glass,[1] and they espy two ships engaged in close fight, about three miles off. At length one gave the other a shot between wind and water, which sunk her to the bottom. Candide and Martin could plainly perceive a hundred men upon deck, who, with their hands lifted up to heaven, made most terrible outcries, and the next moment were swallowed up by the sea.

"Well," said Martin, "you see in what manner mankind treats one another."

"It is true," said Candide, "this is a diabolical affair." And as he spoke these words, he espied something red and shining, which swam close to the vessel. They put out the shallop,[2] and it proved to be one of his sheep. At the recovery of this animal, Candide was more rejoiced than he had been grieved at the loss of the other hundred, though laden with the large diamonds of El Dorado.

The French captain quickly perceived that the victorious ship belonged to the crown of Spain and that the other was a Dutch pirate, and the very same captain who robbed Candide. The immense plunder which this villain had amassed was buried with him in the deep, and out of the whole only one sheep was saved.

"You see," said Candide to Martin, "that vice sometimes meets with condign[3] punishment; the Dutch skipper has met with the fate he deserved."

---

1   A spyglass or telescope.
2   A small, shallow boat; a skiff.
3   Deserved, appropriate.

"Yes," said Martin. "But why should the passengers be doomed also to destruction? God has punished the knave, and the devil has drowned the rest."

The French and Spanish ships continued their course, while Candide went on conversing with Martin. They disputed fifteen days successively, and at the end of those fifteen days they were as far advanced as when they began. However, they chatted, they communicated their ideas, and consoled each other. Candide made much of his sheep: "Since I have found thee again," said he, "I may likewise chance to find my Cunegonde."

Chapter XXI

Candide and Martin draw near the coast of France,
and reason with each other

At length they descried the coast of France, when Candide said to Martin, "Sir, were you ever in France?"

"Yes," said Martin, "I have been in several provinces of that kingdom. In some, one half of the people are fools, in others they are too cunning; in some they are weak and simple, in others they affect to be witty. In all their ruling passion is love, the next is slander, and the next to that is to talk nonsense."

"But, Mr. Martin, pray were you ever at Paris?"

"Yes, sir, it is a city that partakes of all the several species you have been describing. It is a chaos, a confused multitude, where everybody seeks for pleasure without being able to find it, at least as far as I have observed. I made some short stay there. At my arrival I was robbed of all I had in the world by pickpockets and sharpers[1] at the fair of St. Germain. I was taken myself for a robber, and confined eight days in prison, after which I served as corrector of the press, in order to get a little money towards defraying my expenses back to Holland on foot. I knew the whole tribe of scribblers, with the malcontents, and fanatics. It is said that there are very polite people in that city, and I am apt to believe it."

"For my part, I have no curiosity to see France," said Candide. "You may easily imagine that after spending a month at El Dorado, I can desire to behold nothing upon earth but Miss Cunegonde. I am going to meet her at Venice; we shall pass through France on our way to Italy. Will you bear me company?"

---

1 Cheating gamblers, such as cardsharps.

"With all my heart," said Martin. "It is said that Venice is fit only for its own nobility, but that strangers, however, meet with a very good reception, if they have a good deal of money. I have none; you have. Therefore, I'll follow you all over the world."

"But do you believe," said Candide, "that the earth was originally a sea, as we find it asserted in that large book belonging to the captain?"

"I do not believe a word of it," said Martin, "no more than I do of a thousand reveries, which have been published lately."[1]

"But," said Candide, "for what purpose or design was this world originally framed?"

"To plague us to death," answered Martin.

"Are not you greatly surprised," continued Candide, "at the passion of the two girls in the country of the Oreillons, for those monkeys, with whose story I made you acquainted?"

"Not at all," said Martin. "I find nothing extraordinary in it; I have seen so many strange things, that there is nothing strange to me at present."

"Do you believe," said Candide, "that mankind used always to cut one another's throats; that they were always liars, cheats, traitors, and ungrateful; always robbers, fools, inconstant, cowards, envious, gluttons, drunkards, misers, swayed by ambition, bloody-minded, calumniators,[2] debauchees,[3] fanatics, and hypocrites?"

"Do you believe," said Martin, "that hawks always eat pigeons, when these came in their way?"

"Yes, surely," said Candide.

"Well then," said Martin, "if hawks have always had the same nature, why should you pretend that mankind changed theirs?"

"Oh!" said Candide, "there is a vast deal of difference, for free-will ..." Reasoning thus they arrived at Bordeaux.

Chapter XXII
What happened in France to Candide and Martin

Candide made no longer stay at Bordeaux than was necessary for selling a few of the pebbles of El Dorado and for hiring a good

---

1 Voltaire is a bit obscure in this passage. The book is probably not the *Bible* (Genesis 1, the formation of the earth, or 7:6, the story of Noah); it is perhaps a book that Voltaire was reading as he composed *Candide*, but could not expect other readers to know: Charles de Brosses, *Histoire des navigations aux terres australes* (1756).

2 Slanderers, defaming gossips.

3 Pleasure-seekers or libertines.

vehicle to hold two passengers, for he could not bear to be without his philosopher Martin. He was only vexed to part with his sheep, which he left to the academy of sciences at Bordeaux. The academy proposed as a subject for this year's prize, the reason why this sheep's wool was red, and the prize adjudged to a learned man in the North, who demonstrated by A, plus B, minus C, divided by Z, that the sheep must be red, and die of the rot.

In the mean time the passengers whom Candide met in the several inns upon the road told him they were all going to Paris. This general impatience of seeing the capital, inspired him at length with the same desire, and it was not much out of his way to Venice.

No sooner was Candide arrived at his inn than he found himself a little out of order, occasioned by his great fatigue. As he had a very large diamond ring on his finger, and the people of the inn had taken notice of a prodigious heavy box among his baggage, there were two physicians to attend him, though he had never sent for them, a few intimate friends, who never stirred from him, and two devotees, who warmed his broths and jellies. Martin said, "I remember to have been sick at Paris in my first voyage, but as I was very poor, I had neither friends, devotees, nor physicians. Yet I recovered."

However, what by physic and bleeding, Candide's distemper was become a very serious affair. The parson of the parish came with great modesty to ask for a bill for the other world payable to the bearer. Candide would do no such thing, but the devotees assured him it was the fashion.[1] He made answer that he did not trouble his head about fashions. Martin was going to throw the priest out of the window. The priest swore that Candide should not have Christian burial. Martin swore he would bury the priest, if he continued to be troublesome. They began to be over-heated, when Martin took hold of the priest by the shoulders, and turned him out of doors, which occasioned great scandal and a lawsuit.

Candide got well again. During his convalescence he had very genteel company to sup with him. They played very deep, and

---

1 At mid-century in France, dying Catholics were required to sign a bill of confession before absolution could be given. The bill cleared them of association with the ideas of Cornelius Jansen, Bishop of Ypres (1585-1638) and the Jansenist heretical sect, which was especially prominent in some Parisian intellectual circles.

Candide was surprised he could never throw ambs-ace,[1] but Martin was not surprised at all.

Among those who did him the honours of the town was a little abbé[2] of Perigord, one of those busy bodies, who are ever alert, officious, forward, fawning and complaisant; who watch for strangers in their passage through the capital, tell them the scandalous history of the town, and offer them pleasures at all sorts of prices.

This man began with carrying Candide and Martin to the playhouse, where a new tragedy was to be acted. Candide happened to be seated near some of the *beaux esprits*,[3] but this did not prevent his shedding tears at some scenes that were well acted. One of those critics, who sat in the next box, spoke thus to him between the acts, "Your tears are greatly misplaced: that's a shocking actress, the actor who plays with her is a worse performer than herself, and the play is worse still than the actors. The author does not understand a word of Arabic, yet the scene is in Arabia. Besides, he is a man that does not believe in innate ideas, and to-morrow I'll venture to show you twenty pamphlets written against him."[4]

"Sir," said the little abbé de Perigord, "did you take notice of that young creature, with such a killing countenance and so delicate a shape? You may have her for ten thousand livres a month, and fifty thousand crowns in diamonds."

"I could not stay with her above a day or two," answered Candide, "because I have a rendezvous that calls me directly to Venice."

After supper, the insinuating abbé showed himself still more officious in paying his courtship to Candide. "And so, sir, you have a rendezvous at Venice?"

"Yes, monsieur l'Abbé," answered Candide. "I must absolutely wait upon Miss Cunegonde." And then the pleasure of talking

---

1   The lowest possible throw of the dice, "snake eyes."
2   Educated man with some limited training in ecclesiastical practice but, in this era, with little necessary association with the Church beyond education; not to be confused with an abbot.
3   French: Witty people, perhaps also libertines.
4   One playwright who fits this description is Voltaire, and the reference to innate ideas connects to John Locke's philosophy, about which Voltaire wrote in the *Letters Concerning the English Nation*. In 1761, Voltaire added a section of several pages to this chapter starting at this point, to expand upon the treatment of Paris, for the pleasure of his French audience. The added section is appended, following chapter thirty.

about the object he loved induced him to relate, according to custom, part of his adventures with that fair Westphalian.

"I believe," said the abbé, "Miss Cunegonde has a great deal of wit and that she knows how to write an excellent letter?"

"I never had any from her," answered Candide, "for being expelled from the castle upon her account, I had not an opportunity to write to her. Soon after that I heard she was dead, then I found her alive, then I lost her again, and last of all, I sent an express to her a thousand five hundred leagues hence, and I wait for an answer."

The abbé listened attentively, and seemed to be in a brown study.[1] He soon took his leave of the two foreigners, after a most tender embrace. The next morning, when Candide awaked, he received a letter in the following terms.

My dear Candide—I have been ill these eight days in town; and have heard of your arrival. I would fly to your arms, were I able to stir or move. I was informed of your passage at Bordeaux, where I left faithful Cacambo and the old woman, who are to follow me very soon. The governor of Buenos Aires has taken everything from me but your heart, which still remains. Come, your presence will either give me life, or kill me with pleasure.

At the receipt of this charming, this unexpected letter, Candide felt the utmost transports of joy; though on the other hand, the indisposition of his dear Cunegonde overwhelmed him with grief. Divided between those two passions, he takes his gold and his diamonds and hurries away with Martin to the hotel, where Miss Cunegonde was lodged. Upon entering the room, he trembles in every limb, his heart beats, his tongue falters. He undraws the curtain, and calls for a light to the bedside.

"Take care what you do," said the servant-maid. "The light is offensive to her." Immediately she draws the curtain again.

"My dear Cunegonde," said Candide dissolved in tears, "how do you do? If you cannot bear the light, speak to me at least."

"She cannot speak," said the maid. The lady then puts her plump hand out of bed, and Candide first bathes it with tears, then fills it with diamonds, leaving a purse of gold upon the easy chair.

Whilst he is indulging his transports, in comes an officer followed by the abbé, and a file of musqueteers. "There," said he, "are the two suspected foreigners." At the same time he orders them to be seized, and carried to prison.

---

1 Deep in thought.

"Travellers are not treated after this manner in El Dorado," said Candide.

"I am more a Manichean now than ever," said Martin.

"But pray sir, where are you going to carry us?" said Candide.

"To a dungeon," answered the officer.

Martin having recovered himself a little, judged that the person who acted the part of Cunegonde was a cheat; that monsieur l'abbé de Perigord was a knave who had imposed upon the honest simplicity of Candide; and that the officer was another knave, whom they might easily silence.

Candide, directed by Martin's advice, and impatient to see the real Cunegonde, rather than expose himself to a court of justice, proposes to the officer to give him three small diamonds, each of them worth about three thousand pistoles.[1] "Ah, sir," said he, "had you committed ever so much villainy, this would render you in my eye the honestest man in the world: three diamonds, worth three thousand pistoles each! Sir, instead of carrying you to jail, I would lose my life to serve you. There are orders for arresting all strangers. But let me alone; I have a brother at Dieppe[2] in Normandy; I'll conduct you thither, and if you have ever a diamond to give him, he'll take as much care of you as myself."

"And why," said Candide, "should all strangers be arrested?"

The abbé de Perigord then made answer and said, "It is because a poor devil of the county of Artois[3] heard somebody talk nonsense, and this induced him to commit a parricide, not such as that of the month of May 1610, but such as that of 1594, in the month of December, and such as have been perpetrated in other months and years by other poor devils, who had heard nonsense spoken."[4]

The officer then explained what the abbé meant. "Horrid monsters!" cried Candide aloud. "Is it possible that such scenes should be transacted among a dancing, singing nation? Is there

---

1 Foreign coin; in some uses of the expression, foreign coin valued at ten francs.

2 A town in Northern France (Normandy region).

3 A district and town in Northeastern France (Pas-de-Calais region).

4 In 1757, Robert François Damiens, a French-born Jesuit, failed to assassinate Louis XV, the "father" of France. The dates noted refer to successful and unsuccessful attempts, respectively, on the life of Henri IV. Voltaire's letters show he was greatly enraged by Damiens's attempt and blamed religious fanaticism; others concurred, or speculated on English designs. The details of the event and subsequent trial suggest that Damiens was mentally disturbed.

no getting immediately out of this country, where monkeys provoke tigers? I have seen bears in my country; but men I have beheld nowhere except in El Dorado. In the name of God, sir," said he to the officer, "conduct me to Venice, where I am to wait for Miss Cunegonde."

"I can conduct you no farther than to Lower Normandy," said the officer.

Immediately he orders his irons to be struck off, acknowledges himself mistaken, sends away his men, sets out with Candide and Martin for Dieppe, and consigns them to the care of his brother. There was then a small Dutch ship in the harbour. The Norman—grown the most officious man in the world by virtue of the three other diamonds—puts Candide and his attendants on board a vessel that was just ready to set sail for Portsmouth. This was not the way to Venice, but Candide thought he had made his escape out of hell, and he reckoned he should soon have an opportunity of resuming his voyage to Venice.

Chapter XXIII
Candide and Martin touch upon the English coast;
and what they see there

"Ah Pangloss! Pangloss! Ah Martin! Martin! Ah my dear Cunegonde! What sort of a world is this?" said Candide, when he got on board the Dutch ship.

"Something very foolish and abominable," answered Martin.

"You are acquainted with England. Are they as great fools in that country as in France?"

"They have a different kind of folly," said Martin. "You know that these two nations are at war, for a few acres of barren land in the neighbourhood of Canada,[1] and that they have spent a great deal more in the prosecution of this war than all Canada is worth. To tell you exactly, whether there are more inhabitants fit to send to a madhouse in one country than the other is what my imperfect intelligence will not permit. I only know in general that the people we are going to see are very atrabilarious.[2]

---

1 This disparagement ("ces deux nations sont en guerre pour quelques arpents de neige vers le Canada") is one of Voltaire's few references to North America, and to hostilities in the St. Lawrence region that preceded (1754-56) and then accompanied (1756-63) the European Seven Years' War.

2 Melancholic or sad, and perhaps hypochondriac as well.

As they were talking in this manner, they arrived at Portsmouth. The coast was lined with a multitude of people whose eyes were fixed on a lusty[1] man on board one of the men of war in the harbour, who was upon his knees, and blindfolded. Four soldiers stood opposite to this man; each of them fired three balls at his head, with all the calmness in the world, and the whole assembly went away very well satisfied.

"What is all this?" said Candide. "And what demon is it that exercises his tyrannic sway in every country?" He then asked who was that lusty man, who had been killed with so much ceremony.

They answered, "He was an admiral."

"And why should you kill your admiral?"

"Because he did not take care to kill a sufficient number of men himself. He gave battle to a French admiral, and it has been proved that he was not near enough to him."

"But," replied Candide, "the French admiral was as far from the English admiral."

"There is no doubt of it," said they, "but in this country, it is proper now and then to kill one admiral, in order to make the others fight."[2]

Candide was so shocked at what he saw and heard, that he would not set foot on shore, but made a bargain with the Dutch skipper (were he even to rob him, like the captain at Surinam) to carry him directly to Venice.

The skipper was ready in two days. They sailed the coast of France, and passing within sight of Lisbon, Candide trembled. From thence they proceeded to the Straights, entered the Mediterranean, and after a long passage arrived at Venice. "God be praised," said Candide, embracing Martin. "Here I shall see once more my beloved Cunegonde. I put as much trust in Cacambo as in myself. All is well, all very well, all as well as possible."

---

1 Lively, robust.
2 The original line ends with "pour encourager les autres." A better translation brings out what has since become a classic witticism: "In this country, it is good to shoot an admiral from time to time, to encourage the others." In 1757, Voltaire protested the pending execution of Admiral John Byng, charged with neglect of duty in his leadership after a retreat allowed the French to take Port Mahon on the Mediterranean island of Minorca, at that time a British possession. Voltaire asked his friend the duke of Richelieu, who was the opposing leader in the battle, to testify on the valor of Byng's efforts, but the English court martial was not swayed.

Chapter XXIV
Of Paquette and friar Giroflée

Upon their arrival at Venice, he went to search for Cacambo at every inn and coffeehouse and among all the ladies of pleasure, but to no purpose. He sent every day to inquire what ships were come in. "Strange!" said he to Martin, "that I should have had time to perform a voyage from Surinam to Bordeaux, to travel from thence to Paris and Dieppe, to pay a visit to Portsmouth, to sail along the coast of Portugal and Spain, and up the Mediterranean, to spend some months at Venice, and that my lovely Cunegonde should not be yet arrived. Instead of her, I only met with a Parisian wench, and an abbé of Perigord!

"Cunegonde is certainly dead, and I have nothing more to do but to follow her to her grave. Alas! How much better would it have been for me to have remained in the paradise of El Dorado, than to come back to this cursed Europe? You are in the right, my dear Martin! All is misery and deceit."

He was seized with a deep melancholy, and neither went to see the opera, nor any of the other diversions of the carnival. Nay, he was proof against the charms of the fair sex.

Martin said to him, "You are very simple indeed to imagine that a mongrel valet, entrusted with five or six millions, will go in search of your mistress to the other end of the world, and bring her to you to Venice. If he finds her, he will keep her to himself; if he does not find her, he will get another. I advise you to forget your valet Cacambo, and your fair Cunegonde."

Martin's advice was not very consolatory; Candide's melancholy increased; and Martin continued to prove to him that there was very little virtue or happiness upon earth, except perhaps in El Dorado, where no body could gain admittance.

While they were disputing on this important subject, and waiting for Cunegonde, Candide saw a young Theatine[1] friar in the piazza di St. Marco, holding a girl under his arm. The Theatine looked fresh coloured, plump, and vigorous; his eyes sparkled, his air, his gait, were bold and lofty. The girl was very pretty and was singing a song; she looked languishingly[2] on her Theatine, and sometimes pinched his fat cheeks.

"At least you will allow me," said Candide to Martin, "that these two are happy. Hitherto I have met with none but unfortu-

---

1 A monastic order focused especially on missionary work.
2 Near the point of fainting, swooning.

nate people in the whole habitable globe, except in El Dorado, but as to this pair, I would venture to lay a wager that they are very happy."

"I lay you they are not," said Martin.

"We need only desire them to dine with us," said Candide, "and you will see whether I am mistaken or not."

Immediately he accosts them, and with great complaisance invites them to his inn, to eat some macaroni, with Lombard partridges, and caviar, and to drink some Montepulciano, Lacryma Christi, Cyprus, and Samos wine.

The girl blushed, the Theatine accepted the invitation, and she followed him, casting her eyes on Candide with confusion and surprise, and dropping a few tears. No sooner had she set her foot in Candide's apartment, than she cried out, "So, Mr. Candide, do not you know Paquette again!"

Candide had not viewed her as yet with attention, his thoughts being entirely taken up with Cunegonde. But recollecting her as she spoke these words, "Alas!" said he. "Poor girl, was it you that reduced Doctor Pangloss to the sad plight I saw him in?"

"It was I, sir, indeed," answered Paquette. "I find you have heard the whole story. I have been informed of the sad disasters that befell the family of my lady Baroness, and the fair Cunegonde. My fate, I vow, has been equally cruel.

"I was very innocent, when you knew me. A Cordelier, my confessor, easily seduced me. The consequences were terrible: I was obliged to quit the castle a little after the Baron kicked you out of doors. If a famous surgeon had not taken compassion of me, I must have perished. For some time I was this surgeon's mistress, merely out of gratitude. His wife was as jealous as the devil and used to beat me every day most unmercifully; she was a very fiend of hell. The surgeon was one of the ugliest men I ever saw in my life, and I the most wretched of women, to be thus continually buffeted and bruised for the sake of a man whom I did not love. You know, sir, what a dangerous thing it is for an ill-natured woman to be married to any of the medical tribe. Incensed at the behaviour of his wife, he one day gave her so effectual a remedy to cure her of a little cold that she died two hours after, in most horrid convulsions. The wife's relations prosecuted the husband, who was obliged to fly, and I was thrown into jail.

"My innocence would not have saved me, if I had not been handsome. The judge set me free, on condition of his succeeding the surgeon. I was soon supplanted by a rival, turned out of doors quite destitute, and obliged to continue this abominable trade, which appears so pleasant to you men, while to us women, it is the utmost pitch of misery. At length I came to follow the business at Venice. Ah! sir, if you did but know what it is to be obliged to lie with every fellow, with old merchants, with counselors, monks, watermen, and abbés; to be exposed to all their abuse and insolence; to be often necessitated to borrow a petticoat, only to gratify the lust of a disagreeable rascal; to be robbed by one gallant of what we have earned of the other; to be subject to the extortions of civil-magistrates; and to have in prospect the frightful scene of old age, an hospital, or a dunghill; you would conclude, that I am one of the most unhappy wretches upon earth."

Thus did Paquette open her mind to honest Candide, in his closet, in the presence of Martin, who took occasion to say to him, "You see I have won one half the wager."

Friar Giroflée stayed in the parlour and drank a glass or two of wine while he was waiting for dinner. "But," said Candide to Paquette, "you looked so gay and content when I met you; you sung, and you behaved so lovingly to the Theatine, that you seemed to me as happy, as you pretend to be now the reverse."

"Ah! sir," answered Paquette, "this is one of the miseries of the trade. Yesterday I was robbed and abused by an officer; yet today I must put on a good humour to please a friar."

Candide wanted no more to be convinced; he owned that Martin was in the right. They sat down to table with Paquette and the Theatine; the repast was entertaining, and towards the end, they conversed with all the ease and freedom in the world. "Father," said Candide to the friar, "you seem to me to enjoy a state of happiness that even kings might envy; your countenance is the picture of health and jollity, you have a very pretty girl to divert you, and you appear to be well satisfied with your condition as a Theatine."

"Faith, sir," said friar Giroflée, "I heartily wish that all Theatines were at the bottom of the sea. I have been tempted a thousand times to set fire to the convent, and to go and turn Turk.[1] My parents obliged me, at the age of fifteen, to put on this detestable habit, only to increase the fortune of a cursed elder brother of mine, whom God confound. Jealousy, discord and fury reside in our convent. It is true, I have preached a few paltry sermons, whereby I got a little money, part of which the prior robs me of, and the other helps to pay for my girls, but at night,

---

1 To convert to Islam (in more recent idiom, to switch sides).

when I go home to my convent, I am ready to dash my brains against the walls of the dormitory. And this is the very case with all the fraternity."

Martin, turning towards Candide with his usual coolness, said, "Well, what do you think? Have I won the wager?"

Candide gave two thousand piasters to Paquette, and a thousand to friar Giroflée, saying, "I'll answer now, that this will make them happy."

"I believe no such thing," said Martin. "Perhaps this money will only render them more wretched."

"Be that as it may," said Candide. "But one thing consoles me: I see that we often meet with those whom we expected never to see more, so perhaps, as I have found my red sheep and Paquette, it may be my good fortune to meet also with Cunegonde."

"I wish," said Martin, "she may one day make you happy, but I doubt it very much."

"You are very hard of belief," said Candide.

"It is because," answered Martin, "I know something of life."

"You see those watermen," said Candide. "Are not they perpetually singing?"

"You do not see them," said Martin, "at home, with their wives and brats. The doge[1] has his chagrins, the watermen theirs. Not but I believe that upon the whole, the waterman's life is preferable to that of a doge. However, I look upon the difference as so trifling, that it is not worth the trouble of examining."

"People talk," said Candide, "of the senator Pococurante, who lives in that fine palace on the Brenta,[2] where he entertains foreigners in the most polite manner. They pretend that this man never felt any uneasiness."

"I should be glad to see so extraordinary a phenomenon," said Martin. On which Candide sent his compliments to the senator, desiring leave to wait upon him the next day.

Chapter XXV
Candide and Martin pay a visit to the senator Pococurante,
a noble Venetian

Candide and Martin went in a gondola on the Brenta, and arrived at the palace of the noble signor Pococurante. The

---

1 Elected chief magistrate of Venice.
2 A river dotted with villas that links Padua and Venice.

gardens were laid out in taste, and adorned with fine marble statues; the palace was built according to the most regular architecture. The master of the house was a man of sixty, and very rich; he received the two travellers with a polite indifference, which put Candide a little out of countenance, but was not at all disagreeable to Martin.[1]

The first thing they saw was two pretty girls, very neatly dressed, who served them with chocolate which was frothed extremely well. Candide could not help commending their beauty, grace, and address. "The creatures are well enough," said the senator; "I make them lie with me sometimes, for I am tired of the town-ladies. I am tired of their coquetry, their jealousy, their quarrels, their humours, their monkey-tricks, their pride, their folly; I am tired of making sonnets, or of ordering sonnets to be made for them. But after all, these two girls begin to grow tiresome to me."

After breakfast, Candide walked into a long gallery, where he was struck with the fine paintings. He asked, "By what master were the two first?"

"They are by Raphael," said the senator. "I bought them at a monstrous price some years ago, merely out of vanity. They are said to be the finest things in Italy, but they do not please me at all: the colours are dead, the figures not finished, nor do they appear with *relief* enough, the drapery is very bad. In short, let people say what they will, I do not look upon it as a true imitation of nature. I approve of no drawing, except where I think I see nature itself, and there are none of this sort. I have a great many pictures, but I take no manner of notice of them."

---

1 Pococurante (Italian: "few cares") lives in a fine, removed estate like Voltaire (who was sixty-four and very rich) but he cares a great deal less about the state of the world than Voltaire does. Pococurante expresses some ideas about the arts that Voltaire writes of elsewhere, and diverges from some as well. The catalog of painting, music, and literature that follows in this chapter includes very well known artists and works, and perhaps some less well known: Raphael (1483-1520); Homer (before 700 BCE); Virgil (70-19 BCE); Torquato Tasso (1544-95) Italian epic poet, author of *La Gerusalemme Liberata*; Ludovico Ariosto (1474-1533) Italian epic poet, author of *Orlando Furioso*; Horace (65-8 BCE) Latin poet, author of *Satires* (which get mixed reviews from Pococurante), *Epodes and Odes*; Marcus Tullius Cicero (106-43 BCE) Latin rhetor; Seneca the younger (4 BCE-65 CE) Latin stoic philosopher; John Milton (1608-1674) author of *Paradise Lost*; Plato (429-347 BCE) author of *Republic*.

While they were waiting for dinner, Pococurante ordered a concert. Candide praised the music to the skies.

"This noise," said the senator, "may amuse one for half an hour; but if it was to last longer, it would grow tiresome to everybody, though they durst not own it. Music is become the art of executing difficulties. Now, whatever is difficult cannot be long pleasing.

"Perhaps I should be fonder of an opera, if they had not made such a monster of it as really shocks me. Let who will go to see wretched tragedies set to music, where the scenes are contrived for no other end than to introduce, preposterously, three or four ridiculous songs, which set off the pipe of an actress. Let who will, or who can, die away with pleasure at the sight of an eunuch quavering the majestic part of Caesar, or a Cato, and awkwardly strutting along the stage. For my part, I have long ago renounced those paltry entertainments, which constitute the glory of modern Italy and are so dearly purchased by sovereigns." Candide disputed the point, but discreetly; Martin was entirely of the senator's opinion.

They sat down to dinner, and after they had been elegantly entertained they retired to the library. Candide, spying a Homer, richly bound, commended Illustrissimo's[1] taste. "There," said he, "is a book, that was once the delight of the great Pangloss, the best philosopher in Germany."

"He is no favourite of mine," answered Pococurante very coolly. "They used heretofore to make me believe that I took a pleasure in reading him. But that continual repetition of battles, so extremely like one another; those gods that are always bustling, without coming to any decisive blow; that Helen, who is the fire-brand of the war, and yet hardly acts a single character in the whole performance; that Troy, which sustains so long a siege without being taken: all this together renders the poem very insipid to me.

"I have asked some learned men whether they were not as much tired as myself with reading that poet. Those who were sincere have frankly acknowledged to me that he made them fall asleep, and yet it was proper to have him in their library, as an ancient monument, or like those rusty medals which are no longer of use in commerce."

"But your excellency," said Candide, "does not form the same opinion of Virgil?"

---

1 The illustrious or distinguished gentleman (Italian).

"I grant," said the senator, "that the second, fourth, and sixth book of the Aeneid are excellent, but as for his pious Aeneas, his strong Cloanthus, his friend Achates, his little Ascanius, his silly king Latinus, his burgess Amata, his insipid Lavinia, I think there can be nothing more flat and disagreeable. I prefer Tasso a good deal; or even the soporiferous[1] tales of Ariosto."

"May I presume to ask you, sir," said Candide, "whether you do not receive a great deal of pleasure from reading Horace?"

"There are maxims in this writer," answered Pococurante, "from which a man of the world may reap great benefit, and being comprised in laconic verse, they are more easily imprinted in the memory. But I set very little value upon his journey to Brundusium, and his account of a bad dinner, or on his dirty low quarrel between one Rupilius, whose words, he says, were full of poisonous filth, and another, whose language was imbued with vinegar. I have been very much offended with his indelicate verses against old women and witches, nor do I see any merit in telling his friend Maecenas, that if he will but rank him in the choir of lyric poets, his lofty head shall touch the stars. Fools are apt to admire everything in an author of reputation. For my part, I read only to please myself; I like nothing but what makes for my purpose."

Candide, having been educated with a notion of never judging for himself, was very much surprised at what he heard, but Martin found there was a good deal of reason in Pococurante's remarks.

"O! Here is Tully," says Candide. "Here is the great man, whom I fancy you are never tired of reading."

"I never read him at all," replied the Venetian. "What is it to me, whether he pleads for Rabirius or Cluentius? I try causes enough myself: his philosophical works seem to me better, but when I found that he doubted of everything, I concluded that I knew as much as he, and that I had no need of a guide to learn ignorance."

"Ha! Here are fourscore volumes," cried Martin, "of the academy of sciences; perhaps there is something valuable in this collection."

"There might," said Pococurante, "if only one of those rakers of rubbish had shown how to make pins, but in all those voluminous pieces, there is nothing but chimerical systems, and not one single article conducive to real use."

---

1 Producing sleep, soporific.

"What a number of theatrical performances do I behold," said Candide, "in Italian, Spanish, and French!"

"Yes," replied the senator, "there are three thousand, and not three dozen of them good for anything. As to those huge volumes of theology, and those collections of sermons, which all together are not worth a single page of Seneca, you may well imagine, that neither myself nor anybody else ever opens them."

Martin saw some shelves filled with English books. "I have a notion," said he, "that a republican must be vastly pleased with most of these books, which are written with a spirit of freedom."

"Yes," answered Pococurante, "it is noble to write as one thinks; this is the privilege of humanity. All over Italy we write only what we do not think, so that they who inhabit the country of the Caesars and the Antoninuses dare not acquire a single idea without the permission of a Dominican[1] friar. I should be pleased with the liberty of the English nation if the good effects of it were not entirely frustrated by passion and the spirit of party."

Candide, observing a Milton, asked whether he did not look upon this author as a great man? "Who?" said Pococurante. "That barbarian, who writes a long commentary in ten books of rough verse on the first chapter of Genesis? That coarse imitator of the Greeks, who disfigures the creation by making the Messiah take a pair of compasses from the armoury of heaven to circumscribe this world, whereas Moses represents the Eternal producing the universe by his word? How can I have any esteem for a writer who has spoiled Tasso's hell and the devil; who transforms Lucifer, sometimes into a toad, and other times into a pygmy; who makes him repeat the same things a hundred times, who turns him into a school divine; who, by a serious imitation of Ariosto's comic invention of fire arms, represents the devils cannonading in heaven? Neither I, nor any man in Italy, could take pleasure in those melancholy reveries, but the marriage of sin and death, and the snakes brought forth by sin, are enough to turn any person's stomach, that has the least delicacy of taste. This obscure, whimsical, and disagreeable poem, was despised upon its first publication and I only treat the author now as he was treated in his own country by his contemporaries. You are to observe, I say what I think, but I trouble my head very little, whether others think with me or not."

Candide was grieved at this speech, for he had a respect for Homer, and was fond of Milton. "Alas!" said he softly to Martin,

---

1 A Catholic religious order, the Dominicans were the directors of the Inquisition.

"I am afraid this man holds our German poets in very great contempt."

"There would not be much harm in that," answered Martin.

"O, what a surprising man!" continued Candide to mumble to himself. "What a great genius is this Pococurante! Nothing can please him."

After having taken a survey of the library, they went down into the garden, where Candide commended its several beauties. "I know nothing upon earth laid out in so bad a taste," said the master. "All you see is childish and trifling, but I shall have another laid out tomorrow, upon a nobler plan."

As soon as the two travellers had taken leave of his excellency, "Well," said Candide to Martin, "you will agree that this is the happiest of mortals, for he is above everything he possesses."

"But do not you see," answered Martin, "that he has taken a dislike to everything he possesses? Plato observed a long while ago, that the best stomachs are not those which reject all sorts of aliments."

"But is there not a pleasure," said Candide, "in criticizing everything? In pointing out faults, where others fancy nothing but beauties?"

"That is," replied Martin, "there is a pleasure in having no pleasure."

"Well, well," said Candide, "I find that I shall be the only happy man, when I am blessed with the sight of my dear Cunegonde."

"You are in the right to hope," said Martin.

Yet days and weeks passed away, and no news of Cacambo. Meanwhile, Candide was so overwhelmed with grief that he did not reflect on the behaviour of Paquette and friar Giroflée, who never so much as returned to give him thanks.

Chapter XXVI
How Candide and Martin supped with six strangers, and who they were

One evening that Candide and Martin were going to sit down to supper with some foreigners, who lodged in the same inn, a man whose complexion was as black as soot, came behind Candide, and taking him by the arm, said, "Get yourself ready to go along with us; do not fail."

Upon this he turns about, and sees Cacambo. Nothing but the

presence of Cunegonde could have surprised or pleased him more. He was just ready to run mad for joy. After he had embraced his dear friend, "Cunegonde is come with you," said he, "to be sure—where is she? Carry me to her, that I may die with joy in her company."

"Cunegonde is not here," answered Cacambo, "she is at Constantinople."

"O heavens! At Constantinople! But if she was in China, I'll fly thither. Let's be gone, quick."

"We shall set out after supper," replied Cacambo. "I can say no more to you; I am a slave, my master waits for me, I must attend him at table. Do not say a word, eat your supper, and get ready."

Candide felt himself distracted between grief and pain. On the one hand, he was charmed to see his faithful agent, and on the other, he was surprised to behold him in servitude. In this fluctuation of thought, his heart palpitating, his understanding confused, but firmly hoping to recover his dear Cunegonde, he sat down to table along with Martin—who saw all these scenes quite unconcerned—and with six strangers who were to spend the carnival at Venice.

Cacambo waited at table upon one of those strangers. Towards the end of the entertainment he drew near his master and whispered him in the ear, "Sire, your majesty may go when you please: the vessel is ready."

On saying these words he went out. The company in great surprise looked at one another without speaking a word, when another domestic approached his master and said to him, "Sire, your majesty's chaise[1] is at Padua, and the boat is ready." The master gave a nod, and the servant went away.

The company all stared at one another again, for their surprise was greatly increased. A third valet came up to a third stranger, saying, "Sire, depend upon it, your majesty ought not to stay here any longer. I am going to get everything ready," and immediately he disappeared.

Candide and Martin made no manner of doubt but this was a masquerade of the carnival. Then a fourth domestic said to the fourth master, "Your majesty may depart whenever you please," and saying this he went away like the rest.

The fifth valet said the same to the fifth master, but the sixth valet spoke in a different strain to the sixth stranger, who sat near

---

1 Horse-drawn carriage.

to Candide. His words were, "Faith, sir, they will trust your majesty no longer, nor myself neither, and we may both of us chance to be sent to jail this very night; therefore I will take care of myself. Adieu."

The servants being all gone, the six strangers, with Candide and Martin, remained in a profound silence. At length, Candide said, "Gentlemen, this is a very good joke indeed; but why should you be all kings? For my part I own to you that neither Martin nor I have any kingdoms."[1]

Cacambo's master then gravely answered in Italian. "I am not at all joking. my name is Achmet III. I was grand sultan a great many years. I dethroned my brother; my nephew dethroned me. My viziers[2] were beheaded, and I am condemned to end my days in the old Seraglio. My nephew the great sultan Mahmoud permits me to travel sometimes for my health, and I am come to spend the carnival at Venice."

A young man, who sat next to Achmet, spoke then as follows: "My name is Ivan. I was once emperor of all the Russias, but was dethroned in my cradle. My parents were confined, and I was

---

1   In *Candide*, even kings have sad stories to tell, and Voltaire's details—excepting Venetian vacations—are largely correct. The rulers are, respectively: (1) Sultan Ahmed III of Turkey (1673-1736) reigned 1703-30. (2) Ivan VI of Russia (1740-64) was declared emperor as an infant in 1740 by Anna Ivanovna, his mother's aunt. After a year-long reign under two regents and an overthrow by Elizabeth Petrovna in 1741, Ivan was exiled, eventually imprisoned, and finally assassinated by Catherine II. (3) Charles Edward Stuart (1720-88), the Young Pretender, was grandson of James II of England. (4) Augustus III (1696-1763) King of Poland (1733-63) also held the name and title Frederick Augustus II, Elector of Saxony. He fled from Saxony in 1756 as a result of early successes in the Seven Years' War by troops of Frederick II, King of Prussia, and he only returned in the year of his death. (5) Stanislaw Leszczynski (1677-1766) elected King of Poland (1704-09) after the Great Northern War and deposed by Augustus II; elected King again (1733-35) contrary to Augustus III in the War of the Polish Succession (1733-35). Voltaire visited Leszczynski's exiled court in Lorraine for a period in 1749. (6) The German born soldier of fortune Theodore Neuhoff (1694-1756) became king of Corsica for eight months in an effort undertaken through private commercial sponsorship before he fled in 1736. Theodore made much news in Europe in his many attempts to return to power and he eventually languished in a London debtors' prison from 1750 to shortly before his death.

2   High administrative official in the Ottoman Empire.

educated in prison. Yet I am sometimes allowed to travel in company with persons who act as guards, and I am come to spend the carnival at Venice."

The third said: "I am Charles-Edward, king of England. My father has resigned all his regal rights to me. I have fought in defense of them, and above eight hundred of my adherents have been hanged, drawn, and quartered. I have myself been confined in prison. I am going to Rome, to pay a visit to the king my father—who was dethroned as well as myself and my grandfather—and am come to spend the carnival at Venice."

The fourth spoke thus in his turn: "I am the king of Poland. The fortune of war has stripped me of my hereditary dominions; my father underwent the same vicissitudes. I resign myself to Providence in the same manner as Sultan Achmet, the Emperor Ivan, and King Charles-Edward, whom God long preserve. And I am come to the carnival at Venice."

The fifth said: "I am king of Poland also. I have been twice dethroned, but Providence has given me another country, where I have done more good, than all the Sarmatian kings were ever capable of doing on the banks of the Vistula.[1] I resign myself likewise to Providence, and am come to pass the carnival at Venice."

It was now the sixth monarch's turn to speak. "Gentlemen," said he, "I am not so great a prince as any of you; however, I am a crowned head. I am Theodore, elected king of Corsica. I had the title of majesty, and now I am hardly treated as a gentleman. I have coined money, and now am not worth a farthing. I have had two secretaries of state, and now I have scarce a valet. I was once seated on a throne, and since that I have for some time laid upon straw in a common jail in London. I am afraid I shall meet with the same treatment in Venice, though I am come like your majesties to divert myself at the carnival."

The other five kings listened to this speech with a generous compassion; each of them gave twenty zequins[2] to King Theodore to buy him clothes and linen, and Candide made him a present of a diamond worth two thousand zequins.

"Who can this private person be," said the five kings to one

---

1 Sarmatia is a region bordered on the west by the Vistula River, near the northern reaches of the Black and Caspian seas.
2 Venetian gold coins.

another, "who is able to give, and really has given, a hundred times as much as any of us?"[1]

Just as they rose from table, in came four serene highnesses, who had also been stripped of their territories by the fortune of war, and were come to spend the carnival at Venice. But Candide took no manner of notice of those new-comers: his thoughts were entirely employed on his voyage to Constantinople, in search of his beloved Cunegonde.

Chapter XXVII
Candide's voyage to Constantinople

The faithful Cacambo had already prevailed with the Turkish captain to take Candide and Martin on board his ship, which was to reconduct sultan Achmet to Constantinople. They both embarked, after paying their obeisance to his miserable highness. As Candide was on his way, he said to Martin, "You see we supped in company with six dethroned kings, and out of those six there was one to whom I gave charity. Perhaps there are a great many other princes more unfortunate still. For my part, I have lost only a hundred sheep, and now I am flying into Cunegonde's arms. My dear Martin, once more I must says it, Pangloss was in the right, everything is for the best."

"I wish it," answered Martin.

"But," says Candide, "it was a very strange adventure we met with at Venice. There never was an instance, for six dethroned kings to sup together at a public inn."

"This is not more extraordinary," said Martin, "than most of the things that have happened to us. It is a very common thing for kings to be dethroned, and as for the honour we have had to sup in their company, there is nothing in it. It is a trifle, not worth our attention."

No sooner had Candide got on board the vessel, than he flew to his old valet and friend Cacambo, and tenderly embraced him. "Well," said he, "what news of Cunegonde? Is she still as beauti-

---

1   Voltaire was very wealthy, and lent money of a value beyond five hundred thousand pounds to members of the noble classes across Europe. In a manuscript version of this chapter, Voltaire goes further, perhaps too far, for he decides against publishing the following: the kings ask Candide, "Sir, are you a king also?" and he replies, "No, nor have I any desire to be one."

ful as ever? Does she love me still? How does she do? No doubt but you purchased a palace for her at Constantinople?"

"My dear master," answered Cacambo, "Cunegonde washes dishes on the banks of the Propontis, in the service of a prince who has very few dishes to wash. She is a slave in the family of an ancient sovereign, named Ragotsky, to whom the grand sultan allows three crowns[1] a day in his exile.[2] But what is worst of all, she has lost her beauty, and is grown confounded ugly."

"Well! Handsome or ugly," replied Candide, "I am a man of honour, and it is my duty to love her still. But in the name of wonder, how came she to be reduced to so abject a state, with the five or six millions that you carried to her?"

"Ah!" said Cacambo, "was not I to give two millions to signor Don Fernando d'Ibara y Figueora y Mascarenes y Lampourdos y Souza, governor of Buenos Aires, for permitting Miss Cunegonde to come away? And did not a Corsair bravely rob us of the rest! Did not this Corsair carry us to cape de Matapan, to Milo, to Nicaria, to Samas, to Petra, to the Dardanels, to Marmora, to Scutari? Cunegonde and the old woman are servants to the prince I now mentioned to you, and as for myself, I am slave to the dethroned sultan."

"What a chain of shocking calamities!" cried Candide. "But after all, I have some diamonds left, and I may easily pay Cunegonde's ransom. Yet it is pity she is grown so ugly."

Then turning towards Martin, "Who do you think," says he, "is most to be pitied: the emperor Achmet, the emperor Ivan, King Charles-Edward, or I?"

"How should I know!" answered Martin. "I must see into your breasts, to be able to tell."

"Ah!" said Candide, "if Pangloss was here, he could tell."

"I know not," said Martin, "in what sort of scales your Pangloss would weigh the misfortunes of mankind, and set a just estimate on their sorrows. All that I can venture to say is that there are millions of people upon earth whose case is harder a hundred times than that of King Charles-Edward, the emperor Ivan, or the sultan Achmet."

"That may be," said Candide.

---

1 English unit of money: five shillings, one-fourth of a pound each.
2 Francis II Rákóczy (1676-35) was elected Prince of Hungary for a time, then exiled in Turkey from 1717 forward. His court in exile was on the shores of the Sea of Propontis, a body of water that connects the Aegean and Black Seas, now called the Sea of Marmara.

In a few days they reached the Bosphorus,[1] and Candide began with paying a very high ransom for Cacambo: then without losing time, he and his companions went on board a galley, in order to search for his Cunegonde, on the banks of the Propontis, notwithstanding her deformity.

Among the crew there were two slaves who rowed very ill, and to whose bare shoulders the captain would now and then apply a bull's pizzle.[2] Candide, from a natural sympathy, looked at these two slaves more attentively than at any of the rest, and drew towards them with an eye of pity. Their features, though greatly disfigured, seemed to resemble those of Pangloss and the unhappy Jesuit and Westphalian Baron, brother of Miss Cunegonde. This idea made him melancholy.

He looked at them again more attentively. "Indeed," said he to Cacambo, "if I had not been present when master Pangloss was hanged, and if I had not been so unfortunate as to kill the Baron myself, I should think it was they that were rowing."

Upon mentioning the name of the Baron and Pangloss, the two galley slaves gave a loud shriek, held fast by the seat, and let drop their oars. The captain ran up to them, and applied the bull's pizzle harder than ever. "Hold your hand, hold your hand, sir," cried Candide, "I will give you what money you please."

"Lord! It is Candide!" said one of the slaves.

"Lord! It is Candide!" said the other.

"Do I dream?" said Candide. "Am I awake? Or am I on board a galley? Is this the Baron, whom I killed? Is this master Pangloss, whom I saw hanged?"

"It is we, it is we," answered they.

"Well! Is this the great philosopher?" said Martin.

"Harkee, captain," said Candide, "what ransom will you take for monsieur de Thunder-ten-tronckh, one of the principal Barons of the empire, and for monsieur Pangloss, the profoundest metaphysician in Germany?"

"You Christian dog," answered the captain, "since these two dogs of Christian slaves are Barons and metaphysicians, which I make no doubt but are a high dignity in their country, you shall give me fifty thousand zequins."

"You shall have them, sir. Carry me back this minute to Constantinople, and you shall receive the money directly. No, carry me first to Miss Cunegonde." But upon the first proposal made

---

1 The strait between the Sea of Marmara (at Istanbul) and the Black Sea.

2 A whip made from a stretched and dried bull's penis.

by Candide, the captain had already tacked about, and he made the crew ply their oars quicker than a bird cleaves the air.

Candide embraced the Baron and Pangloss a hundred times. "And how happened to it, my dear Baron, that I did not kill you? And my dear Pangloss, how came you to life again, after being hanged? And what has made both of you slaves in a Turkish galley?"

"And is it true that my dear sister is in this country?" said the Baron.

"Yes," answered Cacambo.

"Then I behold once more my dear Candide," cried Pangloss.

Candide presented Martin and Cacambo to them. They embraced each other, and all spoke at the same time.

The galley flew like lightning, and now they were got back to the port. Instantly Candide sent for a Jew, to whom he sold for fifty thousand zequins a diamond worth a hundred thousand, though the fellow swore to him by Abraham that he could give him no more. He immediately laid down the ransom for the Baron and for Pangloss. The latter threw himself at the feet of his deliverer, and bathed them with his tears. The former thanked him with a nod, and promised to return him the money the first opportunity.

"But is it possible," said he, "that my sister should be in Turkey?"

"Nothing is more possible," answered Cacambo, "for she scours the dishes in the service of a Transylvanian prince."

Candide sent directly for two Jews and sold them some more diamonds; and then they all set out together in another galley to deliver Cunegonde from slavery.

Chapter XXVIII
What happened to Candide, Cunegonde, Pangloss, and Martin, &c

"I ask your pardon once more," said Candide to the Baron. "Your pardon, reverend father, for running you through the body."

"Say no more about it," answered the Baron, "I was a little too hasty I own, but since you want to know by what fatality I came to be a galley slave, I will inform you. After I had been cured of the wound you gave me by the apothecary[1] of the college, I was attacked and carried off by a party of Spanish troops who confined me in prison at Buenos Aires, at the very same time my

---

1   Pharmacist and medical practitioner.

sister was setting out from thence. I asked leave to return to Rome, to the general of my order, who appointed me chaplain to the French ambassador at Constantinople. I had not been eight days in this employment, when one evening I met with a young Ichoglan,[1] who was a very handsome fellow. The weather was warm, the young man wanted to bathe, and I took this opportunity to bathe also. I did not know it was a crime for a Christian to be found naked in company with a young Mussulman.[2] I was carried before a cadi,[3] who ordered me a hundred bastinados,[4] and condemned me to the galleys. I do not think there ever was a greater act of injustice. But I should be glad to know in what manner my sister came to be scullion[5] to a Transylvanian prince, who has taken shelter among the Turks!"

"But you, my dear Pangloss," said Candide, "how came my eyes to be so fortunate as to behold you again?"

"It is true," said Pangloss, "you saw me hanged. I should have been burnt, but you may remember it rained exceeding hard, when they were going to roast me. The storm was so violent, that they despaired of lighting the fire, so I was hanged, because they could do no better. A surgeon purchased my body, carried it home, and dissected me. He began with making a crucial incision on me from the umbilicus to the clavicula.[6] It was impossible for a man to have been hanged in a more scurvy manner than I was. The executioner of the holy inquisition was a subdeacon, and knew how to burn people very well, but he was not accustomed to hanging. The cord being wet did not slip properly, and besides the noose was not well tied—in short, I still drew my breath, when the crucial incision made me give such a frightful scream, that my surgeon fell flat upon his back. Imagining he had been dissecting the devil, he ran away, and tumbled down stairs in the fright. His wife hearing the noise, flew from the next room. Seeing me stretched upon the table with my crucial incision, she was seized with a greater trepidation than her husband, and betaking herself to flight, she tumbled over him. When they came to themselves a little, I overheard the wife say to her husband, 'My dear, how could you take it into your head to dissect a heretic? Do not you know that those people have always the devil

---

1 Young male page in the Turkish royal court.
2 Old variant of "Muslim."
3 Judge of Islamic religious law (variant of qadi).
4 Strokes of a cane upon the soles of the feet.
5 Scullery worker, kitchen drudge.
6 From the navel to the collarbone (Latin terminology).

in their bodies? I will go and fetch a priest this minute to exorcise[1] him.' At this proposal I shuddered, and mustering up what little strength I had still remaining, I cried out aloud, 'Have mercy on me!'

"At length the Portuguese barber plucked up his spirits, and sowed up my wound; the wife nursed me, and I was upon my legs again in fifteen days. The barber got me to be lackey[2] to a Knight of Malta, who was going to Venice, but finding my master had no money to pay me my wages, I entered the service of a Venetian merchant, and went with him to Constantinople.

"One day I took it into my head to step into a mosque, where I saw only an old imam, and a very pretty young devotee, who was saying her paternosters.[3] Her breast was uncovered, and in her bosom she had a beautiful nosegay of tulips, roses, windflowers, ranunculas, hyacinths, and auriculas. She let drop her nosegay;[4] I took it up immediately, and presented it to her with the most profound reverence. I was so long in delivering it, that the imam began to be angry, and seeing I was a Christian, he cried out for help. They carried me before the cadi, who ordered me a hundred bastinados, and sent me to the galleys.

"I was chained to the very same galley, and the same bench with the Baron. On board this galley there were four young men from Marseilles, five Neapolitan priests, and two monks of Corfu,[5] who told us that the like adventures happened daily. The Baron pretended that he had undergone a more unjust treatment than myself; and I insisted that it was far more innocent to take up a nosegay, and place it again on a woman's bosom, than to be found stark naked with an Ichoglan. We were continually disputing, and received twenty lashes a day with a bull's pizzle, when the concatenation of sublunary events brought you on board our galley, and you was so good as to ransom us from slavery."

"Well, my dear Pangloss," said Candide to him, "when you were hanged, dissected, whipped, and tugging at the oar, did you always think that everything in this world happens for the best?"

"I am still of my first opinion," answered Pangloss. "For after all, I am a philosopher, and it does not become me to retract, especially as Leibniz could never be in the wrong and besides, the

---

1   To expel an evil spirit who possesses and influences an individual.
2   Footman or other servant.
3   The Lord's prayer (Latin, "Our Father").
4   A small bouquet of fragrant flowers.
5   A small island off the west coast of Greece and Albania.

pre-established harmony is the finest thing in the world, and so is his *plenum* and *materia subtilis*."[1]

Chapter XXIX
How Candide found Cunegonde and the old woman again

While Candide, the Baron, Pangloss, Martin and Cacambo were relating their several adventures and reasoning on the contingent or non-contingent events of the universe—on effects and causes; on moral and physical evil; on liberty and necessity, and on the comforts a slave may feel on board a Turkish galley—they arrived at the house of the Transylvanian prince on the banks of the Propontis. The first thing they saw was Cunegonde and the old woman, who were hanging up napkins to dry.

The Baron grew pale at this sight. Even Candide, the tender lover, upon seeing his fair Cunegonde thus changed into a tawny Moor, with blear eyes, withered neck, wrinkled face, and red scaly arms, was greatly shocked and drew back, but advanced afterwards out of good manners. She embraced Candide and her brother; they embraced the old woman, and Candide ransomed them both.

There was a small farm in the neighbourhood, which the old woman proposed to Candide to make a shift with till the company could be provided for in a better manner. Cunegonde did not know she had grown ugly, for nobody had told her of it, and now she reminded Candide of his promise in so positive tone, that the good man durst not refuse her. He therefore intimated to the Baron that he would shortly marry his sister.

"I will not suffer," said the Baron, "such meanness on her part, and such insolence on yours. I shall never have it said to me by way of reproach, that my nephews are not qualified for the first ecclesiastical dignities in Germany. No. My sister shall never marry any person lower than a Baron of the empire."[2]

Cunegonde flung herself at his feet, and bedewed them with her tears; still he was inflexible.

---

1 Pangloss is a bit addled at this point: *Plenum* (a substance with no gaps in it) and *materia subtilis* (the very fine material that fills apparent gaps) are discussed by Leibniz, but are more closely associated with Descartes's physics, which Voltaire wrote against in his *Elements of the Philosophy of Newton*.

2 Some monasteries of Europe made a distinction of class, and would only admit monks of noble background.

"Thou foolish fellow," said Candide, "I have delivered thee out of the galleys, I have paid thy ransom, and thy sister's also. She was a scullion, and is very ugly, yet I am so condescending as to marry her, and dost thou pretend to oppose the match? I should kill thee again, were I only to consult my anger."

"Thou may'st kill me again," said the Baron, "but thou shalt not marry my sister, at least while I am living."

Chapter XXX
The CONCLUSION

Candide in his own mind had no great desire to marry Cunegonde. But the extreme impertinence of the Baron determined him to conclude the match, and Cunegonde on the other hand pressed him so hard that he could not go back from his word. However, he consulted Pangloss, Martin, and the faithful Cacambo. Pangloss drew up an excellent memorial, wherein he proved that the Baron had no right over his sister, and that, according to the laws of the empire, she might marry Candide with her left hand.[1] Martin was for throwing the Baron into the sea; Cacambo determined it would be better to deliver him up again to the captain of the galley, with directions to send him by the first ship to the general of the order at Rome. The advice was well received, the old woman approved of it, they said not a word to his sister; the thing was executed for a little money, and they had the pleasure of entrapping a Jesuit, and punishing the pride of a German Baron.

It is natural to imagine that Candide, after such vicissitudes of life—being now married to the woman he had long adored, and living under the same roof with the philosophers Pangloss and Martin, the prudent Cacambo and the old woman, and especially as he had brought so many diamonds with him from the country of the ancient Incas—must have led a very happy life. But he was so greatly imposed upon by the Jews, that he had nothing left except his small farm; his wife grew uglier every day, and was withal grown intolerably peevish; the old woman was infirm, and even more fretful and ill-humoured than Cunegonde herself. Cacambo worked in the garden, and carried legumes to Con-

---

1 Pangloss's memorial (memo) cited an obscure article of German protocol to preserve state control of land. Marrying with the left hand allowed an important landowner to guarantee hereditary titles, but not the transfer of property, to his children.

stantinople, but fatigued with the drudgery, he often cursed his hard fate. Pangloss was ready to despair, because he did not make a figure in some German university. As to Martin, he was firmly persuaded that it would fare with him as ill anywhere else, so that he took things patiently.

Candide, Martin, and Pangloss sometimes disputed about morality and metaphysics. They often saw under the farm windows boats full of effendis, bashaws, and cadis who were going into banishment to Lemnos, Mitylene, or Erzerum.[1] And they saw other cadis, bashaws, and effendis coming to supply the place of the exiles, and afterwards exiled in their turn. They saw heads decently impaled, which were to be presented to the sublime port. Such spectacles as these increased the number of their dissertations, and when they did not dispute, time hung so heavy upon their hands that one day the old woman ventured to say to them, "I want to know which is worse: to be ravished a hundred times by negro pirates, to have a buttock cut off, to run the gauntlet among the Bulgarians, to be whipped and hanged at an Auto-da-fé, to be dissected, to be a galley-slave—in short, to go through all the miseries that we have undergone, or to stay here and have nothing to do?"

"It is a very difficult question," said Candide.

This discourse gave rise to new reflections, and Martin especially concluded that man was born to live either in a state of distracting inquietude, or of lethargic disgust. Candide did not quite agree to that, but he affirmed nothing. Pangloss owned that he had gone through a terrible deal of hardship, but as he had once asserted that everything went wonderfully well, he still maintained the same opinion, though he did not believe it to be true.

What helped to confirm Martin in his detestable principles, to stagger Candide more than ever, and to puzzle Pangloss, was that one day they saw Paquette and friar Giroflée land at the farm in the greatest misery imaginable. They soon squandered their three thousand piasters, parted, were reconciled, quarreled again, were

---

1 Under the Ottoman empire, 'bashaw,' or pasha, referred to a governor or general of the Ottoman Empire, 'cadi' referred to a judge of religious law who might also have other administrative duties in the empire, and 'effendi' was a civil term of respect, used much like 'sir,' that might also denote official status. The various respected persons were bound for exile on two smaller islands in the Aegean Sea, and in a backwater province of Turkey. Voltaire may be referring loosely to a spate of political instability in the Ottoman Empire that followed the fall of Sultan Osmann III in 1757.

thrown into jail, had made their escape, and friar Grioflée at length had turned Turk. Paquette continued her trade, wherever she went, but made nothing of it.

"I foresaw it," said Martin to Candide, "that your presents would soon be squandered away, and only make them more miserable. You have rolled in millions of money, you and Cacambo, and yet you are not happier than friar Giroflée and Paquette."

"Ha!" said Pangloss to Paquette, "providence has then brought you amongst us again, my poor child! Do you know that you cost me the tip of my nose, an eye, and an ear, as you may see you have? What a world is this!" And now this new adventure engaged them to philosophize more than ever.

In the neighbourhood lived a very famous dervish,[1] who was esteemed the best philosopher in all Turkey, and him they went to consult. Pangloss was the speaker. "Master," said he, "we are come to beg you will let us know for what end so strange an animal as man was formed?"

"What is that to you?" answered the dervish. "Is it any business of thine?"

"But reverend father," said Candide, "there is a vast deal of evil in this world."

"What signifies it," said the dervish, "whether there be good or evil? When his highness sends a ship to Egypt, does he trouble his head, whether the rats on board are at their ease or not?"

"What then must we do?" said Pangloss.

"Hold your tongue," answered the dervish.

"I was in hopes," said Pangloss, "that I should reason with you a little about causes and effects, about the best of possible worlds, the origin of evil, the nature of the soul, and the pre-established harmony."

At these words the dervish shut the door in their face.

During this conversation, the news spread that two vizirs and the mufti,[2] had been strangled at Constantinople, and that several of their friends had been impaled. This catastrophe made a great noise for some hours. Pangloss, Candide and Martin, returning to the little farm, saw a good looking old man taking the fresh air at his door under an orangebower. Pangloss, whose curiosity was equal to his philosophy, asked the old man, "What was the name of the strangled mufti?"

---

1 A Muslim holy man, much like a monk.
2 A high Muslim scholar, appointed by the Ottoman Sultan who interprets religious law, and whose interpretations are to be applied by the cadi (judge).

"I do not know," answered the good man, "and what's more, I never knew the name of any mufti, or of any vizir. I am entirely ignorant of the event you have been mentioning; I presume in general that they who meddle with the administration of public affairs die sometimes miserably, and that they deserve it, but I never trouble my head about what is transacting at Constantinople. I content myself with sending my fruits thither, the produce of my gardens, which I cultivate with my own hands."

He had no sooner said these words than he invited the strangers into his house. His two sons and two daughters presented them with several sorts of sherbets, which they made themselves, besides kaimak[1] enriched with the peels of candied citrons,[2] oranges, lemons, ananas,[3] pistachio nuts, and Mocha coffee, unadulterated with the bad coffee of Batavia, or the American islands. After which the two daughters of the honest Mussulman perfumed the strangers' beards.

"You must have a very fine estate," said Candide to the Turk.

"I have no more than twenty acres of land," answered the old man. "I cultivate the whole myself, with the help of my children, and our labour preserves us from three great evils, idleness, vice, and want."

Candide on his way home made profound reflections on the old man's conversation. "This honest Turk," said he to Pangloss and Martin, "seems to be in a situation preferable to that of the six kings, with whom we had the honour of supping."

"Human grandeur," said Pangloss, "is extremely precarious, according to the testimony of philosophers. For, in short, Eglon king of Moab was assassinated by Ehud; Absalom was hanged by the hair of the head, and pierced through with three darts. King Nadab, the son of Jeroboam, was killed by Baasa; king Ela by Zimri; Ahaziah by Jehu; Athaliah by Jehoiada; the kings Jehoiakim, Jeconiah, and Zedekiah were led into captivity. You know what was the fate of Croesus, Astyages, Darius, Dionysius of Syracuse, Pyrrhus, Perses, Hannibal, Jugurtha, Ariovistus, Caesar, Pompey, Nero, Otho, Vitellius, Domitian, Richard II of England, Edward II, Henry VI, Richard III, Mary Queen of Scots, Charles I, the three Henries of France, the emperor Henry IVth? You know ..."

---

1 A cream-based drink.
2 Citrus fruit, much like lemons.
3 Pineapple.

"—I know also," said Candide, "that we must take care of our garden."

"You are in the right," said Pangloss, "for when our first parent was placed in the garden of Eden, he was put there *ut operaretur eum*,[1] to cultivate it, which shows that man was not born to be idle."

"Let us work," said Martin, "without disputing: it is the only way to render life tolerable."

Hereupon the whole society entered into this laudable design, according to their different abilities. Their little piece of ground produced them a plentiful crop. Cunegonde indeed was very ugly, but she became an excellent pastry-cook, while Paquette worked at embroidery and the old woman looked after the linen. They were all, not excepting friar Giroflée, of some service or other, for he made a good carpenter, and became a very honest man.

Pangloss used sometimes to say to Candide, "there is a concatenation of events in this best of all possible worlds, for if you had not been kicked out of a magnificent castle on account of miss Cunegonde, if you had not been thrown into the inquisition, if you had not rambled all over America on foot, if you had not run the Baron through the body, if you had not lost all your fine sheep of El Dorado, you would not be here to eat preserved citrons and pistachio nuts."

"All that is very well," answered Candide, "but let us take care of our garden."[2]

FINIS

---

1 Altered passage of Genesis 2:15, "Dominus Deus hominem et posuit eum in paradiso voluptatis ut operaretur et custodiret illum." "And the Lord God took the man and put him in the garden of Eden to do work in it and take care of it."

2 This is certainly Voltaire's most famous line: "Cela est bien dit," répondit Candide, "mais il faut cultiver notre jardin." For an interpretation, see p. 29.

Candide, Chapter XXII, revised version[1]
What Happened to Candide and Martin in France

Candide stayed no longer at Bordeaux than was necessary to dispose of a few of the pebbles he had brought from Eldorado, and to provide himself with a post-chaise for two persons, for he could no longer stir a step without his philosopher Martin. The only thing that gave him concern was the being obliged to leave his sheep behind him, which he intrusted to the care of the Academy of Sciences at Bordeaux, who proposed, as a prize subject for the year, to prove why the wool of this sheep was red; and the prize was adjudged to a northern sage, who demonstrated by A *plus* B, *minus* C, *divided* by Z, that the sheep must necessarily be red, and die of the mange.

In the mean time, all travellers whom Candide met with in the inns, or the road, told him to a man, that they were going to Paris. This general eagerness gave him likewise a great desire to see this capital; and it was not much out of his way to Venice.

He entered the city by the suburbs of St. Marceau, and thought himself in one of the vilest hamlets in all Westphalia.

Candide had not been long at his inn, before he was seized with a slight disorder, owing to the fatigue he had undergone. As he wore a diamond of an enormous size on his finger, and had among the rest of his equipage a strong box that seemed very weighty, he soon found himself between two physicians, whom he had not sent for, a number of intimate friends whom he had never seen, and who would not quit his bedside, and two female devotees, who were very careful in providing him hot suppings.

"I remember," said Martin to him, "that the first time I came to Paris I was likewise taken ill; I was very poor, and accordingly I had neither friends, nurses, nor physicians, and yet I did very well."

---

1 In 1761 Voltaire made minor revisions to the text of *Candide*, and greatly supplemented the treatment of Paris in chapter twenty-two, tripling its length. This change was not reflected in the second editions of extant English editions of *Candide*—presumably, the improvements were less important to English readers. The new version was probably first rendered into English in the translation here presented, from the edition of *The Works of M. de Voltaire. Translated from the French with Notes, Historical and Critical by T. Smollett, M.D., T. Francklin, M.A., and Others.* Printed for J. Newbery [*et al.*], at Salisbury (1761-74, 34 vols.). vol. 18, 1762. Names, spellings, and some punctuation have been modernized.

However, by dint of purging and bleeding, Candide's disorder became very serious. The priest of the parish came with all imaginable politeness, to desire a note of him, payable to the bearer in the other world.[1] Candide refused to comply with his request; but the two devotees assured him that it was a new fashion. Candide replied, that he was not one that followed the fashion. Martin was for throwing the priest out of the window. The clerk swore Candide should not have Christian burial. Martin swore in his turn, that he would bury the clerk alive if he continued to plague them any longer. The dispute grew warm; Martin took him by the shoulders, and turned him out of the room, which gave great scandal, and occasioned a verbal process.

Candide recovered; and till he was in a condition to go abroad, had a great deal of very good company to pass the evenings with him in his chamber. They played deep. Candide was surprised to find he could never turn a trick; and Martin was not at all surprised at the matter.

Among those who did him the honours of the place was a little spruce abbé of Perigord, one of those insinuating, busy, fawning, impudent, necessary fellows, that lay [in] wait for strangers on their arrival, tell them all the scandal of the town, and offer to minister to their pleasures at various prices. This man conducted Candide and Martin to the play-house: they were acting a new tragedy. Candide found himself placed near a cluster of wits: this, however, did not prevent him from shedding tears at some parts of the piece which were most affecting, and best acted.

One of these talkers said to him between the acts, "You are greatly to blame to shed tears; that actress plays horribly, and the man that plays with her still worse, and the piece itself is still more execrable than the representation. The author does not understand a word of Arabic, and yet he has laid his scene in Arabia, and, what is more, he is a fellow who does not believe in innate ideas. Tomorrow I will bring you a score of pamphlets, that have been wrote against him."[2]

"Pray, sir," said Candide to the abbé, "how many theatrical pieces have you in France?"

"Five or six thousand," replied the other.

"Indeed! that is a great number," said Candide, "but how many good ones may there be?"

---

1   This probably alludes to the present disputes in France about subscribing to the bull Unigenitus, without which ceremony a man is refused the sacraments *in articulo mortis*. [This footnote in the original.]
2   At this point begins the added material of Voltaire's second edition.

"About fifteen or sixteen."

"Oh! that is a great number," said Martin.

Candide was greatly taken with an actress, who performed the part of Queen Elizabeth in a dull kind of tragedy that is played sometimes. "That actress," said he to Martin, "pleases me greatly; she has some sort of resemblance to Miss Cunegonde. I should be very glad to pay my respects to her."

The abbé of Perigord offered his service to introduce him to her at her own house. Candide, who was brought up in Germany, desired to know what might be the ceremonial used on those occasions, and how a queen of England was treated in France. "There is a necessary distinction to be observed in these matters," said the abbé. "In a country town we take them to a tavern; here in Paris, they are treated with great respect during their life-time, provided they are handsome, and when they die we throw their bodies upon a dunghill."

"How?" said Candide, "throw a queen's body upon a dunghill!"

"The gentleman is quite right," said Martin, "he tells you nothing but the truth. I happened to be at Paris when Miss Monimia made her exit, as one may say, out of this world into another. She was refused what they call here the rites of sepulture; that is to say, she was denied the privilege of rotting in a churchyard by the side of all the beggars in the parish.[1] They buried her at the corner of Burgundy street, which must certainly have shocked her extremely, as she had very exalted notions of things."

"This is acting very unpolitely," said Candide.

"Lord!" said Martin, "what can be said to it; it is the way of these people. Figure to yourself all the contradictions, all the inconsistencies possible, and you may meet with them in the government, the courts of justice, the churches, and the public spectacles of this odd nation."

"Is it true," said Candide, "that the people of Paris are always laughing?"

"Yes," replied the abbé, "but it is with anger in their hearts;

---

1 Voltaire here refers to his own experiences. An early love of Voltaire's, Adrienne Lecouvreur, began her theatrical career playing Monimia in Racine's *Mithridate*, and went on to interpret roles for Voltaire. Despite Lecouvreur's great popularity and largesse to the Church, actresses, like prostitutes, were automatically excommunicated, and Lecouvreur was denied burial in Church ground in 1730.

they express all their complaints by loud bursts of laughter, and commit the most detestable crimes with a smile on their faces."

"Who was that great overgrown beast," said Candide, "who spoke so ill to me of the piece with which I was so much affected and of the players who gave me so much pleasure?"

"A very good for nothing sort of a man I assure you," answered the abbé, "one who gets his livelihood by abusing every new book and play that is written or performed; he abominates to see anyone meet with success, like eunuchs, who detest everyone that possesses those powers they are deprived of; he is one of those vipers in literature who nourish themselves with their own venom; a pamphlet-monger."

"—A pamphlet-monger!" said Candide, "what is that?"

"Why, a pamphlet-monger," replied the abbé, "is a writer of pamphlets—a f——."[1]

Candide, Martin, and the abbé of Perigord, argued thus on the staircase, while they stood to see the people go out of the playhouse. "Though I am very anxious to see Miss Cunegonde again," said Candide, "yet I have a great inclination to sup with Miss Clairon, for I am really much taken with her—."

The abbé was not a person to show his face at this lady's house, which was frequented by none but the best company. "She is engaged this evening," said he, "but I will do myself the honour to introduce you to a lady of quality of my acquaintance, at whose house you will see as much of the manners of Paris, as if you had lived here for forty years."

Candide, who was naturally curious, suffered himself to be conducted to this lady's house, which was in the suburbs of St. Honore. The company was engaged at basset;[2] twelve melancholy punters held each in his hand a small pack of cards, the corners of which doubled down, were so many registers of their ill fortune. A profound silence reigned throughout the assembly, a pallid dread had taken possession of the countenances of the punters, and restless inquietude stretched every muscle of the face of him who kept the bank; and the lady of the house, who was seated next to him, observed with lynx's eyes every parole, and *sept-le-va* as they were going, as likewise those who tallied,

---

1 In the original French, Voltaire explicitly names "Fréron" at this point. Elie Fréron (1719-76) wrote a review of *Candide* shortly after its publication and was Voltaire's most vocal long-term literary opponent.

2 A high-risk card game. This paragraph contains various terms related to the game and to card playing.

and made them undouble their cards with a severe exactness, though mixed with a politeness, which she thought necessary not to frighten away her customers. This lady assumed the title of Marchioness of Parolignac.[1] Her daughter, a girl of about fifteen years of age, was one of the punters, and took care to give her mamma an item, by signs, when any one of them attempted to repair the rigour of their ill fortune by a little innocent deception. The company were thus occupied when Candide, Martin, and the abbé, made their entrance: not a creature rose to salute them, or indeed took the least notice of them, being wholly intent upon the business in hand.

"Ah!" said Candide, "My Lady Baroness of Thunder-ten-tronckh would have behaved more civilly."

However, the abbé whispered the Marchioness in the ear, who half raising herself from her seat, honoured Candide with a gracious smile, and gave Martin a nod of her head, with an air of inexpressible dignity. She then ordered a seat for Candide, and desired him to make one of their party at play: he did so, and in a few deals lost near a thousand pieces; after which they supped very elegantly, and everyone was surprised at seeing Candide lose so much money, without appearing to be the least disturbed at it. The servants in waiting said to each other, "This is certainly some English lord."

The supper was like most others of this kind in Paris. At first everyone was silent; then followed a few confused murmurs, and afterwards several insipid jokes passed and repassed, with false reports, false reasonings, a little politics, and a great deal of scandal. The conversation then turned upon the new productions in literature. "Pray," said the abbé, "good folks, have you seen the romance written by the Sieur Gauchat, Doctor of Divinity?"

"Yes," answered one of the company, "but I had not patience to go through it. The town is pestered with a swarm of impertinent productions, but this of Dr. Gauchat's outdoes them all. In short, I was so cursedly tired of reading this vile stuff that I even resolved to come here, and make a party at basset."

"—But what say you to the Archdeacon T——'s miscellaneous collection?"[2] said the abbé.

"Oh my God!" cried the Marchioness of Parolignac, "never mention the tedious creature! Only think what pains he is at to

---

1 "Parolignac" refers to *paroli*, a play in the card game of basset.
2 Abbé Gabriel Gauchat and Abbé Nicolas Trublet, like Fréron, had written criticism of Voltaire's work.

tell one things that all the world knows, and how he labours an argument that is hardly worth the slightest consideration! How absurdly he makes use of other people's wit! How miserably he mangles what he has pilfered from them! The man makes me quite sick! A few pages of the good archdeacon are enough in conscience to satisfy any one."

There was at the table a person of learning and taste, who supported what the Marchioness had advanced. They next began to talk of tragedies. The lady desired to know how it came about that there were several tragedies, which still continued to be played, which there was no reading. The man of taste explained very clearly, how a piece may be in some manner interesting, without having a grain of merit. He showed, in a few words, that it is not sufficient to throw together a few incidents that are to be met with in every romance, and that dazzle the spectator; the thoughts should be new, without being far-fetched; frequently sublime, but always natural: the author should have a thorough knowledge of the human heart, and make it speak properly; he should be a complete poet, without showing any affectation of it in any of the characters of his piece; he should be a perfect master of his language, speak it with all its purity, and with the utmost harmony, and yet so as not to make the sense a slave to the rhyme. "Whoever," added he, "neglects any one of these rules, though he may write two or three tragedies with tolerable success, will never be reckoned in the number of good authors. There are very few good tragedies; some are idylls, in well-written and harmonious dialogue; and others a chain of political reasonings that set one asleep, or else pompous and high-flown amplifications, that disgust rather than please. Others again are the ravings of a madman, in an uncouth style, unmeaning flights, or long apostrophes to the deities, for want of knowing how to address mankind: in a word, a collection of false maxims and dull common-place."

Candide listened to this discourse with great attention, and conceived a high opinion of the person who delivered it; and as the Marchioness had taken care to place him near her side, he took the liberty to whisper her softly in the ear and ask who this person was that spoke so well. "It is a man of letters, replied Her Ladyship, who never plays, and whom the abbé brings with him to my house sometimes to spend an evening. He is a great judge of writing, especially in tragedy: he has composed one himself, which was damned, and has written a book that was never seen out of his bookseller's shop, excepting only one copy, which he sent me with a dedication, to which he had pre-fixed my name."

"Oh the great man!" cried Candide, "he is a second Pangloss." Then turning towards him, "Sir," said he, "you are doubtless of opinion that everything is for the best in the physical and moral world, and that nothing could be otherwise than it is?"

"Me, sir!" replied the man of letters, "I think no such thing, I assure you; I find that all in this world is set the wrong end upper-most. No one knows what is his rank, his office, nor what he does, nor what he should do; and that except our evenings, which we generally pass tolerably merrily, the rest of our time is spent in idle disputes and quarrels, Jansenists against Molinists, the Par-liament against the Church, and one armed body of men against another; courtier against courtier, husband against wife, and rela-tions against relations. In short, this world is nothing but one continued scene of civil war."

"Yes," said Candide, "and I have seen worse than all that; and yet a learned man, who had the misfortune to be hanged, taught me that everything was marvelously well, and that these evils you are speaking of were only so many shades in a beautiful picture."[1]

"Your hempen sage," said Martin, "laughed at you; these shades, as you call them, are most horrible blemishes."

"It is men who make these blemishes," rejoined Candide, "and they cannot do otherwise."

"Then it is not their fault," added Martin.

The greatest part of the gamesters, who did not understand a syllable of this discourse, amused themselves with drinking, while Martin reasoned with the learned gentleman; and Candide enter-tained the lady of the house with a part of his adventures.

After supper the Marchioness conducted Candide into her dressing-room, and made him sit down under a canopy. "Well, said she, are you still so violently fond of Miss Cunegonde of Thunder-ten-tronckh?"

"Yes, madam," replied Candide.

The Marchioness says to him with a tender smile, "you answer me like a young man born in Westphalia; a Frenchman would have said, 'It is true, madam, I had a great passion for Miss Cune-

---

1 Compare: "... shadows enhance colours; and even a dissonance in the right place gives relief to harmony. ... And is it not most often necessary that a little evil render the good more discernible, that is to say, greater?" Leibniz, *Theodicy*, Part 1, section 12.

gonde; but since I have seen you, I fear I can no longer love her as I did.'"

"Alas! madam," replied Candide, "I will make you what answer you please."

"You fell in love with her, I find, in stooping to pick up her handkerchief which she had dropped; you shall pick up my garter."

"With all my heart, madam," said Candide, and he picked it up.

"But you must tie it on again," said the lady. Candide tied it on again. "Look ye, young man," said the Marchioness, "you are a stranger, I make some of my lovers here in Paris languish for me a whole fortnight; but I surrender to you the first night, because I am willing to do the honours of my country to a young West-phalian." The fair one having cast her eye on two very large diamonds that were upon the young stranger's finger, praised them in so earnest a manner, that they were in an instant transferred from his finger to hers.

As Candide was going home with the abbé he felt some qualms of conscience for having been guilty of infidelity to Miss Cunegonde. The abbé took part with him in his uneasiness; he had but an inconsiderable share in the thousand pieces Candide had lost at play, and the two diamonds which had been in a manner extorted from him; and therefore very prudently designed to make the most he could of his new acquaintance, which chance had thrown in his way. He talked much of Miss Cunegonde; and Candide assured him, that he would heartily ask pardon of that fair one for his infidelity to her, when he saw her at Venice.

The abbé redoubled his civilities, and seemed to interest himself warmly in everything that Candide said, did, or seemed inclined to do. "And so, sir, you have an engagement at Venice?"

"Yes, Monsieur l'Abbé," answered Candide, "I must absolutely wait upon Miss Cunegonde ..."[1]

---

1 From here forward, chapter twenty-two continues along the lines of Voltaire's first edition.

Appendix A: Poetic Contexts

[The supplementary readings selected for this edition of *Candide* are intended to sketch the intellectual background and the social context in which Voltaire published his comic masterwork. These readings place the work within contemporary discussions of the philosophical problem of evil, a problem that is displayed in *Candide* by the pervasiveness of deadly disease, natural disaster, and religious persecution within the creation of a supposedly good God. Extended discussion of each of the supplementary readings is presented in section two of the introduction (pp. 15-29).

Before *Candide*, Alexander Pope's *Essay on Man* (1734) presented a lengthy poetic argument to "vindicate the ways of God to Man." Pope's poem would become a topic of intellectual discussion throughout Europe for decades, and Voltaire entered the conversation with a similar poetic argument, prompted by a disastrous earthquake that appeared to rain unjustifiable, indiscriminate slaughter on innocents while they prayed in church on All Saints' Day, 1 November 1755, in Lisbon, Portugal. Voltaire's *Poem upon the Destruction of Lisbon* (1756) received responses by many essayists, including another leading thinker of the time, Jean-Jacques Rousseau. Rousseau's *Letter to Voltaire on Optimism* (1756) soon became another important document in Europe's discussion of the problem of evil.]

1. From Alexander Pope, *An Essay on Man* (1734)[1]

EPISTLE I. Of the Nature and State of Man, with respect to the Universe

Awake, my St. John![2] leave all meaner things
To low ambition, and the pride of Kings.
Let us (since Life can little more supply

---

1 This edition closely follows selections from the first complete edition of the *Essay on Man*, 1734. The most useful complete text for a reader to consult is Alexander Pope, *An Essay On Man*, ed. Maynard Mack (London: Methuen, 1950).

2 Pope's *Essay* is dedicated to his friend and intellectual peer, Henry St. John, First Viscount Bolingbroke. Bolingbroke was, at the time, in the late stages of a tumultuous political career.

Than just to look about us and to die)
Expatiate free o'er all this scene of Man;
A mighty maze! but not without a plan;
A Wild, where weeds and flow'rs promiscuous shoot,
Or Garden tempting with forbidden fruit.
Together let us beat this ample field,
Try what the open, what the covert yield;   10
The latent tracts, the giddy heights explore
Of all who blindly creep, or sightless soar;
Eye Nature's walks, shoot Folly as it flies,
And catch the Manners living as they rise;
Laugh where we must, be candid where we can;
But vindicate the ways of God to Man.[1]

I. Say first, of God above, or Man below
What can we reason, but from what we know?
Of Man, what see we, but his station here,
From which to reason, or to which refer?   20
Thro' worlds unnumber'd tho' the God be known,
'Tis ours to trace Him only in our own.
He, who thro' vast immensity can pierce,
See worlds on worlds compose one universe,
Observe how system into system runs,
What other planets circle other suns,
What vary'd being peoples ev'ry star,
May tell why Heav'n has made us as we are.
But of this frame the bearings, and the ties,
The strong connections, nice dependencies,   30
Gradations just, has thy pervading soul
Look'd thro'? or can a part contain the whole?[2]
  Is the great chain, that draws all to agree,
And drawn supports, upheld by God, or thee?

II. Presumptuous Man! the reason wouldst thou find,
Why form'd so weak, so little, and so blind!
First, if thou canst, the harder reason guess,
Why form'd no weaker, blinder, and no less!

---

1 This line echoes John Milton, *Paradise Lost*, Book 1 line 26. Pope refers
   more subtly to many classical and modern authors throughout the
   Essay, most frequently Erasmus, Milton, and John Dryden.
2 Part and whole—reflected especially in the inability of the limited individual to survey the whole of the universe—and the Great Chain of
   Being that connects all things to God (noted in the following line), are
   two ideas that govern the argument of much of Pope's *Essay*.

Ask of thy mother earth, why oaks are made
Taller or stronger than the weeds they shade?   40
Or ask of yonder argent fields above,
Why Jove's satellites are less than Jove?[1]
    Of Systems possible, if 'tis confest
That Wisdom infinite must form the best,
Where all must full or not coherent be,
And all that rises, rise in due degree;
Then, in the scale of reas'ning life, 'tis plain
There must be, somewhere, such a rank as Man;
And all the question (wrangle e'er so long)
Is only this, if God has plac'd him wrong?   50
    Respecting Man, whatever wrong we call,
May, must be right, as relative to all.
In human works, tho' labour'd on with pain,
A thousand movements scarce one purpose gain;
In God's, one single can its end produce;
Yet serves to second too some other use.
So Man, who here seems principal alone,
Perhaps acts second to some sphere unknown,
Touches some wheel, or verges to some goal;
'Tis but a part we see, and not a whole.   60
    When the proud steed shall know why Man restrains
His fiery course, or drives him o'er the plains;
When the dull Ox, why now he breaks the clod,
Is now a victim, and now Egypt's God:[2]
Then shall Man's pride and dulness comprehend
His actions', passions', being's, use and end;
Why doing, suff'ring, check'd, impell'd; and why
This hour a slave, the next a deity.
    Then say not Man's imperfect, Heav'n in fault;
Say rather, Man's as perfect as he ought;   70
His knowledge measur'd to his state and place,
His time a moment, and a point his space.
If to be perfect in a certain sphere,
What matter, soon or late, or here or there?
The blest today is as completely so,
As who began a thousand years ago.

...

---

1 Jove: more commonly known as Jupiter (from the Latin, *Iouis pater*, or
    God, the father). In Pope's time, the planet had four known moons.
2 Apis, the bull-deity of Memphis.

IV. Go, wiser thou! and, in thy scale of sense
Weigh thy Opinion against Providence;
Call Imperfection what thou fancy'st such,
Say, here he gives too little, there too much;   80
Destroy all creatures for thy sport or gust,
Yet cry, If Man's unhappy, God's unjust;
If Man alone ingross not Heav'n's high care,
Alone made perfect here, immortal there:
Snatch from his hand the balance and the rod,
Re-judge his justice, be the God of God!
  In Pride, in reas'ning Pride, our error lies;
All quit their sphere, and rush into the skies.
Pride still is aiming at the blest abodes,
Men would be Angels, Angels would be Gods.   90
Aspiring to be Gods, if Angels fell,
Aspiring to be Angels, Men rebel;
And who but wishes to invert the laws
Of Order, sins against th' Eternal Cause.
V. Ask for what end the heav'nly bodies shine,
Earth for whose use? Pride answers, "'tis for mine:
"For me kind Nature wakes her genial pow'r,
"Suckles each herb, and spreads out ev'ry flow'r;
"Annual for me, the grape, the rose renew
"The juice nectareous, and the balmy dew;   100
"For me, the mine a thousand treasures brings;
"For me, health gushes from a thousand springs;
"Seas roll to waft me, suns to light me rise;
"My foot-stool earth, my canopy the skies."
  But errs not Nature from this gracious end,
From burning suns when livid deaths descend,
When earthquakes swallow, or when tempests sweep
Towns to one grave, whole nations to the deep?
"No, ('tis reply'd) the first Almighty Cause
"Acts not by partial, but by gen'ral laws;[1]   110
"Th' exceptions few; some change since all began,
"And what created perfect?"—Why then Man?
If the great end be human Happiness,
Then Nature deviates; and can Man do less?

---

1 That God works through general laws provides a third prevalent idea in
   Pope's effort to "vindicate" God's choices. That argument directs the
   Essay to the topic of human attempts to characterize the laws of nature,
   in the Second Epistle.

As much that end a constant course requires
Of show'rs and sun-shine, as of man's desires;
As much eternal springs and cloudless skies,
As men for ever temp'rate, calm, and wise.
If plagues or earthquakes break not Heav'n's design,
Why then a Borgia, or a Catiline?[1]   120
Who knows but He, whose hand the light'ning forms,
Who heaves old Ocean, and who wings the storms,
Pours fierce ambition in a Caesar's mind,
Or turns young Ammon loose to scourge mankind?[2]
From pride, from pride, our very reas'ning springs;
Account for moral, as for nat'ral things:
Why charge we Heav'n in those, in these acquit?
In both, to reason right is to submit.
    Better for Us, perhaps, it might appear,
Were there all harmony, all virtue here;   130
That never air or ocean felt the wind;
That never passion discompos'd the mind:
But ALL subsists by elemental strife;
And passions are the elements of Life.
The gen'ral Order, since the whole began,
Is kept in Nature, and is kept in Man.[3]

...

VIII. See, thro' this air, this ocean, and this earth,
All matter quick, and bursting into birth.
Above, how high progressive life may go!
Around, how wide! how deep extend below!   140
Vast chain of being, which from God began,
Natures Ethereal, human, angel, man,
Beast, bird, fish, insect! what no eye can see,
No glass can reach! from Infinite to thee,

---

1 Roderic Borgia (1431-1503) became Pope Alexander VI and is frequently considered the most corrupt Pope in history; his son Cesare
   (1475-1507) was a particularly ruthless politician, and Machiavelli's
   hero. Catiline (108-62 BCE) headed a failed conspiracy to overthrow
   the Roman Republic.
2 In his youth, Alexander the Great (356-323 BCE) was acknowledged by
   the priests of Ammon as descended from that god.
3 Pope's reference to "general order" presents a fourth governing idea for
   the *Essay*, indicating humanity's place and limit, and allowing Pope to
   incorporate discussion of science and of universal law.

From thee to nothing! On superior pow'rs
Were we to press, inferior might on ours:
Or in the full creation leave a void,
Where, one step broken, the great scale's destroy'd:
From Nature's chain whatever link you strike,
Tenth or ten thousandth, breaks the chain alike.   150
      And if each system in gradation roll,
Alike essential to th' amazing whole;
The least confusion but in one, not all
That system only, but the whole must fall.
Let earth unbalanc'd from her orbit fly,
Planets and Suns run lawless thro' the sky,
Let ruling angels from their spheres be hurl'd,
Being on being wreck'd, and world on world,
Heav'n's whole foundations to their centre nod,
And Nature tremble to the throne of God: 160
All this dread Order break—for whom? for thee?
Vile worm!—Oh, Madness! Pride! Impiety!

IX. What if the foot, ordain'd the dust to tread,
Or hand, to toil, aspir'd to be the head?
What if the head, the eye, or ear repin'd
To serve mere engines to the ruling mind?
Just as absurd for any part to claim
To be another, in this gen'ral frame:
Just as absurd, to mourn the tasks or pains
The great directing Mind of All ordains.   170
      All are but parts of one stupendous whole,
Whose body Nature is, and God the soul;
That, chang'd thro' all, and yet in all the same,
Great in the earth, as in th' ethereal frame,
Warms in the sun, refreshes in the breeze,
Glows in the stars, and blossoms in the trees,
Lives thro' all life, extends thro' all extent,
Spreads undivided, operates unspent;
Breathes in our soul, informs our mortal part,
As full, as perfect, in a hair as heart;   180
As full, as perfect, in vile Man that mourns,
As the rapt Seraph that adores and burns;
To him no high, no low, no great, no small;
He fills, he bounds, connects, and equals all.

X. Cease, then, nor Order Imperfection name:
Our proper bliss depends on what we blame.
Know thy own point: This kind, this due degree

Of blindness, weakness, Heav'n bestows on thee.
Submit—In this, or any other sphere,
Secure to be as blest as thou canst bear: 190
Safe in the hand of one disposing Pow'r,
Or in the natal, or the mortal hour.
All Nature is but Art, unknown to thee;
All Chance, Direction, which thou canst not see;
All Discord, Harmony not understood;
All partial Evil, universal Good:
And, spite of Pride, in erring Reason's spite,
One truth is clear, "Whatever Is, is Right."

EPISTLE II. Of the Nature and state of Man, with respect to
Himself, as an Individual

I. Know, then, thyself, presume not God to scan;
The proper study of Mankind is Man.
Plac'd on this isthmus of a middle state,
A being darkly wise, and rudely great:
With too much knowledge for the Sceptic side,
With too much weakness for the Stoic's pride,
He hangs between; in doubt to act, or rest,
In doubt to deem himself a God, or Beast;
In doubt his Mind or Body to prefer,
Born but to die, and reasoning but to err;   10
Alike in ignorance, his reason such,
Whether he thinks too little, or too much:
Chaos of Thought and Passion, all confus'd;
Still by himself abus'd, or disabus'd;
Created half to rise, and half to fall;
Great lord of all things, yet a prey to all;
Sole judge of Truth, in endless error hurl'd:
The glory, jest, and riddle of the world!
    Go, wond'rous creature! mount where Science guides,[1]
Go, measure earth, weigh air, and state the tides;   20
Instruct the planets in what orbs to run,
Correct old Time, and regulate the Sun;

---

1 Pope begins here to assess the merits and limits of science, and moves
   on to practical knowledge in alchemy and agriculture in section three.
   The sciences that follow particularly include contemporary physical sciences and astronomy, represented especially in the work of Isaac
   Newton (1643-1727).

Go, soar with Plato to th' empyreal sphere,
To the first good, first perfect, and first fair;
Or tread the mazy round his follow'rs trod,
And quitting sense call imitating God;
As Eastern priests in giddy circles run,
And turn their heads to imitate the Sun.[1]
Go, teach Eternal Wisdom how to rule—
Then drop into thyself, and be a fool!   30
  Superior beings, when of late they saw
A mortal Man unfold all Nature's law,
Admir'd such wisdom in an earthly shape.
And shew'd a Newton as we shew an ape.
  Could he, whose rules the rapid Comet bind,
Describe or fix one movement of his Mind?
Who saw its fires here rise, and there descend,
Explain his own beginning, or his end?
Alas, what wonder! Man's superior part
Uncheck'd may rise, and climb from art to art: 40
But when his own great work is but begun,
What Reason weaves, by Passion is undone.
  Trace Science, then, with Modesty thy guide;
First strip off all her equipage of Pride;
Deduct what is but Vanity or Dress,
Or learning's Luxury, or Idleness;
Or tricks to shew the stretch of human brain,
Mere curious pleasure, or ingenious pain:
Expunge the whole, or lop th' excrescent parts
Of all, our Vices have created Arts: 50
Then see how little the remaining sum,
Which serv'd the past, and must the times to come!

...

III. ... Yes, Nature's road must ever be prefer'd;
Reason is here no guide, but still a guard:
'Tis hers to rectify, not overthrow,
And treat this passion more as friend than foe:
A mightier Pow'r the strong direction sends,
And sev'ral Men impels to sev'ral ends.
Like varying winds, by other passions tost,
This drives them constant to a certain coast.   60
Let pow'r or knowledge, gold or glory, please,

---

1 Pope refers here to Plato's astronomical ideas in *Timaeus*, and to
   whirling dervishes, the Sufi Muslim practitioners.

Or (oft more strong than all) the love of ease;
Thro' life 'tis followed, even at life's expence;
The merchant's toil, the sage's indolence,
The monk's humility, the hero's pride,
All, all alike, find Reason on their side.
  Th' Eternal Art, educing good from ill,
Grafts on this Passion our best principle:[1]
'Tis thus the Mercury of Man is fix'd,
Strong grows the Virtue with his nature mix'd;   70
The dross cements what else were too refin'd,
And in one interest body acts with mind.
  As fruits, ungrateful to the planter's care,
On savage stocks inserted, learn to bear;
The surest Virtues thus from Passions shoot,
Wild Nature's vigour working at the root.
What crops of wit and honesty appear
From spleen, from obstinacy, hate, or fear!
See anger, zeal and fortitude supply;
Ev'n av'rice, prudence; sloth, philosophy;   80
Lust, thro' some certain strainers well refin'd,
Is gentle love, and charms all womankind:
Envy, to which th' ignoble mind's a slave,
Is emulation in the learn'd or brave;
Nor Virtue, male or female, can we name,
But what will grow on Pride, or grow on Shame.
  Thus Nature gives us (let it check our pride)
The virtue nearest to our vice ally'd:
Reason the byass turns to good from ill,
And Nero reigns a Titus, if he will.   90
The fiery soul abhor'd in Catiline,
In Decius charms, in Curtius is divine.[2]
The same ambition can destroy or save,
And makes a patriot as it makes a knave.

IV. This light and darkness in our chaos join'd,
What shall divide? The God within the mind.

---

1 What follows in this stanza is metaphor drawn from alchemy (the precursor to chemistry), famous for efforts to turn lead into gold and less
   well known as a general search for purification and perfection in material things.
2 Catiline led an anti-democratic rebellion, and Nero was a particularly
   abhorrent Roman Emperor; the reputations of Emperor Titus and the
   Decii emperors were the reverse. The Roman youth Marcus Curtius is
   said to have sacrificed himself for the Roman people.

Extremes in Nature equal ends produce,
In Man they join to some mysterious use;
Tho' each by turns the other's bound invade,
As, in some well-wrought picture, light and shade,   100
And oft so mix, the diff'rence is too nice
Where ends the Virtue or begins the Vice.
 Fools! who from hence into the notion fall,
That Vice or Virtue there is none at all.
If white and black blend, soften, and unite
A thousand ways, is there no black or white?
Ask your own heart, and nothing is so plain;
'Tis to mistake them, costs the time and pain.

...

EPISTLE III. Of the Nature and state of Man, with respect
to Society

Here then we rest: "The Universal Cause
Acts to one end, but acts by various laws."
In all the madness of superfluous health,
The trim of pride, the impudence of wealth,
Let this great truth be present night and day;
But most be present, if we preach or pray.
 Look round our World; behold the chain of Love
Combining all below and all above.
See plastic Nature working to this end,
The single atoms each to other tend,   10
Attract, attracted to, the next in place
Form'd and impell'd its neighbour to embrace.
See Matter next, with various life endu'd,
Press to one centre still, the gen'ral Good.
See dying vegetables life sustain,
See life dissolving vegetate again:
All forms that perish other forms supply,
(By turns we catch the vital breath, and die)
Like bubbles on the sea of Matter borne,
They rise, they break, and to that sea return.   20
Nothing is foreign: Parts relate to whole;
One all-extending, all-preserving Soul
Connects each being, greatest with the least;
Made Beast in aid of Man, and Man of Beast;
All serv'd, all serving! nothing stands alone;

The chain holds on, and where it ends, unknown.
  Has God, thou fool! work'd solely for thy good,
Thy joy, thy pastime, thy attire, thy food?
Who for thy table feeds the wanton fawn,
For him as kindly spread the flow'ry lawn.   30
Is it for thee the lark ascends and sings?
Joy tunes his voice, joy elevates his wings.
Is it for thee the linnet pours his throat?
Loves of his own and raptures swell the note:
The bounding steed you pompously bestride,
Shares with his lord the pleasure and the pride:
Is thine alone the seed that strews the plain?
The birds of heav'n shall vindicate their grain:
Thine the full harvest of the golden year?
Part pays, and justly, the deserving steer: 40
The hog, that ploughs not nor obeys thy call,
Lives on the labours of this lord of all.
  Know, Nature's children all divide her care;
The fur that warms a monarch, warm'd a bear.
While man exclaims, "See all things for my use!"
"See man for mine!" replies a pamper'd goose:
And just as short of reason he must fall,
Who thinks all made for one, not one for all.

...

EPISTLE IV. Of the Nature and State of Man, with respect to
Happiness

...

II. ... Order is Heav'n's first law; and this confest,
Some are, and must be, greater than the rest,
More rich, more wise; but who infers from hence
That such are happier, shocks all common sense.
Heav'n to Mankind impartial we confess,
If all are equal in their Happiness:
But mutual wants this Happiness increase;
All Nature's diff'rence keeps all Nature's peace.
Condition, circumstance is not the thing;
Bliss is the same in subject or in king,   10
In who obtain defence, or who defend,
In him who is, or him who finds a friend:

Heaven breathes through every member of the whole
One common blessing, as one common soul.
But Fortune's gifts if each alike possest,
And each were equal, must not all contest?
If then to all Men Happiness was meant,
God in Externals could not place Content.
    Fortune her gifts may variously dispose,
And these be happy call'd, unhappy those;   20
But Heav'n's just balance equal will appear,
While those are plac'd in Hope, and these in Fear:
Nor present good or ill, the joy or curse,
But future views of better or of worse,
    Oh, sons of earth! attempt ye still to rise,
By mountains pil'd on mountains, to the skies?
Heav'n still with laughter the vain toil surveys,
And buries madmen in the heaps they raise. ·

III. Know, all the good that individuals find,
Or God and Nature meant to mere Mankind,   30
Reason's whole pleasure, all the joys of Sense,
Lie in three words, Health, Peace, and Competence.
But Health consists with Temperance alone,
And Peace, oh, Virtue! Peace is all thy own.
The good or bad the gifts of Fortune gain;
But these less taste them, as they worse obtain.
Say, in pursuit of profit or delight,
Who risk the most, that take wrong means, or right?
Of Vice or Virtue, whether blest or curst,
Which meets contempt, or which compassion first?   40
Count all th'advantage prosp'rous Vice attains,
'Tis but what Virtue flies from and disdains:
And grant the bad what happiness they wou'd,
One they must want, which is, to pass for good.

...

VII. Know, then, this truth (enough for Man to know)
"Virtue alone is Happiness below."
The only point where human bliss stands still,
And tastes the good without the fall to ill;
Where only Merit constant pay receives,
Is blest in what it takes, and what it gives;   50
The joy unequal'd, if its end it gain,
And if it lose, attended with no pain:

Without satiety, though e'er so blest,
And but more relished as the more distress'd:
The broadest mirth unfeeling Folly wears,
Less pleasing far than Virtue's very tears:
Good, from each object, from each place acquir'd,
For ever exercis'd, yet never tired;
Never elated, while one man's oppress'd;
Never dejected while another's bless'd;   60
And where no wants, no wishes can remain,
Since but to wish more Virtue, is to gain.
    See! the sole bliss Heav'n could on all bestow;
Which who but feels can taste, but thinks can know:
Yet poor with fortune, and with learning blind,
The bad must miss; the good, untaught, will find;
Slave to no sect, who takes no private road,
But looks thro' Nature up to Nature's God;
Pursues that Chain which links th' immense design,
Joins heaven and earth, and mortal and divine;   70
Sees, that no being any bliss can know,
But touches some above, and some below;
Learns, from this union of the rising Whole,
The first, last purpose of the human soul;
And knows, where Faith, Law, Morals, all began,
All end, in Love of God, and Love of Man.
    For him alone, Hope leads from goal to goal,
And opens still, and opens on his soul,
'Till lengthen'd on to Faith, and unconfin'd,
It pours the bliss that fills up all the mind.   80
He sees, why Nature plants in Man alone
Hope of known bliss, and Faith in bliss unknown:
(Nature, whose dictates to no other kind
Are giv'n in vain, but what they seek they find)
Wise is her present; she connects in this
His greatest Virtue with his greatest Bliss;
At once his own bright prospect to be blest,
And strongest motive to assist the rest.
    Self-love thus push'd to social, to divine,
Gives thee to make thy neighbour's blessing thine.   90
Is this too little for the boundless heart?
Extend it, let thy enemies have part:
Grasp the whole worlds of Reason, Life, and Sense,
In one close system of Benevolence:
Happier as kinder, in whate'er degree,

And height of Bliss but height of Charity.
  God loves from whole to parts: but human soul
Must rise from Individual to the Whole.
Self-love but serves the virtuous mind to wake,
As the small pebble stirs the peaceful lake;   100
The centre mov'd, a circle straight succeeds,
Another still, and still another spreads,
Friend, parent, neighbour, first it will embrace,
His country next, and next all human race,
Wide and more wide, th'o'erflowings of the mind
Take ev'ry creature in, of ev'ry kind;
Earth smiles around, with boundless bounty blest,
And Heav'n beholds its image in his breast.
  Come, then, my Friend! my Genius, come along,
Oh, master of the poet, and the song!   110
And while the Muse now stoops, or now ascends,
To Man's low passions, or their glorious ends,
Teach me, like thee, in various nature wise,
To fall with dignity, with temper rise;
Form'd by thy converse, happily to steer
From grave to gay, from lively to severe;
Correct with spirit, eloquent with ease,
Intent to reason, or polite to please.
Oh! while along the stream of Time thy name
Expanded flies, and gathers all its fame,   120
Say, shall my little bark attendant sail,
Pursue the triumph, and partake the gale?
When statesmen, heroes, kings, in dust repose,
Whose sons shall blush their fathers were thy foes,
Shall then this verse to future age pretend
Thou wert my guide, philosopher, and friend?
That urg'd by thee, I turned the tuneful art
From sounds to things, from fancy to the heart;
From Wit's false mirror held up Nature's light;
Shew'd erring Pride, Whatever Is, Is Right;   130
That Reason, Passion, answer one great aim;
That true Self-Love and Social are the same;
That Virtue only makes our Bliss below;
And all our Knowledge is, Ourselves To Know.

2. From Voltaire, *Poem upon the Destruction of Lisbon: Or, an inquiry into the Maxim, Whatever is, is right* (1756)[1]

The Author's Preface

If the question concerning physical evil ever deserves the attention of men, it is in those melancholy events which put us in mind of the weakness of our nature; such as plagues, which carry off a quarter of the inhabitants of the known world; the earthquake which swallowed up four hundred thousand of the *Chinese* in 1699, that of *Lima* and *Callao*, and, in the last place, that of *Portugal* and the kingdom of *Fez*. The maxim, *whatever is, is right*, appears somewhat extraordinary to those who have been eye-witnesses of such calamities: All things are doubtless arranged and set in order by providence, but it has long been too evident, that its superintending power has not disposed them in such a manner as to promote our temporal happiness....

The author of the *Poem upon the Destruction of Lisbon* does not write against the illustrious *Pope*, whom he always loved and admired; he agrees with him in almost every particular, but compassionating the misery of man; he declares against the abuse of the new maxim, *whatever is, is right*.[2] He maintains that ancient and sad truth acknowledged by all men, that *there is evil upon earth*; he acknowledges that the words, *whatever is, is right*, if understood in a positive sense, and without any hopes of a happy future state, only insult us in our present misery....

He acknowledges with all mankind that there is evil as well as good upon the earth: he owns that no philosopher has ever been able to explain the nature of moral and physical evil. He asserts that Bayle, the greatest master of the art of reasoning that ever

---

1 *Poème sur le Désastre de Lisbonne*, originally published 1756. From the edition of *The Works of M. de Voltaire. Translated from the French with Notes, Historical and Critical by T. Smollett, M.D., T. Francklin, M.A., and Others.* Printed for J. Newbery [*et al.*], at Salisbury (1761-74, 34 vols.). Vol. 33. Spelling has been modernized in the prose preface only, which has been reproduced only in excerpts for this edition. Many of Voltaire's extended footnotes to the poem have also been excluded, as most of the argument they contain is better represented in other material included in this volume.

2 Voltaire refers to the closing line of Epistle I of Pope's *Essay on Man*, "One truth is clear, 'Whatever Is, is Right'" (p. 149).

wrote, has only taught to doubt, and that he combats himself; he owns that man's understanding is as weak as his life is miserable. He lays a concise abstract of the several different systems before his readers. He says that Revelation alone can untie the great knot which philosophers have only rendered more puzzling; and that nothing but the hope of our existence being continued in a future state can console us under our present misfortunes; that the goodness of Providence is the only asylum in which man can take refuge in the darkness of reason, and in the calamities to which his weak and frail nature is exposed.

P.S. Readers should always distinguish between the objections which an author proposes to himself, and his answers to those objections, and should not mistake what he refutes for what he adopts.

Poem upon the Destruction of Lisbon

Oh wretched man, earth-fated to be curst;
Abyss of plagues, and miseries the worst!
Horrors on horrors, griefs on griefs must shew,
That man's the victim of unceasing woe,
And lamentations which inspire my strain,
Prove that philosophy is false and vain.
Approach in crowds, and meditate awhile
Yon shatter'd walls, and view each ruin'd pile,
Women and children heap'd up mountain high,
Limbs crushed which under pond'rous marble lie;   10
Wretches unnumber'd in the pangs of death,
Who mangl'd, torn, and panting for their breath,
Bury'd beneath their sinking roofs expire,
And end their wretched lives in torments dire.
Say, when you hear their piteous, half-form'd cries,
Or from their ashes see the smoak arise,
Say, will you then eternal laws maintain,
Which God to cruelties like these constrain?
Whilst you these facts replete with horror view,
Will you maintain death to their crimes was due?   20
And can you then impute a sinful deed
To babes who on their mothers bosoms bleed?
Was then more vice in fallen Lisbon found,
Than Paris, where voluptuous joys abound?

Was less debauchery to London known,
Where opulence luxurious holds her throne?
Earth Lisbon swallows; the light sons of France
Protract the feast, or lead the sprightly dance.
Spectators who undaunted courage shew,
While you behold your dying brethren's woe;   30
With stoical tranquillity of mind
You seek the causes of these ills to find;
But when like us Fate's rigors you have felt,
Become humane, like us you'll learn to melt.
When the earth gapes my body to entomb,
I justly may complain of such a doom.
Hem'd round on every side by cruel fate,
The snares of death, the wicked's furious hate,
Prey'd on by pain and by corroding grief
Suffer me from complaint to find relief.   40
'Tis pride, you cry, seditious pride that still
Asserts mankind should be exempt from ill.
The awful truth on Tagus banks explore,[1]
Rummage the ruins on that bloody shore,
Wretches interr'd alive in direful grave
Ask if pride cries, *Good Heaven, thy creatures save.*
If 'tis presumption that makes mortals cry,
Heaven on our sufferings cast a pitying eye.
All's right, you answer, the eternal cause
Rules not by partial, but by general laws.   50
Say what advantage can result to all,
From wretched Lisbon's lamentable fall?
Are you then sure, the power which could create
The universe and fix the laws of fate,
Could not have found for man a proper place,
But earthquakes must destroy the human race?
Will you thus limit the eternal mind?
Should not our God to mercy be inclin'd?
Cannot then God direct all nature's course?
Can power almighty be without resource?   60
Humbly the great Creator I intreat,
This gulf with sulphur and with fire replete,
Might on the deserts spend its raging flame,
God my respect, my love weak mortals claim;
When man groans under such a load of woe,

---

1 The Tagus river runs through Lisbon.

He is not proud, he only feels the blow.
Would words like these to peace of mind restore
The natives sad of that disast'rous shore?
Grieve not, that others' bliss may overflow,
Your sumptuous palaces are laid thus low;   70
Your toppled towers shall other hands rebuild;
With multitudes your walls one day be fill'd;
Your ruin on the North shall wealth bestow,
For general good from partial ills must flow;
You seem as abject to the sov'reign power,
As worms which shall your carcasses devour.
No comfort could such shocking words impart,
But deeper wound the sad, afflicted heart.
When I lament my present wretched state,
Alledge not the unchanging laws of fate;   80
Urge not the links of the eternal chain,
'Tis false philosophy and wisdom vain.
The God who holds the chain can't be enchain'd;
By His blest will are all events ordain'd:
He's just, nor easily to wrath gives way,
Why suffer we beneath so mild a sway:[1]
This is the fatal knot you should untie,
Our evils do you cure when you deny?
Men ever strove into the source to pry,
Of evil, whose existence you deny.   90
If he whose hand the elements can wield,
To the winds' force makes rocky mountains yield;
If thunder lays oaks level with the plain,
From the bolts' strokes they never suffer pain.
But I can feel, my heart oppressed demands
Aid of that God who formed me with His hands.
Sons of the God supreme to suffer all
Fated alike; we on our father call.
No vessel of the potter asks, we know,
Why it was made so brittle, vile, and low?   100
Vessels of speech as well as thought are void;
The urn this moment formed and that destroy'd,
The potter never could with sense inspire,
Devoid of thought it nothing can desire.

---

1 *Sub Deo justo nemo miser nisi mereatur.*—St. Augustine. The meaning of
  this *ipse dixit* [unsupported claim] of the Saint is, no one is miserable
  under the government of a just God, unless deserving to be so.
  [Voltaire's note.]

The moralist still obstinate replies,
Others' enjoyments from your woes arise,
To numerous insects shall my corps give birth,
When once it mixes with its mother earth:
Small comfort 'tis that when Death's ruthless power
Closes my life, worms shall my flesh devour.   110
Remembrances of misery refrain
From consolation, you increase my pain:
Complaint, I see, you have with care represt,
And proudly hid your sorrows in your breast.
But a small part I no importance claim
In this vast universe, this gen'ral frame;
All other beings in this world below
Condemn'd like me to lead a life of woe,
Subject to laws as rigorous as I,
Like me in anguish live and like me die.   120
The vulture urg'd by an insatiate maw,
Its trembling prey tears with relentless claw:
This it finds right, endu'd with greater powers
The bird of Jove the vulture's self devours.[1]
Man lifts his tube, he aims the fatal ball
And makes to earth the tow'ring eagle fall;
Man in the field with wounds all cover'd o'er,
Midst heaps of dead lies weltering in his gore,
While birds of prey the mangled limbs devour,
Of Nature's Lord who boasts his mighty pow'r.   130
Thus the world's members equal ills sustain,
And perish by each other born to pain:
Yet in this direful chaos you'd compose
A gen'ral bliss from individuals woes?
Oh worthless bliss! in injur'd reason's spight,
With fault'ring voice you cry, "What is, is right."
The universe confutes your boasting vain,
Your heart retracts the error you maintain.
Men, beasts, and elements know no repose
From dire contention; earth's the seat of woes: 140
We strive in vain its secret source to find,
Is ill the gift of our Creator kind?

---

1 Voltaire writes of "an eagle," and the translator has artfully inserted a
   classical reference to the eagle as the "bird of Jove," or of Jupiter. "The
   eagle ... Jupiter is thought to have singled out from among birds,
   because it alone, men say, strives to fly straight into the rays of the rising
   sun." Gaius Julius Hyginus, *De Astronomia* 2.16.

Do then fell Typhon's[1] cursed laws ordain
Our ill, or Arimanius[2] doom to pain?
Shocked at such dire chimeras, I reject
Monsters which fear could into Gods erect.
But how conceive a God, the source of love,
Who on man lavish'd blessings from above,
Then would the race with various plagues confound
Can mortals penetrate his views profound?   150
Ill could not from a perfect being spring,
Nor from another,[3] since God's sov'reign king;
And yet, sad truth! in this our world 'tis found,
What contradictions here my soul confound!
A God once dwelt on earth amongst mankind,
Yet vices still lay waste the human mind;
He could not do it, this proud sophist cries,
He could, but he declined it, that replies;
He surely will, ere these disputes have end,
Lisbon's foundations hidden thunders rend,   160
And thirty cities' shatter'd remnants fly,
With ruin and combustion thro' the sky,
From dismal Tagus' ensanguin'd shore,
To where of Cadiz' sea the billows roar.
Or man's a sinful creature from his birth,
And God to woe condemns the sons of earth;
Or else the God who being rules and space,
Untouch'd with pity for the human race,
Indifferent, both from love and anger free,
Still acts consistent to His first decree: 170
Or matter has defects which still oppose
God's will, and thence all human evil flows;
Or else this transient world by mortals trod,
Is but a passage that conducts to God.
Our transient sufferings here shall soon be o'er,
And death will land us on a happier shore.
But when we rise from this accurst abyss,
Who by his merit can lay claim to bliss?
Dangers and difficulties man surround,
Doubts and perplexities his mind confound.   180
To nature we apply for truth in vain,

---

1 The author of evil according to the ancient Egyptians. [Voltaire's note.]
2 The author of evil according to the ancient Persians. [Voltaire's note.]
3 From another principle. [Voltaire's note.]

God should His will to human kind explain.
He only can illume the human soul,
Instruct the wise man, and the weak console.
Without him man of error still the sport,
Thinks from each broken reed to find support.
Leibnitz can't tell me from what secret cause
In a world govern'd by the wisest laws,
Lasting disorders, woes that never end
With our vain pleasures real suff'rings blend;   190
Why ill the virtuous with the vicious shares?
Why neither good nor bad misfortunes spares?
I can't conceive that *what is, ought to be,*
In this each doctor knows as much as me.
We're told by Plato, that man, in times of yore,
Wings gorgeous to his glorious body wore,
That all attacks he could unhurt sustain,
By death ne'er conquer'd, ne'er approached by pain.
Alas, how chang'd from such a brilliant state!
He crawls 'twixt heav'n and earth, then yields to fate.   200
Look round this sublunary world, you'll find
That nature to destruction is consign'd.
Our system weak which nerves and bone compose,
Cannot the shock of elements oppose;
This mass of fluids mix'd with temper'd clay,
To dissolution quickly must give way.
Their quick sensations can't unhurt sustain
Th' attacks of death and of tormenting pain,
This is the nature of the human frame,
Plato and Epicurus I disclaim.   210
Nature was more to Bayle than either known:
What do I learn from Bayle, to doubt alone?[1]
Bayle, great and wise, all systems overthrows,
Then his own tenets labors to oppose.
Like the blind slave to Dalilah's commands,
Crush'd by the pile demolish'd by his hands.[2]
Mysteries like these can no man penetrate,
Hid from his view remains the book of fate.
Man his own nature never yet could sound,

---

1 Bayle ... has left the controversy concerning the *origin of evil* undecided
... but he never gives his own opinion. [Excerpt from Voltaire's note.]
2 Judges 16 concludes the story of Samson, betrayed by Delilah and delivered to the Philistines. Samson ultimately crushes himself, along with
many Philistines, by pulling down the pillars of a house.

He knows not whence he is, nor whither bound.   220
Atoms tormented on this earthly ball,
The sport of fate, by death soon swallow'd all,
But thinking atoms, who with piercing eyes
Have measur'd the whole circuit of the skies;
We rise in thought up to the heavenly throne,
But our own nature still remains unknown.
This world which error and o'erweening pride,
Rulers accurst between them still divide,
Where wretches overwhelm'd with lasting woe,
Talk of a happiness they never know,   230
Is with complaining fill'd, all are forlorn
In seeking bliss; none would again be born.
If in a life midst sorrows past and fears,
With pleasure's hand we wipe away our tears,
Pleasure his light wings spreads, and quickly flies,
Losses on losses, griefs on griefs arise.
The mind from sad remembrance of the past,
Is with black melancholy over-cast;
Sad is the present if no future state,
No blissful retribution mortals wait,   240
If fate's decrees the thinking being doom
To lose existence in the silent tomb.
All may be well; that hope can man sustain,
All now is well; 'tis an illusion vain.
The sages held me forth delusive light,
Divine instructions only can be right.
Humbly I sigh, submissive suffer pain,
Nor more the ways of Providence arraign.
In youthful prime I sung in strains more gay,
Soft pleasure's laws which lead mankind astray.   250
But times change manners; taught by age and care
Whilst I mistaken mortals' weakness share,
The light of truth I seek in this dark state,
And without murmuring submit to fate.[1]
A caliph once when his last hour drew nigh,

---

1   George Havens has argued that Voltaire's first manuscript versions of the
    poem closed at this line, which readers found too dismal. Voltaire obliged
    his critics, adding the last six lines as well as a final footnote, reproduced
    below. Voltaire toyed with concluding the poem with a question at the final
    line (roughly, "Could one add 'hope', man's sole bliss below?") rather than
    the assertion that is there, and much of the final footnote appears to be
    entirely disingenuous, and it varies greatly among editions of the poem.

Pray'd in such terms as these to the most high:
Being supream, whose greatness knows no bound,
I bring thee all that can't in thee be found;
Defects and sorrows, ignorance and woe.
Hope he omitted, man's sole bliss below.[1]   260

3. From Jean-Jacques Rousseau, *Letter to Voltaire on Optimism* (1756)[2]

18 August 1756

Your last two poems, sir, have come to me in my solitude.[3] ... I will not tell you that all in them appears to me equally good, but the things that displeased me only inspire me with more confidence in the things that swept me away. It is not without difficulty that I sometimes defend my reason against the charms of your poetry, but to make my admiration more worthy of your works I fight not to admire every part of them. ...

All my criticism, then, is against your Poem on the Lisbon dis-

---

1   Most nations entertained this hope even before they had the assistance of revelation. The hope of existing after death is founded upon the desire of existing during life; it is founded upon the probability that what thinks now shall think hereafter. Of this there is no demonstration, because the contrary of whatever is demonstrated is a contradiction and because there never was any dispute concerning demonstrable truths. Lucretius, in his third book, offers arguments of a force which must afflict those who wish for a life to come, in order to destroy this hope: but he does no more than oppose probabilities to probabilities more strong. Many of the Romans thought like Lucretius; and these words, in a chorus of Seneca the Tragedian, were sung upon the Roman stage; *Post mortem nihil est, there remains nothing after death.* But instinct, reason, the desire of consolation, and the good of society prevailed, and men have always hoped in a life to come: this hope has, however, been generally accompanied with doubt. Revelation destroys that doubt, and makes it give place to certainty. [Voltaire's note.]

2   First published in 1759 as *Lettre de J. J. Rousseau à Monsieur de Voltaire.* Selections translated for this edition by Eric Palmer, from the French in Besterman, ed., *The Complete Works of Voltaire* (Oxford: Voltaire Foundation, 1972). Letter D6973, vol. 101 pp. 280-92.

3   In 1755, Rousseau sent Voltaire a copy of his newly published *Discourse on the Origin and Foundations of Inequality Among Men.* Voltaire thanked Rousseau in a witty and acid letter for the gift of "his new book against the human race." Voltaire returned the favor in 1756 by sending Rousseau the *Poem on the Law of Nature* and the *Poem upon the Destruction of Lisbon.*

aster, for I expected it would have effects that were more appropriate to the concern for humanity that appears to have inspired you to write it. You reproach Pope and Leibniz for condemning the evils we suffer while claiming that all is well, and you present such a broad sweep of misery that you make us more miserable than before. In place of the consolations that I hoped for, you further afflict me; one might say that you fear that I am not aware of how unhappy I am, and it seems that you may believe that you calm me by proving to me that all is bad.

Do not deceive yourself, sir: the result is exactly the opposite of what you intend. This optimism that you find so cruel consoles me especially when I suffer the same miseries that you treat as overwhelming. Pope's poem calms my suffering and brings me patience; yours increases my suffering, moves me to complain, and, taking away all but a shattered hope, reduces me to despair. A strange tension resides between what you establish and what I experience—so calm the perplexity that agitates me and tell me whether sentiment or reason is in the wrong.

"Humans, have patience," Pope and Leibniz tell me, "your ills are a necessary consequence of your nature and of the construction of this universe. The eternal and beneficent Being who governs it would have wished to have guarded you from them. Of all the possible Economies, he chose the one that would unite the least evil with the most good; or, to say the same thing, but more crudely: if this was the result, then he has not done better because he could not do so."

Now, what does your poem tell me? "Suffer forever, you unhappy ones. If there is a God who created you, without doubt he is all-powerful, and could have prevented all your ills. Do not hope that they will ever end, then, for one cannot discern why you exist, if it is not to suffer and die." I do not see how such a doctrine could be more consoling than optimism, or fatalism; for my part, I assert that it seems to me still more cruel than Manicheism. If the problem of the entry of evil into the world demands that you alter any of God's perfections, why would you defend his power at the expense of his goodness? If one must choose between two errors, I much prefer the first.

...

I do not see that one could look for the origins of moral evil anywhere but in man: free and perfect, so also corrupted. For, concerning physical suffering: if sensitive yet impassive matter is a contradictory concept, as it seems to me to be, it is inevitable in any account that includes human beings, and thus the concern is not why human beings are not perfectly happy, but why they exist. Moreover, I believe I have shown that, apart from death (which is hardly an evil, except for the process that precedes it) most of the physical evils we experience are really of our own making.[1] Without straying from your subject of Lisbon, for example, consider that it was not nature that there gathered twenty thousand houses of six or seven floors, and if the inhabitants of this great city had been dispersed more evenly and had lived in lesser buildings, the destruction would have been much less, and perhaps even nothing at all. All would have flown at the first trembling, and one would have found them the next day twenty leagues away and as happy as if nothing had happened. But they had to stay, stubbornly squatting on their ruins, exposing themselves to new shocks, because what they would be leaving behind was worth much more that what they could carry away. How many miserable ones died in this disaster, one wanting to return for clothes, another for papers, a third for money? Is it not clear that the person of each has become the least important part of what he is, and that it seems to be hardly worth the effort to save it when he has lost everything else?

You would have wanted the earthquake to have arisen in the middle of a desert, rather than in Lisbon. Is there any doubt that they also happen in deserts? We do not mention them at all, because they do no harm to the Gentlemen of the Cities, the only people who we think matter. They do little to the animals and savages who live scattered about such remote places, and who are little troubled by roofs falling or houses burning. What does such an attitude suggest? Could it mean that the order of nature must change according to our whims, that nature must be submitted to our laws, and that, to stop an earthquake from occurring in a particular place, we would just have to build a city there?

Some events strike us more or less according to the features we consider, and lose much of the horror that they inspire at first glance when they are examined further. I found in *Zadig*[2]—and

---

1 Rousseau presents such argument in the seventh note to the *Discourse on the Origin and Foundations of Inequality Among Men* (1755).

2 *Zadig* is, like *Candide*, one of Voltaire's moral tales. In the culminating chapter, an angel in possession of the Book of Destiny kills a boy, then explains to Zadig that the death was in service of divine providence, to avert worse evils that would have resulted from the child's actions during adulthood. This explanation is not fully satisfying to Zadig, however, and the angel's imperious commands and swift departure leave a note of uncertainty in Zadig that he appears to suppress.

events confirm this day after day—that an early death is not always a genuine evil, and that it can sometimes pass as relatively good. Of the many people smashed under the ruins of Lisbon, without doubt, many escaped worse misfortune, and—despite such lively description and how touchingly it provides for poetry—it is not certain that even one of these unfortunates suffered more than if he had followed the ordinary course of things, suffering the long agonies of a different, surprising death. Was it a sadder end than that of someone wasting through useless ministrations, crowded about by lawyer and heirs, killed in his own bed by doctors at their ease, upon whom barbarous preachers ply their craft, to make the contemplation of death yet more vivid? For my part, I see in all this that the sufferings to which we are subjected by nature are less cruel than those we add to them.

But no matter how ingenious we can be at increasing our miseries through the work of our great institutions, to this point, we have not perfected ourselves to the degree that we have turned life into a burden for most of us, making death preferable to this existence, since depression and despair would quickly have snatched the greater number, and the human species would not have been able to survive for long. But if it is better for us to be than not to be, then that would be enough to justify our existence, even if there were no reparations in the future for the ills that we have suffered, and even if these ills are as grand as you depict.

...

Regarding the rest, you have given a much needed corrective to Pope's system when you observe that there can be no proportional gradation between the Creatures and the Creator, and that, if the chain of created beings ends at God, it is because he holds the end of it, not because he is the end of it.

On the good of the whole being preferable to the good of a part, you have men say, "I must be as important to my master— I, who think and feel—as the planets, which probably do not feel at all. Doubtless this material universe must not be more important to its creator than even one creature that thinks and feels."[1]

---

1 Quotation marks have been introduced in this paragraph (by the editor) for clarity. Rousseau does not attribute this view to Voltaire, but rather to a fictional naïve speaker, to whom Voltaire also refers in the preface to the *Poem upon the Destruction of Lisbon*.

But the system of this universe that produces, maintains, and perpetuates all the Beings that think and feel must be more important to him than a single one of these beings; therefore, he can, despite his goodness, or rather by reason of his goodness, sacrifice some part of the happiness of some individuals to conserve the whole. "I believe, I hope that, I am of more value in the eyes of God than the earth of some planet,"—but if the planets are inhabited, as seems probable, then why should I be of more value in his eyes than all the inhabitants of Saturn? Such a view is easily ridiculed, for it is certain that the argument is on their side, and only human pride opposes the idea. If such inhabitants are supposed, then the conservation of the universe even seems to present a moral obligation for God to multiply accounts by the number of inhabited worlds.

That a man's corpse provides nourishment for worms, wolves, or plants is not, I admit, any recompense for his own death; but if, in the system of this Universe, it is necessary for the conservation of the human species that there should be a circulation of substance among human beings, animals, and vegetables, then the particular harm to one individual contributes to the good of all. I die, I am eaten by worms, but my children, my brothers, will live on as I have lived; my body fertilizes the earth of which they partake, and I do, through the workings of nature and to the benefit of all to come, as Codrus, Curtius, the Decies, the Philaeni, and a thousand others willing have done for a small part of humanity.[1]

To get back, sir, to the system that you attack, I believe one cannot examine it appropriately without distinguishing carefully the harm to the particular, the existence of which has been denied by no philosopher, from harm in general, which is denied by the optimist. It is not a question of knowing whether each of us suffers or not, but of knowing whether it is good that the universe exists, and whether our suffering was inevitable in its constitution. Thus the addition of a definite article would render the proposition more exact, and in place of *all is well*, it might be better to say *the whole is well* or *all is well, on the whole*. ...

The philosophers, for their part, do not appear any more reasonable to me when I see them crying to the heavens that they are

---

1 King Codrus of Greece, the Roman youth Marcus Curtius, the Roman Emperor Trajan, Emperor Decius and his son, and the Carthaginian brothers called "the Philaeni," were storied heroes who sacrificed their lives for the good of their people.

not tougher, lamenting that all is lost when toothache strikes, or that they are poor, or that they have been robbed, since they charge God with protecting their knapsacks, as Seneca wrote.[1] If some tragic accident had ended the life of Cartouche or Caesar in infancy, they would have asked, what did they do?[2] These two thieves did live, and we ask, why were they allowed to stay alive? On the other side, a devout Christian would say, in the first case, God wished to punish a father by taking his child from him; and in the second, that God kept the child to punish the nation. Whatever nature might do, providence is always in the right for the devout, and always wrong for the philosophers. Perhaps, in the order of things human, there is neither right nor wrong, because everything falls under the common universal law of nature, and there is no exception for anyone. That is to say: that particular events are insignificant in the eyes of the master of the Universe; that his providence is only universal; that he contents himself with conserving the general and the species and with presiding over the whole without concern for the way in which each individual passes this short life. Need a wise King, who wants everyone to live happily in his kingdom, concern himself whether the inns are good? The traveller complains for an evening if they are bad, and laughs the rest of his days at such misplaced impatience. *Nature has willed that we be on earth as guests in passage, not as permanent residents.*[3]

To think straight in this regard, it seems that things must be considered relatively for physics, and absolutely for morality: the finest idea of providence I see is that each material being would be arranged in the best possible relation to all, and each intelligent and sensitive being arranged in the best possible relationship to itself; in other words, for those beings that feel their existence, it is better to exist than not to exist. But the rule must apply to the entirety of the life of each sensitive being, not to some par-

---

1 By "philosophers," Rousseau clearly intends to point to Voltaire and his intellectual circle. Theodore Besterman notes that the reference to the knapsack and Seneca (*De providentia, VI.i*) may be poking fun right at Voltaire, who was greatly concerned with fine possessions, and who wrote at length, in his earlier letter to Rousseau, of others making profits by pilfering his old writing.

2 Cartouche (Louis Dominique Bourguignon) was a famous French bandit of the early eighteenth century. Julius Caesar (100-44 BCE) moved Rome away from limited democracy to dictatorship.

3 *Commorandi enim natura diversorium nobis, non habitandi dedit.* Cicero, *Cato Maior de Senectute*, XXIII.

ticular moment in its entire existence, such as its life as a human being. This shows how the question of providence is tied to that of the immortality of the soul, in which I have the good fortune to believe, despite that there are reasonable grounds for doubt, and tied to that of the doctrine of eternal damnation, in which neither you, nor I, nor any man who thought well of God would ever believe.

If I reduce these questions to their common principle, it seems to me that they all connect to that of the existence of God. If God exists he is perfect; if he is perfect he is wise, powerful and just; if he is wise and powerful, all is well; if he is just and powerful, my soul is immortal; if my soul is immortal, thirty years on earth amount to nothing for me, and might be necessary in the processes of this universe. If the first principle is conceded, one cannot leave those that follow from it; if it is denied, then there is no point in arguing over these consequences.

Neither of us denies the key principle. At least, so far as I can gather from reading the body of your writing, the greater part offers grand, sweet, and consolatory ideas of divinity, and I love a Christianity like yours far more that of the Sorbonne.[1]

As for me, I openly admit to you that neither side of the argument appears to be demonstrated conclusively by reason, and that, if the theist grounds an opinion solely upon probability, the atheist's ground is even less, seeming to rely on opposed possibility. Moreover, the objections of either side against the other can never be refuted because they depend on topics about which human beings have no real idea. I accept all of this, yet I believe in God as strongly as I believe any other truth, because believing and not believing are the things over which I have the least control in this world. The state of doubt is far too stressful for my soul, and when my reason runs away, my faith is incapable of remaining for long in suspense, and settles itself without reason, so finally, a thousand preferences attract me to the more consoling view, and tie the weight of hope to the balance of reason.

Here, then, there is a truth from which we both start: with its support, you must recognize how easy it is to defend optimism and justify providence, and I need not reiterate to you the famil-

1 Rousseau was a theist, more sympathetic to Voltaire than he would be to a scholarly Roman Catholic intellectual of the University of Paris (the Sorbonne). Rousseau tended to ground true religious understanding in deep sentiment, as he indicates in the next sentence, not at all in the sort of technical argument he has attempted in the previous paragraph, and not substantially in the general argument that this letter provides.

iar but solid arguments that have been given so frequently on this subject. Regarding philosophers who do not acknowledge the principle, there is no disputing these matters with them, for what is for us an argument based in sentiments cannot become a logical demonstration for them, and it is not a reasonable move to say to someone, *You must believe this because I do.* They on their side should, similarly, refrain from arguing with us about these matters, which are nothing but consequences of the key principle, which is one that a fair adversary should not debate; and in their position they would also be wrong to expect that we prove the conclusions independently of the proposition from which it is drawn. I think they must refrain for a further reason, that it is inhumane to trouble placid souls, and to devastate people to no purpose at all, when what one would teach them is neither certain nor useful. In short, I am in agreement with your example, one could not overdo attacking the superstitious beliefs that distress society, nor show too much respect for the religious faith that sustains it.

...

It would be dishonest, sir, for me not to note here a singular opposition between you and me, regarding the subject of this letter. Stuffed with glory, beyond the limits of society, you live freely in a nest of abundance; assured of your literary immortality, you philosophize in peace concerning the nature of the soul, and if your body or your heart suffers, you have Tronchin as your doctor and friend. Yet, you find nothing but evil on the earth! And I, a man of no note, poor, and tormented by an illness that cannot be cured, meditate with pleasure in my retreat and find that all is well. From where do these apparent contradictions come? You have provided the explanation yourself: you play at this game, while I hope, and hope makes everything beautiful.[1]

I have as much difficulty finishing this boring letter as you will have reading it to its end. Pardon me, great man, my perhaps indiscreet zeal, which I would not vent upon you if I thought less

---

1 Voltaire has "provided the explanation" for their differences in attitude in a reference to hope in the last line of his poem. Rousseau's melodramatic closing may have been spurred by a very bad report on his health that indicated impending death, but ultimately led to chronic discomfort over an ordinary lifespan. Voltaire was similarly afflicted over a remarkably long life, hence his efforts to keep an excellent doctor close at hand. Rousseau was at this time at a high point in his considerable fame, but could not boast the social significance, or the abundant wealth, of Voltaire.

of you. It would not please God if I were to offend a fellow whose talents I honour the most, and whose writings speak best to my heart, but it is for the cause of providence, from which I expect everything. After having drawn so long from your lessons of consolation and of courage, I find it hard that you refuse me them now, offering nothing but an uncertain and vague hope, more as a palliative than as a promise of the future. No, I have suffered too much in this life not to expect another. All the subtleties of metaphysics will not make me doubt for a moment the immortality of the soul and a beneficent providence. I feel it, I believe it, I wish it, I hope for it, I will defend it to my last breath, and this will be, of all the disputes that I have entered, the only one where my own interests will not be left aside.

I am, with respect, sir ...

Appendix B: Philosophical Contexts

[*Candide* is a philosophical dessert. It follows upon heavier discussion of the problem of evil that Voltaire also considered in his *Philosophical Dictionary*. The problem of evil gets its classic characterization in philosophy from writing by the Roman-African scholar Lactantius (240-*ca*. 320 CE), who attributes the argument to the Greek thinker Epicurus (341-270 BCE):

> God, says Epicurus, is either willing to remove evil, and is not able: or else he is both willing and able. If he is willing and not able, he must then be weak, which cannot be affirmed of God. If he is able and not willing, he must be envious, which is likewise contrary to the nature of God. If he is neither willing nor able, he must be both envious and weak, and consequently, not God. If he is both willing and able, which only can agree with the notion of God, whence then proceeds evil? (Lactantius quoted in Pierre Bayle, "Paulicians")

Pierre Bayle brought the problem of evil to the attention of Europe through many challenging arguments presented in several articles of his *Historical and Critical Dictionary* (first edition, 1697). Bayle indicates that the problem is even older in the history of religion, and is resolved by the Zoroastrian faith, and later by Christian sects referred to generally as 'Manichean,' through the claim that the world we see is the product of two gods in battle, representing good and evil.

Bayle's reflections on the problem of evil prompted Gottfried Leibniz to write extensive responses into his lengthy *Essays of Theodicy* (1710), which presents the position that evil is a result of necessary constraints upon God, called the eternal truths, that are part of the one world that a good God has created, which is "the best among all possible worlds." A very different line of thinking focuses almost exclusively on demonstrating that much or all apparent evil is actually good, and can be understood better through the study of nature. This line, called physico-theology, has more scientific roots, since it begins from observation of the complexity of nature, rather than from philosophical argument concerning the nature of good and evil. Isaac Newton and Robert Boyle argued this position rather abstractly in the previous century, but that work was soon taken up in popular writing, and in Voltaire's time it reached its peak in the very successful *Spectacle of Nature* of Noël Pluche (eight volumes, 1732-50).

In *Candide*, the character of Pangloss illustrates Voltaire's ridicule of both philosophical and popular scientific thought on evil, and is meant to reflect Leibniz explicitly and Pluche implicitly. In the *Philosophical Dictionary*, reworked and augmented many times after its appearance in 1764, Voltaire engages in reasoned arguments that reflect the influences of the three authors of these supplementary readings. "Of Good and Evil, Physical and Moral" attempts to build an account of God's qualities, with obvious roots in Pierre Bayle's skeptical arguments. "Theist" is a brief and clearly sympathetic portrayal of a religious position that skeptically dismisses both Bayle's and Leibniz's philosophical intricacies. "Final Causes" is Voltaire's attempt to sort out the confusions of Pluche in particular, and of much physico-theology generally, by distinguishing inconstant from constant features of nature. Since stone houses appear not to have been a basic product within the order of nature from time immemorial, we should not draw the conclusion that such a use for stones was intended by the Creator when nature's order was created. Concerning purposes (or intentions, ends, and final causes—all these terms have closely related meanings), the Creator's are expressed only in what is present through all time, and are most evident in the abiding presence of laws of nature. Perhaps God had the purpose of creating clever people, but it was the clever people who had the purpose of sheltering themselves aptly with stone houses.

Voltaire's positions in these three articles of the *Philosophical Dictionary* do not appear consistent, if he wishes to assert them as his own views of metaphysics rather than as lessons in clear argument. In "Of Good and Evil" Voltaire argues that the Supreme Being is "incomprehensible," and this position conflicts with many claims in "Theist." "Of Good and Evil" undermines support for even the limited claims regarding God's purposes and goodness that will be presented again in the readings of Appendix C.]

1. From Pierre Bayle, *Historical and Critical Dictionary* (1697)[1]

Manicheans:[2] heretics whose infamous sect, founded by one Manes, began in the third century and established itself in several provinces and subsisted a very long time. They taught such doctrines, as ought to inspire us with the greatest horror. Their weakness did not consist, as at first it may seem, in their doctrine of two principles, one good, and the other bad, but in the particular explications they gave of it and in the practical consequences they drew from it. It must be confessed that this false tenet—which is much more ancient than Manes and cannot be maintained by any one who admits the Holy Scripture either in whole or in part—would not easily be refuted, if it were maintained by Pagan Philosophers well skilled in disputing....

According to the Manicheans,[3] the two principles fought together, and this conflict occasioned a mixture of good and evil. Ever after the good principle laboured to separate what belonged to him, he spread his virtue among the elements, to make in them this separation....

The heavens and the rest of the universe declare the glory, power, and the unity of God; man alone—that masterpiece of his creation among things visible—man alone, I say, affords the greatest objection against the unity of God. The matter is thus:

Man is wicked and unhappy: every one knows it by what he feels in himself, and by the intercourse he is obliged to have with

1   First edition published in 1697. This text follows the second edition of 1702, in *The Dictionary Historical and Critical of Mr Peter Bayle*, trans. P. Desmaizeaux, (London: Knapton *et al.* 1734, reprinted: New York: Garland Publishing, 1984). The more ordinary 'Manicheans' here replaces the term 'Manichees' from Desmaizeaux's translation, and some word ordering and punctuation have been modernized in this edition. Bayle's footnotes are presented, with the exception of cross-references internal to the *Dictionary*. Square brackets in the footnotes of this section indicate further information as well as translations of quotations provided by the editor.

2   [Zoroaster (*ca.* 1000 BCE) was a Persian prophet who provided the root idea here presented of two Gods locked in battle. Manes (216-274 CE), or Mani, is often considered the partially Christian origin of Christian versions of this dualism, which are generally called Cathar or Manichean. Important Manichean movements included the Paulicians (seventh century, Armenia) and the Albigensians (twelfth to thirteenth centuries, southern France).]

3   Augustine, *On Heresy*, ch. 96.

his neighbours. He who lives only five or six years may be perfectly convinced of these two things, and they who live long and are much engaged in worldly affairs know this still more clearly....

There are everywhere some things that are physically good and morally good; some examples of virtue, and some examples of happiness. And this is that which makes the difficulty, for if there were none but evil and unhappy men, there would be no occasion to have recourse to the hypothesis of two principles. It is the mixture of happiness and virtue with misery and vice which requires this hypothesis, and this is the strong hold of the sect of Zoroaster....

In order to make it appear how difficult it would be to refute this false system, and that we may conclude that it is necessary to have recourse to revelation to overthrow it, let us feign here a dispute between Melissus[1] and Zoroaster, who were both Pagans, and great Philosophers.... Let us hear Zoroaster continuing his discourse:

If man is the creature of one principle perfectly good, most holy and omnipotent, can he be exposed to diseases, to heat and cold, hunger and thirst, pain and grief? Can he have so many bad inclinations? Can he commit so many crimes? Can perfect holiness produce a criminal creature? Can perfect goodness produce an unhappy creature? Would not omnipotence, joined with infinite goodness, furnish his own work plentifully with good things and secure it from every thing that might be offensive or vexatious?

If Melissus consults the notions of order, he will answer that man was not wicked when God made him. He will say that man was created by God in a happy state, but that he—not following the light of his conscience, which was intended by the author of his Being to conduct him in a way of virtue—became wicked, and deserved that God, who is perfectly just as well as perfectly good, should make him feel the effects of his wrath. God, therefore, is not the cause of moral evil, but he is the cause of physical evil, i.e., of the punishment of moral evil; a punishment which is so far from being inconsistent with a principle perfectly good that it flows necessarily from one of his attributes—I mean from his justice, which is no less essential to him than his goodness.

---

1 [Melissus of Samos (*fl.* 433 BCE) wrote as a philosopher especially on the origin of contrary properties. The arguments opposed to Zoroaster's two principles that Bayle presents in Melissus' name have the character of more recent Christian thought, however, and might be considered consistent with Molinism, about which see note 2, p. 183.]

This answer, which is the best that Melissus could make, is good and sound at the bottom, but it may be opposed by reasons that have something more specious and dazzling, for Zoroaster would not fail to represent that, if man were the work of a principle infinitely good and holy, he ought to have been created not only without any actual evil, but also without any inclination to evil, since that inclination is such a defect as could not have such a principle for its cause. It remains, therefore, that we say that man, coming out of the hands of his Creator, had only the power of determining himself to evil, and that having determined himself to it, he was the sole cause of the crime which he committed, and of the moral evil which has introduced itself into the world.

But, first, we have no distinct idea that can make us understand that a Being which does not exist by itself can nevertheless act by itself. Zoroaster, therefore, will say that the free will which was given to man is not able actually to determine itself, since it exists continually and totally by the action of God.

Second, he will put this question: Did God foresee that man would make an ill use of his free will? If you answer yes, he will say that it seems not possible that any thing can foresee that which depends wholly upon an indeterminate cause. But I will grant you, he will say, that God did foresee the sin of his creature, and from thence I conclude that he would have hindered him from the sinning, for the ideas of order will not suffer us to believe that a cause infinitely good and holy, which can hinder the introduction of moral evil, should not hinder it—especially since, by permitting it, God was obliged severely to punish his own work. If God did not foresee the fall of man, yet at least he must think it possible.... For if a goodness so bounded as that of earthly fathers necessarily requires that they should prevent, as much as is possible, the bad use their children may make of the good things they give them, much more will an infinite and almighty goodness prevent the ill effects of his gifts. Instead of giving them free will, it will always effectually watch over them, to keep them from sinning.

I believe indeed that Melissus would not remain silent, but all that he could answer would be presently opposed by reasons as plausible as his, and so there would be no end of the dispute.... If he had no recourse to retortion, he would very much perplex Zoroaster, but by once granting him his two principles he would leave himself an open way to come at the explication of the origin of evil. Zoroaster would go back to the time of the chaos, which is a state as to his two principles very like that which Hobbes[1] calls the state of nature, and which he supposes to have preceded the first establishment of societies. In this state of nature one man was a wolf to another, and everything belonged to the first possessor: none was master of anything, except he was the strongest. To get out of this confusion, everyone agreed to quit his right to the whole, that he might have a property in something; they transacted together and the war ceased. The two principles, weary of the chaos wherein each confounded and overthrew what the other would do, came at last to an agreement: each of them yielded something, each had a share in the production of man and in the laws of the union of the soul.[2] The good principle obtained those which procure to man a thousand pleasures, and consented to those which expose man to a thousand sorrows, and if it were consented that moral good should be infinitely less in mankind than moral evil, he repaired the damage in some other kind of creatures wherein vice should be much less than virtue. If many men in this life have more misery than happiness, this is recompensed in another state: what they have not under a human shape they shall recover under another.[3] By means of this agreement, the chaos was disembroiled—the chaos, I say: a passive principle which was the field of battle between these two active principles. The poets have represented this disembroiling under the image of a quarrel ended.[4]

This is what Zoroaster might allege, boasting that he does not attribute to the good principle the production at his own pleasure of a creature which was to be so wicked and miserable, but only after he had found by experience that he could do no better, nor better oppose the horrible designs of the evil principle. To

---

1 [Thomas Hobbes (1588-1679) maintained that men adopt the political solution to the state of nature as a rational response to fear. Bayle suggests that their motivation is to escape from "confusion" regarding possessions, but Hobbes clearly indicates that the principal motivation is fear of death. No such acute threat is available to motivate the two Gods to settle their dispute in the Zoroastrian case.]

2 Apply here what Juno says to Venus in Virgil, Aeneid 4.98: "Let discord be no more, but peace eternal succeed; and, when the nuptial band is tied, One common people be our common care."

3 [Manicheans as well as Zoroastrians generally accepted metempsychosis, which is the transmigration of souls and reincarnation, including, perhaps, reincarnation of souls in non-human animals.]

4 "Nature, and nature's God, this strife composed." Ovid, Metamorphoses I.21.

render his hypothesis the less offensive, he might have denied that there was a long war between the two principles, and laid aside all those fights and prisoners which the Manicheans speak of. The whole might be reduced to the certain knowledge of the two principles, that one could never obtain from the other but such and such conditions. And thus an eternal agreement might be made upon this footing.

A thousand great difficulties might be objected to this Philosopher; but as he would find answers, and after all desire to be furnished with a better hypothesis, pretending to have solidly refuted that of Melissus, he would never be brought back into the way of truth. Human reason is too weak for this end: it is a principle of destruction, and not of edification; it is only fit to start doubts, and to turn itself all manner of ways, to perpetuate a dispute. I think I am not mistaken if I say of natural revelation—that is, of the light of reason—what divines say of the Mosaic economy. They say that it was only fit to discover to man his weakness and the necessity of a redeemer, and of a law of mercy. It was a schoolmaster (they are their own words)[1] to bring men to Jesus Christ. Let us say the same of reason; it can only discover to man his ignorance and weakness, and the necessity of another revelation, which is that of the scripture. There we find what is sufficient to refute unanswerably the hypothesis of two principles, and all the objections of Zoroaster.

Paulicians: The reasons for the permission of sin—which are not taken from the mysteries revealed in Scripture—have this defect:[2] how good soever they be, they may be opposed by other reasons more specious, and more agreeable to the ideas we have

---

1 Bayle's reference to the "Mosaic economy" is to Galatians 3:24, "the law hath been our tutor [or schoolmaster] *to bring us* unto Christ, that we might be justified by faith"; his reference to "their own words" is to that of many scholastic philosophers who similarly held philosophy to be a preliminary guide to faith, beginning particularly with Clement of Alexandria (died 215) in *Stromata* Book 1, Ch.5: "Perchance, too, philosophy was given to the Greeks directly and primarily, till the Lord should call the Greeks. For this was a schoolmaster to bring 'the Hellenic mind,' as the law, the Hebrews, 'to Christ.'" [Roberts-Donaldson, trans. Loeb Classical Library.]

2 To this may be referred what a father of the Church said: "Happy fault, that procured such a redeemer." [This is a phrase found in the Latin Mass, referring to Romans 5:20, "But where sin abounded, grace did abound more exceedingly."]

of order. For instance, if you say that God permitted sin to manifest his wisdom, which shines the more brightly by the disorders which the wickedness of men produces every day, it may be answered that this is to compare the Deity to a father who should suffer his children to break their legs on purpose to show to all the city his great art in setting their broken bones, or to a king who should suffer seditions and factions to increase through all his kingdom, that he might purchase the glory of quelling them.[1] The conduct of this father and monarch is so contrary to the clear and distinct ideas according to which we judge of goodness and wisdom and in general of the whole duty of a father and a king, that our reason cannot conceive how God can make use of the same. But you will say, the ways of God are not our ways. Keep to that then, this is a text of Scripture,[2] and do not reason any more....

Those who say that God permitted sin, because he could not hinder it without destroying free will, which he had given to man, and which was the best present he had made him, venture very much. The reason they have is specious, there is in it *I know not what*, which dazzles the eyes: something that appears great, but nevertheless it may be opposed by such reasons as are more suited to the capacity of all men, and more founded upon good sense and the ideas of order. Without having read the fine treatise of Seneca concerning benefits, any one knows, by the light of nature, that it is essential to a benefactor not to bestow such favours which he knows will be abused in such a manner that they will serve only to the ruin of him on whom they are bestowed. There is no enemy so inveterate who would not upon these terms load his enemy with favours. It is essential to a benefactor to spare nothing to make the person happy with his benefits, whom he honours with them. If he could confer on him the knowledge of making good use of them and should refuse it him, he would very ill sustain the character of a benefactor; neither would he better sustain it, if being able to keep his client from abusing benefits, he should not hinder him by curing his bad inclinations. These are ideas which are known as well to the common people as to the Philosophers. I confess that if one could not prevent the ill use of a favour but by breaking the arms and

---

1 "Who will say that Aeneas is righteous if he wished his native city to be captured in order that he might rescue his father from captivity?..."
   Seneca, *On Benefits* VI.36. [John Basore, trans. Loeb Classical Library.]
2 "For my thoughts are not your thoughts, neither are my ways your ways, saith the Lord." Isaiah 55:8.

legs of one's clients, or by shackling their feet with irons in a dungeon, one would not be obliged to prevent it; it were better to refuse them the benefit. But if one can prevent it by changing the heart, and by giving a man a relish of good things, one ought to do it. Now this is what God might easily do, if he would....

By these reasons it would be easy to show that the free will of the first man—which was preserved to him sound and entire, in the circumstances wherein he was to make use of it to his own loss, to the ruin of mankind, to the eternal damnation of the greatest part of his posterity, and to the introduction of a terrible deluge of evils, of guilt and punishment—was not a good gift. We shall never understand that this privilege could be preserved to him by an effect of goodness, and out of love for holiness. Those who say that it was necessary there should be free Beings, to the end that God might be loved with a love of choice,[1] are conscious to themselves that this hypothesis does not satisfy reason, for when it is foreseen that those free Beings will choose not the love of God but sin, one may plainly perceive that the intended end is defeated, and that therefore it is no wise necessary that free will should be preserved....

[According to the Manichean,] if you examine your system carefully, you will acknowledge that you as well as I admit two principles, the one good, and the other evil—but instead of placing them as I do, in two subjects, you join them together in one and the same substance, which is monstrous and impossible. The one only principle which you admit—determined from all eternity, according to you—is that man should sin, and that the first sin should be infectious,[2] that it should produce without end and without intermission all imaginable crimes over the face of the whole earth, in consequence whereof he prepared for mankind in this life all the miseries that can be conceived, such as pestilence, war, famine, pain, vexation, and after this life an Hell, wherein all men almost shall be eternally tormented after such a manner as makes our hair stand on end when we read the

---

1 See the *Treatise of Morality* of Father Malebranche [Nicolas Malebranche (1638-1715)].

2 According to the Molinists, he [God] decreed to place men in such circumstances wherein he certainly knew they would sin, and he could either have put them in more favourable circumstances, or not have put them in these. [Molinists attempted to reconcile Divine grace with a human will that can freely choose the good under those circumstances. The principal author was Father Luis Molina (1535-1600), and this philosophical position was adopted by the Jesuits.]

descriptions of it. If such a principle is, besides, perfectly good and loves holiness infinitely, must we not acknowledge that the same God is at one and the same time perfectly good and perfectly bad, and that he loves vice no less than he does virtue? Now is it not more reasonable to divide these two opposite qualities, and to give all that is good to one principle, and all that is bad to another principle?

Human history will prove nothing to the disadvantage of the good principle. I [the Manichean] do not say as you do, that, of his own will and only because it was his good pleasure, he subjected mankind to sin and misery, when nothing hindered him from making them holy and happy: I suppose he did not consent to this but to shun a greater evil, and that he did it as it were in his own defense. This clears him of guilt. He saw that the evil principle would destroy all; he opposed him as much as he could, and by agreement he obtained the state to which things are now reduced. He acted like a monarch, who, to avoid the ruin of all his dominions, is obliged to sacrifice one part of them to the good of the other. This is a grand inconveniency, and which at first frightens human reason, to talk of a first principle and a necessary Being as of a thing that does not all it has a mind to, and which is forced for want of power to submit to conjectures. But it is yet a greater imperfection to resolve voluntarily to do evil when one can do good. This is what might be said by this heretic.

I shall conclude with the good use for which I made these remarks. It is more useful than one would think to humble the reason of man by showing him with what force the most foolish heresies—such as those of the Manicheans are—may confound it, and embroil the most fundamental truths.... What must be done then? Men must captivate their understandings to the obedience of faith, and never dispute about some things; particularly, they must not oppose the Manicheans but by the Scripture, and by the principle of submission, as St. Augustine does:

> Their Doctors who were Philosophers (or rather Sophists) professing to follow nothing but reason, without paying any deference to authority, very easily entangled by their reasoning and the deceitful subtleties of a Philosophy merely human those who had not knowledge enough to answer them, and could only oppose to them the scripture, and the authority of the church, to which it belongs to interpret scripture according to its true sense. Thus by promising to their disciples that they would discover the truth to them by the mere natural

light of good sense and reason, and making everything pass for an error which is above it, as our mysteries are, they perverted many.[1]

...

It has been a constant opinion amongst the Christians from the beginning that the Devil is the author of all false religions, that he deprived Adam and Eve of their innocence, that he moves the Heretics to dogmatize, and inspires men with errors, superstitions, schisms, lewdness, avarice, intemperance—in a word, with all the crimes that are committed among men—from whence it follows that he is the cause of moral evil, and of all the miseries of man. He is therefore the first principle of evil, but because he is not eternal nor uncreated, he is not the first ill principle in the sense of the Manicheans, which afforded those Heretics I know not what matter of boasting and insulting over the orthodox. They might have told them, your doctrine is much more injurious to the good God than ours, for you make him the cause of the ill principle. You assert that he produced him, and that though he could have stopped him at the first step he made, yet he permitted him to usurp so great a power in this world that mankind having been divided into two cities—that of God and that of the Devil[2]—the first was always very small, and even so small for many ages, that it had not two inhabitants, when the other had two millions. We are not obliged to enquire into the cause of the wickedness of our ill principle, for when an uncreated being is so or so, one cannot say why it is so: it is its nature; one must necessarily stop there. But as for the qualities of a creature, one ought to inquire into the reason of them, and it cannot be found but in its cause. You must therefore say that God is the author of the devil's malice, that he himself produced it such as it is or sowed the seeds of it in the soil that he created, which is a thousand times more dishonourable to God than to say that he is not the only necessary and independent being. This brings in again the abovementioned objections concerning the fall of the first man.

It is not therefore necessary to insist any longer upon it. We must humbly acknowledge that Philosophy is here at a stand, and that its weakness ought to lead us to the light of revelation, where we shall find a sure and steadfast anchor. Note that those

---

1 Augustine, *On the Usefulness of Faith.*
2 See St. Augustine, *City of God.*

Heretics made an ill use of some passages of the holy Scripture, wherein the Devil is called the prince[1] and the God of this world.[2]

An explanation: That which has been said of Scepticism in this Dictionary cannot prejudice religion.

... Divines ought not to be ashamed to confess that they cannot enter the lists with such disputants, and that they will not expose the gospel-truths to such an encounter. The vessel of Jesus Christ is not made to float upon that tempestuous sea, but to ride secure from this tempest in the haven of faith. It has pleased the Father, the Son, and the Holy Ghost, Christians must say, to lead us by the way of faith, and not of science, or disputation. They are our instructors and directors, we cannot err having such guides, and reason itself commands us to prefer them before its own direction....

A true Believer—a Christian who well understands the spirit of his religion—does not expect to see it agree with the aphorisms of the Lyceum,[3] nor to find it able by the mere strength of reason, to confute the difficulties of reason. He well knows that natural things have no proportion to the supernatural, and that if a Philosopher was desired to level and adjust the mysteries of the Gospel with the Aristotelian axioms, it would be requiring of him what is inconsistent with the nature of things. You must necessarily make an option betwixt Philosophy and the Gospel: if you will believe nothing but what is evident and agreeable to common notions, choose Philosophy, and leave Christianity; if you will believe the incomprehensible mysteries of religion, take Christianity and leave Philosophy. For to enjoy at the same time evidence and incomprehensibility is a thing impossible; the conjunction of these two things is no less impossible than the conjunction of the properties of a square and of a circle. You must necessarily make an option between them: if the conveniences of a round table do not satisfy you, make a square one, and do not pretend that the same table should furnish you with the conveniences both of a round and of a square table. Once more, a true Christian well instructed in the character of supernatural truths, and well grounded in the principles peculiar to the Gospel, will

---

1 John 14:30.
2 2 Corintians 4:4.
3 [The Lyceum was Aristotle's school of philosophy. Aristotelian thought provides much of the philosophical framework of scholastic theology.]

laugh at the subtleties of Philosophers, and especially of the Sceptics. Faith will place him above the regions wherein the storms of disputation rage. He will find himself in a post from whence, being calm and undisturbed, he can hear the thunder of argumentations and distinctions roar below him. A post that will prove the true Olympus of the Poets;[1] and the true temple of the sages,[2] from whence he will see in a perfect tranquility the weakness of reason, and the errors of men who have no other guide. Every Christian who suffers himself to be startled and offended with the objections of unbelievers is in the same lamentable condition as they are....

Most men so little examine the nature of divine Faith, and reflect so seldom upon this act of their mind, that they want to be roused from their negligence by a long enumeration of the difficulties that encompass the doctrines of the Christian Religion. It is by a lively sense of those difficulties we learn the excellency of Faith and of this gift of God. Hereby we learn also to mistrust reason, and have recourse to grace. They who know nothing of the great contest between reason and faith and are ignorant of the force of Philosophical objections have but an imperfect sense of God's goodness to them; and of the manner of triumphing over all the temptations of incredulous and presumptuous reason.

The true way of humbling it is to know that if it be capable of inventing objections, it is incapable of resolving them, and, in a word, that it is not by reason that the gospel was established:

It is Faith alone that can teach that Divine Philosophy, which none of the princes of this world had known.[3] Whoever opens his eyes to so pure a light is truly enlightened. It was not by strength

---

1 "but as the lofty summit of Olympus, far removed from the winds and tempests of the lower air, its eternal bright serene untroubled by any cloud, is lifted above the rain storms and hears the hurricane rushing beneath its feet while it treads upon the thunder's roar; so thy patient mind, unfettered by cares so manifold, rises high above them ..." Claudian, *On the Consulship of Flavius Manlius Theodorus*, v. 206. [Maurice Platnauer, trans. Loeb Classical Library.]

2 "But above all, 'tis pleasantest to get/ The top of High Philosophy, and sit/ On the calm, peaceful, flourishing head of it;/ Whence we may view deep, wondrous deep below,/ How poor mistaken mortals wandering go,/ Seeking the path to happiness." Lucretius *On the Nature of Things* Book ii, v. 7. (Creech) [Thomas Creech, trans.]

3 "Truth came by Christ." John 1:17. "Speak wisdom ... which none of the rulers of this world knoweth." Paul, 1 Corinthians 2:6-8.

of syllogisms and argumentations that this Philosophy recommended itself to men, but by its simplicity and the ignorance of those who preached it to the world.... Faith, having discovered to men the false glimpses that shone in the Heathen Philosophy, accustomed them not to them, that it is better to be ignorant of what God has been pleased to conceal, and with a respectful ignorance to adore the secrets he has not revealed, than to attempt to fathom this abyss of light by the rashness of our conjectures and the faint views of our reason. It was to this Divine ray of Faith that the Christian took pleasure to sacrifice that insolent curiosity which made him too rashly examine the works of God by examining the effects of nature, and stifle all the views of that proud reason which fixes him to the creatures and makes him a rebel against the Creator. It was by the rays of this celestial light that the Christian perceived it was better to yield than to argue in point of religion; that narrowness of wit is more advantageous to a Christian than all the force and penetration of the mind, and that the simplicity of Faith is preferable to all the pomp of science. Since, after all, the works of God which bear the most the stamp of his omnipotence and his character are those we the least comprehend, therefore nothing is more just than to humble our reason and submit it to the light of eternal reason, which is the rule of all reasons. And indeed there is no science but requires submission for the establishment of its principles.[1]

...

This, I think, is more than sufficient to remove the scruples which the pretended triumph of the Sceptics had raised in the minds of some of my readers.

2. From Voltaire, "Of Good and Evil, Physical and Moral," *Philosophical Dictionary* (1764)[2]

We here treat of a question of the greatest difficulty and importance. It relates to the whole of human life. It would be of much greater consequence to find a remedy for our evils; but no

---

1 Rapin, *Réflexions sur la Philosophie*, pag. m. 447.

2 From the *Dictionnaire Philosophique Portatif*, originally published in 1764, which received numerous augmentations and retitlings by Voltaire, well into the 1770s. This text is from Voltaire, *Philosophical Dictionary*, vols. 3-7 of *The Works of Voltaire, A Contemporary Version*, trans. William F. Fleming (New York: E.R. DuMont, 1901). Spellings have been modernized.

remedy is to be discovered, and we are reduced to the sad necessity of tracing out their origin. With respect to this origin, men have disputed ever since the days of Zoroaster, and in all probability they disputed on the same subject long before him. It was to explain the mixture of good and evil that they conceived the idea of two principles—Oromazes, the author of light, and Arimanes, the author of darkness; the box of Pandora; the two vessels of Jupiter; the apple eaten by Eve; and a variety of other systems.[1] The first of dialecticians, although not the first of philosophers, the illustrious Bayle, has clearly shown how difficult it is for Christians who admit one only God, perfectly good and just, to reply to the objections of the Manicheans who acknowledge two Gods—one good, and the other evil.

The foundation of the system of the Manicheans, with all its antiquity, was not on that account more reasonable. Lemmas,[2] susceptible of the most clear and rigid geometrical demonstrations, should alone have induced any men to the adoption of such a theorem as the following: "There are two necessary beings, both supreme, both infinite, both equally powerful, both in conflict with each other, yet, finally, agreeing to pour out upon this little planet— the one, all the treasures of his beneficence, and the other all the stores of his malice." It is in vain that the advocates of this hypothesis attempt to explain by it the cause of good and evil: even the fable of Prometheus explains it better.[3] Every hypothesis which only serves to assign a reason for certain things, without being, in addition to that recommendation, established upon indisputable principles, ought invariably to be rejected.

---

1 Oromazes (also called Ahura Mazda) and Arimanes (Angra Mainyu) are the paired principles of good and evil in Zoroastrian religion, and the root of a similar division for the Manicheans (see Pierre Bayle's selection in this volume). Zeus's (or Jupiter's) gift of a good (mixed with complications) was Pandora herself, the first woman, and the gift of evil was Pandora's box, which contained disorder and evil that Pandora let out when she looked inside. (Hesiod, *Works and Days* (ll. 53-104)) The two urns of Jupiter (or Zeus) may be accounted for as sources used to create Pandora and her box. (Homer, *Iliad*, 24. 527-33)

2 A lemma is a preliminary logical proof used along the way to another proof. Voltaire's use of the technical language of logic, including his discussion of a few examples of "contradiction" a few paragraphs down, is inflated rhetoric: strictly speaking, Voltaire does not sketch arguments in detail sufficient to pass for demonstrations.

3 Zeus sent good and evil things to men, who were Prometheus's creation, by way of Pandora, after Prometheus stole fire to provide them warmth.

The Christian doctors—independently of revelation, which makes everything credible—explain the origin of good and evil no better than the partner-gods of Zoroaster....

A father who kills his children is a monster; a king who conducts his subjects into a snare, in order to obtain a pretext for delivering them up to punishment and torture, is an execrable tyrant. If you conceive God to possess the same kindness which you require in a father, the same justice that you require in a king, no possible resource exists by which, if we may use the expression, God can be exculpated; and by allowing Him to possess infinite wisdom and infinite goodness you, in fact, render Him infinitely odious; you excite a wish that He had no existence; you furnish arms to the atheist, who will ever be justified in triumphantly remarking to you: Better by far is it to deny a God altogether, than impute to Him such conduct as you would punish, to the extremity of the law, in men.

We begin then with observing that it is unbecoming in us to ascribe to God human attributes. It is not for us to make God after our own likeness. Human justice, human kindness, and human wisdom can never be applied or made suitable to Him. We may extend these attributes in our imagination as far as we are able, to infinity; they will never be other than human qualities with boundaries perpetually or indefinitely removed; it would be equally rational to attribute to Him infinite solidity, infinite motion, infinite roundness, or infinite divisibility. These attributes can never be His.

Philosophy informs us that this universe must have been arranged by a Being incomprehensible, eternal, and existing by His own nature; but, once again, we must observe that philosophy gives us no information on the subject of the attributes of that nature. We know what He is not, and not what He is.

With respect to God, there is neither good nor evil, physically or morally. What is physical or natural evil? Of all evils, the greatest, undoubtedly, is death. Let us for a moment consider whether man could have been immortal.

In order that a body like ours should have been indissoluble, imperishable, it would have been necessary that it should not be composed of parts; that it should not be born; that it should have neither nourishment nor growth; that it should experience no change. Let any one examine each of these points; and let every reader extend their number according to his own suggestions, and it will be seen that the proposition of an immortal man is a contradiction.

If our organized body were immortal, that of mere animals would be so likewise; but it is evident that, in the course of a very short time, the whole globe would, in this case, be incompetent to supply nourishment to those animals; those immortal beings which exist only in consequence of renovation by food, would then perish for want of the means of such renovation. All this involves contradiction. We might make various other observations on the subject, but every reader who deserves the name of a philosopher will perceive that death was necessary to everything that is born; that death can neither be an error on the part of God, nor an evil, an injustice, nor a chastisement to man.

Man, born to die, can no more be exempt from pain than from death. To prevent an organized substance endowed with feeling from ever experiencing pain, it would be necessary that all the laws of nature should be changed; that matter should no longer be divisible; that it should neither have weight, action, nor force; that a rock might fall on an animal without crushing it; and that water should have no power to suffocate, or fire to burn it. Man, impassive, then, is as much a contradiction as man immortal.

This feeling of pain was indispensable to stimulate us to self-preservation, and to impart to us such pleasures as are consistent with those general laws by which the whole system of nature is bound and regulated....

Moral evil, upon which so many volumes have been written is, in fact, nothing but natural evil. This moral evil is a sensation of pain occasioned by one organized being to another. Rapine, outrage, etc., are evil only because they produce evil. But as we certainly are unable to do any evil, or occasion any pain to God, it is evident by the light of reason—for faith is altogether a different principle—that in relation to the Supreme Being and as affecting Him, moral evil can have no existence.

As the greatest of natural evils is death, the greatest of moral evils is, unquestionably, war. All crimes follow in its train; false and calumnious declarations, perfidious violation of the treaties, pillage, devastation, pain, and death under every hideous and appalling form.

All this is physical evil in relation to man, but can no more be considered moral evil in relation to God than the rage of dogs worrying and destroying one another. It is a mere commonplace idea, and as false as it is feeble, that men are the only species that slaughter and destroy one another. Wolves, dogs, cats, cocks, quails, all war with their respective species: house spiders devour one another; the male universally fights for the female. This warfare is the result of the laws of nature, of principles in their very blood and essence; all is connected; all is necessary.

Nature has granted man about two and twenty years of life, one with another; that is, of a thousand children born in the same month, some of whom have died in their infancy, and the rest lived respectively to the age of thirty, forty, fifty, and even eighty years, or perhaps beyond, the average calculation will allow to each the above-mentioned number of twenty-two years.

How can it affect the Deity, whether a man die in battle or of a fever? War destroys fewer human beings than smallpox. The scourge of war is transient, that of smallpox reigns with paramount and permanent fatality throughout the earth, followed by a numerous train of others; and taking into consideration the combined, and nearly regular operation of the various causes which sweep mankind from the stage of life, the allowance of two and twenty years for every individual will be found in general to be tolerably correct.

Man, you say, offends God by killing his neighbor; if this be the case, the directors of nations must indeed be tremendous criminals; for, while even invoking God to their assistance, they urge on to slaughter immense multitudes of their fellow-beings, for contemptible interests which it would show infinitely more policy, as well as humanity, to abandon. But how—to reason merely as philosophers—how do they offend God? Just as much as tigers and crocodiles offend him. It is, surely, not God whom they harass and torment, but their neighbor. It is only against man that man can be guilty. A highway robber can commit no robbery on God. What can it signify to the eternal Deity, whether a few pieces of yellow metal are in the hands of Jerome, or of Bonaventure?[1] We have necessary desires, necessary passions, and necessary laws for the restraint of both; and while on this our ant-hill, during the little day of our existence, we are engaged in eager and destructive contest about a straw, the universe moves on in its majestic course, directed by eternal and unalterable laws, which comprehend in their operation the atom that we call the earth.

---

1   St. Bonaventure (1221-74 CE) was a member of the Franciscan Order, and St. Jerome (*ca.* 347-420) might be taken to represent the spiritual father of the Dominican order. If this reflects Voltaire's intention, then he is referring to a debate of doctrine from two centuries before that affected the popularity of the two orders, and so had financial effects on charity. See *Essay on Mores*, chapter 129.

3. From Gottfried Leibniz, *Essays of Theodicy on the Goodness of God, the Freedom of Man, and the Origin of Evil* (1710)[1]

Preface

... Our souls have the same perfections as God, but He possesses them without limit: He is an ocean, from which we have only received drops. While there is in us some power, some knowledge, and some goodness, these qualities are complete in God. Order, proportions, and harmony enchant us, and painting and music exemplify these qualities; God is order itself, He always keeps the right proportions, He makes universal harmony: all beauty emanates from Him....

Even if God did not concur in evil actions, there would still be a problem in the fact that He foresees and permits them, despite the fact that He could prevent them in virtue of His omnipotence. This is why some philosophers and even some theologians have preferred to deny God's providence and foreknowledge rather than to admit something that they believed conflicted with His goodness. The Socinians ... incline towards this opinion.... While there is no doubt that they are quite mistaken, others are no less wrong, who, convinced that nothing happens except in virtue of God's will and power, attribute to Him intentions and actions so unworthy of the greatest and best of all beings, that it might even be said that such authors have in effect renounced the dogma that recognizes the justice and the goodness of God. They believed that because God is the sovereign master of the universe, He could cause sins to be committed without compromising His holiness, just because it pleased Him to do so, or in order to have the pleasure of punishing, and they believed that He could even take pleasure in eternally tormenting innocents, without committing any injustice, because no one has the right or power to limit His actions. Some have even gone so far as to say that God actually uses His power in this way, and under the pretext that we are nothing in comparison with Him, they compare us to earthworms, that human beings do not hesitate to crush underfoot

---

1 Selections translated for this edition by Sean Greenberg, University of California, Irvine, copyright 2009. Translated from C. I. Gerhardt, ed., *G. W. Leibniz: Die Philosophischen Schriften* (Hildesheim: Georg Olms, 1978), vol. 6, pp. 27, 34-37 *et. seq.* Footnotes are a collaborative effort of translator and editor.

while walking, or in general with animals from a different species, whom we have no scruple about mistreating.[1]

I believe that many otherwise well-meaning people share these thoughts, because they do not clearly enough grasp their consequences. They do not see that it is actually to destroy God's justice: for what content can we give to this sort of justice, that has only the will as its rule, that is to say, where the will is not determined by rules of goodness, and tends directly to evil? Unless this is the idea contained in that tyrannical definition advanced by Plato's Thrasymachus, who said that 'just' is nothing else than what pleases the most powerful.[2] All those who ground obligation on constraint and consequently take power to be the basis of right return unthinkingly to this definition. But these very strange maxims, so unfit to make human beings good and charitable in the image of God, will be soon abandoned when it has been well considered that a God who would take pleasure in the evil of others would be no different than the evil principle of the Manicheans, assuming that this principle had become the sole master of the universe, and that consequently feelings must be attributed to the true God that make Him worthy of being called the good principle.

Happily these outrageous dogmas hardly persist among theologians: nevertheless, some clever people, who enjoy causing problems, revive them. They seek to increase our discomfort, by combining the controversies that arise from Christian theology with philosophical disputes. Philosophers have considered the questions of necessity, freedom, and the origin of evil; theologians have added to these the questions of original sin, grace, and predestination.[3] The original corruption of the human race,

---

1 Pierre Bayle considers possibilities like these, but, as he is a skeptic, does not assert them. The view has a vague precedent in Psalms 8: "O Lord, our Lord ... You make him [man] ruler over the works of your hands, you put everything under his feet...."

2 Plato, *Republic* 338c; a more developed argument of this form may be found in Plato, *Gorgias* 482d.

3 The philosophers' topics that Leibniz notes are introduced by Bayle in his selections in this volume; the theologians' topics, first or original sin, grace, and predestination, will be introduced by Leibniz later in these excerpts. One concept, predestination, is key to explaining the two others. It may appear that an all-seeing (omniscient) God has the power of knowing our actions, and so perhaps of deciding our fates before we ourselves make our choices. Thus it appears that our futures are foreordained: we would appear to be predestined in our actions, rather than

derived from the first sin, seems to us to have imposed a natural necessity of sinning, without the aid of divine grace: but insofar as necessity is incompatible with punishment, it will be inferred that sufficient grace ought to have been given to all human beings, which does not seem to be in keeping with experience.

But the difficulty is great, especially with respect to God's intention about human salvation. There are few who are saved or elected; God does not therefore have the express will[1] to elect many. And since it is admitted that those whom He has chosen do not merit it any more than the others, and are not in the end any less evil, at the root, since whatever goodness is in them only comes from the grace of God, the difficulty is even increased. Where is His justice (one might say), or, at least, where is His goodness? Partiality or preference of people goes against justice, and one who limits His goodness without reason surely is not good enough. It is true that those who are not elected are lost by their own fault, and they lack either good will or lively faith, but it was up to God to give it to them. It is obvious that, besides internal grace, it is usually external circumstances that differentiate human beings, and that education, conversation, and example often correct or corrupt natural inclinations. But wouldn't there be reason to be surprised that God should prepare circumstances favorable to some and should abandon others to circumstances that contribute to their downfall? ...

It is hoped that all these difficulties will be resolved. It will be shown that absolute necessity, which is also called logical, metaphysical, and even sometimes geometrical, and which would be the only sort of necessity to be feared, is not to be found in free actions. And thus freedom is exempt, not only from constraint, but also from true necessity. It will be shown that even God, although He always chooses the better, does not act by absolute necessity, and that the laws of nature that God prescribed to Himself, which are grounded on their suitability, occupy the

---

the initiators of our choices. Furthermore, if God is also good and omnipotent, then it would appear that there is no room for God to allow us to make sinful choices, and so, even the first sins of Adam and Eve, called the original sin, would appear to be God's responsibility, and not theirs (nor ours, their children's). If these are God's responsibility, then it does not appear that we should require grace, God's forgiveness, to enter heaven. In the selections from the First Part of the *Theodicy*, below, Leibniz attempts to solve some of these problems.

1 *Volonté décretoire* appears to be novel terminology introduced by Leibniz; it is here translated as "express will."

middle ground between geometrical, absolutely necessary truths, and arbitrary decrees: this has not been properly understood by Monsieur Bayle and other new philosophers. It will also be shown that there is an indifference in freedom, because there is no absolute necessity for one side or the other, but that there is nevertheless never an indifference of perfect equilibrium. Finally, it will be shown that there is a perfect spontaneity in free actions, that goes beyond what has been granted up to this point.

Preliminary Dissertation on the Conformity of Faith and Reason

2. Now there are two kinds of truths of reason. The first kind are called *eternal truths*, which are absolutely necessary, so that their denial implies a contradiction: truths of this kind are logically, metaphysically, or geometrically necessary, and cannot be denied without falling into absurdity. The second kind can be called *positive truths*, because they are laws that it pleased God to give to nature, or because they depend on those laws. We learn them, either from experience, that is to say, *a posteriori*, or from reason and *a priori*, that is to say, from considerations of the suitability that made it the case that they were chosen. This suitability also has its rules and its reasons, but it is the free choice of God, and not geometrical necessity, that makes what is suitable preferred, and that brings it into existence. Hence it can be said that *physical necessity* is based on *moral necessity*, that is, on the choice of the wise one worthy of his wisdom, and both physical and moral necessity must be distinguished from *geometrical necessity*. This physical necessity constitutes the order of nature, and consists in laws of motion and certain other general laws that it pleased God to give to things when He created them. It is therefore true that it is not without reason that God has given these laws, for He chooses nothing by caprice and as it were by lot or by a pure indifference. But the general reasons of goodness and order that led Him to choose them can be overcome in certain cases by more significant reasons derived from a higher order.

3. The foregoing shows that God can release creatures from the laws that He prescribed to them and can produce in them something that goes beyond their nature when He works a *miracle*. And when creatures are raised to perfections and capacities more noble than those to which they can attain in virtue of

their nature, the scholastics[1] call such capacities *obediential powers*, that is to say, capacities that the thing acquires by obeying the commandment of Him, who can give what the creature does not have, although the scholastics ordinarily give examples of such powers that I hold to be impossible, such as when they maintain that God can give a creature the capacity to create. It may be that there are miracles that God works through the agency of angels, where the laws of nature are no more violated than when human beings aid nature through art, for the artifice of angels only differs from ours in virtue of its degree of perfection. Nevertheless it always remains the case that the laws of nature are subject to the dispensation of the legislator, whereas eternal truths, such as the truths of geometry, are altogether indispensable, and they cannot even be contravened by faith....

32. One thing that could have contributed the most to making M. Bayle believe that the problems raised by reason against faith cannot be satisfactorily resolved is the fact that he seems to require that God be justified in a way similar to that ordinarily employed to plead the cause of an accused person before a judge. But he has not remembered that in human tribunals, which cannot always penetrate all the way to the truth, it is often necessary to judge on the basis of signs and *probabilities*, and especially on the basis of *assumptions* and *prejudices*, whereas it is agreed, as we have already remarked, that mysteries are not probable.[2] For example, M. Bayle does not think that the goodness of God in the permission of sin can be justified, because probability would be against a person who found himself in a case that would appear similar. God foresees that Eve will be deceived by the serpent when he puts her in the circumstances in which she has since found herself; and nevertheless he put her there. Now if a father or a tutor acted in the same way towards his child or his student, or a friend acted the same way towards a young person whose conduct depended on him, the judge would not grant the pleas of a lawyer who said that the evil was only permitted, but was not done or willed, and he would even take this permission as a sign

---

1 The scholastics are Aristotelian philosophers in the orders of the Catholic church. The account of obediential powers (*potentia obedientialis*) reaches back especially to Thomas Aquinas (*ca.* 1225-74).

2 Leibniz remarks that religious mysteries are not probable, but nevertheless, events such as that in the example are known to have occurred. As Leibniz indicates, an event that is a mystery would be judged highly *im*probable— and if it were not, it would not be likely to be judged mysterious.

of an evil will, and he would consider it to be a sin of omission, which would render the one proven guilty the accessory of another's sin of commission.

33. But it must be considered that when one has foreseen an evil that one did not prevent, even though it seems that the evil could easily have been prevented, and that one has even done things that facilitated that evil, it does not for all that follow *necessarily* that one is an accessory to it: this is only a strong presumption, which ordinarily takes the place of truth in human affairs, but which could be demolished by an exact discussion of the fact, if we were capable of such a discussion in the case of God. For jurisprudence calls *presumption* what may pass provisionally for the truth, just in case the contrary cannot be proven, and it is something more than *conjecture*, although the dictionary of the Academy has not yet marked the difference. Now there is undoubtedly reason to judge that one would learn from such a discussion if it could be held that very just reasons, stronger than those that seem contrary, have obliged the most wise one to permit the evil, and even to do the very things that facilitated it. Several examples will be given below.

34. It is not unproblematic, I admit, that a father, a tutor, or a friend might have such reasons in the case under consideration. Nevertheless it is not absolutely impossible, and a skillful novelist could perhaps find an extraordinary case that would even justify a person in the circumstances that I just noted. But in the case of God, there is no need to imagine or to check the particular reasons that could have led Him to permit the evil: general reasons suffice. It is known that the whole universe, all of whose parts are linked together, is under His charge, and it should thereby be inferred that He had an infinity of considerations that together led Him to judge that it was not right to prevent certain evils.

35. It even ought to be said that it must be necessarily the case that there were important, or rather invincible reasons, that led the divine wisdom to the permission of the evil that surprises us, in virtue of the very fact that this permission was granted, for nothing can come from God that is not in perfect conformity with goodness, justice, and holiness. Thus we can judge from the event (or *a posteriori*) that this permission was indispensable, although it would not be possible for us to prove (*a priori*) by the detail of the reasons that God may have had to permit this, just as it is no more necessary that we prove this in order to justify it. M. Bayle himself quite rightly says, with respect to this topic

(*Response to the Questions of a Provincial*, ch. 165, volume 3, p. 1067): "Sin entered the world, thus God was able to permit it without going against His perfections: *from the actual to the possible is a valid consequence.*"[1] With respect to God, the following argument is sound: He did it, therefore He did it well. It is therefore not the case that we do not have any idea of justice in general that can also apply to God, and it is no more the case that God's justice has other rules than human justice, but it is rather that the case in question is altogether different from those common to human beings. Universal law is the same for God and for human beings, but the fact is altogether different in the case in question....

First Part

Essays on the Justice of God and on the Liberty of Man in the Origin of Evil

1. After having settled the rights of faith and of reason in a way that makes reason serve faith, rather than being contrary to it, we will see how they exercise these rights in order to sustain and to reconcile what the natural light and the revealed light teach us about God and about man with respect to evil. The *difficulties* may be distinguished into two classes. One sort of difficulty arises from human freedom, which seems to be incompatible with the divine nature; nevertheless freedom is judged to be necessary for human beings to be judged guilty and punished for their misdeeds. The other sort of difficulty concerns the conduct of God, since He seems to play too much of a part in the existence of evil, even if human beings are free and also take part in it. This conduct seems to be contrary to God's goodness, to His holiness, and to divine justice, since God concurs with both physical and moral evil, and He concurs with the one and the other both in a moral fashion and in a physical fashion, and it seems that these evils are manifest in the order of nature, as well as in the order of grace, and in the future and eternal life, as well as and even more than in this transitory life.[2]

---

1 "*Ab actu ad potentiam valet consequentia*"—a standard logician's expression that indicates a claim that is obviously true: whatever really exists must also be judged to be possible.
2 Moral evil includes decisions that are wrong, and that may lead to physical evil: to pain and suffering. See p. 22 of the introduction to this edition for further clarification.

2. In order to summarize these difficulties, it must be noted that freedom appears to be undermined by any sort of determination or certainty, and nevertheless the common dogma of our philosophers maintains that the truth of future contingents is determined. God's foreknowledge also renders the entire future certain and determined, but His providence and His preordination, on which His foreknowledge even seems to be based, makes it even more the case that the future is certain and determinate. For God is not like a human being who can look at events with indifference, and who can suspend his judgment, since nothing exists except as a consequence of the decrees of His will and by the activity of His power. And even if one abstracts from God's concurrence, everything is perfectly linked in the order of things, since nothing can happen without there being a cause disposed as it must be in order to produce the effect: this is no less the case in voluntary actions than in all other actions. From which it seems that human beings are compelled to do the good and evil that they do, and as a consequence of this, they merit neither reward nor punishment for their actions, which destroys the morality of actions and destabilizes all human and divine justice.

3. But even if this freedom that human beings assume to their own detriment were granted to them, the conduct of God would not fail to provide matter for criticism, sustained by the presumptuous ignorance of human beings, who would wish to exonerate themselves of all responsibility at God's expense. It is objected that all the reality, and what is called the substance of the act, even in sin, is a production of God, since all that is real in creatures and in their actions comes from God. Whence it may well be inferred, not only that God is the physical cause of sin, but also that He is its moral cause, since He acts very freely, and He does not do anything without a perfect knowledge of the thing and of the consequences that it can have. And it is not enough to say that God has given Himself a law to concur with human wills or resolutions, whether this is understood in accordance with the common opinion, or in accordance with the system of occasional causes. For besides the fact that it would be strange that He had given Himself such a law, whose consequences He could not fail to know, the chief difficulty is that it seems that even an evil will could not exist without His concurrence, and even without some predetermination on His part, that contributes to give rise to this will in a human being or in some other rational creature, for an action, despite being evil, is no less dependent on God. Hence one might finally want to conclude that God does everything

indifferently, both good and evil, unless one wants to say, with the Manicheans, that there are two principles, the one good, and the other bad. Moreover, following the common opinion of theologians and philosophers, that conservation is a continued creation, it will be said that human beings are continually created corrupted and sinning.[1] Moreover, there are some modern Cartesians who claim that God is the only actor, for Whom created beings are only purely passive organs, and M. Bayle stresses that claim.

4. But even if God should concur with actions only by means of a general concurrence, or even if He were not to concur with actions at all, at least not with evil actions, it will be said that the fact that nothing happens without His permission is enough for the actions to be attributable to Him and to make Him the moral cause of sin. To say nothing of the fall of the angels, He knows everything that will happen if He places a human being in such-and-such circumstances after having created him, and He does not hesitate to place him in those circumstances. The human being is exposed to a temptation to which it is known that he will succumb, and it is known that in this way he will be the cause of an infinity of horrible evils, and the whole human race will be infected by this fall and placed in a kind of necessity of sinning, which is called the original sin. The world will be thus thrown into a strange confusion, and by this means death and sickness will be introduced into the world, along with a thousand other misfortunes and miseries that ordinarily afflict both good and evil people—even evil will rule and virtue will be oppressed here on Earth, and thus it will almost not seem that Providence governs things. But it is much worse when one considers the life to come, since there will only be a small number of human beings who will be saved, and all the others will perish eternally, besides the fact that those people destined for eternal salvation will have been selected from the corrupted mass by a choice made for no reason, regardless of whether it is claimed that in choosing them, God looked to their good future actions, or to their faith, or to their works, and also regardless of claims that He wished to give them these good qualities and these actions, because He had predestined them for salvation....

---

1 The doctrine of continuous creation suggests that God not only created our universe, but that God's continued concurrence is required to maintain it in its existence through time. One follower of Descartes, alluded to in the next sentence, is Nicolas Malebranche (1638-1715).

5. So that it is a terrible judgment that God having given His only son for the whole human race, the sole author and master of the salvation of mankind, nevertheless saves so few and abandons all the others to His enemy the devil, who torments them eternally and makes them blaspheme their creator, although they had all been created to reflect and to manifest His goodness, His justice, and His other perfections. And this is all the more frightening because all these human beings are unhappy for all eternity only because God exposed their parents to a temptation that He knew they would not resist; this sin is inherent in and imputed to human beings before their will even plays a part; this hereditary vice determines their wills to commit actual sins; and an infinity of human beings, children and adults, who have never heard of Jesus Christ, the savior of the human race, or who have not heard enough about him, die before having received the aids necessary to draw back from the oblivion of sin, and are condemned to be forever rebels against God and plunged into the most horrible miseries, with the worst of all creatures, although at bottom these human beings were no worse than others, and although many of them were perhaps less guilty than some of this small number of elect who were saved by an unfounded grace, and who thereby enjoy eternal felicity that they did not merit. Here is a summary of the difficulties that many authors have already discussed; but M. Bayle was one of those who has pressed these difficulties the furthest, as it will appear in what follows, when we examine passages from his work. At present I believe that I have reported what is essential in his difficulties, but I judged it appropriate to refrain from certain expressions and exaggerations that could have scandalized the reader and that would not have made the objections any stronger.

6. Let us now turn the coin, and let us also present what one can reply to these objections, which it will be necessary to explain by means of a lengthier discourse, for many objections can be raised in few words, but to discuss them, one must go on at length. Our goal is to distance human beings from the false ideas that represent God to them as an absolute prince, using a despotic power, scarcely suitable to be loved and little worthy of being loved. These notions are all the worse with respect to God, since the essence of piety is not only to fear Him, but all the more to love Him above all things, which cannot be done without knowing all the perfections capable of arousing the love that He merits and which constitute the happiness of those who love Him. Finding ourselves animated with a zeal that cannot fail to

please Him, we have reason to hope that He will enlighten us, and that He Himself will aid us in the execution of an enterprise undertaken for His glory and for the good of mankind....

7. *God is the first reason of things*: for those things that are limited, like everything that we see and experience, are contingent and have nothing in themselves that makes their existence necessary, it being obvious that time, space, and matter, united and uniform in themselves and indifferent to everything, could receive altogether different movements and figures, and in a different order. *The reason for the existence of the world*, which is the entire assembly of *contingent* things, must therefore be sought, and it must be sought in a *substance that bears the reason for its existence within itself*, and which consequently is *necessary* and eternal.[1] It must also be the case that this cause is *intelligent*, for given the fact that this world that exists is contingent, and an infinity of other worlds are equally possible and equally claim existence, as it were, just as much as this one, it must be the case that the cause of the world has a concern for or a relation to all these possible worlds, in order to settle on one. And this connection or relation of an existing substance to simple possibilities cannot be anything other than the *understanding* that has ideas of these possibilities; and determining one of these possibilities cannot be anything other than the act of the *will* that chooses. And it is the *power* of this substance that makes its will efficacious. Power is directed to *being*, wisdom or understanding is directed to the *true*, and the will is directed to the *good*. And this intelligent cause must be infinite in every respect and absolutely perfect in *power*, in *wisdom*, and in *goodness*, since it extends to everything that is possible. And since everything is connected, there is no reason to admit more than one such being. His understanding is the source of *essences*, and His will is the origin of *existences*. Here in few words is the proof of a unique God with His perfections, and by this a proof of the origin of things.

8. Now this supreme wisdom, joined to a goodness that is no less infinite than it, cannot have failed to choose the best. For since a lesser evil is a kind of good, so too a lesser good is a kind

---

1 The necessary and eternal substance, which Leibniz indicates is distinguishable from the contingent world that we see, is God. In the difficult passage that follows, Leibniz argues that the "power" of this particular substance can bring the substance itself into being. Leibniz's argument reflects longstanding views that God is a self-creating substance, or the cause of itself, and God is the will that intelligently chooses the best and the single created world that we do experience from among an infinity of possible worlds that God conceives.

of evil, if it hinders a greater good, and there would be something to correct in the actions of God, if He could have done better than He did. Just as in mathematics, when there is no *maximum* or *minimum*, nothing in fact distinct, everything is done equally, or when this cannot be done, nothing is done: the same thing can be said of the perfect wisdom, which is no less governed than mathematics, that if there were no best (*optimum*) among all possible worlds, God would not have produced any world. I call 'world' the whole succession and the entire collection of all existing things, in order that it not be said that several worlds could exist in different times and different places. For these must all be counted together in order to form a world, or if you prefer, a universe. And even if all the times and all the places were filled, it always remains true that they could have been filled in an infinity of ways, and that there are an infinity of possible worlds of which it is necessary that God chose the best, since He can do nothing without acting in accordance with supreme reason.

9. Some adversary, unable to answer this argument, will perhaps answer the conclusion by a counter-argument, by saying that the world could have existed without sin and without suffering, but I deny that it would therefore have been *better*. For it must be known that everything is linked in each possible world: the universe, whatever it may be, is all of a piece, like an ocean, and the smallest movement there extends its effect to whatever distance there may be, although this effect becomes less sensible in proportion to the distance that it travels. So God has determined everything there in advance once and for all, having foreseen the prayers, the good and bad actions, and everything else, and each thing contributed *ideally* before its existence to the decision that was taken regarding the existence of all things. So that nothing can be changed in the universe (no more than in a number), except its essence, or if you prefer, except its *numerical identity*. Thus if the least evil that occurs in the world were lacking, it would not be this world, which, all things together, with no allowance made, was found to be the best by the creator Who chose it.

10. It is true that possible worlds without sin and without unhappiness can be imagined, and one could make them like novels, like utopias, like the Sevarites, but these very worlds would be very much inferior in goodness to our own.[1] I cannot

1 'Sevarites' refers to the imaginary nation of which Denis Veiras writes in the *Histoire des Séverambes*, published in English in 1675 and in French in 1677. The work is one of the many utopian libertine writings of the seventeenth century.

make you see this in detail, for can I know and can I represent to you infinities and compare them together? But you ought to judge with me from the effect,[1] since God chose this world as it is. Besides, we know that often an evil causes a good, which would not have arrived without this evil. Often even two evils have made a great good:

And if the fates will it, two poisons taken together have a favorable effect.[2]

Just as two liquors sometimes produce a dry body, witness the spirit of wine and the spirit of urine mixed by van Helmont; or just as two cold and dark bodies produce a great fire, witness an acid liquor and an aromatic oil combined by M. Hofmann. The general of an army sometimes makes a happy mistake, that leads to victory in a great battle; and in churches of the Roman Catholic confession, is it not sung the day before Easter:

O truly necessary sin of Adam,
Which the death of Christ has blotted out!
O happy fault,
That merited such and so great a Redeemer![3]

...

22. But someone will say to me: Why do you speak to us about *permitting*? Is it not the case that God does evil and wills it? It is here that it will be necessary to explain what *permission* is, in order that it may be seen that it is not without reason that this term is employed. But first the nature of the will, which has degrees, must be explained: and in the general sense, it can be said that the will consists in an inclination to do something and its strength varies in proportion to the goodness of the action. This will is called *antecedent* when it is detached, and considers each good individually as a good. In this sense, it can be said that God tends to all good insofar as it is good, *to the simply simple per-*

---

1 Original in Latin: "*ab effectu.*" This and many of the brief Latin expressions that follow are standard logicians' and theologians' terms.

2 Original in Latin: "*Et si fata volunt, bina venena juvant.*"

3 A portion of a hymn still used in the Catholic Easter proclamation. Original in Latin: "*O certe necessarium Adae peccatum,/Quod Christi morte deletum est!/O felix culpa, quae talem ac tantum/Meruit habere Redemptorem!*"

fection,[1] to speak scholastically, and this by means of an antecedent will. He has a sincere inclination to sanctify and save all human beings, to expel sin and prevent damnation. It can even be said that this will is efficacious *in itself* (*per se*): that is to say such that the effect would follow, if there were no stronger reason that prevented it, for this will does not extend to the final effort (*ad summum conatum*), otherwise it would never fail to produce its full effect, since God is the master of all things. The entire and infallible success pertains only to what is called the *consequent will*. It is that which is complete, and with respect to it this *rule* holds, that one never fails to do what one wills to do when one can do it. Now this consequent, final, and decisive will results from the conflict of all the antecedent wills, as much those that tend towards the good as those that repel evil, and it is from the concurrence of all these particular wills that the total will comes ...

23. From this it follows that God wills *antecedently* the good and *consequently* the best. As for evil, God does not at all will moral evil, and He does not will absolutely physical evil or suffering: it is for this reason that there is no absolute predestination to damnation, and it can be said of physical evil that God often wills it as a pain due to the guilty, and often also as a means appropriate to an end, that is to say, to prevent greater evils or to obtain greater goods. Pain also serves as a penalty and as an example, and evil often allows the good to be better appreciated, and sometimes also it contributes to a greater perfection of he who suffers, just as grain that is sown is subject to a kind of corruption in order to germinate: this is a beautiful comparison that Jesus Christ himself used.[2]

24. As for sin or moral evil, although it also very often happens that it can serve as a means for obtaining a good or for hindering another evil, it is not however this that makes an object sufficient for the divine will or even a legitimate object for a created will: it must be the case that it is neither admitted or permitted except insofar as it is seen as a certain consequence of an indispensable duty. So it should not be the case that one who would not will to permit another's sin would himself fail to fulfill some obligation, as if an officer who ought to guard an important post left it, especially in a time of danger, to break up a quarrel in the town between two soldiers from the garrison ready to kill each other.

---

1 Original in Latin: "*ad perfectionem simpliciter simplicem.*"
2 John 12:24.

25. The rule that holds that "evil must not be done in order that good may come"[1] and that forbids even permitting a moral evil in order to obtain a physical good, is here confirmed, far from being violated, and both the source and the meaning of this rule is shown. It would not be acceptable if a queen were to claim to save the state in committing or even in permitting a crime. The crime is certain, and the harm to the state is doubtful, despite the fact that this way of authorizing crimes, if it were admitted, would be worse than the overthrow of some country, which happens enough without this, and would maybe even be more likely to happen through such a means as would be chosen to prevent it from happening. But with respect to God, nothing is doubtful, nothing could be opposed to *the rule of the best*, which admits of no exception and makes no exception. And it is in this sense that God permits sin, for He would fail in something that He owes himself, in what He owes to His wisdom, to His goodness, and to His perfection, if He were not to follow the great result of all His tendencies towards the good, and if He were not to choose that which is absolutely the best, notwithstanding the pain of repentance, which is found enveloped there by the supreme necessity of the eternal truths. From this it must be concluded that God wills all good in itself *antecedently*, that He wills the best *consequently* as an end, that He sometimes wills the indifferent and physical evil as a means, but that He will only permit moral evil if it is absolutely required[2] or from some hypothetical necessity that links it with the best. This is why the *consequent will* of God, which has sin as its object, is only permissive.

26. It is still good to consider that moral evil is such a great evil only because it is a source of physical evils that are found in one of the most powerful creatures, with the greatest capacity for committing such evils. For an evil will is in its realm what the evil principle of the Manicheans would be in the universe, and reason, which is an image of the divinity, furnishes evil souls with great means to cause much evil. Just one Caligula, or Nero, does more evil than an earthquake.[3] An evil person enjoys causing suffering and destruction, and he finds only too many opportunities

---

1 Original in Latin: "*non esse facienda mala, ut eveniant bona.*" This passage is derived from Saint Paul's Letter to the Romans 3:8 (reproduced above in the rendering of the King James Bible).

2 Original in Latin: "*sine qua non.*"

3 The Roman Emperors Caligula (reigned 37-41 CE) and Nero (reigned 54-68 CE) were particularly depraved and tyrannical rulers, especially as depicted in the perhaps sensationalist accounts of historian Suetonius (*ca.* 69-130 CE).

to do so. But God being led to produce the most good that is possible, and having all the knowledge and all the power necessary for this, it is impossible that there might be in Him fault, guilt, or sin, and when He permits sin, it is wisdom, it is virtue.

4. Voltaire, "Theist," *Philosophical Dictionary* (1764)[1]

The theist is a man firmly persuaded of the existence of a Supreme Being equally good and powerful, who has formed all extended, vegetating, sentient, and reflecting existences; who perpetuates their species, who punishes crimes without cruelty, and rewards virtuous actions with kindness.

The theist does not know how God punishes, how He rewards, how He pardons; for he is not presumptuous enough to flatter himself that he understands how God acts; but he knows that God does act, and that He is just. The difficulties opposed to a providence do not stagger him in his faith, because they are only great difficulties, not proofs; he submits himself to that providence, although he only perceives some of its effects and some appearances; and judging of the things he does not see from those he does see, he thinks that this providence pervades all places and all ages.

United in this principle with the rest of the universe, he does not join any of the sects, who all contradict themselves; his religion is the most ancient and the most extended; for the simple adoration of a God has preceded all the systems in the world. He speaks a language which all nations understand, while they are unable to understand each other's. He has brethren from Peking to Cayenne, and he reckons all the wise his brothers. He believes that religion consists neither in the opinions of incomprehensible metaphysics, nor in vain decorations, but in adoration and justice. To do good—that is his worship; to submit oneself to God—that is his doctrine. The Muslim cries out to him: "Take care of yourself, if you do not make the pilgrimage to Mecca." "Woe be to thee," says a Franciscan, "if thou dost not make a journey to our Lady of Loreto."[2] He laughs at

---

1 From Voltaire, *Philosophical Dictionary*. In *The Works of Voltaire, A Contemporary Version*, trans. William F. Fleming (New York: E.R. DuMont, 1901). Vols. 3-7. Spellings have been modernized.

2 Mecca, birthplace of the prophet Muhammad, is the most important site of pilgrimage for the Muslim. Loreto, Italy, is an important Christian pilgrimage site, held to be the final location to which the house of the Virgin Mary moved by miraculous means.

Loreto and Mecca; but he succors the indigent and defends the oppressed.

5. From Abbé Noël Antoine Pluche, *The Spectacle of Nature* (1750)[1]

Selection from "Letter from the Prior to the Chevalier touching the extension and limits of reason," in which the arrangement of all is shown to be intended by God for humanity's purpose

'Tis true, indeed, Man is not invigorated with the Agility of birds, who are every Moment wafted by their Wings to a large Distance. He is not fortified with the Strength of those Animals who are armed with Horns, strong Talons, and destructive Teeth; much less is he arrayed, like them, by the Hands of Nature: he neither comes into the World with Furs, or Plumes, or Scales, to defend him from Injuries of the Air. Does such a Destitution comport with the Lord of the Earth? But he has received the Gift of Reason, and is therefore rich and strong, and plentifully accommodated with all wants. This informs him that whatever Animals enjoy, 'tis all for his Use; that in Reality they are his Slaves, their Lives and Services are at his Disposal. Is he desirous of game for his Regale? He dispatches his Dog or Falcon, who are trained up for that Purpose, and, without any Trouble of his own he is accommodated with all he wants. Would he, in one Season, change the Habit that clothes him in another? The Sheep resigns to him her Fleece, and the Silk-Worms spin, for his Use, a more light and gorgeous Robe. The Animals sustain him, and keep Sentry at his Door; they combat for him, they cultivate his Lands, and carry his Loads.

Nor do the Animals alone lend him their Agility and Vigour; Reason makes the most insensible Creatures contribute to his

---

1   Originally published as *Spectacle de la Nature, ou, Entretiens sur les particularités de l'histoire naturelle, Qui ont paru les plus propres à rendre Jeunes-Gens curieux, et à leur former l'esprit,* 8 volumes, 1732-50. This text follows *Spectacle de la Nature: or, Nature Display'd. Being Discourses on such particulars of natural history as were thought most proper to excite the curiosity and form the minds of youth.* The Eighth Edition, Revised and Corrected. London, R. Franklin, et al., 1757. Translated from the Original *French* by Mr. HUMPHREYS. Spelling and punctuation modernized for ease of reading; original headings augmented for clarity. Vol. 1, 200-03; 2, 218-19; 3, 394-96; 3, 397-98; 2, 294; 3, 374-79.

Service; it causes the Oaks to descend from the Mountains, and forces the Stones to start from their Quarries, to furnish him with a Habitation. Would he change the Climate, cross the Seas to distant Lands, and either carry any of his Superfluities thither, or bring back from hence what he wants? He makes the Mobility of the Waves and Winds subservient to his Designs. Reason places Elements and Metals in Subjection to his Necessities, and every Object around him is submissive to his Laws....

To such valuable Productions and precious Advantages, Reason joins a Set of Privileges that still ennoble her the more. She is the Center of the Works of God on Earth; she is their End, and constitutes their Harmony. Let us take Reason but a Moment from the World, and suppose Mankind destitute of her Influence; all Union would cease to subsist among the Works of the Deity, and a general Confusion be introduced through the Whole. The Sun enlightens the Earth, but this Earth is insensible, and wants none of that Luster. The Rain and Dews, aided by the Warmth of that amiable Orb, give Vegetation to the Seed and cover the Fields with Harvests and Fruits; but these are all lost Riches, and there are none to gather or consume them. The Earth, I contest, will nourish the Animals, but these Animals are insignificant for want of a Master to exercise their good qualities, and concentrate their Services. The Horse and Ox have Strength sufficient to enable them to draw or carry very weighty Loads, their feet are armed with Horn, capable of resisting the most rugged Ways; but they neither needed so much Force, nor so strong a Horn, to qualify them for grazing in the Meadows where they seek their Pasture. The sheep is charged with the Weight and Impurities of her Fleece, and the Cow and Goat are incommoded with the Redundancy of their Milk. Disadvantage or Contradiction reigns through the Whole. The Earth incloses in her Bosom Stones fit for Building, and Metal proper for the formation of all Sorts of Vessels. But she has no Guest to Lodge, nor any Workmen to employ these Materials. Her surface is a Spacious Garden, but not beheld by any Spectator; all Nature is a charmed Prospect, but afforded to none. Let us restore Man, and replace Reason on the Earth; Intelligence, Relations, and Unity will immediately reign through every Part, and the very Things which did not seem created for Man, but more immediately for Plants, or Animals, will have some Relation to him by the Services he receives from those Animals and Plants. The Gnat deposits her eggs in the Water, and they produce a Species of vermin that live a considerable time, before they inhabit Air, and are the usual

Sustenance of Fish and Water-Fowl. All these are made for Man; 'tis therefore to his Advantage that Gnats should exist. In the same manner he approaches all other Beings. His preference is the Band that connects such a Variety of Parts into the Whole, and He is the Soul by which they are animated.

In a word, Reason not only renders Man the Center of the creatures who surround him, but likewise constitutes him their Priest: He is the Minister and Interpreter of their Gratitude, and it is by his Mouth that they offer their Tribute of Praise to him who has formed them for his Glory. The diamond is neither acquainted with its own value, nor knows from whom it received its trembling Luster. Animals are ignorant of him who clothes and sustains them. The Sun himself is insensible of his Author. Reason alone discovers him, and as she is placed between the Deity and Creatures of no Understanding, she is conscious that in using these Creatures, Gratitude to God, Adoration and Love, are incumbent on her. Without her Presence, all Nature would be mute, but by her Meditation every Part of it proclaims that Glory of that Being from whom they received their Existence and Admirable Qualities. Reason alone is sensible she is in his Presence; she alone knows what she receives from his Bounty, and enjoys the inestimable Happiness of being able to adore him, for all that is either in or around her; and as there is Reason upon Earth, consequently there ought to be Religion, and Man should be devout in proportion to his rationality. It is apparent that his Religion is only weak according as Reason is sunk and perverted, which always happens when he obstinately desires Attainments that surpass him, or neglects to enrich himself with what was intended for his Instruction and Exercise.

The Divine purposes of Volcanoes and Earthquakes

The same Causes that produce the Evaporations of the Water and all those Meteors[1] that roll over our Heads do also produce other Effects no less dreadful under our Feet; I mean Earthquakes and the Eruption of Volcanoes. As the Agency therefore of the same Water and air are equally necessary both in the one and the other of these Productions, they naturally fall under the same Subject of Discourse.

The Vapors, being condensed and falling down in Rain on the Surface of the Earth, mix with the Salt-peter which the air has there

---

1   In older English usage, 'meteor' refers to anything in the near sky (e.g., clouds—hence, 'meteorology').

deposited, the different Salts, with which the bodies of Animals abound, Oil, Dung, Sweepings, and many different Compositions, which soak with the Water into the Earth through ten thousand different Drains and Fissures, sometimes steering their Course over Strata of Salt, sometimes over Beds of Sulfur, at one time passing through Mines of Iron, at another Layers of Vitriol, dissolving and carrying away parts of these Bodies as they pass along. These subterraneous Rivers, the Existence of which we before demonstrated, cast up on the Sides of their Channels greater or smaller Quantities of these inflammable Materials, which dry and incrustate in Layers one upon another as the Water lessens and falls away. The Composition being thus formed, the least Particle of Fire (brought thither by the Wind, or kindled by any other means, whether by Fermentation, which is very common betwixt Sulfurous and Mineral Bodies, or by some Mass of burning Sulfur in the subterraneous Caverns) inflames those particles of Oil which are contiguous to it, and those communicate it from one Train of sulfur to another. The Combustion being thus begun, the mineral Particles dissolve; the Air conveyed under Ground in its Vehicle of Water is dilated, and violently repels the Salt-peter, which is the most forcible and powerful of all the combustible Ingredients. Thus the Rarefaction of the Air, and the Projection of those Salts, with which it is impregnated, conspire to act with such amazing Vehemence and Fury that whenever they meet with any Resistance to obstruct their Passage, they make the very Earth to shake and tremble from the Center to the Surface, and overthrow whole Towns, and lay in Ruin whole Kingdoms. But Providence, which weighs both the Usefulness and dangerous Effects of these Tremendous forces, set Bounds to their Power by opening at Proper distances certain Volcanoes or Vent-Holes, through which the imprisoned Air and all those combustible Ingredients that kindle so dreadful a War in the Bowels of the Earth may discharge their Fury. By being dispersed in the open Air they lose Strength, which when united and collected in one Body acts with such irresistible Force on everything that opposes its way. So that we may see how these Volcanoes, which are looked upon as so many Plagues and Calamities in those Countries where they are, are appointed by God for their Safety and Preservation.

The Divine Design, even in those things which are seemingly hurtful: Wood Rot

But where is the Goodness, it may be objected, in having created so many hurtful Insects, those destructive Worms, for Example, which insensibly eat and consume the Sides of our Ships, the piles of our Dikes, and the Timber of our Houses?

These Worms, like all others, do by the Corruption of one thing contribute to the Generation of another, and serve to promote the general Circulation of the Commodities and Productions of different Countries, on which Commerce necessarily depends. So mean an Animal in Appearance as the Pipe-Worm, by usefully employing the vigilance of the Dutch, not only maintains but brings Riches to the inhabitants of Sweden and to those who live on the borders of the White Sea. Were they not under a perpetual Necessity of tarring and sometimes repairing their Vessels and Dikes at Amsterdam, in vain would the Muscovite and Norwegian barrel up the Pitch, which distills from their Pines; in vain would the Swedes cut down the Oaks and Lofty Fir-Trees that grow in their Forests. Thus does this little Animal, which we so much complain of as troublesome and injurious to us, become the very Cement which unites these distant Nations in one common Interest, and as some Insects are continually at work at Amsterdam for the Advantage of Stockholm and Archangel, so are there others in the North whose Labour is no less profitable to the Hollanders, inasmuch as they promote the Consumption of their Salt, Spices and other Grocery Wares, which are sent thither to season their Provisions, to preserve them from being corrupted by those Insects, and to cure their Fish, which they often use instead of Bread.

But let us not lose our Time and Labour in answering the Cavillings and Objections of those dissatisfied People, who are ever complaining and murmuring. To undertake a Defense of God's Conduct in the Government of the World is both unreasonable and unbecoming us, seeing his Providence does not stand in need of our Justifications. His Wisdom and Bounty are eminently conspicuous in all his Administrations, and the Difficulty we may sometimes meet with in discovering the particular End of some of his Works argues the Narrowness of our Understandings, not any Defect in his Goodness. The Prospect we have taken of Nature does in every part sufficiently prove that the Good of Man was the chief End proposed by Providence in the Works of the Creation, even in those very things which seem hurtful or offensive; and that what we call an Evil is oftentimes a real Good, and almost always designed to administer Occasion to the Exercise of Some Virtue which is more beneficial to us than a State of Indolence and Inaction. Every thing is calculated by Divine Wisdom to make us richer, wiser, or better; this is a Truth which does not want so much to be proved as attended to, and is the Sum and Substance of true Philosophy. In vain does our shallow Reason attempt to fathom the Mysteries of Nature, and to pry into the Secrets of the Almighty, whose *Judgments are unsearchable and his ways past finding out*; nay, the Eye of a little Worm is a Subject capable of exhausting all our boasted Speculations, an Abyss wherein we lose ourselves, whereas the Contemplation of the goodness and condescension of God, so visibly displayed in the Wonders of the Creation, cannot fail of making us both wiser and better; and though his Goodness be infinite as well as his Wisdom and Power, yet we can in some Measure keep Pace with this Attribute, by making returns of boundless Love and Gratitude. And indeed, God seems to have laid the highest Claim to this Tribute of Love by the Care he has taken to Manifest his goodness in the most open Manner, while at the same time he has concealed from us the most curious Particulars with Regard to the Structure and Essence of his Works; and to this our Ignorance of the Nature and Properties of Bodies it is owing that we sometimes look upon one thing as useless, and another as incompatible with Justice, whereas a thorough Sense and Persuasion of the Divine Goodness can alone satisfy all our Doubts, and resolve our Scruples. Some few Instances will illustrate my Meaning....

The Divine purpose in those things which seem unjust,
as eating the Flesh of Animals

The same goodness and Condescension will help us to clear up another Difficulty seemingly of greater Force, how to reconcile the Creation of Animals for Slaughter with the Justice of God. The Necessity of killing them is agreed upon by all, for the Earth would cease to be habitable were the Number of them not retained; but then it may be asked, is it agreeable to the Justice of God to have created them to be butchered?

To find Fault with this Order of Providence is to find Fault with the Hand that has enriched us, 'tis complaining that it has created Animals fit to clothe and feed us, and, in short, that it has provided for our Wants. An Ox is not only delicious Meat, but it is a living Banquet that moves from Place to Place, is sustained by its own Labour, and surrenders itself to be a Feast for Man, when he has Occasion for it. Thus does it become doubly serviceable to us. The Many Animals which we see all around us, and which serve either our Nourishment, our Clothing, or Ornament, only live and grow that they may more effectually answer these Ends of their Creation; for this purpose has Nature provided them with Teeth to eat, and Stomachs to digest their Meat; with Arms to defend themselves; with Wings, Feet, Fins & the better to preserve and subsist themselves in their respective ways of Life till Man has Occasion for them.

Objection

But it may happen that these Animals so nourishing and salutary may increase and multiply in too great Abundance, that the Number of them may exceed our Wants, or be greater than the Fruits of the Earth can sustain, so that their dead Bodies, by lying unburied above Ground, may infect the Air and Cause a Contagion.

Answered, from the being of Carnivorous Animals

All this was not only foreseen but provided against, Nature having sufficiently stocked both the external and internal Part of the Earth, and also the Waters, with Animals of Prey and of the carnivorous Kind, to prevent such like Inconveniences, the which may properly be stiled so many living Charnel-Houses or animated Sepulchres continually devouring whatever might be useless or hurtful to us. He, who created these Animals with such voracious Appetites did well foresee that their Services would sometimes exceed our desires, but he also knew that they were only proportionable to our Wants, for Man stands as much in need of being punished, or forewarned, as of having his immediate Wants supplied; nay, it is more for his good to be labourious, prudent and vigilant, than to live in a State of Indolence and careless Security.

The Souls of Beasts

There always have been some murmuring and dissatisfied People, who, instead of praising and thanking God, as they ought, for having made all nature subservient to their use, turn the Prerogative and Dignity with which man is honoured into matter of Complaint, calling his Right of Dominion over all other Animals Usurpation and Tyranny; nay, not content with degrading themselves, they preach up for the natural Rights of brute Beasts, and proceed so far as to allow them the Privilege of Reason, which is only peculiar to Man.[1]

We shall not have Recourse to the Philosophy of *Descartes* for Arguments to confute this unreasonable Supposition. To say that we have an absolute Right to dispose of all kinds of Animals as our Occasions require because they are mere Machines is to found a certain Right on uncertain Principles. Man is conscious to himself that he was born to inhabit the Earth, to cultivate it, and to enjoy the Benefit of its Productions, and the same natural Relations or Fitness of things that informs him of the Lawfulness of eating the Fruits of the Earth, does also instruct him how to use the Skins and Flesh of Animals. It is not necessary for him to philosophize on the Nature of these Things in order to make a right Use of them, any more than he is obliged to have a thorough Knowledge of the Body of the Sun before he ventures to walk by the Light of it, of the Properties and Formation of Stones before he uses them to build with, or of the Nature of Straw before he lays it on his Land to manure it. The Essences of things are concealed from us, but we are sufficiently acquainted with their Uses; and the great Care, which the sovereign Being has taken to proportion them to our Wants, and to keep up a constant Succession of them in our favour, is a sufficient Indication that he has commissioned us to use them.

Savagery in Animals

The Deity causes all these Animals to exhibit to Mankind the Appearance, either of an advantageous Prey, a formidable Foe, or some acquirable Conquest. He strengthens him by the Exercises of the Chase, and qualifies him for opposing a more dangerous Enemy, in any necessary Conjuncture. He habituates him, by an innocent Probation, to defend himself in the most effectual manner against a lawless Invader of his Property.

---

1 The extent of reason in beasts, and its comparison with human reason, is a classical topic that was well-considered in the Enlightenment, especially beginning with Montaigne's *Apology for Raymond Sebond* (1580). Descartes argued, in *Discourse on Method* (1637), that beasts lack the rational souls of men, and so, are merely complex machinery; Bayle's article "Rorarius" (1697) was another important addition to the discussion. Voltaire's writing strongly suggests a tendency toward promotion of animal rights, though Voltaire appears not to have been so radical as to have practiced vegetarianism, which he nonetheless applauded in his discussion of Hindu culture (see pp. 221, 232).

Were a Savage of *America* possess'd of a Watch, and had, by frequent Observations on the Movements, attained to a thorough Knowledge of the Action of the Wheels, the disposition and correspondence of the several Parts of it, and without knowing the Division of Time, or any Use of his Watch, he would in Reality be more ignorant with regard to all the Intents and Purposes of this Machine than a *European*, who knows how to inform himself by it of the Time and Hour of the Day, without having made any Observations on the Mechanism and Structure of it. Just so it is with him who has spent his Life in the Study of Natural History and taken no Pains to acquaint himself with the ends and Designs of Providence in the Economy of the New World. This Philosopher, notwithstanding all his Study and Learning, is more devoid of useful knowledge than the illiterate upright Man, who, without having made any curious Researches into the Laws of Motion, or the Particular Structure and Frame of the Universal System, sees enough to lead him to pay his constant Adorations and Thanks to that great and good Being, who created and sustains this wonderful Machine for his Use, and continues to shower down daily his Gifts and Blessings on Mankind.

We may, then, collect and treasure up Rarities from the four Quarters of the World, cast out the Number of the Stars, calculate the Motions of the Planets, and venture to foretell the Return of Comets; we may be able to dissect Insects with all imaginable Art, anatomize the Elements themselves, even trace Nature through all its curious *Phenomena*, and yet remain profoundly ignorant. The Whole system of Nature may very aptly be compared to a large Watch, the Springs and Movements of which are employed to teach us something more than is visibly represented by them; and therefore the Naturalist who spends his whole Time in barely observing the Play and Actions of these movements without carrying his Enquires farther is no better than our *American* Savage: he labours to find out what is not necessary for him to know and perhaps impossible for him to comprehend, and neglects the only main Point, which is to know what the Watch is good for.

What then shall we say of the Use and Design of Nature? Shall we compare it to a Looking Glass, which is made to represent something more than the Glass itself, or to an Enigma, which under remote Similitudes and Terms conceals some Meaning which we are glad to find out? This is the most inadequate idea we can frame of it. Both Reason and Religion conspire to engage our Attention to the language of the Heavens, of the Earth, and the Whole Universe, which with one common Voice proclaim the glory of God from one End of the Creation to the other; they clearly point out to us his invisible Perfections in the visible Operations of his Hands. The Prospect of Nature, then, is a kind of vulgar Theology, in which all Men may learn those Truths which it is of the highest Consequence and Importance for them to know.

The first Use which a great number of learned men have thought fit to make of natural Philosophy has been to prove the Existence of God; but however laudable the Design of these Men may seem, in being at the Pains to deduce from hence regular Demonstrations of his Being, yet I cannot help thinking such a Labour useless and unnecessary. Who ever thought it useful to draw out his Watch to prove there is such a Trade as Watchmaking? Who ever saw a beautiful Machine and doubted at the same time whether it was contrived from some skillful Artist?[1] There is no Occasion for any Force of Argument to show the necessary Connexion of these two Ideas, and were any Man to dispute whether my Watch had a maker, I should not think it worthwhile to convince him. The many Large Volumes which have been written to prove the Existence of God, of which every Reasonable Man is thoroughly convinced as of his own; the many Sermons and theological Lectures which are founded in some Countries to establish this Truth, which common sense will teach every Man—these are so many Discourses, in some sort, affronting to the Understanding of their Auditors and Readers, at best unprofitable and needless, seeing the Authors of them suppose there to be such Persons as Atheists when there are really none; or granting this, they are addressing the Reason of those who are resolved not to be convinced, and therefore undeserving of such a Compliment.

If the whole World is, as must be granted, one great Picture in which are displayed the Perfections of God, the Use of this Rep-

---

1 The following sections of Pluche's argument, and this sentence especially, provide anticipations of watchwork analogies that William Paley would develop in his proof for God's existence in *Physico Theology* (1802). The arguments to follow have their descendants in the recent and continuing argument that the design of the universe is tuned for the possibility of life (see John Barrow and Frank Tipler, *The Anthropic Cosmological Principle*, Oxford: Oxford UP, 1987).

resentation is not to prove that he is the Author of it, but to demonstrate his Unity, his Power, his Wisdom, his Independence, his goodness, and his Providence. It is, as it were, an agreeable School, where we need only open our Eyes and receive Instruction, and where Truth even prevents out Inquires by presenting itself to us in so visible and inviting a Dress that it cannot fail to charm its Beholders.

The Unity of God proved from the Union and Harmony of all the Parts of Nature

The Unity of that first Principle which created the Universe demonstrates itself to the Senses of all Men in the Harmony and Union which they cannot but see in all the Parts of Nature; in that one simple End to which it is directed; and in the Uniformity of those Means which conduce thereto.

Which way soever we direct our Observation, we discern either simple Elements or compound Bodies which have all different Actions and Offices. What the Fire inflames the water extinguishes, what one Wind freezes another thaws, and what the Sun dries the Rain moistens. But all these Operations and a thousand others so seemingly repugnant to each other do all concur in a wonderful Manner to produce one Effect. Some serve to assist, some to qualify and correct the Violence of others, and are all so necessarily useful to carry on the main Design, that, were the Agency of any one of these Causes destroyed, the Ruin of the whole, or at least an Interruption of the Order and Harmony of the Creation, would immediately ensue....

As all the Parts of Nature therefore were constituted for the mutual Service and Assistance of each other, so do they undeniably prove the Unity of their omniscient Creator. If one Almighty Being had created the Sun and another the Earth, then as the Views and Ends which they proposed by these Acts of Creation would be different, he that made the sun would not submit that so glorious a Body should be entirely subservient to the Use of the Earth, and consequently, they would be like the fabulous Deities in *Homer*, always at Variance. The Order and Government of the World do therefore necessarily suppose one only first Principle, who has established such a Correspondence between all the Parts of it, and made them so dependent on each other that the Annihilation or Subduction of any one of them would destroy the Beauty and Economy of the whole Machine, and superinduce an universal Disorder.

The Unity of God Proved from the general End of the
whole System of Nature

The same Truth receives still stronger Confirmation when we reflect on the general End to which all the Parts of Nature are directed. It could only be one and the same intelligent Being who has impressed upon them all the same Tendency and has used the Concurrence of so many different Causes and Actions to produce one Effect. In my earlier Letter to you on the Extent and Bounds of Reason, I believe I sufficiently convinced you that Man is the Center of all works of God, and that if we exclude him from the Creation, whatever Beauty and Comeliness is in the World would no longer serve to any beneficial Purpose. We proved in our subsequent Discourse that whatever is produced on the Surface of the Earth, or formed within the bowels of it, is for the use and Service of Man. The same beneficent Intention appears throughout the whole, and universally proclaims the unity of our common Benefactor.

6. From Voltaire, "Final Causes," *Philosophical Dictionary* (1764)[1]

Section III

It would appear that a man must be supposed to have lost his senses before he can deny that stomachs are made for digestion, eyes to see, and ears to hear.

On the other hand, a man must have a singular partiality for final causes, to assert that stone was made for building houses, and that silkworms are produced in China that we may wear satins in Europe.

But, it is urged, if God has evidently done one thing by design, he has then done all things by design. It is ridiculous to admit Providence in the one case and to deny it in the others. Everything that is done was foreseen, was arranged. There is no arrangement without an object, no effect without a cause; all, therefore, is equally the result, the product of the final cause; it is, therefore, as correct to say that noses were made to bear spectacles, and fingers to be adorned with rings, as to say that the ears were formed to hear sounds, the eyes to receive light.

---

1 From Voltaire, *Philosophical Dictionary*. In *The Works of Voltaire, A Contemporary Version*, trans. William F. Fleming (New York: E.R. DuMont, 1901). Vols. 3-7. Spellings have been modernized.

All that this objection amounts to, in my opinion, is that every-thing is the result, nearer or more remote, of a general final cause; that everything is the consequence of eternal laws. When the effects are invariably the same in all times and places, and when these uniform effects are independent of the beings to which they attach, then there is visibly a final cause.

All animals have eyes and see; all have ears and hear; all have mouths with which they eat; stomachs, or something similar, by which they digest their food; all have suitable means for expelling the feces; all have the organs requisite for the continuation of their species; and these natural gifts perform their regular course and process without any application or intermixture of art. Here are final causes clearly established; and to deny a truth so universal would be a perversion of the faculty of reason.

But stones, in all times and places, do not constitute the materials of buildings. All noses do not bear spectacles; all fingers do not carry a ring; all legs are not covered with silk stockings. A silkworm, therefore, is not made to cover my legs, exactly as your mouth is made for eating, and another part of your person for the "garderobe."[1] There are, therefore, we see, immediate effects produced from final causes, and effects of a very numerous description, which are remote productions from those causes.

Everything belonging to nature is uniform, immutable, and the immediate work of its author. It is he who has established the laws by which the moon contributes three-fourths to the cause of the flux and reflux of the ocean, and the sun the remaining fourth. It is he who has given a rotatory motion to the sun, in consequence of which that orb communicates its rays of light in the short space of seven minutes and a half to the eyes of men, crocodiles, and cats.

But if, after a course of ages, we started the inventions of shears and spits, to clip the wool of sheep with the one, and with the other to roast in order to eat them, what else can be inferred from such circumstances, but that God formed us in such a manner that, at some time or other, we could not avoid becoming ingenious and carnivorous?

Sheep, undoubtedly, were not made expressly to be roasted and eaten, since many nations abstain from such food with horror. Mankind are not created essentially to massacre one another, since the Brahmins, and the respectable primitives

---

1 "et votre derrière pour aller à la garderobe": and your behind for defecating.

called Quakers, kill no one. But the clay out of which we are kneaded frequently produces massacres, as it produces calumnies, vanities, persecutions, and impertinences. It is not precisely that the formation of man is the final cause of our madnesses and follies, for a final cause is universal, and invariable in every age and place; but the horrors and absurdities of the human race are not at all the less included in the eternal order of things. When we thresh our corn, the flail is the final cause of the separation of the grain. But if that flail, while threshing my grain, crushes to death a thousand insects, that occurs not by an express and determinate act of my will, nor, on the other hand, is it by mere chance; the insects were, on this occasion, actually under my flail, and could not but be there.

It is a consequence of the nature of things that a man should be ambitious; that he should enroll and discipline a number of other men; that he should be a conqueror, or that he should be defeated; but it can never be said that the man was created by God to be killed in war....

Appendix C: Humanistic Contexts

[The efforts of Pope, Leibniz, Pluche and others to reconcile the problem of evil in poetic, philosophical, and popular scientific writing set the context for one of Voltaire's last major essays, *We Must Take Sides*, composed in 1772 or 1773. Voltaire presents an extended argument concerning the nature of God, followed by a debate among representatives of different religious views, and a conclusion concerning right human action. Voltaire's suggestion that God is "a single, universal and powerful intelligence" is tempered by other claims that indicate an otherwise total ignorance of God, even of God's goodness. Voltaire argues that all in human affairs is not well, but that it is our responsibility to work to make the world the best place possible. Such a view is the essence of humanism. For a more comprehensive introduction to *We Must Take Sides*, see the closing paragraphs of section two of the introduction (pp. 27-29).

Does Voltaire believe that God is good? The final selection presents a different answer, in a colorful vignette by the eminent English writer James Boswell, relating his visit to Voltaire's home in 1764. Boswell finds Voltaire to be highly unorthodox and certainly not Christian, yet Voltaire's bold humanism is also tempered, perhaps sincerely, by a "love" of God, the "Authour of Goodness."]

1. From Voltaire, *We Must Take Sides, or, the Principle of Action* (1772)[1]

Introduction
It is not a question of taking sides between Russia and Turkey; for these States will, sooner or later, come to an understanding without my intervention.

It is not a question of declaring oneself in favour of one English faction and against another; for they will soon have disappeared, to make room for others.

---

1 First published 1772 as *Il Faut Prendre un Parti: Ou le Principe d'Action et de l'Eternité des Choses: Diatribe*. In *Toleration and Other Essays by Voltaire*. Translated, with an Introduction, by Joseph McCabe (New York: G.P. Putnam's Sons, 1912). Spellings have been modernized.

I am not endeavouring to choose between Greek and Armenian Christians, Eutychians and Jacobites, Christians who are called Papists and Lutherans, Calvinists, Anglicans, the primitive folk called Quakers, Anabaptists, Jansenists, Molinists, Socinians, Pietists, and so many other *ists*. I wish to live in peace with all these gentlemen, whenever I may meet them, and never dispute with them; because there is not a single one of them who, when he has a crown to share with me, will not know his business perfectly, or who would spend a single penny for the salvation of my soul or his own....

The subject I have in mind is but a trifle—namely, the question whether there is or is not a God; and I am going to examine it in all seriousness and good faith, because it interests me, and you also.

I. Of the principle of action
Everything is in motion, everything acts and reacts, in nature.

Our sun turns on its axis with a rapidity that astonishes us; other suns turn with the same speed, while countless swarms of planets revolve round them in their orbits, and the blood circulates more than twenty times an hour in the lowliest of our animals.

Everything, even death, is active. Corpses are decomposed, transformed into plants, and nourish the living, which in their turn are the food of others. What is the principle of this universal activity?

This principle must be unique. The unvarying uniformity of the laws which control the march of the heavenly bodies, the movements of our globe, every species and genus of animal, plant, and mineral, indicates that there is one mover.[1] If there were two, they would either differ, or be opposed to each other, or like each other. If they were different, there would be no harmony; if opposed, things would destroy each other; if like, it would be as if there were only one—a twofold employment.

I am encouraged in this belief that there can be but one principle, one single mover, when I observe the constant and uniform laws of the whole of nature.

---

1 'First mover' is a standard, minimally descriptive term in philosophy for a creator of the world, usually introduced in general *a priori* arguments. Voltaire will also use the term in more specific *a posteriori* argument, which infers God's nature from observation of the creation, as, for example, in the first paragraph of chapter two.

The same gravitation reaches every globe, and causes them to tend towards each other in direct proportion, not to their surfaces, which might be the effect of an impelling fluid, but to their masses.

The square of the revolution of every planet is as the cube of its distance from the sun (which proves, one may note, what Plato had somehow divined, that the world is the work of the eternal geometrician).

The rays of light are reflected and refracted from end to end of the universe. All the truths of mathematics must be the same on the star Sirius as in our little home....

Assuredly the oak and the nut have come to no agreement to be born and to grow in the same way, any more than Mars and Saturn have come to an understanding to observe the same laws. There is, therefore, a single, universal, and powerful intelligence, acting always by invariable laws.

No one doubts that an armillary sphere, landscapes, drawings of animals, or models in coloured wax, are the work of clever artists. Is it possible for the copyists to be intelligent and the originals not? This seems to me the strongest demonstration; I do not see how it can be assailed.

II. Of the necessary and eternal principle of action
This single mover is very powerful, since it directs so vast and complex a machine. It is very intelligent, since the smallest spring of this machine cannot be equaled by us, who are intelligent beings.

It is a necessary being, since without it the machine would not exist.

It is eternal, for it cannot be produced from nothing, which, being nothing, can produce nothing; given the existence of something, it is demonstrated that something has existed for all eternity. This sublime truth has become trivial. So great has been the advance of the human mind in our time, in spite of the efforts to brutalize us which the masters of ignorance have made for so many centuries.

III. What is this principle?
... Having therefore recognized from movement that there is a mover; having proved from action that there is a principle of action; I seek the nature of this universal principle. And the first thing I perceive, with secret distress but entire resignation, is that, being an imperceptible part of the great whole ... it will be impos-

sible for me to understand this great whole, which hems me in on every side, and its master.

Yet I am a little reassured on seeing that I am able to measure the distance of the stars, and to recognize the course and the laws which keep them in their orbits. I say to myself: Perhaps, if I use my reason in good faith, I may succeed in discovering some ray of probability to lighten me in the dark night of nature. And if this faint dawn which I seek does not come to me, I shall be consoled to think that my ignorance is invincible; that knowledge which is forbidden me is assuredly useless to me; and that the great Being will not punish me for having sought a knowledge of him and failed to obtain it.

IV. Where is the first principle? Is it infinite?

I do not see the first motive and intelligent principle of the animal called man, when he demonstrates a geometrical proposition or lifts a burden. Yet I feel irresistibly that there is one in him, however subordinate. I cannot discover whether this first principle is in his heart, or in his head, or in his blood, or in his whole body. In the same way I have detected a first principle in nature, and have seen that it must necessarily be eternal. But where is it?

If it animates all existence, it is in all existence: that seems to be beyond doubt. It is in all that exists, just as movement is in the whole body of an animal, if one may use so poor a comparison....

V. That all the works of the eternal being are eternal

The principle of nature being necessary and eternal, and its very essence being to act, it must have been always active. If it had not been an ever-active God, it would have been an eternally indolent God, the God of Epicurus, the God who is good for nothing.[1] This truth seems to me to be fully demonstrated.

Hence the world, his work, whatever form it assume, is, like

---

1 In the cosmology of Epicurus (341-270 BCE), atoms in the world move mechanically, according to laws. His analysis was intended to separate explanation of the natural order from all reference to Gods, who, if they exist at all, have no regard for human affairs. Voltaire's effort to link the "first principle" to a "single mover" that is "ever-active" suggests that he is attempting to introduce process into his metaphysics, using the term 'principle of action.' Voltaire appears to be reaching, with limited success, toward an account partly inspired by Leibniz, whose idea that entities contain the "seeds" of all of their own changes within themselves was developed into the theory of monads. See Leibniz, *Discourse on Metaphysics* (section eight onwards) and *Monadology*.

him, eternal; just as the light is as old as the sun, movement as old as matter, and food as old as the animals; otherwise the sun, matter, and the animals would be, not merely useless, but self-contradictory things, chimaeras.

What, indeed, could be more contradictory than an essentially active being that has been inactive during an eternity; a formative being that has fashioned nothing, or merely formed a few globes some years ago, without there being the least apparent reason for making them at one time rather than another? The intelligent principle can do nothing without reason; nothing can exist without an antecedent and necessary reason. This antecedent and necessary reason has existed eternally; therefore the universe is eternal.

We speak here a strictly philosophical language; it is not our part even to glance at those who use the language of revelation.

VI. That the eternal being, and first principle, has arranged all things voluntarily

It is clear that this supreme, necessary, active intelligence is possessed of will, and has arranged all things because it willed them. How can one act, and fashion all things, without willing to fashion them? That would be the action of a mere machine, and this machine would presuppose another first principle, another mover. We should always have to end in a first intelligent being of some kind or other. We wish, we act, we make machines, when we will; hence the great very powerful Demiourgos has done all things because he willed.[1]

Spinoza himself recognizes in nature an intelligent, necessary power.[2] But an intelligence without will would be an absurdity, since such an intelligence would be useless; it would do nothing, because it would not will to do anything. Hence the great necessary being has willed everything that it has done.

I said above that it has done all things necessarily because, if its works were not necessary, they would be useless. But does this

---

1   "Demiourgos" (demiurge) is the creator of the universe, and the word sometimes implies that a lesser god acts under the authority of a greater god (though apparently not in Voltaire's use here). Voltaire has used the expression "very powerful" and has not elected to write "omnipotent"; he may have employed the expression "demiourgos" to underscore the suggestion of possible limits to God's power.

2   Benedictus de Spinoza (1632-77), in his *Ethics*, linked God's activity so closely to nature's workings that some found the two indistinguishable in his writing, and so considered his view to be atheism.

necessity deprive it of will? Certainly not. I necessarily will to be happy, but I will it none the less on that account; on the contrary, I will it all the more strongly because I will it irresistibly.

Does this necessity deprive it of liberty? Not at all. Liberty can only be the power to act. Since the supreme being is very powerful, it is the freest of beings.

We thus recognize that the great artisan of things is necessary, eternal, intelligent, powerful, possessed of will, and free....

IX. Of the principle of action in sentient beings

There comes at length a time when a greater or smaller number of perceptions, received in our mechanism, seem to present themselves to our will. We think that we are forming ideas. It is as if, when we turn the tap of a fountain, we were to think that we cause the water which streams out. We create ideas, poor creatures that we are! It is evident that we had no share in the former, yet we would regard ourselves as the authors of the latter. If we reflect well on this vain boast of forming ideas, we shall see that it is insolent and absurd.

Let us remember that there is nothing in external objects with the least analogy, the least relation, to a feeling, an idea, a thought. Let an eye or an ear be made by the best artisan in the world; the eye will see nothing, the ear will hear nothing. It is the same with our living body. The universal principle of action does everything in us. He has not made us an exception to the rest of nature....

X. Of the principle of action called the soul

But, some centuries later in the history of man, it came to be imagined that we have a soul which acts of itself; and the idea has become so familiar that we take it for a reality.

We talk incessantly of "the soul," though we have not the least idea of the meaning of it.

To some the soul means the life; to others it is a small, frail image of ourselves, which goes, when we die, to drink the waters of Acheron; to others it is a harmony, a memory, an entelechy.[1]

1　In Homer's *Odyssey*, Odysseus meets the souls or shadows of the dead at the Acheron river, linked to the river Styx (Book 10). This and many other theories of the soul that Voltaire notes are discussed in Plato's *Phaedo*. 'Entelechy' is a technical term in Aristotle, later adapted in Leibniz, intended to classify those things that are complete in themselves, or develop according to their own nature (such as the growth of a plant from seed).

In the end it has been converted into a little being that is not body, a breath that is not air; and of this word "breath," which corresponds to "spirit" in many tongues, a kind of thing has been made which is nothing at all.

Who can fail to see that men uttered, and still utter, the word "soul" vaguely and without understanding, as we utter the words "movement," "understanding," "imagination," "memory," "desire," and "will"? There is no real being which we call will, desire, memory, imagination, understanding, or movement; but the real being called man understands, imagines, remembers, desires, wills, and moves. They are abstract terms, invented for convenience of speech. I run, I sleep, I awake; but there is no such physical reality as running, sleep, or awakening. Neither sight, nor hearing, nor touch, nor smell, nor taste, is a real being; I hear, I see, I smell, I taste, I touch. And how could I do this if the great being had not so disposed all things; if the principle of action, the universal cause—in one word, God—had not given us these faculties?

We may be quite sure that there would be just as much reason to grant the snail a hidden being called a "free soul" as to grant it to man. The snail has a will, desires, tastes, sensations, ideas, and memory. It wishes to move towards the material of its food or the object of its love. It remembers it, has an idea of it, advances towards it as quickly as it can; it knows pleasure and pain. Yet you are not terrified when you are told that the animal has not a spiritual soul; that God has bestowed on it these gifts for a little time; that he who moves the stars moves also the insect. But when it comes to man you change your mind. This poor animal seems to you so worthy of your respect—that is to say, you are so proud—that you venture to place in its frail body something that seems to share the nature of God himself, yet something that seems to you at times diabolical in the perversity of its thoughts; something wise and foolish, good and execrable, heavenly and infernal, invisible, immortal, incomprehensible. And you have familiarized yourself with this idea, as you have grown accustomed to speak of movement, though there is no such being as movement; as you use abstract words, though there are no abstract beings.

XI. Examination of the principle of action called the soul
There is, nevertheless, a principle of action in man. Yes, there is one everywhere. But can this principle be anything else than a spring, a secret first mover which is developed by the ever-active first principle—a principle that is as powerful as it is secret, as

demonstrable as it is invisible, which we have recognized as the essential cause in the whole of nature?

If you create movement or ideas because you will it, you are God for the time being; for you have all the attributes of God—will, power, and creation. Consider the absurdity into which you fall in making yourself God.

You have to choose between these two alternatives: either to be God whenever you will, or to depend continually on God. The first is extravagant; the second alone is reasonable.

If there were in our body a little god called "the free soul," which becomes so frequently a little devil, this little god would have to be regarded either as having been created from all eternity, or as created at the moment of your conception, or during your embryonic life, or at birth, or when you begin to feel. All these positions are equally ridiculous.

A little subordinate god, existing uselessly during a past eternity and descending into a body that often dies at birth, is the height of absurdity.

If this little god-soul is supposed to be created at the moment of conception, we must consider the master of nature, the being of beings, continually occupied in watching assignations, attentive to every intercourse of man and woman, ever ready to despatch a sentient and thinking soul into a recess between the entrails. A fine lodging for a little god! When the mother brings forth a still-born child, what becomes of the god-soul that had been lodged in the abdomen? Whither has it returned?

The same difficulties and absurdities, equally ridiculous and revolting, are found in connection with each of the other suppositions. The idea of a soul, as it is usually and thoughtlessly conceived by people, is one of the most foolish things that has ever been devised.

How much more reasonable, more decent, more respectful to the supreme being, more in harmony with our nature, and therefore truer, is it not to say:

"We are machines made successively by the eternal geometrician; machines made like all the other animals, having the same organs, the same needs, the same pleasures, the same pains; far superior to all of them in many things, inferior to them in others; having received from the great being a principle of action which we cannot penetrate; receiving everything, giving ourselves nothing; and a million times more subject to him than the clay is to the potter who moulds it"?

Once more, either man is a god or he is precisely as I have described him....

XIII. Of the Liberty of Man, and of Destiny

A ball that drives another, a hunting-dog that necessarily and voluntarily follows a stag, a stag that leaps a great ditch not less necessarily and voluntarily, a roe that gives birth to another roe, which will bring a third into the world—these things are not more irresistibly determined than we are to do all that we do. Let us remember always how inconsistent and absurd it would be for one set of things to be arranged and the other not.

Every present event is born of the past, and is father of the future; otherwise the universe would be quite other than it is, as Leibniz has well said, more correct in this than in his pre-established harmony. The eternal chain can be neither broken nor entangled. The great being who necessarily sustains it cannot let it hang uncertainly, nor change it; for he would then no longer be the necessary and immutable being, the being of beings; he would be frail, inconstant, capricious; he would belie his nature, and exist no longer.

Hence, an inevitable destiny is the law of nature, as the whole of antiquity felt. The dread of depriving man of some false liberty, robbing virtue of its merit, and relieving crime of its horror, has at times alarmed tender souls; but as soon as they were enlightened they returned to this great truth, that all things are enchained and necessary.

Man is free, we repeat, when he can do what he wills to do; but he is not free to will; it is impossible that he should will without cause. If this cause is not infallibly followed by its effect, it is no cause. It would not be more absurd for a cloud to say to the wind: "I do not wish to be driven by you." This truth can never injure morality. Vice is always vice, as disease is always disease. It will always be necessary to repress the wicked; if they are determined to evil, we must reply that they are equally predestined to chastisement....

XV. Of evil and, in the first place, the destruction of beasts

We have never had any idea of good and evil, save in relation to ourselves. The sufferings of an animal seem to us evils, because, being animals ourselves, we feel that we should excite compassion if the same were done to us. We should have the same feeling for a tree if we were told that it suffered torment when it was cut; and for a stone if we learned that it suffers when it is dressed. But we should pity the tree and the stone much less than the animal, because they are less like us. Indeed, we soon cease to be touched by the awful destiny of the beasts that are intended for our table.

Children who weep at the death of the first chicken they see killed laugh at the death of the second.

It is only too sure that the disgusting carnage of our butcheries and kitchens does not seem to us an evil. On the contrary, we regard this horror, pestilential as it often is, as a blessing of the Lord; and we still have prayers in which we thank him for these murders. Yet what can be more abominable than to feed constantly on corpses?

Not only do we spend our lives in killing, and devouring what we have killed, but all the animals slaughter each other; they are impelled to do so by an invincible instinct. From the smallest insects to the rhinoceros and the elephant, the earth is but a vast battle-field, a world of carnage and destruction. There is no animal that has not its prey, and that, to capture it, does not employ some means equivalent to the ruse and rage with which the detestable spider entraps and devours the innocent fly. A flock of sheep devours in an hour, as it crops the grass, more insects than there are men on the earth.

What is still more cruel is that in this horrible scene of reiterated murder we perceive an evident design to perpetuate all species by means of the bloody corpses of their mutual enemies. The victims do not expire until nature has carefully provided for new representatives of the species. Everything is born again to be murdered.

Yet I observe no moralist among us, nor any of our fluent preachers or boasters, who has ever reflected in the least on this frightful habit, which has become part of our nature. We have to go back to the pious Porphyry and the sympathetic Pythagoreans to find those who would shame us for our bloody gluttony; or we must travel to the land of the Brahmins.[1] Our monks, the caprice of whose founders has bade them renounce the flesh, are murderers of soles and turbots, if not of partridges and quails. Neither among the monks, nor in the Council of Trent, nor in the assemblies of the clergy, nor in our academies, has this universal butchery ever been pronounced an evil. There has been no more thought given to it in the councils of the clergy than in our public-houses.

Hence the great being is justified of these butcheries in our eyes; or, indeed, we are his accomplices.

---

1 Porphyry (233-309) wrote in support of vegetarianism, and vegetarianism was also linked to Pythagorean practices of living in ancient Greece, as well as Hindu practices, up to the present.

XVI. Of evil in the animal called man

So much for the beasts; let us come to man. If it be not an evil that the only being on earth that knows God by his thoughts should be unhappy in his thoughts; if it be not an evil that this worshipper of the Deity should be almost always unjust and suffering, should know virtue and commit crime, should so often deceive and be deceived, and be the victim or the executioner of his fellows, etc.; if all that be not a frightful evil, I know not where evil is to be found.

Beasts and men suffer almost without ceasing; men suffer the more because, not only is the gift of thought often a source of torture, but this faculty of thinking always makes them fear death, which the beast cannot foresee. Man is a very miserable being, having but a few hours of rest, a few moments of satisfaction, and a long series of days of sorrow in his short life. Everybody admits and says this; and it is true.

They who have protested that all is well are charlatans. Shaftesbury,[1] who set the fashion in this, was a most unhappy man. I have seen Bolingbroke torn with grief and rage;[2] and Pope, whom he induced to put this miserable joke into verse, was one of the most pitiable men I have ever known, misshapen in body, unbalanced in temperament, always ill and a burden to himself, harassed by a hundred enemies until his last moment.[3] At least let us have happy beings saying that all is well....

---

1 Anthony Ashley Cooper, Third Earl of Shaftesbury (1671-1713), was a moral philosopher who Voltaire often credits as the first in a series of three English philosophical optimists that includes Lord Henry St. John, First Viscount Bolingbroke (1678-1751), and Alexander Pope (1688-1744). Pope learned from the other two and Voltaire alludes in the next sentence to Pope's dedication of his *Essay on Man* to Bolingbroke.

2 Contemporary reports suggest that Voltaire's estimation of Shaftesbury's and Bolingbroke's general happiness is misleading, and perhaps deliberately so. Voltaire did not know Shaftesbury, but he knew Bolingbroke from early in his own life and reported being highly impressed by Bolingbroke's good nature. Voltaire to Thieriot, 4 December 1722, in Besterman, ed., *The Complete Works of Voltaire* (Oxford: Voltaire Foundation, 1972).

3 Voltaire met Alexander Pope during his trip to England (1726-28) and he remained impressed throughout his life by Pope's poetry, though not by his philosophy. A disease left Pope with a hunchback from his youth, which explains Voltaire's estimation of him as "misshapen." On this particular subject and others Pope may rightly have been considered very testy and he was a very bad enemy to have, particularly due to his sharp satirical wit and its copious expression in published writing such as the *Dunciad* (1728). In this respect, Pope was much like Voltaire.

Say the word, if you dare, in connection with Alexander VI and Julius II;[1] say it over the ruins of a hundred towns that have been swallowed up by earthquakes, and amid the twelve millions of Americans who are being assassinated, in twelve million ways, to punish them for not being able to understand in Latin a papal bull that the monks have read to them. Say it today, the 24th of August, 1772; a day on which the pen trembles in my fingers, the two-hundredth anniversary of the massacre of St. Bartholomew.[2] Pass from these innumerable theatres of carnage to the equally unnumbered retreats of sorrow that cover the earth, to that swarm of diseases which slowly devour so many poor wretches while they yet live; think of that frightful ravage of nature which poisons the human race in its source, and associates the most abominable of plagues with the most necessary of pleasures.... To complete this true and horrible picture, fancy yourself amid the floods and volcanoes that have so often devastated so many parts of the world; amid the leprosy and the plague that have swept it. And do, you who read this, recall all that you have suffered, admit that evil exists, and do not add to so many miseries and horrors the wild absurdity of denying them.

XVII. Romances invented to explain evil
Of a hundred peoples who have sought the cause of physical and moral evil, the Hindus are the first whose romantic imaginations are known to us. They are sublime, if the word "sublime" be taken to mean "high." Evil, according to the ancient Brahmins, comes of a quarrel that once took place in the highest heavens, between the faithful and the jealous angels. The rebels were cast out of heaven into Ondera for millions of ages. But the great being pardoned them at the end of a few thousand years; they were turned into men, and they brought

---

1   Roderic Borgia (1431-1503), who became Pope Alexander VI, is frequently considered the most corrupt Pope in history; his violent reign was followed by that of the "Warrior Pope," Julius II (Giuliano della Rovere, 1443-1521).

2   The St. Bartholomew's day massacre began as an assassination plot advanced by Catherine de' Medici against prominent French Protestants gathered in Paris for her wedding to Henri of Navarre (later King Henri IV). The massacre spread uncontrolled throughout France, leading to the death of perhaps as many as thirty thousand Protestants over the course of several months.

upon the earth the evil that they had engendered in the empyraean. We have elsewhere described at length this ancient fable, the source of all fables.[1]

It was finely imitated by gifted nations, and grossly reproduced by barbarians. Nothing, indeed, is more spiritual and agreeable than the story of Pandora and her box. If Hesiod has had the merit of inventing this allegory, I think it as superior to Homer as Homer is to Lycophron.[2]

This box of Pandora, containing all the evils that have issued from it, seems to have all the charm of the most striking and delicate allusions. Nothing is more enchanting than this origin of our sufferings. But there is something still more admirable in the story of Pandora. It has a very high merit, which seems to have escaped notice: it is that no one was ever commanded to believe it.

XVIII. Of the same romances, imitated by barbaric nations

... The Syrians ... told that man and woman, having been created in heaven, desired one day to eat a certain cake; and that they then asked an angel to show them the place of retirement. The angel pointed to the earth. They went thither; and God, to punish them for their gluttony, left them there. Let us also leave them there, and their dinner and their ass and their serpent. These inconceivable puerilities of ancient Syria are not worth a moment's notice. The detestable fables of an obscure people should be excluded from a serious discussion.[3]

Let us return from these miserable legends to the great saying of Epicurus, which has so long alarmed the whole earth, and to which there is no answer but a sigh: "Either God wished to

---

1 Voltaire relies here on scholarship concerning what is now considered a text of doubtful authenticity (the *Shasta*). Such a story of the fall of angels that parallels Jude 1:6 and other biblical passages is not likely to have been present in the Hindu literature. See Daniel S. Hawley, "L'Inde de Voltaire," *Studies on Voltaire and the Eighteenth Century*, vol. 120, pp. 139-78.

2 Pandora's story may be found in Hesiod, *Works and Days*. Lycophron (*fl.* 285 BCE) earned the title "Lycophron the obscure" for his poem *Alexandria*.

3 Voltaire is again drawing on historical scholarship that is difficult to trace, to argue that Genesis 3 has historical origins. See footnote 16 to "Bien, Tout Est," in the *Dictionnaire Philosophique*, vol. 35, p. 423 of *The Complete Works of Voltaire* (Oxford: Voltaire Foundation, 1968-present).

prevent evil and could not do so; or he was able to do so, and did not wish."[1]

A thousand bachelors and doctors of divinity have fired the arrows of the school at this unshakeable rock; in this terrible shelter have the Atheists taken refuge. Yet the Atheist must admit that there is in nature an active, intelligent, necessary, eternal principle, and that from this principle comes all that we call good and evil. Let us discuss the point with the Atheist.

XIX. Discourse of an Atheist on all this

An Atheist says to me: It has been proven, I admit, that there is an eternal and necessary principle. But from the fact that it is necessary I infer that all that is derived from it is necessary; you have been compelled to admit this yourself. Since everything is necessary, evil is as inevitable as good. The great wheel of the ever-turning machine crushes all that comes in its way. I have no need of an intelligent being who can do nothing of himself, and who is as much a slave to his destiny as I am to mine. If he existed, I should have too much with which to reproach him. I should be obliged to call him either feeble or wicked. I would rather deny his existence than be discourteous to him. Let us get through this miserable life as well as we can, without reference to a fantastic being whom no one has ever seen, and to whom it would matter little, if he existed, whether we believed in him or not. What I think of him can no more affect him, supposing that he exists, than what he thinks of me, of which I am ignorant, affects me. There is no relation, no connection, no interest between him and me. Either there is no such being or he is an utter stranger to me. Let us do as nine hundred and ninety-nine mortals out of a thousand do; they work, generate, eat, drink, sleep, suffer, and die, without speaking of metaphysics, or knowing that there is such a thing.

XX. Discourse of a Manichaean

A Manichaean, hearing the Atheist, says to him: You are mistaken. Not only is there a God, but there are necessarily two. It has been fully proved that the universe is arranged intelligently,

---

1 The formulation of the problem of evil that is traditionally attributed to Epicurus (341-270 BCE) has not been found in writing earlier than its statement by a much later thinker, Lactantius (240-*ca.* 320 CE). The full argument is quoted in the article "Paulicians" in Pierre Bayle's *Historical and Critical Dictionary* and is reproduced in the introduction to Appendix B (p. 175).

and there is an intelligent principle in nature; but it is impossible that this intelligent principle, which is the author of good, should also be the author of evil. Evil must have its own God. Zoroaster was the first to proclaim this great truth, about two thousand years ago; and two other Zoroasters came afterwards to confirm it.[1] The Parsis have always followed, and still follow, this excellent doctrine. Some wretched people or other, called the Jews, at that time in bondage to us, learned a little of our science, together with the names of Satan and Knatbul. They recognized God and the devil; and the devil was so powerful, in the opinion of this poor little people, that one day, when God had descended into their country, the devil took him up into a mountain.[2] Admit two gods, therefore; the world is large enough to hold them and find sufficient work for them.

XXI. Discourse of a Pagan

Then a Pagan arose, and said: If we are to admit two gods, I do not see what prevents us from worshipping a thousand. The Greeks and Romans, who were superior to you, were polytheists. It will be necessary some day to return to the admirable doctrine that peoples the universe with genies and deities; it is assuredly the only system which explains everything—the only one in which there is no contradiction. If your wife betrays you, Venus is the cause of it. If you are robbed, put the blame on Mercury. If you lose an arm or a leg in battle, it was arranged by Mars. So much for the evil. In regard to the good, not only do Apollo, Ceres, Pomona, Bacchus, and Flora load you with presents, but occasionally the same Mars will rid you of your enemies, the same Venus will find you mistresses, the same Mercury may pour

---

1   Zoroaster (*ca.* 1000 BCE) was a Persian prophet who provided the root idea of Manichaeism, that this world is the field of battle for two Gods, Ormuzd (also called Ahura Mazda) and Ahriman (Angra Mainyu). Mani (216-274 CE) is often considered the partially Christian origin of Christian versions of this dualism, which had a later great leader in the founder of the Paulician sect of Christianity, Constantine-Silvanus (*fl.* 657). The migration of a Zoroastrian community to India, probably after the beginning of the eighth century, marked the origin of the Parsis.

2   The passage mentioned is Matthew 4:8. Voltaire's reference to Knatbul as an alias of Satan appears to be a confusion he gained while reading a biblical commentator: see footnote 8 to "Carême," p. 435 in the *Dictionnaire Philosophique*, vol. 35 of *The Complete Works of Voltaire* (Oxford: Voltaire Foundation, 1968-present).

all your neighbours' gold into your coffers, provided your hand comes to the assistance of his wand.

It was much easier for these gods to agree in governing the universe than it seems to be to this Manichaean to reconcile his Ormuzd, the benevolent, and Ahriman, the malevolent, two mortal enemies, so as to maintain both light and darkness. Many eyes see better than one. Hence all the poets of antiquity are continually calling councils of the gods. How can you suppose that one god is enough to see to all the details of life on Saturn and all the business of the star Capella? What! You imagine that everything on our globe, except in the houses of the King of Prussia and the Pope Ganganelli, is regulated by councils, and there is no council in heaven! There is no better way of deciding things than by a majority of votes. The deity always acts in the wisest way....

But he confides to the subordinate gods the care of the stars, the elements, the seas, and the bowels of the earth. His wife, who represents the expanse of space that he fills, is Juno. His daughter, who is eternal wisdom, his word, is Minerva. His other daughter, Venus, is the lover of the poetical generation. She is the mother of love, inflaming all sensitive beings, uniting them, reproducing by the attraction of pleasure all that necessity devotes to death. All the gods have made presents to mortals. Ceres has given them corn, Bacchus the vine, Pomona fruit; Apollo and Mercury have taught them the arts....

But everything becomes corrupt in time. Religion changed. The splendid name of Son of God—that is to say, just and benevolent—was afterwards given to the most unjust and cruel of men, because they were powerful. The ancient piety, which was humane, was displaced by superstition, which is always cruel. Virtue had dwelt on the earth as long as the fathers of families were the only priests, and offered to Jupiter and the immortal gods the first of their fruits and flowers; but all this was changed when the priests began to shed blood and wanted to share with the gods. They did share, in truth; they took the offerings, and left the smoke to the gods. You know how our enemies succeeded in crushing us, adopting our earlier morals, rejecting our bloody sacrifices, calling men to the Church, making a party for themselves among the poor until such time as they should capture the rich. They took our place. We are annihilated, they triumph; but, corrupted at length like ourselves, they need a great reform, which I wish them with all my heart.

XXII. Discourse of a Jew

Take no notice of this idolatrous Pagan who would turn God into a Dutch president, and offer us subordinate gods like members of parliament.

My religion, being above nature, can have no resemblance to others.

The first difference between them and us is that the source of our religion was hidden for a very long time from the rest of the earth. The dogmas of our fathers were buried, like ourselves, in a little country about a hundred and fifty miles long and sixty in width. In this well dwelt the truth that was unknown to the whole world, until certain rebels, going forth from among us, took from it the name of "truth" in the reigns of Tiberius, Caligula, Claudius, and Nero; and presently boasted that they were establishing a new truth.[1] ...

God, the creator of all men, is not the father of all men, but of one family alone. This family, always wandering, left the fertile land of Chaldaea to wander for some time in the neighbourhood of Sodom; from this journey it acquired an incontestable right to the city of Jerusalem, which was not yet in existence.[2]

Our family increases at such a rate that seventy men produce, at the end of two hundred and fifty years, six hundred and thirty thousand men bearing arms; counting the women, children, and old men, that amounts to about three millions. These three millions live in a small canton of Egypt which cannot maintain twenty thousand people. For their advantage God puts to death in one night all the first-born of the Egyptians; and, after this massacre, instead of giving Egypt to his people, God puts himself at their head to fly with them dry-foot across the sea, and cause a whole generation of Jews to die in the desert.[3]

We have seven times been in slavery in spite of the appalling miracles that God works for us every day, causing the moon to

---

1 That is, Christians.

2 Chaldaea is the homeland of Abraham, whose father began the migration to Canaan (Genesis 11:27-32). On Sodom, see Genesis 12:14; on the right to Jerusalem, see Genesis 22:14.

3 This paragraph primarily concerns the story of Exodus, and mentions the wanderings in the desert characterized in the following three books of the Tanak (Leviticus, Numbers, Deuteronomy). Voltaire appears to have the timespan reduced by 180 years (Exodus 12:40, though see an even briefer span of four generations stated in Genesis 15:16). On the population count, see Exodus 1:5 and 12:37; on the death of firstborn males and the flight from Egypt, see Exodus 12 and Numbers 14:16-23.

stand still in midday, and also the sun. Ten out of twelve of our tribes perished for ever. The other two are scattered and in misery.[1] ...

Unhappily, we were not well known to other nations until we were nearly annihilated. It was our enemies, the Christians, who made us known when they despoiled us. They built up their system with material taken from a bad Greek translation of our Bible. They insult and oppress us to this day; but our turn will come. It is well known how we will triumph at the end of the world, when there will be no one left on the earth.

XXIII. Discourse of a Turk
When the Jew had finished, a Turk, who had smoked throughout the meeting, washed his mouth, recited the formula "Allah Illah," and said to me:[2] ...

The miracles of Muhammad were victories. God has shown that he was a favourite by subjecting half our hemisphere to him. He was not unknown [to Europe] for two whole centuries. He triumphed as soon as he was persecuted.

His religion is wise, severe, chaste, and humane. Wise, because it knows not the folly of giving God associates, and it has no mysteries; severe, because it prohibits games of chance, and wine, and strong drinks, and orders prayer five times a day; chaste, because it reduces to four the prodigious number of spouses who shared the bed of all oriental princes; humane, because it imposes on us almsgiving more rigorously than the journey to Mecca.[3]

Add tolerance to all these marks of truth. Reflect that we have in the city of Istanbul alone more than a hundred thousand Christians of all sects, who carry out all the ceremonies of their cults in peace, and live so happily under the shelter of our laws that they never deign to visit you, while you crowd to our imperial gate.

---

1 The stopping of sun and moon are found at Joshua 10:12-13. The fall of Samaria to the Assyrians in 722 BCE led to the subjugation of Israel, and the dispersion of all the tribes except those of the southern kingdom, Judah and Benjamin (2 Kings 17).
2 "La Ilaha Ill Allah ..." is the first half of the Shahada, the Islamic profession of monotheistic faith: "There is no god but God ..."
3 Voltaire has added the upper limit of four wives (Qur'an 4:3) and the prohibition of gambling and alcohol (2:219) to four of the five pillars of Islam (profession of faith, prayer, fasting, pilgrimage, charity).

XXIV. Discourse of a Theist

A Theist then asked permission to speak, and said:

Everyone has his own opinion, good or bad. I should be sorry to distress any good man. First, I ask pardon of the Atheist; but it seems to me that, compelled as he is to admit an excellent design in the order of the universe, he is bound to admit an intelligence that has conceived and carried out this design. It is enough, it seems to me, that, when the Atheist lights a candle, he admits that it is for the purpose of giving light. It seems to me that he should also grant that the sun was made to illumine our part of the universe. We must not dispute about such probable matters.

The Atheist should yield the more graciously since, being a good man, he has nothing to fear from a master who has no interest in injuring him. He may quite safely admit a God; he will not pay a penny the more in taxes, and will not live less comfortably.

As to you, my pagan friend ... I confess that I see no impossibility in the existence of several beings far superior to us, each of whom would superintend some heavenly body. Indeed, it would give me some pleasure to prefer your Naiads, Dryads, Sylvans, Graces, and Loves to St. Fiacre, St. Pancratius, Sts. Crepin and Crepinien, St. Vitus, St. Cunegonde, or St. Marjolaine. But, really, one must not multiply things without need; and as a single intelligence suffices for the regulation of the world, I will stop at that until other powers show me that they share its rule.

As to you, my Manichaean friend, you seem to me a duellist, very fond of fighting. I am a peaceful man, and do not like to find myself between two rivals who are ever at war. Your Ormuzd is enough for me; you can keep your Ahriman.

I shall always be somewhat embarrassed in regard to the origin of evil; but I suppose that the good Ormuzd, who made everything, could not do better. I cannot offend him if I say to him: You have done all that a powerful, wise, and good being could do. It is not your fault if your works cannot be as good and perfect as yourself. Imperfection is one of the essential differences between you and your creatures. You could not make gods; it was necessary that, since men possessed reason, they should display folly, just as there must be friction in every machine. Each man has his dose of imperfection and folly, from the very fact that you are perfect and wise. He must not be always happy, because you are always happy. It seems to me that a collection of muscles, nerves, and veins cannot last more than eighty or a hundred years at the most, and that you must be for ever. It seems to me impossible that an animal, necessarily compacted of desires and wills, should not at times wish to serve his own purpose by doing evil to his neighbour. You only never do evil. Lastly, there is necessarily so great a distance between you and your works that the good is in you, and the evil must be in them.

As for me, imperfect as I am, I thank you for giving me a short span of existence, and especially for not having made me a professor of theology.

That is not at all a bad compliment. God could not be angry with me, seeing that I do not wish to displease him. In fine, I feel that, if I do no evil to my brethren and respect my master, I shall have nothing to fear, either from Ahriman, or Cerberus and the Furies, or Satan, or Knatbul, or St. Fiacre and St. Crepin; and I shall end my days in peace and the pursuit of philosophy.

I come now to you, Mr. Abrabanel and Mr. Benjamin.[1] You seem to me to be the maddest of the lot. The Kaffirs, Hottentots, and blacks of New Guinea are more reasonable and decent beings than your Jewish ancestors were. You have surpassed all nations in exorbitant legends, bad conduct, and barbarism. You are paying for it; it is your destiny. The Roman Empire has fallen; the Parsis, your former masters, are scattered. The Armenians sell rags, and occupy a low position in the whole of Asia. There is no trace left of the ancient Egyptians. Why should you be a power?

As to you, my Turkish friend, I advise you to come to terms as soon as possible with the Empress of Russia, if you wish to keep what you have usurped in Europe.[2] I am willing to believe that the victories of Muhammad, son of Abdala, were miracles; but Catherine II also works miracles. Take care that she does not some day perform the miracle of sending you back to the deserts from which you came. In particular, continue to be tolerant; it is the true way to please the being of beings, who is alike the father of Turks and Russians, Chinese and Japanese, black and yellow man, and of the whole of nature.

---

1 Benjamin of Tudela (*fl.* 1165) Isaac Abravanel (1437-1508), and Uriel Dacosta (*ca.* 1585-1640) (who is also mentioned in Voltaire's text, but is left out by the translator), were a traveller, a financier, and a failed reformer of Jewish religious practice, respectively. Their backgrounds and influences are diverse, so perhaps Voltaire names them simply as representatives of intellectual Jewry.

2 Russia, under Catherine II (1762-96), and the Ottoman Empire, under Sultan Mustafa III (1757-74), were engaged in a war that began in 1768 and would conclude in Russia's favor in 1774.

XXV. Discourse of a citizen

When the Theist had spoken, a man arose and said: I am a citizen, and therefore the friend of all these gentlemen. I will not dispute with any of them. I wish only to see them all united in the design of aiding and loving each other, in making each other happy, in so far as men of such different opinions can love each other, and contribute to each other's happiness, which is as diffi-cult as it is necessary.

To attain this end, I advise them first to cast in the fire all the controversial books which come their way, especially those of the Jesuits; and also the ecclesiastical gazette, and all other pamphlets which are but the fuel of the civil war of fools.

Next, each of our brethren, whether Theist, Turk, Pagan, Greek Christian, Latin Christian, Anglican, Scandinavian, Jew, or Atheist, will read attentively several pages of Cicero's *De Officiis*, or of Montaigne, and some of La Fontaine's *Fables*.[1]

The reading of these works insensibly disposes men to that concord which theologians have hitherto held in horror. Their minds being thus prepared, every time that a Christian and a Muslim meet an Atheist they will say to him: "Dear brother, may heaven enlighten you"; and the Atheist will reply: "When I am converted I shall come and thank you."

The Theist will give two kisses to the Manichaean woman in honour of the two principles. The Greek and Roman woman will give three to each member of the other sects, even the Quakers and Jansenists. The Socinians need only embrace once, seeing that those gentlemen believe there is only one person in God; but this embrace will be equal to three when it is performed in good faith....

These preliminaries being settled, if any quarrel occur between members of two different sects, they must never choose a theologian as arbitrator, for he would infallibly eat the oyster and leave them the shells.

To maintain the established peace nothing shall be offered for sale, either by a Greek to a Turk, a Turk to a Jew, or a Roman to a Roman, except what pertains to food, clothing, lodging, or pleasure. They shall not sell circumcision, or baptism, or burial,

---

1 Cicero (106-43 BCE) wrote *On Obligation* to outline the duties of the good citizen. Montaigne (1533-92) worked to undermine the certainty of different religious sects, and so to promote tolerance and extinguish religious war, in *Apology for Raymond Sebond*. Jean de la Fontaine (1631-95) was an early Enlightenment thinker who wrote fables that conveyed radical ethical and political lessons.

or permission to turn round the black stone in the Kaaba, or to harden one's knees before Our Lady of Loreto, who is still blacker.[1]

In all the disputes that shall arise it is expressly forbidden to treat any person as a dog, however angry one may be—unless indeed we treat dogs as men when they steal our dinner or bite us.

2. James Boswell, On Voltaire (1764)[2]

He was all Brilliance. He gave me continued flashes of Wit. I got him to speak english, which he does in a degree that made me now and then start up and cry upon my soul this is astonishing. When he talked our language He was animated with the Soul of a Briton. He had bold flights. He had humour. He had extravagance, he had a forcible oddity of stile that the most comical of our *dramatis Personae* could not have exceeded. He swore bloodily, as was the fashion when he was in England. He hum'd a ballad; He repeated nonsense.—Then he talked of our Constitution with a noble enthusiasm. I was proud to hear this from the mouth of an illustrious Frenchman. At last we came upon religion. Then did he rage. The company went to Supper. M. de Voltaire and I remained in the drawing-room with a great Bible before us; and if ever two mortal men disputed with vehemence we did. Yes—upon that occasion he was one Individual and I another. For a certain portion of time there was a fair opposition between Voltaire and Boswell. The daring bursts of his Ridicule confounded my understanding. He stood like an Orator of ancient Rome. Tully was never more agitated than he was. He went too far. His aged frame trembled beneath him. He cried, "O I am very sick; My head turns round" and he let himself gently fall upon an easy chair. He recovered. I resumed our conversa-

---

1 The Black Stone is one of the cornerstones of the Kaaba in Mecca, the earthly duplicate of the house of Allah. The Kaaba is a site of pilgrimage required of all practicing Muslims who are capable of reaching it. A dark statue of Mary, mother of Christ, is found at Loreto, Italy, in the house of Mary, which was miraculously transported to that place from its origin in Nazareth, following Muslim conquest in 1291.

2 Selection of a letter from James Boswell to William Johnson Temple, 28 December 1764. *The Correspondence of James Boswell and William Johnson Temple*, ed. Thomas W. Crawford, 2 vols. (Edinburgh: Edinburgh UP, 1997), vol.1, pp. 124-25.

tion, but changed the tone. I talked to him serious and earnest. I demanded of him an honest confession of his real sentiments. He gave it me with candour and with a mild eloquence which touched my heart. I did not believe him capable of thinking in the manner that he declared to me was "from the bottom of his heart." He exprest his veneration his love of the Supreme Being, and his entire Resignation to the will of Him who is allwise. He exprest his desire to resemble the Authour of Goodness by being good himself. His sentiments go no farther. He does not inflame his mind with grand hopes of the immortality of the Soul. He says it may be; but he knows nothing of it. And his mind is in perfect tranquillity. I was moved; I was sorry. I doubted his Sincerity. I called to him with emotion, "Are you sincere? Are you really sincere?" He answered, "Before God, I am." Then with the fire of him whose Tragedies have so often shone on the Theatre of Paris, he said. "I suffer much. But I suffer with Patience and Resignation; not as a Christian—But as a Man."

Select Bibliography

Most of the information on Voltaire's life presented in the introduction for this volume may be found in five detailed biographies of Voltaire: Theodore Besterman, *Voltaire*, third edition (U of Chicago P, 1976); Haydn Mason, *Voltaire: A Biography* (Johns Hopkins UP, 1981); Jean Orieux, *Voltaire*, translated by Helen Lane (Doubleday, 1979); Roger Pearson, *Voltaire Almighty: A Life in Pursuit of Freedom* (Bloomsbury, 2005); and Ira O. Wade, *The Intellectual Development of Voltaire* (Princeton UP, 1979). Two less exact biographies are centered upon Voltaire's personal relationships: Ian Davidson, *Voltaire in Exile* (Grove Press, 2006) and David Bodanis, *Passionate Minds* (Crown Publishers, 2006).

Voltaire's writings are collected, primarily in French, in *The Complete Works of Voltaire* (Voltaire Foundation, 1968 to present). The correspondence (vols. 85-135) is complete, and the whole work, projected at more than 150 volumes, is approaching completion. The most relevant academic journal, *SVEC* (formerly *Studies on Voltaire and The Eighteenth Century*), is also published by the Voltaire Foundation. (See www.voltaire.ox.ac.uk.) An English translation of most writing, excluding correspondence, is *The Works of Voltaire, A Contemporary Version*, translated by William F. Fleming (E.R. DuMont, 1901: issued in twenty-two double volumes *or* forty-two volumes).

Volume forty-eight of *The Complete Works of Voltaire* (all in French, edited by René Pomeau in 1980) contains the most exact study of the history of *Candide*. *Candide* was referred to in its time as a *conte*: a fantastic story, or an adventurer's story, often incorporating a moral. The most famous French *contes* include the fairy tales of Charles Perrault (1628-1703), who wrote the familiar *Goldilocks* and others. An excellent collection of five of Voltaire's *contes* may be found in Voltaire, *Candide and Other Stories*, translated by Roger Pearson (Oxford UP, 1990). Good editions to introduce other aspects of Voltaire's writing include *Philosophical Dictionary*, translated and edited by Theodore Besterman (Penguin, 1972); *Letters Concerning the English Nation*, edited by Nicholas Cronk (Oxford UP, 1994); *Political Writings*, edited by David Williams (Cambridge, 1994); *Treatise on Tolerance and Other Writings*, edited by Simon Harvey (Cambridge, 2000); *Selected Letters of Voltaire*, translated by Richard A. Brooks (New York UP, 1973). For history writing, poetry and plays, see volumes in *The Works of Voltaire, A Contemporary Version.* A good collection at a low price is *The Portable Voltaire,* edited by Ben Ray Redman (Penguin, 1977).

Very brief surveys that provide a critical introduction to Voltaire's writing in all its forms are Haydn Mason, *Voltaire* (St. Martin's Press, 1975) and Peyton Richter and Ilona Ricardo, *Voltaire* (Twayne, 1980). For more detail on Voltaire's writing, especially in the context of his life, see J.H. Brumfitt, *Voltaire, Historian* (Oxford UP, 1958) and Peter Gay, *Voltaire's Politics: The Poet as Realist,* second edition (Yale UP, 1988). For deeper research on Voltaire, begin with the biographies noted above and other books in the bibliography of Roger Pearson's *Voltaire Almighty,* or consider the topical essays collected in Nicholas Cronk, editor, *The Cambridge Companion to Voltaire* (Cambridge UP, 2009). For deeper research into *Candide,* begin with Ira O. Wade, *Voltaire and Candide: A Study in the Fusion of History, Art, and Philosophy* (Princeton UP, 1959); Roger Pearson, *The Fables of Reason: A Study of Voltaire's* Contes Philosophiques (Clarendon Press, 1993); Robin Howell, *Disabled Powers: A Reading of Voltaire's* Contes (Rodopi, 1993); and turn to the sources noted in Robin Howell, "Voltaire's *contes*: a review of studies 1969-1993," *SVEC,* vol. 320, 1994, pp. 229-82.

Information on the diffusion of editions of *Candide* is in Ira O. Wade, *Voltaire and Candide,* and René Pomeau, *The Complete Works of Voltaire* (vol. 48). An intriguing, detailed cultural history of clandestine book publishing, which is supplemented by three surprising novels of the time, is Roger Darnton's *The Forbidden Best-Sellers of Pre-Revolutionary France* (W.W. Norton, 1996).

For the history of the problem of evil as it is addressed in philosophical theodicy in Europe and America, see the collection of readings edited by Mark Larrimore, *The Problem of Evil: A Reader* (Blackwell, 2001); and see studies of this history in Susan Neiman, *Evil in Modern Thought* (Princeton UP, 2004) and Peter Dews, *The Idea of Evil* (Blackwell, 2007). For a narrower focus that is near to Voltaire's time, see W.H. Barber, *Leibniz in France: From Arnauld to Voltaire* (Clarendon, 1955). For twentieth-century philosophical thought on this problem, see Michael Peterson, editor, *The Problem of Evil* (Notre Dame UP, 1992), and William L. Rowe, editor, *God and the Problem of Evil* (Blackwell Press, 2001); for new philosophical thinking, see Peter van Inwagen, *The Problem of Evil* (Oxford UP, 2004), and Alan D. Schrift, editor, *Modernity and the Problem of Evil* (Indiana UP, 2005).

For other recent philosophical work, some of which does not concern a theological context, and some of which enters "post-metaphysical" terrain, see the authors in Jennifer L. Geddes, *Evil After Postmodernism* (Routledge, 2001), and those in María Pía Lara, *Rethinking Evil: Contemporary Perspectives* (U of California P, 2001). Note also the monographs of Mary Midgley, *Wickedness*, second edition (Routledge, 2001), María Pía Lara, *Narrating Evil* (Columbia UP, 2007), Susan Neiman, *Moral Clarity* (Harcourt, 2008), and Susan Sontag, *Regarding the Pain of Others* (Farrar, Straus & Giroux, 2003).

Index

Listings for characters within the text of *Candide* usually reflect their first appearance in the text; listings of places and events indicate page numbers reflecting the presence of main characters in those situations.